EVERLY

BOOK ONE OF THE EVERLY SERIES

by Meg Bonney

pandamoon
publishing

www.pandamoonpublishing.com

Jacket design and illustrations © Pandamoon Publishing

Art Direction by Matthew Kramer: Pandamoon Publishing
Illustrations by Ayush Pokharel: Pandamoon Publishing
Editing by Zara Kramer, Rachel Schoenbauer, and Rachel Lee Cherry: Pandamoon Publishing

Pandamoon Publishing and the portrayal of a panda and a moon are registered trademarks of Pandamoon Publishing.

Library of Congress Cataloging-in-Publication Data is on file at the Library of Congress, Washington, D.C.

Edition: 1, Version 1.01

ISBN-10: 1-945502-08-8
ISBN-13: 978-1-945502-08-8

DEDICATION

For my daughters. Keep being weird.

EVERLY

CHAPTER 1

Nine days. Nine days until I was free. Nine days until I could sit in my room for hours, speaking to absolutely no one. Nine days until high school was over and I could escape the false applause, the empty high fives, and one very stupid nickname.

Nine days.

"Madison Rosewood! How are those legs, Mad Dash?" Mr. Hillman, the husky gym teacher, asked as he checked off something on his clipboard and paced.

I flared my nostrils and forced a smile.

Running. All anyone ever wanted to talk to me about was my running. Not coffee, Frodo Baggins, Joss Whedon shows, or anything else that I actually cared about.

"Great. Pretty anxious to walk the hell out of high school, Mr. Hillman," I joked as I stared down at the water sloshing in the pool.

"Watch the language, kid."

"Sorry, sir."

Mr. Hillman stopped pacing the lineup of my gym class and stood between me and the pool. He always gave me and the other top athletes extra attention, and today was no exception.

"You know, after you win the state championship this weekend, you'll walk out of here a legend. This school is proud of you," Mr. Hillman said in a firm voice.

"I just want to walk out of here, period," I answered under my breath, but Mr. Hillman had already moved on down the line of students.

"You! What's your name?" Mr. Hillman asked the tall, lanky boy a few people down from me.

"Bryan Mendez," he answered.

I rolled my eyes. Bryan had been in this class with us all year, but he wasn't a sporty dude and, therefore, he wasn't on Mr. Hillman's radar.

Mr. Hillman nodded and walked to the end of the line. My classmates looked as uncomfortable as I felt. And, like me, they were also sporting horrifically tragic Greenrock High School-issued black swimsuits.

"All right, class. This is the last day of the swimming unit. For those of you who have not completed your swimming skills test, please line up on the deep end of the pool. The rest of you, go the shallow end and have free play. Don't kill each other," he bellowed.

The pool house erupted with chatter as nearly everyone hurried past me to the shallow end of the pool, but I did not move. Since starting the swimming unit in gym class, I had skillfully avoided getting into the deep end of the pool, but in order to complete my skills test and pass this stupid unit, I needed to.

I anxiously adjusted a strap of the swimsuit. One of the straps was fine, but the other was super stretched out and wouldn't stay on my shoulder. Swimming was literally the last thing in the world I wanted to be doing, ever. Unlike most of my fellow Floridians, I couldn't swim. Every time I had tried, I sank like a rock.

I followed Mr. Hillman to the deep side of the pool.

"Ready, Mad Dash?" Mr. Hillman asked.

"I'm a runner, Mr. Hillman," I replied. "Not a swimmer."

Mr. Hillman looked me over and raised his eyebrow. He had to see how nervous I was.

"What do I always say, kid?" Mr. Hillman asked as he rested his hand on the rounded silver pool ladder.

"Always be ready," I grumbled as I stayed firmly planted about six feet away from him and the deep end of the pool.

"That's right!" Mr. Hillman exclaimed. His usually unamused eyes lit up. Mr. Hillman never looked happier than when he got to share his "wisdom" with us.

"And when your destiny comes knocking, what do you say?" he asked with a grin.

"Go away?" I replied with one raised eyebrow.

"Nope! You open that door and say, 'I'm ready!'" Mr. Hillman pumped his fist in the air enthusiastically.

I let out a sigh of defeat and walked to where Mr. Hillman stood by the ladder of doom.

The problem was, I wasn't ready. I took one more step toward the rippling water below. If swimming was my destiny, then I was for sure not ready.

"Mr. Hillman, I will never need to know this, I promise." I was desperate now. "And if I ever do find myself submerged in a body of water, it will be a cold day in hell. I don't go swimming and I don't plan to."

"Okay, fine. But swimming skills are essential. You live on an island in the Gulf. Water is all around us, so we need to know how to survive it. If not for you, do it for others," Mr. Hillman replied.

"What do you mean?" I squinted and tried to think of a way that swimming was, in any way, a charitable activity.

"What if someone needs your help, or someday you have kids and one of them falls in a pool?" Mr. Hillman asked.

"Kids are overrated. I'll adopt cats," I shot back.

Mr. Hillman sighed.

"Water safety is a must, Rosewood." He had a knack for giving an explanation that didn't feel like a lecture.

"Maybe I'll move somewhere really cold and then all the water will be frozen. Boom, problem solved!"

Mr. Hillman didn't answer that one. Instead, he let out a slow sigh.

Just then, Shawn Milton, my lifelong nemesis, knocked into my shoulder and stood next to Mr. Hillman. *Gross.* I sneered at Shawn and his stupid face. We had hated each other ever since I broke his nose in middle school for lifting up my skirt at lunch. Jerks like him didn't deserve straight noses and wide nasal passages.

"Damn, Mad Dash, looking good." He laughed.

I gave him a dirty look but didn't respond to his taunting. In no universe would Shawn Milton give me an actual compliment—not that I cared.

Shawn made a kissy face at me, and my stomach churned. His eyes scanned me up and down as I balled my fists at my sides.

"Pipe down, Milton. Sorry, Rosewood, you know how boys are," Mr. Hillman remarked.

"Mr. Hillman, it's a penis, not a free pass to be a pervert."

"All right, all right, shut up, both of you. Ladies first." Mr. Hillman slapped the ladder and his Greenrock High School ring clanged loudly against it.

I swallowed hard and stepped back. "Actually, Mr. Hillman, I'm not feeling so great. Can I go to the nurse?" I covered my stomach with my arms.

"Rosewood…" Mr. Hillman shook his head.

Shawn turned back to me and squinted his stupid, too-close-together eyes at me. "You are so full of sh—"

"Shawn, shut up," Mr. Hillman interrupted. "Rosewood, if you don't complete this test, I will have to fail you for this unit. That will pull your whole grade down."

Normally, who cared? It was just a stupid gym grade. But ever since Principal Grayson had made us sign the Student Athletic Code Agreement, I needed to keep a

C or better in each of my classes to compete in any student sporting events. Like the state track championships this Saturday.

"I know the strokes. Can I just show you here...on this impeccably dry land?" I took another step back from the pool. I felt like my heart was going to burst out of my chest as I weighed my options.

Truth was, I didn't really care about the track meet itself, but I needed to be on that bus on Saturday. The team would get off of Greenrock Island for the whole day, and that was all I needed, whether that meant running in the race or not. And I knew that if I was disqualified from competing in the meet, I was still the team captain, and my coach would still make me attend—although, if Aunt Ruth got wind of me failing this class, I could kiss that bus ride good-bye. She would either ground me or kill me. Both would be detrimental to my plans.

"Rosewood, it's a swimming unit. You need to get in the water. No more excuses. No more wisecracks." Mr. Hillman clapped his hands.

"No more wisecracks? I did not consent to that."

"Now!" Mr. Hillman barked.

"Shawn can go first." I spun around and walked to the wooden bench next to window.

"Fine. Milton, go," Mr. Hillman ordered.

I sat with my back to the pool and looked out at the trees as they swayed in the wind. The rustle of the wind in the trees was one of the greatest sounds in the world, if you asked me. I wanted to be out there in the fresh air so badly. Really, I wanted to be anywhere but here.

I thumbed the silver window frame, willing it to open so I could escape, but the windows remained tightly closed. I took a deep breath. The pool house was hot and humid and smelled heavily of chlorine. It made me long for the fresh air even more.

Be calm, Maddy. Be calm.

I exhaled loudly.

I glanced back over to Mr. Hillman and Shawn, but as I did, something out the window caught my eye.

At the edge of the tree line was a guy dressed in all black, standing with his feet shoulder width apart, facing the school. His face was not familiar. Unfamiliar at this school was uncommon.

And it was like he was looking right at me.

"Weird," I said aloud. This side of school rarely had any traffic. The only people who went into those woods were the potheads.

4

Just then, a loud ringing noise pierced the air. I flinched and cupped my hands over my ears because it was the kind of sound that almost hurt to hear. I felt like my eardrums were going to burst from the pressure.

Still holding my ears, I turned, expecting to see everyone reacting like me, but nobody else looked bothered by the noise. It got louder and increasingly shrill while they all splashed and played like nothing was happening. I could hear nothing over the ringing noise.

I looked back to the window.

The guy in all black was now at the window, also holding his ears. He was inches from the glass. Inches from me. I jumped in surprise and fell off the bench onto the cold tile floor with a painful thud.

And then the noise stopped.

"Oh, crap. Rosewood, are you okay over there?" Mr. Hillman called over to me. I looked around the pool house. Everyone in the shallow end was still playing and splashing around. Shawn was doing the butterfly in the deep end.

Nobody else had noticed me or my fall, thankfully.

I hopped to my feet and adjusted the strap of the swimsuit before it slid down my shoulder again. Because that was all I needed to end my high school career—a nip slip.

I stood up and turned back to the window.

Gone. The guy was gone.

I took a step closer to the window and leaned over the bench as I searched the area for the person. I looked to the woods, to the left and right. Nothing.

"Rosewood?" I heard Mr. Hillman ask again.

"Yes, I'm fine," I answered.

"No, it's your turn, Rosewood. Come here, please."

"Oh, what?" I snapped back into reality.

"Your turn," Mr. Hillman replied.

Shawn climbed the ladder out of the pool and pushed the water out of his stupid hair. He twirled his goggles on his index finger.

"Milton, you passed. Go ahead down to free play." Mr. Hillman wrote something on the clipboard.

I gave Shawn another evil glance as he adjusted his swim trunks. He puckered his lips at me and walked past me to join the lucky folks in the shallow end of the pool.

"Eat it, Shawn," I replied with disdain. I quickly adjusted my focus back to the looming horror of the swimming pool in front of me. Hating Shawn Milton would have to wait. This was it. I walked to the edge of the pool and lined my unpolished toes up to the edge of the tile.

Okay, I was out of jokes. I was out of quips.

Hello, paralyzing fear! It's me, Madison.

I took a half step back.

Maybe if I explained everything to Mr. Hillman, he wouldn't make me get in the water. Or I could tell him that today was my birthday. That alone deserved a pass out of gym class swimming, right? He seemed like a nice enough guy. I couldn't be the only person in the history of time who didn't want to get in the deep end.

Just then, without warning, I felt two hands hit me sharply in the back and thrust me toward the water below. I flailed my arms to catch something but had no such luck. Into the water I went with a hard splash.

This is it. This is how I am going to die.

I kicked my legs wildly and thrashed my arms as fast as I could, but it didn't help. Sinking to the bottom like a rock in a pond, I opened my eyes. *Somebody help me!* On the shallow side of the pool, I could see the legs of the other students just as my own feet hit the bottom.

I could hear the noises of everyone yelling and playing in an echoed, distorted way. The water above me was unmoved. Nobody was coming to save me, but it didn't matter. I couldn't hold my breath any longer, and I sucked in a bit of water.

My lungs burned and I squeezed my eyes and mouth shut. My panic faded and I felt almost tranquil for a moment as I thought of Jason, my best friend. My only friend. I heard his laugh and saw his smile.

This is it.

Just then, I felt a hand on my arm, and I was rapidly pulled from the pool's floor. My head breached the surface and I began coughing violently. Somebody's arms were around me and I was being pulled to the side of the pool. I tried to breathe. My throat ached and I began coughing up water.

"Rosewood, can you hear me?" Mr. Hillman's voice called out over the chatter of my peers. "Watch your step, there's glass on the ground!"

More chatter.

I kept my eyes shut as I was lifted out of the water and plopped onto the tile floor. It felt like my lungs were filled with rocks and acid.

I couldn't stop coughing as the water and air bubbles escaped my throat.

"You there—who are you? Somebody call the nurse!" Mr. Hillman hollered. "Get the Principal in here, we need to go on lock down, now."

Everything sounded like it was really far away, at the end of an endless tunnel or something.

I blinked a few times and opened my chlorine-stung eyes to see someone right in front of me. It was the guy from the window. He was hunched over me, and the only things that weren't blurry were his vibrantly green eyes.

"You—you," I sputtered with an aching throat.

I flinched as a sharp pain shot through my arm. My rescuer reached down and tugged something out of my arm, just above my elbow. I moved my arm to escape his touch as he held up a piece of glass covered in my blood and tossed it away from me. It skittered across the tile.

"Ah, crap. She's bleeding. Where is the damn nurse?" Mr. Hillman hollered.

I didn't look at Mr. Hillman or the chaos around me; I kept my eyes on the boy who pulled me from the water. He leaned closer to my face as drops of water fell from his nose onto me. "The noise. You heard it, too," he said. It was less of a question and more of a statement.

I narrowed my eyes at him and nodded a little. "What are—" I started to ask, but I was overcome by the violent coughing again.

My rescuer smiled softly and stood up.

The glass beneath Mr. Hillman's shoes crunched as he directed students to leave the pool house. I squeezed my eyes shut. It felt like I had razor blades in my throat. I took a weak breath and opened my eyes just in time to see the green-eyed boy jump out through the broken window that I had been sitting near a few minutes ago.

Ignoring the pain in my left elbow, I propped myself up as Mr. Hillman crouched down next to me. "Oh, kid. I am so sorry. Everything happened so fast. We'll get that elbow looked at, too."

I nodded. People were still crowding around, even though they had been told to disperse.

"Just don't move, okay? There's glass everywhere. That lunatic came out of nowhere. Good thing, though, I suppose. You're okay, right?" Mr. Hillman spoke fast and his eyes were wide and frantic.

"I'm okay." A few teachers ran over to clear the students out. The new history teacher stopped and bent over me. Her brown hair fell forward as she leaned down. "What's your name, dear?" she asked sweetly.

"Rosewood. Madison Rosewood."

"Don't worry, Madison, we will call your parents," the teacher said sympathetically, patting my shoulder.

"Yeah, I don't have any of those," I replied abruptly. My voice sounded hoarse now.

"I'll take care of it. Hang tight, okay?" Mr. Hillman insisted and stood. He walked the clueless teacher away from me and leaned closer to talk to her. He was giving her the lowdown on my lack of parents, no doubt.

I shifted but stayed put. It wasn't as if I could actually go anywhere. The floor was covered in broken glass. And to make matters worse, the blood from my arm had mixed with the water that was pooling under me, making it spread over the white tiles of the pool house floor.

Despite Mr. Hillman's efforts to get them to leave, many of my classmates remained. Just staring. Gawking at me. *Joy*.

"Mr. Hillman?"

He hurried back over to me. "What is it?"

"Did I pass?"

Mr. Hillman let out a solitary chuckle and smiled sympathetically down at me. "Shut up, Rosewood."

CHAPTER 2

I walked sluggishly to my locker, taking my time. The lockdown was lifted almost immediately. It was decided that my rescuer wasn't a threat. He saved my life. By now, the entire school had heard about the mysterious window-smashing dude who had pulled me from the pool. It was all over social media, with a bunch of people recounting how "terrifying" it was for them.

These were the same people who didn't even know me other than the fact that I was a runner. The ace runner in the 100 meters. Madison "Mad Dash" Rosewood. It was all I was known for at this school and in this town. Being known for something that you find incredibly dull is as lovely as it sounds.

Apparently, nearly drowning had its perks, though. My aunt Ruth chewed Principal Grayson a new one and demanded that I be sent home to rest. We lived two blocks from school, so footing it home was no big deal.

I rummaged through the contents of my locker. With the end of school near, I was finding myself less and less motivated to keep it clean or organized. There was really only one thing that I needed from my locker today, my eighteenth birthday. I carefully pulled out a plain thin manila folder.

Inside this folder was the key to finding my parents—my real parents. Today, I was a legal adult, which meant that I could go file the paperwork requesting the release of my adoption file.

Aunt Ruth had adopted me as a little girl because my parents couldn't take care of me. My mother was her sister.

That was it. That was all I knew about my real parents. Two lousy sentences.

But not now! Now, I didn't have to ask Aunt Ruth. I didn't have to attempt to get closer to her and her icy personality to find answers. I was going to find them on my own. It was something I had thought about almost daily. Every time I won a race and my parents weren't there to cheer me on. Every holiday. Every birthday, I thought about them.

And now, I could find them. I had the power to find my parents. That notion gave me more excitement than any race I had ever been in. It was how I planned to spend all my time now that I was eighteen. It was all that mattered.

The bell rang loudly overhead. I stuck the folder in my messenger bag.

"Hello, gorgeous! I heard you went for a swim!"

The curls of my damp ponytailed hair caught on my eyelashes as I turned.

"Yes, I do love a good swim, you know."

It was my best friend, Jason Vega. He was the picture of high school perfection as he adjusted his varsity letterman jacket. He smiled, but I could see the apprehension in his deep brown eyes. His eyes always gave him away.

It was the same look I would have if it had been Jason at the bottom of that pool. Actually, no, I would probably just look pissed and ready to kill whoever pushed him.

"Seriously. Are you okay, Mads?" He lowered his chin and his shoulder-length dark hair fell from behind his ears.

"I'm fine," I insisted. "It was that idiot Shawn Milton, I know it. He pushed me and I wasn't ready. And I got this handy souvenir!"

I held up my elbow to show him the large beige bandage that the nurse had put on it.

"Yikes."

I shrugged. "It barely hurts." A total lie. It hurt every time I moved my arm.

"Well, that's good. And I have seen you try to swim. Ready or not, you sink like a rock." Jason raised his eyebrows. "What about that dude who busted through the window to save you?"

"Bite your tongue, sir. He didn't save me. I would have gotten to the surface eventually," I lied, lowering my voice. The other students were leaving their classrooms and scattering into the hall. I could feel their eyes on me, something that I hated on a normal day. This was worse somehow.

"Well, I'm glad you're okay." Jason clamped his arm firmly around my shoulder. "Can't have my little Maddy stuck at the bottom of the pool!" He nuzzled against my cheek.

"You are so bizarre. You know that, right?" I asked with a chuckle and pushed his face away from mine.

"Something's wrong." Jason's face fell serious. He knew me too well, so hiding anything from him was a waste of time, really.

"You're going to think I'm crazy," I warned.

"Already do, but go on," he replied.

"Okay, so I was in the pool house, and I saw this guy outside—the guy who ended up pulling me out of the pool—and then I heard this really loud ringing noise, but it was like nobody else heard it. And then when the guy pulled me out of the water, he asked me if I had heard it, too," I recounted.

"I thought the crazy part of this story would be that you nearly drowned. But ringing, huh?" He looked at me with genuine concern. "Are you okay, like, seriously? Do you want me to walk you home?"

"No, I'm okay, really. It was just super weird."

Jason paused and chewed on the inside of his cheek, like he always did when he was worried.

"I'm fine."

He sighed and squinted at me.

"Subject change?" Jason asked.

He always knew. "Yes, please," I answered gratefully.

"We need to talk about your yearbook entry."

"Okay, what about my entry?" I turned to lean on a locker as two sophomore girls walked past and pointed at me. Gossiping, the two girls stared as I promptly held out my middle finger and glared back at them.

"Maddy, you listed 'none' under your interests," Jason said as he lowered my offending hand without comment. The two girls scoffed and continued walking.

"Yeah, so? Lots of people listed 'none,'" I shot back.

Jason laughed. "Yeah, but Maddy, you are the captain of the school's track team. You are the reigning state champion in the 100 meters. You are the fastest runner in the state of frickin' Florida. And you listed your interests as 'none.'"

"Well…running doesn't interest me." I shrugged.

Jason pressed his lips together. "I know you don't love it like I love playing sports, but come on, Mads."

"Nope. I just do it. It doesn't interest me." I shook my head like a stubborn child.

"You're going to college on a track scholarship, and you're competing in the statewide championship meet this weekend to defend your title."

"Correct."

"But running isn't one of your interests."

"Ding, ding, ding." I pointed my finger and poked him with each *ding*.

Jason pouted and rubbed his forearm with his palm. "Ow! Stop it. You know I bruise like a peach."

"So sorry." I laughed as we started walking down the long bustling hallway.

"We have to get you out of this funk, Maddy," Jason insisted.

11

"Funk shmunk." I shook my head.

"I have Yearbook now, and then I'll be headed your way. Are you going home now?"

I nodded. "Yep. I get to go relax and recuperate in an empty house. Best part of all of this."

My cousin Lacy waved from the other side of the hall. "Hey, guys! Pardon me," she said to a group of people blocking her path to us.

"Move!" I shouted at them.

The tallest kid turned to eye me, and I gave my best stink eye. The rest didn't even turn around before they got out of Lacy's way. She was too sweet to yell at them herself. The clump moved along like a tiny unwashed herd of sheep.

"Sorry, thank you!" Lacy called after them and gave me a scowl. She was too nice to tell them to get out her way. I wasn't.

Lacy shoved a yellow flyer in my hand and then turned to give one to Jason.

Judging by her lack of concern-filled hugs, Lacy hadn't heard about her boyfriend trying to drown me earlier. That's right: scumbag Shawn Milton was dating my angel-faced cousin Lacy.

"What's this?" Jason asked, examining the flyer.

"Mayor Milton's Energy Crisis Rally," I read aloud. "Is this flyer my present? Because, wow, it is just so not what I wanted for my birthday."

"Mayor Milton is hosting an event to discuss the island's energy crisis!" Lacy said enthusiastically. "It will be right in the town square, and no, you big nerd, that is not your present. Here."

In her hand was a little black box. I took it as she jumped up and down.

"I was going to give it to you at home, after my swim practice, but I just couldn't wait. Open it!"

I felt my cheeks flush. "Lacy, I was just joking, you didn't ha—"

"Open it!" she shrieked.

I smiled and nodded without saying another word. I carefully opened the little box. In it were two little silver lightning bolt earrings.

"Wow, Lacy, these are great. Thank you!" I showed the box to Jason. They really were adorable. I didn't wear jewelry often, but these were just my speed.

"Those are cool," Jason said.

"Get it? Because you're so fast!" she exclaimed as she took the box from me and put the earrings in my typically vacant pierced ears. Lacy stepped back and clapped once. "Perfect! Happy birthday, Mad Dash!"

"Thank you, Lacy," I replied, trying not to cringe at her use of that stupid nickname because I was fairly confident that she was the one who came up with it in the first place.

"You are very welcome. Now, I'll see you guys at the rally, right?" Lacy practically sang. When she got excited, which was almost hourly, her joy couldn't be contained.

Jason groaned dramatically. "Does your mom know you're getting into politics?"

"That sort of gets in the way of her agenda of turning us into her little super soldiers, doesn't it?" I asked sarcastically.

"It's not politics. The mayor is just hosting. And I do not need my mom's permission to care about the energy crisis! I'll still have time to go to my mom's gym and teach self-defense classes all summer long, don't you worry! This is just important to me. Mayor Milton is going to make some real changes on Greenrock Island! Yes, I realize that the mayoral election is next month, but that's not what this is about. This is about the people around here being so reliant on energy. Boating and cars and blasting the air conditioning all day, every day—it's insane. And with all of the city's blackouts, how can you not see that there's a real problem here?"

"Whoa. Save some of that judgmental berating and anger for the other constituents." I held my hands up and grinned at her.

Lacy rolled her big blue eyes. "Will you come? Please? Look, I'm not asking you to join the campaign team or anything, but at least come and hear what Mayor Milton has to say," Lacy urged us.

It was hard to say no to her when she wanted something, but it was fun to try.

"Meh," I shrugged. "And are you sure that your sudden interest in the town's political race has nothing to do with the fact that you're currently dating Mayor Milton's horrid son?"

"There will be food!" Lacy beamed as she so cleverly tried to appeal to me and my greatest love of all while simultaneously dodging my question.

I raised an eyebrow. "Intrigued."

"Maddy, this is important. Mayor Milton is going to talk about his plans. The island needs to stop relying so much on electricity. We need to find ways to conserve power and—"

"Bah! We'll be there, Lacy, just stop talking." I held my hand up.

"Can't wait!" Jason gave a thumbs-up.

"Thank you, guys. This is really important to me. And, Jason, bring your boyfriend! The more the merrier," she said in her cheeriest voice. She adjusted the thin black headband that held back her meticulously straight ice-blonde hair.

Jason looked up at the black-framed clock on the hallway wall. "Speaking of, I have to go. I told Caleb I'd meet him and walk to Yearbook together. Mads, I'll come over right after school. Bye, Lacy."

I waved as Jason jogged off in the other direction.

Lacy cleared her throat. "Hey, are you excited about the race this weekend?"

"Um, sure. Running is running." I nodded.

"I checked your race times, and you're so early that I don't know if I can make it. Mom and I have that lame Saturday morning class to teach. Don't worry, I'll talk to her."

"I don't think I passed my gym test, so I may get disqualified from competing. I'll still have to go, though."

"Doubtful, Maddy. You would have to do something really big to get disqualified—like, *really* big. I don't think a unit in gym class is reason enough."

Crap! It would be way easier to go over to the courthouse if I were disqualified. I could try to slip away while everyone was competing and be back in time for my race.

Of course I wasn't disqualified; Lacy was right. This school banked on me winning everything. My near-death experience in gym class would likely be the loophole that let me compete this weekend.

Damn loopholes.

My cousin hooked her arm through mine and I tried not to wince. I didn't tell her that she was rubbing her arm against my injury. That would just launch her into a frenzy of worried questions, and I didn't want to deal with that.

Lacy smiled at me as she spoke. "I am so proud of you. You'll win! I know you will. And, my stars, even if you don't, you already have a full scholarship for track. You're set, Maddy."

"Right. Set," I agreed half-heartedly. Truth was, I wasn't as excited as everyone else that my future was all set. I was good at running, sure. I had won every race I had ever been in.

Nobody could beat Mad Dash. Joy of joys.

Lacy was my biggest cheerleader when it came to running. For my last race, she had decorated our shared bedroom with streamers and balloons. She was always so proud of me. I didn't have the heart to tell her that I didn't give a rat's ass about this race.

"I have to get to class. See you at home! Love you, Mad Dash!" Lacy leaned over and kissed my cheek before she disappeared into the crowd.

Time to go home. I pushed open the doors and walked outside into the sun.

Nine more days.

CHAPTER 3

Navigating the lawn outside school between classes was always a bit of a debacle. And it was even harder near my big races. It was like a really annoying, unfun game of Frogger.

Most of the top jocks at my school enjoyed the attention and couldn't wait for somebody to bring up the big game. Me? I would rather punch myself in the face. I suck at small talk and, for some reason, all these kids take an interest in me when it comes to me winning state titles.

A light tap on my shoulder made me stop. "Hey, Madison! I heard you almost died and this guy, like, busted through the window to save you!" Joe Gomez, an impossibly tall boy on my track team, exclaimed.

I smiled and nodded and kept walking. We were teammates, but I barely knew the guy outside of his race times and his constant chatter on the bus rides to meets. Even if I was in the mood to discuss it, which I wasn't, I knew better than to get stuck in a conversation with him.

I kept walking and decided to avoid all eye contact until I made it home.

"Oh my gosh! Why aren't you at the hospital, Mad Dash? Are you okay?" a girl's voice asked from behind me.

I groaned to myself and didn't stop walking or turn around, but to my annoyance, someone stopped right in front of me and blocked my path.

"Hey, Mad Dash," she started. "I heard you almost died and some guy pulled you out of the pool and had to resuscitate you!"

I looked up to see a familiar-looking girl whose name I couldn't remember.

"Shh, I don't like you," I replied, and walked around her.

"Rude," I heard the girl say as I hurried toward my freedom. I stopped and switched paths to avoid a cluster of people a few feet ahead of me.

I passed more people. More eyes. More whispers. I crossed my arms and kept my head down. I exhaled a long, frustrated lungful. My throat still hurt from the whole pool thing.

"Mad Dash! I heard you died!" another person yelled.

Christ.

Before I could respond, I heard voices murmuring behind me. I spun on my heel to face the small crowd that had formed behind me.

"Creepy much?" I asked.

"We heard a ninja shot out a window and saved you from drowning in the pool!" Tommy from my gym class shouted over the other voices.

"What? Tommy, you were there, you moron. That didn't happen. I was fine." My heart was beating faster. I needed to go. I needed to get away from them.

"Maybe it was someone from the Palm City High School track team trying to take out the competition!" one girl theorized.

I shook my head, not sure who was even talking anymore. "It is so hot," I said, and fanned myself. Sweat had collected on my upper lip, and a slow drop rolled down my temple. The voices were fading in and out now. I felt like I was spinning in circles, trapped in an endless loop of predatory stares and uncomfortable questions.

"No, they pulled her out of the pool!" Tommy yelled back to the girl.

"Are you going to able to run this weekend, Maddy?" another gawker asked.

The skin on my arms started to prickle, like goosebumps, but sharper somehow.

"Madison, not Maddy," I muttered, wiping my face.

I waved my hands, urging the crowd to disperse. I felt the heat rising inside me like I had just chugged hot coffee and stepped into a sauna.

"Must you always have an audience, Ms. Rosewood? Be on your way, students," Principal Grayson said condescendingly.

"No, I..." I wiped my face with my hands again and started billowing my shirt back and forth as I tried to cool off. I wanted to scream for him to help me. I was on fire—something was wrong. I felt sick and dizzy. This wasn't normal. *I need help!*

"Go on!" Mr. Grayson ordered the thinning crowd as he turned to face me.

He had a full head of neatly kept gray hair and wore a suit every day. He would make a good banker, or maybe even a ruthless dictator. He certainly had the chops for it.

"Ms. Rosewood, be on your way. I have enough of a mess to deal with today thanks to you," Grayson said.

I scoffed and started fanning myself even faster. "Yes, my god! I apologize for nearly drowning! I was pushed! How rude of me! What a frickin' saint you are!"

"Quiet," Mr. Grayson said dismissively.

"Are you warm? It's so warm," I pulled a half-empty water bottle from my bag and started chugging it. "And I won't be quiet. Shawn pushed me. He did!"

"That is enough, Madison. Nobody saw Milton push you in the water. Now, go on your way. I believe you were excused for the day. Keep this up and I will write you up."

"Sure thing, sir!" I rolled my eyes, not even listening to him anymore. I felt like my skin was going to bubble up and melt off. Grayson was the least of my concerns. I had to get out of here. Something was wrong. This wasn't anxiety; this was something else.

To my relief, the crowd of people had left, and Grayson's focus shifted to a couple attempting to vertically make a baby against the trunk of a tree out on the lawn.

More sweat ran down my cheek. It was warm out, but not this warm. In an attempt to cool down faster, I lifted the water bottle above my head and poured the rest of it on my face.

"Woo-hoo! Yeah, baby! That's what I want to see!" a boy's voice yelled to me from a few yards away.

I angled my head back down as the ineffective water trickled down my face. It was Shawn frickin' Milton. Without hesitation, I walked the few yards to where Shawn stood.

"I know it was you, Shawn." I clenched my jaw.

Shawn laughed and ran his tongue across his teeth.

"Admit it." I clenched my fists at my sides and continued to glare at him. Shawn and his buddies, who flanked him on either side, all wore plaid shorts and polo shirts in different colors. The three of them looked like a really terrible boy band.

"I just like seeing you wet." Shawn winked one of his beady eyes at me.

This pleased the boy band wannabes, and they all started cackling.

I couldn't contain my anger any longer. My fist met his nose with a rather satisfying crack. Shawn's large, muscular body crumbled to the ground like a flimsy piece of wet paper as I stood over him.

"You bitch!" Shawn yelped through his bloody hands.

I shook my hand out. "It's what you get, scumbag!"

It only took a few seconds for Principal Grayson to notice and run back over to where I stood.

"Madison, what did you do?" he demanded.

I watched as a few students and Mr. Grayson crouched down to check on Shawn, who was rolling back and forth on the ground, almost in the fetal position.

Grayson's face was red. He waved his hand, and the security guard started to run toward us. I felt a tiny twinge of guilt as Shawn stood and more blood gushed from his face, but not enough guilt to regret it. He could have killed me, and someone needed to teach him a lesson.

Grayson grabbed me by the elbow. "What is the matter with you, young lady?"

"Me? He tried to drown me. You weren't going to do anything about it, and then he made a pervy comment."

"And you think that your own vigilante justice is the way to solve this?" Grayson tugged my wrist sharply.

I met his angered stare. "It's better than no justice."

"It's broken!" Shawn shrieked from the ground.

Grayson huffed. "Why can't you just behave like a nice young lady for once? Girls do not get into fights!"

"Last I checked, genitals didn't dictate behavior," I said, still very angry. Thankfully, the hot flash seemed be going away now.

"Don't use those swear words with me!" Grayson pointed his finger in my face.

I raised an eyebrow. "What swear word? *Genitals?*"

Did he just say genitals *was a swear word?*

"Marcus! Take her and escort her off campus. She's suspended," Grayson instructed the security guard.

Marcus was a former student and just a couple years older than me. He was also the assistant track coach, and he looked pissed. He walked up and grabbed me by my wrist to pull me away from the scene.

"Hey, Mad Dash! I heard some guy had to give you mouth-to-mouth in the gym! Lucky dude!" a guy from my English class said as he walked past.

I balled my fist, ready to break another nose. "Eat sh—"

"Knock it off," Marcus snapped. It was hard to tell if he was talking to me or the guy from my English class. Marcus had the type of anger that just radiated out to anyone near.

I adjusted my bag as we wove in and out of the trees and students who lurked in small groups on the lawn.

"You are in a lot of trouble, kid. Better start taking this seriously. I mean, really, Madison, what was that back there?" Marcus asked as we reached the property line of the school.

I chewed my lip. "He pushed me in the pool and I almost died."

Marcus let my arm go. "So that makes him a jerk. You punching him puts the wrong right back on you. You need to think about that stuff, or you're going to get in some real trouble someday."

I didn't dare roll my eyes as Marcus towered over me.

"And what about the track meet this weekend? There's no way Coach will let you race after that crap you just pulled. You're benched, Mad Dash."

Perfect.

I placed my hand on my bag, which held the very important papers I would be filing during the meet, and tried not to smile.

CHAPTER 4

I managed to escape the remainder of Marcus's rant and start my walk home. My coach would not be happy with the news, but I didn't really care. Even though we had almost two weeks left before school ended, I was mentally done with high school and ready for the next chapter of my life.

I tried my best to fix my hair as I walked down the sidewalk. I tied the half-dry, half-wet cluster of curls up on top of my head in one big messy knot. At least I didn't have anything I needed to look presentable for today.

Even with Marcus's glower burning through my skull, the rest of my birthday could still be salvageable. That is, until I had to face Aunt Ruth—my very unfunny, unforgiving, un-shenanigan-loving Aunt Ruth.

Who cared? Shawn Milton deserved all the broken noses I could give him.

I shook my head and sighed, thinking of the endless lecturing I would surely endure when Aunt Ruth came home. My aunt had spent the better part of the last decade scolding me for something. Sometimes for things I hadn't even done. I rubbed my forehead with my palm.

Thankfully, at this time of day, she wouldn't be home. Ruth owned a fitness center here in town and also taught a self-defense class for women in Palm City, the next island over. Aunt Ruth had better luck with the folks in Palm City, which was bigger than Greenrock and saw much more crime. Her classes there were always packed with women learning how to throw a mean right hook. Ruth loved teaching them that. That's right: my aunt, who was going to yell at me for punching someone, was the woman who taught me how to throw a punch in the first place.

Ruth was a hard-as-nails lady who you really didn't want to mess with. She wasn't exactly a warm and fuzzy mom to Lacy, but at least she was around, which was more than I could say for my own parents.

We didn't have any other family, just us. I had lived with Aunt Ruth and Lacy for as long as I could remember. Lacy was her daughter; I was just the charity case. I decided long ago that she only took me in so that I could entertain Lacy, like how you don't ever want to get just one cat because that cat will be lonely.

So here I am. Madison Rosewood, the companion cat.

I turned onto Main Street. We lived just off the main road, which was really just seven blocks that contained nearly all the businesses on the island. Our house was on one of the side streets that nobody drove down unless they lived there. The house was small but just big enough for the three of us.

There it was again—the noise. The ringing noise. I stopped suddenly when I heard it again.

"What the hell is that?" I asked aloud.

Before I could figure it out, I felt a buzz coming from my bag. It was my phone, showing a text from Aunt Ruth that simply read "GYM NOW." I guess she didn't want to wait until this evening to rip me a new one. Well, this should be as pleasant as a root canal.

"I thought you were in Palm City," I texted back quickly.

She responded with a simple "Now," and I groaned.

Lucky for me, the gym was on the way home. I hadn't planned to make a stop there, but there was no denying Ruth's orders. Seriously.

I kept walking down the sidewalk until the cozy houses turned to red brick storefronts. There wasn't too much to this side of Main Street: a coffee shop, a diner, a bookstore, a doctor's office, and my aunt's gym.

I stopped in front of the building. The sign was plain with bold black letters. No fuss, no cutesy swirls or flowers like the rest of the establishments around it. Simple and to the point, just like Aunt Ruth.

I pushed through the door and the little silver bell chimed over my head. My eyes wandered around the empty gym. On the back wall, there were treadmills and two elliptical machines. In the middle of the room was a wide blue floor mat where Ruth taught self-defense classes.

This time of day, the place was usually dead. The lights were on, though, so Ruth must have just gotten back from Palm City—either that, or she came back just to rip me apart for breaking the nose of the mayor's son.

"Hello?" I called out.

My bag dropped from my shoulder and fell to the floor in front of the metal lockers lining one wall. I always put my bag there, and my aunt always yelled at me for it. That never stopped me.

I opened my mouth to call for Aunt Ruth again, but before I could speak a word, something struck my back and I flew forward onto the blue mat. The lights in the gym clicked off.

"Seriously?" I huffed. Count on Aunt Ruth for a surprise self-defense drill—especially if she heard I was fighting at school.

My back stung, but I rolled to the side and hopped up into a low crouch. My heart pounded and the sudden darkness was jarring, but I searched the room for my assailant.

A foot drilled into my back, and I fell forward on the mat again. This time, I turned quicker to get a look. Still nobody there. I felt my pulse race as I grew angrier.

"Enough! Just come out!" I called, rubbing my sore back.

"If you had swept your leg around, you would have had me there. You are slow! Maybe if you spent more time training and less time causing trouble at school, you would have had me," Aunt Ruth yelled. I spun to face it.

"He pushed me into a pool!" I protested.

"You didn't need to punch him. That's not self-defense," she said. I tracked the sound of her voice.

"This is stupid!" I yelled and stood, but I kept my arms up in front of me defensively, knowing she could pounce at any minute.

"This is training."

I groaned angrily. "Training for what? You keep telling me I can't use my fighting skills unless someone attacks me. This is Greenrock Island. Nobody is attacking me on Greenrock Island!"

"Focus!" Aunt Ruth commanded. "Do it!"

I closed my eyes before breathing out slowly. I took a defensive position and listened, just like Aunt Ruth had taught me. In the corner, I could hear the plinking of water coming from the bathroom. I tuned it out and slowed my breathing further as I tried to listen for her, for any clues on her position in the gym. The faster I proved I could defend against her, the faster this would be over.

I hated these stupid surprise trainings. There was no merit in them, but that wouldn't make a difference to her, because it never did.

A clink by the door; a rustle on the back wall. She was trying to confuse me, which could only mean one thing. She was about to attack. I crouched down and balled my fists. And even though I hated being surprised by these stupid sessions, I couldn't help but smirk. I loved the competitive nature of it all. It's the only time I wasn't punished for fighting.

Just then, she was on me. No weapons, just stiff jabs and punches that I blocked and dodged in the dark with ease until I misjudged her. I caught an elbow to my jaw and stumbled back. She never hit me with force during these trainings—just enough to highlight my weak spots.

"Good. Now find a weapon," she said.

"You don't have one. Why do I need one? This is a fair fight," I argued.

"No fight you want to win needs to be fair. You take any advantage you can get." Her voice, smooth and even, never seemed to reflect her generally stern personality.

I darted to a storage closet, pulled the wooden double doors open, and reached inside, putting my palms on the empty shelves.

"There isn't anything here!" I turned back around.

"Do you think you'll always be handed a weapon? Find one! Use your resources!"

I huffed again and sprinted to the far side of the dark gym. Three thick black curtains hung in front of the large picture window, blocking the natural light. How the hell would I find a weapon in a pitch-black gym? She hid them; she clearly had the edge. I tripped over the bottom of one of the stiff curtains but caught my balance quickly.

"Sloppy!" she noted. She was on the opposite wall now.

Without hesitation, I reached up and yanked a curtain panel down. Light poured into the modestly sized gym. I slid the black fabric off the thin golden curtain rod and the fabric fell to a heap on the floor, sending dust into the air.

And there she was. Aunt Ruth.

I spun the rod in my hand like an oversized baton and locked eyes with her.

She walked to the center of the gym, and her bare feet made a soft crunch against the mats on the floor. Her blonde hair was tied up in a secure bun on top of her head. Her lean muscles bulged in her tight black shorts, and her lime sports bra was bright against her pale skin.

"If you broke that, it will come out of your paycheck." Aunt Ruth pointed her long index finger and stared down her nose at me.

"You said to find a weapon." I shrugged, unable to hide my smile. I pulled one end of the curtain rod and it came apart in the middle.

"Here," I said and tossed the other half of the rod to her.

"I said it doesn't need to be fair," she said, catching it with a swift, effortless reach. I walked toward her and she stuck a hand on her hip, showing her usual annoyance with me.

"I prefer fair." I gave her a nod. I swung the curtain rod around in front of me and it made a gratifying *whoosh* as it cut the air.

These stupid drills of her hers were nothing new to me. She didn't really do it to Lacy, but any chance she got to catch me off guard, Aunt Ruth did.

She always said she was preparing me to defend myself. I think she was just bored and sometimes weirdly competitive with me. Either way, there wasn't much I could do to get out of it. She was my legal guardian and the only parental type I had—for now, anyway.

I met her in the center of the floor and we both took a defensive stance.

"Did you break it?" Aunt Ruth swung her piece of the curtain rod and met mine with a *ting*.

"No, it slides back together." I lunged, swinging my rod to meet hers.

"I know how curtain rods work. I was talking about his nose. Did you break Shawn Milton's nose?" Aunt Ruth asked as she started to spar faster. I moved my rod to block each of her swings, but then I misjudged her and the curtain rod smacked my arm.

I took a few steps back and grabbed my arm. Most kids would see concern on the face of their family member at this point, but not me. Aunt Ruth's face was as hardened as ever. She lifted her pointed chin and raised her rod.

"Did you break his nose?" she asked again.

I nodded. "He pushed me into the pool, and I almost drowned."

Her eyes narrowed for a moment and she looked out the window. I capitalized on her momentary lack of focus, swung my makeshift weapon, and clipped her shin. She faltered, stepping back, but quickly caught her balance.

I tried not to smirk at her, but I couldn't help myself, and for a split second, I thought I saw her smile back at me. She would never say it, but I had a feeling that she liked when I bested her like that.

Aunt Ruth charged me again, her gray-blue eyes focused and determined. She was going even faster now; she had both hands on the rod and began swinging it quickly, nearly hitting me multiple times before I lost my footing and fell backward.

Before I could get to my feet, she raised the rod over her head and swung down hard, stopping within a quarter-inch of the tip of my nose. I was panting loudly as I held myself up on my elbows. She hovered over me, a flash of delight in her eyes.

She lowered her face toward mine while keeping the rod just a hair away from my nose.

She spoke calmly but quickly. "His actions don't decide what you do. You are in control of your own choices. And today, you chose wrong."

She stood and turned away.

"Don't you even care that I almost died today? You only seem to care about dumbass Shawn Milton and his precious nose."

"You disrespected the principal, broke a young man's nose, and got kicked off campus—suspended. You embarrassed yourself and your family." Aunt Ruth looked back at me and dropped the curtain rod on the floor.

I stood up. "Um, well…not technically in that order."

"Do you even think about how the things you do will impact me? How they impact Lacy?" Ruth put her hands on her hips, her abs even more prominent than usual.

"So this isn't about me. It's about you," I said.

Aunt Ruth shook her head. "Did you even think about your teammates? About how they would feel if you weren't there to lead them at the state championships this weekend?"

I puckered my lips and looked up at the ceiling. "They would be happy that they'll finally have a shot at winning, since I won't be there?"

"Not funny, Madison. You made a commitment to your team. You don't break something like that. You are the leader, and that is not what a leader does. You stick by your team, no matter what you may be feeling."

"Look, I don't care about the stupid state championship, and I don't care about being their leader. I don't. I don't want to do it anymore. That's all anyone ever frickin' talks to me about. I don't want to run. I hate it," I sighed. "I'll be there. I'll still have to go. I just can't run."

"You don't always love what you do. You just do it because you made that promise. And when you have a gift like yours, you don't waste it," Aunt Ruth replied.

"I'm not wasting it. I just…I just don't want to do it. I have zero passion for it, Aunt Ruth," I explained, almost begging for her to finally see my side of something.

"This isn't even about you wasting your talent. It's about you drawing negative attention to yourself. To Lacy. To me! I have a business to run." She undid her bun and ran her fingers through her dark blonde hair.

"It's a gym. Technically, your business *is* to run," I said under my breath.

Ruth sighed. "Life is not some big joke, Madison. You are an adult now. You need to grow up! You have responsibilities. And the sooner you realize that, the better."

I huffed heatedly and clenched my jaw as I stared back at her. "Oh, so you actually remember what today is? That it's my eighteenth birthday?"

"Of course I do. I've been thinking about this day for longer than you will ever understand. Do you think that this is all a game? You cannot behave this way."

Getting yelled at by Ruth was not a new thing for me, but lately she seemed even more "Ruth" than usual, constantly checking in on me and wanting to know where I was at all times. I was two years older than Lacy, and she treated me like the younger one.

"Here is what will happen. You are going to write a letter of apology to Shawn Milton, Principal Grayson, and the school. And then you are going to be my new shadow. You will be with me every day after school. You will wake up, go to school, come to the gym, we will go home, you will do your chores, and then you will sleep so you can do it over again the next day."

"I'm eighteen. I am not—"

Ruth took a step toward me. "Shadow. You will be my shadow. Do I make myself clear?"

She turned and walked toward the lockers on the other side of the gym. I clenched my jaw, too mad to say anything—not that it would help.

"And how many times do I have to tell you to use these damn lockers? You can't just leave your bag wherever you want!"

"Sorry, I'll move it!" I yelled, but not fast enough.

Aunt Ruth crouched to shove the spilled contents of my bag back inside it and stopped. She was silent and still, holding the manila folder open.

"What the hell is this?" she asked softly, without turning around.

"I'm eighteen, an adult, like you said." I walked over to where she was still bent on the floor. My heart raced. Why did this make me so nervous?

"That's not an answer, Madison," Aunt Ruth said, irritation in her voice.

I pulled the folder and the form from her long, thin fingers. She didn't move for a moment, then slowly stood and turned to face me.

"I—I have to go study." I clutched the folder tightly in my hands and turned toward the gym's entrance.

"Don't you dare take another step," Ruth warned me. "What are you doing with that form? I told you to leave it alone."

"Why do you care what I do? I'm just the charity case you took in," I said.

Aunt Ruth looked hurt for a second before giving me her standard scowl. Even that slight flicker of emotion was more than I usually got from Aunt Ruth. We didn't talk about real things like this. We didn't share feelings, talk about my parents or how it was tearing my heart out not to know them. We didn't talk about any of that, ever. School, the gym, chores, and of course, how I was a crushing disappointment to her: those were the topics we hit.

"Look, I know I'm not your mother. But you are my responsibility, and you will be respectful."

"I respect you, Ruth, but respect doesn't mean that I'm going to obey everything you ever say," I insisted.

"I disagree," Aunt Ruth replied. "I am the leader of our family. You obey the leader. Now, tell me. What is that form?" She folded her arms across her chest.

"My parents. I'm eighteen. I'm going to find my parents," I answered calmly. "You can't keep it from me anymore."

I could see the shock in her eyes, but it didn't matter. It couldn't. I had spent more hours than I could count on Jason's computer trying to locate my parents. Because I had nowhere to start, other than my name, I never got very far.

But today, I was legally an adult. That changed things.

Ruth's eyes were closed as she held the bridge of her nose and shook her head.

"I told you, Madison. I told you to leave it alone!" she yelled, breaking the even-toned calmness of our exchange.

"It's not up to you. And no, you didn't! You didn't tell me anything about them. I don't even know their names. You won't tell me anything! You won't ever talk about them. Why? *Why?*" I yelled back, matching her volume.

"Madison, I forbid you to look for them."

"What the hell are you talking about?"

"I forbid you to do this."

"It's my choice, Ruth. I'm an adult, and there is nothing you can do to stop me. I deserve to know! I des—"

"Damn it, Madison!"

"What? Are you afraid that you will lose your niece or that you will lose your employee? I'm doing this."

"You won't find them!"

"Why? Why not?"

"Because they're dead!"

And that's when everything went silent.

My heart jolted, and I felt like the air had been sucked out of my lungs. I panted loudly for a few moments and stared wide-eyed back at Ruth. She looked just as shocked as I felt.

"What?" I managed to utter as my eyes flooded with tears.

Ruth kept her eyes locked on mine but said nothing. Her already fair skin went even more pale.

"They're—they're dead? How could you have not told me?" I shook my head. "At the very frickin' least—why didn't you tell me that? How…how—"

"Madison…" Ruth reached her hand out.

"No," I said through clenched teeth. I grabbed my bag and swept the manila folder and the rest of its contents back inside. "You don't get to pretend to care now. No."

Aunt Ruth took another step toward me and reached out again. I pulled away instantly and looked back into her gray eyes. Her gestures seemed sincere, but the cold stare in her eyes never left, even after she had blurted out something as shattering as that.

"You are horrible," I said with clear articulation and unwavering conviction. "Stay away from me."

I backed away, then swung open the door of the gym and slipped out to the sidewalk. I heard the bell chime as I sprinted down the street, clutching my bag to my chest.

They were dead.

Dead.

I couldn't stop the words from repeating in my mind, and I couldn't stop my tears. I ran as fast as I could, away from Ruth's Gym and away from Aunt Ruth.

They were dead.

CHAPTER 5

I reached the back door and stopped, letting my head rest against the cool metal of the large white door as I waited for my breath to return after running home from the gym. My heartbeat showed no signs of slowing. I pulled my house keys from my bag.

Aunt Ruth's words still stung, like a bee sting to the brain, and I couldn't stop hearing those words over and over.

They're dead.

Before I could put the keys in the lock, I heard that stupid ringing noise again. It was coming from the backyard. I set my bag on the ground by the door and turned around, sniffling and wiping the tears and sweat from my face as I walked toward the sound. I was no longer cautious or worried.

The sound was guiding me, increasing in volume with each step I took. I navigated through the un-kept grove of trees that lined the edge of the backyard. The snap of twigs and the crunch of last year's leaves was barely audible over the persistent ringing sound.

The air felt heavier with moisture back here in a cluster of oak trees. One oak right in the middle seemed to stand out from the rest.

"Whoa," I muttered. The tree. There was something about that particular tree.

The sound stopped as I stepped in front of it. The trunk was particularly wide compared to the others around it. I looked up at the green leaves. They were completely still. That wouldn't be strange on its own, but leaves on all the trees around it moved and rustled in the breeze.

But not this tree. This tree was motionless.

"Okay…" My eyes traced the curves and splits in the bark of the trunk. My body tingled, like that feeling you get when your leg falls asleep, but all over. I felt weightless and heavy at the same time and, as if I was no longer in control, I saw my hand rise up in front of me.

I had to touch it. I had to touch this tree.

Something inside me urged me to. My fingers trembled as I slowly moved my hand to the trunk. I closed my eyes and laid my hand on the rough bark.

And...nothing happened.

I opened one eye and placed my other hand on the trunk of the tree.

That's when it felt like a brick hit me in the temple. I fell to the ground and cradled my head in my hands. I couldn't tell if I was screaming out loud or not because all I could hear was the loud ringing again. Both of my temples jolted with a sharp pain, and my skin got hot again. I felt something warm running down my lips.

I touched my lips and saw that my fingertips were covered with blood.

Stunned, I laid with my face on the musty-smelling ground for a moment. My head pounded, and each hair on my body stood up.

What's happening to me?

Then the ringing stopped.

I rolled over, then backed away from the tree on all fours like a crab. My nose was still gushing, but at least the pounding headache was gone. A big gust of wind rustled the leaves of the trees around me. The leaves on this tree still didn't budge.

What the hell?

I wiped my nose with the back of my hand and sprinted through the trees and the backyard, back up to the house.

My fingers fumbled with the keys before I managed to unlock the door. I slid the strap of my bag onto my shoulder and darted into the kitchen. I checked behind me to make sure I hadn't tracked dirt into the house before running up the stairs to get to my bedroom. Traumatic event or not, Aunt Ruth would flip if I tracked dirt in the house.

With a grunt, I swung my bedroom door closed behind me. The right side of the white room was neat and tidy: a white dresser; a twin bed with a flowered pink comforter, tucked in. In the middle of the floor was a large shaggy pink and gray area rug.

Then I looked at my side of the room, which was a total mess. The strap of my bag was starting to hurt me. I let my bag slip to the floor.

Rubbing my shoulder, I crossed over to the full-length mirror that hung on the back of the closet door. Blood was smeared from my upper lip to my ear like a giant creepy smirk. I plucked an obnoxious amount of tissue from the box on Lacy's dresser and used the sweat from my forehead to wipe the drying blood from my cheek.

How was that for karma? I gave someone a bloody nose and then got one in the span of an afternoon. Even the absurdly strange tree incident, however, couldn't distract me from Aunt Ruth's bombshell.

My birth parents were dead.

I had pictured my parents in my mind for as long as I could remember. I had created this twisted fantasy of a different life that I could lead if I ever did go and find them. How they didn't intend to give me up. That they just lost track of Ruth and me. I pictured teary reunions and long hugs. All things that made me want to barf under any other circumstance, but when I thought about my parents, they didn't sound so bad.

Unlike Aunt Ruth, I wasn't void of emotion. But at the same time, I wasn't all that great at dealing with emotions, either. I felt my skin crawl, like I needed to run or something. Anything to burn off this energy that was building in the pit of my stomach.

My phone buzzed loudly. I pulled it from my back pocket and clenched it in my fist.

It was Aunt Ruth calling. She never called. Calling meant speaking to me and allowing me to answer. Nope, Aunt Ruth was much more of a texter. Texting orders was her thing. I ignored her call.

My parents are dead.

The manila folder peeked out from under the pile of papers sticking out of my bag. I thought about the delusional dreams of Christmas dinners and family vacations, of my dad wrapping me in a big bear hug or my mom brushing my hair. They were people who only existed in my mind, but that didn't stop my grief.

My phone started buzzing again. It was Aunt Ruth again.

I picked up the phone. *"What?"* I screamed into it.

"Madison, calm down!" Aunt Ruth said sternly back. "You need to keep your emotions in check. You need to focus, do you understand?"

"Are you seriously telling me that I need to focus right now? You just told me my parents were dead...on my birthday. I was going to file a petition with the courts to get my records released on Saturday."

"The courthouse won't be open on a Saturday and even it were, Saturday is your track meet, Madison. Not only were you going to defy me, but you were planning to skip your meet?" Aunt Ruth asked with utter disappointment and no remorse, no guilt for what she had just done. She didn't even care.

"Are you frickin' serious? This is a little much, even for you. I don't give a rat's ass about the stupid track meet! The only thing I cared about was finding them, and you just—you just—" My emotions choked out my voice.

"I should have told you, but now you know and you need to move on. There are more important things at hand now. You need to come back to the gym right now. We aren't done here."

"I am done. I am so very done with all of this," I said through a sob.

"You don't understand. You are letting your emotions take hold of you. Focus, Madison."

"What the hell is wrong with you? You are delusional. I am never coming back there!"

"Madison."

"No," I said with a low voice, clenching my teeth. "I hate you."

I whipped my phone against my bedroom wall, and it exploded into shards of black and silver. How could they be dead? How could she have kept it from me? I was going to find them, and they were going to be wonderful.

They were going to be wonderful. They had to be wonderful.

I slid the manila folder out of the cluster of schoolwork with one finger, dragged it across the wood floor, and flicked it open. There it was. The petition for the court to release my adoption records. For so long, it was the only thing that I really cared about. It was my plan.

I had a plan.

This crisp white paper was my eighth attempt at filling out the form, to ensure everything on it was perfect, yet it had never occurred to me to check to make sure the stupid courthouse would be open on a Saturday. But it didn't matter anymore anyway. My fingers traced the loops of my signature before I laid my palm on the center of the page and crumpled it in my fist.

I took a deep breath, holding the paper tightly, then threw it to the center of my bedroom. It landed on the shaggy pink and gray rug.

"Enough." Keeping it together most days meant pushing this crap far, far from my mind.

"Enough," I repeated, leaning my head on my bed next to me.

"Mads?" a voice called. It was Jason. It was like he had a beacon that told him when I needed him. He was outside the window on the far side of the room, opposite me. I didn't move. I didn't need to; he was already there, perched on the branch of the oak tree that stood just outside my bedroom window. He shimmied the screen up and slid through.

Tossing his backpack on the floor, he kept his eyes on mine. We didn't speak as he moved across the room to where I sat slumped against my bed. As soon as he hugged me, my tears swallowed me again.

I laid my head on his shoulder, and we sat in silence for a while. For a few moments, it didn't feel so terrible, and my stomach didn't feel like a giant boulder.

Jason pointed to the shattered pieces of my phone strewn across my floor. "I love what you've done with the place."

I sat up and wiped my face with my hands. "Ha, yeah, thanks."

Jason laughed.

"Did you hear?" I asked.

"Shawn's nose? Oh, yeah, I heard about that. I'm pretty sure my great-aunt Didi in Wisconsin heard about that one."

If only that was the craziest thing that had happened to me today.

I leaned over to grab the balled-up piece of paper and dropped it in Jason's lap.

"Thanks for your help with this, but I won't be needing it anymore. They're dead."

Jason opened it just enough to see what the paper was, then tossed it behind us toward the wall.

"Yeah, Ruth called me," he replied.

Classic Ruth. I got emotional; she couldn't deal, so she called Jason.

Jason patted my knee. "Quite a day for you, huh?"

"Yep. Happy birthday to me."

CHAPTER 6

I woke up slumped down in the ratty brown recliner that sat under the window in the bedroom. Jason had directed me to sit in it while he went to help at his parent's restaurant during the dinner rush, and I fell asleep almost instantly in the cozy chair. It was my favorite spot in the whole house, and even though it was an eyesore, Lacy and Ruth never made me throw it out. The arms of the chair had little jagged lines in the leather that threatened to tear apart at any moment, but it was still as comfy as ever.

I listened to the birds and buzzing bugs that filled the silence of my empty room. My body was numb. I was numb. My nap didn't help clear away any of the crappiness of my afternoon.

"Maddy?" Jason's voice broke the silence as he walked back into the room with his computer bag and food in hand.

"Pizza!"

"I know a crisis when I see one." Jason kicked his shoes off. "My dad's pizza cures all."

I shifted over just as Jason plopped next to me in the chair and set a bag of various snack foods into my lap. He opened the box of pizza from his parents' restaurant. Melted cheese, spicy peppers, and beef. It was my favorite thing they served there. The restaurant was Italian and Puerto Rican fusion, just like Jason.

Having such easy access to free pizza was just one of the perks of Jason being my bestie. The greatest thing about having Jason as my best friend was how well he knew me. Not just that my favorite color was teal or that I was scared of water. Or that I loved anything with chocolate. No, the reason Jason was the greatest was that he didn't make me talk all the time. He knew when to just let me be.

He also hadn't mentioned the worst part of the day—my dead parents.

"Ran into some kids from school at the market." Jason began setting up his computer and picked a TV show.

Great.

"Nobody is talking about the pool incident or the state championships, that's for damn sure," Jason added. "Just that Mad Dash broke the prom king's nose again."

"Now, if we can just shake the stupid Mad Dash part, I'll be happy." I pulled some napkins out of the bag and laid them out on my lap. "Guess I'll be at the race on Saturday after all."

Jason set a slice of pizza on my napkins before taking a huge bite of his own piece. "What are you talking about?"

"They're—they're dead," I mumbled, still hating how that sounded. "There's nobody to find. I would just get their names. And I guess the courthouse is only open during the week. I have no idea how I could make that work."

I chewed my pizza slowly.

Jason shook his head. "So we skip class! School can kiss my ass, Mads. We're still going to file that paper. You deserve to know. You may not get the ending you wanted, but we are going to find them, even if it kills us."

Skipping school? Aunt Ruth would have my head for that. *Even better.* I smiled. "Always be you. You are perfect, you know that?"

"That's what they tell me," he answered with a laugh.

I took a deep breath and kept eating. "I'll think about it."

"Do that. I'll back you, no matter what you decide, Mads."

It was the relaxing end to a crappy day. Just some food, some TV, and Jason. My bedroom door swung open, scaring both of us.

"All right! Who's ready to go to the energy crisis rally tonight?" Lacy exclaimed from the doorway.

"Nope," I replied.

"Second that," Jason chimed in.

Lacy entered our shared room like a perky ray of sunshine in human form. She was always so damn happy.

"Come on!" Lacy encouraged me. "You punched my jerk of an ex-boyfriend. You owe me!"

"Ex?" Jason chimed. "That's new."

"I heard about the pool," Lacy said, looking at me. "I'm glad you're okay."

Was I okay?

"Thanks, Lace." I forced a smile.

Even with that sign of solidarity, I was too upset to go to the rally.

"You guys are in veg mode at 7:30 on Friday night, eating junk food," Lacy said, folding her arms. "You are the worst teenagers on the planet. Get off your butts and let's go out. I am not going to let you turn into a hermit again this summer."

I did my best to hide the sadness that was trying to swallow me whole. I didn't want to talk to Lacy about my parents. She wasn't like Jason. She would make me talk about it, and that was not something I was in the mood for, right now or ever.

"Let's go!" Lacy repeated.

"Like, leave the house?" I narrowed my eyes.

"Yeah."

"But there are people out there."

"We are in a mood, Lacy. We have earned this," Jason said.

I nodded and took a bite of pizza.

"I don't get why Maddy is upset, and I am not even going to try to figure that one out. But, Jason, why are you sad?" Lacy raised an eyebrow.

Jason held up a can of whipped cream and sprayed some in his mouth. "When she hurts, I hurt," he answered with his mouth full. "We are basically one very, very, *very* attractive person. Maddy may or may not be going through something. She is upset and she is handling it with grace, if you ask me!"

Jason then offered me some, which I accepted, of course. My cheeks puffed with whipped cream as the can hissed.

"Yeah. I have grace!" I said, barely understandable through my mouthful of whipped cream.

Lacy sank down onto the foot of my bed and sighed.

"Have you talked to my mom, Maddy?" she asked.

"Unfortunately."

"Did she rip your head off?" Lacy asked, not knowing the full scope of my day's traumas.

Jason spoke before I could. "I know you meant that figuratively, but I am pretty sure Ruth could literally rip a head off. That woman is an animal. She could bench like two of me."

"True story," I replied.

"Maybe even three of me." Jason's eyes widened.

"She has been putting in some crazy hours at the gym lately. One of the other trainers quit, so she's teaching classes all day," Lacy added. She never saw the flaws in her mother, which was a good thing. Lacy seemed to be as well-adjusted and happy as I could hope for. Aunt Ruth was warmer with her, thankfully.

"This is Greenrock Island," Jason said. "There are, like, ten thousand residents on this island in the winter. It's already a ghost town with all the seasonal folks heading back up north. How is she finding all of these people to work out?"

"Who cares? Pass me the gummy bears." I held out my hand.

"Maddy! Stop eating that crap! You are going to feel horrible on our run in the morning," Lacy said, standing up.

"I am not running in the morning. I am never leaving this chair ever again." I shoved a handful of gummy bears in my mouth and handed one to Jason.

"Thank you, m'lady," he sung out.

Lacy stomped her foot. "Seriously, Madison. You have a state championship meet! And ugh, you aren't even going to come to the rally tonight? I am the only one here who seems to care about this energy crisis!"

"The lights flicker now and then. It happens," Jason said.

"You need to care about this!" Lacy argued, crossing her arms.

"Lacy, the only thing I care about right now is whether this hot guy can get out of this deal with the crossroad demon," I shot back, gesturing to the TV show that continued to play on the computer screen.

"Hot guy's brother will save him," Jason replied out of the corner of his mouth.

"I hope so."

"Ugh! You two drive me insane. Maddy, if it wasn't your birthday, I would give you a piece of my mind, but since it is, I will direct this at Jason!"

I looked up to meet the annoyed glare of a red-faced Lacy.

"Your best friend almost screwed up her chance at running in the state championships. Why? I don't know," Lacy started.

"I told you, your pervert boyfriend tried to kill me," I interjected.

"I don't know why Maddy did this, but I think she got scared," Lacy continued, still only speaking to Jason.

"Scared of what?" he asked curiously.

"Don't encourage this." I slapped Jason's knee. "Lacy, leave it alone. You have no idea what you're talking about."

"Maddy worked her butt off for this opportunity. She was the shoo-in to win State, and I think it makes her nervous. I don't know why. I don't know why someone would intentionally screw it up, but I think that is exactly what she did."

"Why do you even care, Lacy?" It wasn't funny anymore. Now I was starting to get mad.

She crossed her arms, looking even more defensive. "I care because it's important! My mother gave up so much to raise us and make sure we had every opportunity. And you were going to just throw it away like it meant nothing!"

"Okay, *Ruth*. Are you done?" I asked, rolling my eyes.

"No! There are real problems in the world. Real problems that won't go away just because you ignore them and binge watch TV shows on a Friday night. The rally is in the town square. You want to stay here and be remembered as the crazy violent girl, that's fine. Or you could make a real difference at this rally tonight. Instead of sitting here like a couple of lazy selfish jerks, you need to get off your butts and go. We are the future, and we are the only ones who can save this place!"

"By all that you hold dear on this good earth, I bid you stand, men of the West!" I exclaimed and pumped my fist in the air, my head leaned back against the recliner and my eyes closed.

Jason chuckled and let out a long, amused sigh. "Listen, Aragorn, she may have a point," he said, turning his head to me.

I dropped my jaw and gasped. "Brutus!"

"Thank god you two have each other. I never know what the heck either of you are talking about." Lacy threw her hands in the air and marched out of the room.

"You seriously want to go to the mayor's dumb rally?" I asked Jason. "I broke his son's nose."

Jason shrugged. Spending my birthday with a bunch of people I didn't know did not appeal to me, but I could already tell by the look on Jason's face that he had made up his mind.

I sighed. "Do you think they have cake?"

"They might have cake," Jason answered with optimism.

I grunted as I pushed myself out of the chair that Jason and I had been so solidly wedged into. "This has been the worst day ever. But I am going to get some damn cake on my birthday."

"That's right. Let's get you some cake." Jason stood. "I have to change. I'll be back in twenty."

I watched as Jason walked out of my room.

"You got it," I said, but he was already gone.

Groaning, I stood up and stretched. Did I need a shower before this shindig? I took my hair down and held a few strands to my nose. Yeah, I needed a shower. Before I left my room to go to the bathroom and get cleaned up, I crossed back over to my window.

"They better have some frickin' cake!" I yelled through the open window.

I heard the faint sound of Jason laughing as he crossed the street to his house. It was the cute blue one right across from ours.

Looking down at the super dull black T-shirt and khaki shorts that I had worn to school, I walked over to my closet. Before I could pick out new clothes, I heard the ringing sound again.

This time, it was unbearably loud. I pressed my hands over my ears, fell to my knees, and screamed.

CHAPTER 7

"Mads?" I heard Jason call out over the obnoxious ring that continued to sound through the air, but thankfully, the volume was decreasing. I was curled up on the floor in front of my closet.

"I heard you screaming." Jason ran to me. "What's going on?"

I couldn't answer him yet. The sound was fading, but the pain in my ears lingered. I pulled my hands away and tried to sit up.

"Are you okay?" Jason knelt in front of me, holding my shoulders. "You weren't downstairs like we said, and then I heard you screaming."

I nodded as the piercing ring finally disappeared. "You said we would meet downstairs in twenty minutes."

"Maddy, it's been twenty-five minutes."

"What?" I asked through my haze. Had I been laying here screaming for more than twenty minutes? "Did you hear that noise?"

Jason shook his head. "You screaming? Yeah, I heard it from outside. What happened?"

"Something...strange is going on," I said nervously.

"What do you mean?"

"I just feel weird."

"You are weird," Jason shot back.

"I'm serious. Something's happening to me, Jay."

"You sound scared, Maddy." His eyes were narrow and pensive, and I could see how worried he was, even with the little light in my room. "Okay. Well, don't worry. I'm here now," he reassured me.

And in typical Jason form, he wrapped his arms around my shoulders and pulled me close to him in an awkward embrace as we both knelt on the floor. Jason was taller than me, and he rested his chin gently on the top of my head, my arms pinned at my sides.

"Off! Off!" I said. My words were muffled by his shirt. "This is super weird."

"Ugh, touching. Ugh, affection," Jason mocked in his best girly voice. "I'm swaddling you, like a baby. It's comforting."

I let out a laugh. Hugging that went on longer than a second or two felt more like suffocation than affection, and this was even worse because I couldn't move at all.

"I'll go grab you a water," Jason said as he released me and left the room.

"Thanks." The setting sun gave the room a yellow glow, but it wasn't bright enough to illuminate anything. Reaching my arm out, I flicked the light switch up. Nothing happened. I grabbed the digital clock on my nightstand next to me, but it was blank. I slipped my red sneakers on.

"Jay, the power's out!" I called out.

He didn't answer.

"Jay?" I called again and moved to the doorway of my room. As I started to walk down the hall toward the stairs, there was a rustling sound behind me. It was coming from my aunt's room.

"Jay?" I whispered. "What are you doing? You know Ruth hates people going into her room."

No answer. I pivoted and slowly walked toward Aunt Ruth's bedroom. There were no windows in the hall, making it almost pitch black—which wasn't a problem. I had snuck out of this house in the dark many, many times, so navigating it blind was pretty easy for me.

"Aunt Ruth?" I called down the hall. Her room was at the end of the hallway, just across from the bathroom.

No answer.

I stopped at the closed door of Aunt Ruth's office, a room she always kept locked.

"Aunt Ruth?" I called again, but there was no response.

My heart pounded in my ears, drowning out all other noises. It was the only thing I could hear now. I stopped in Aunt Ruth's doorway.

There was an unnerving stillness in the room. The window was covered in a sheer white curtain, letting some light filter in, but not enough to see well.

"If this is another one of your stupid drills, I am not in the mood, Aunt Ruth."

I clenched my fist and took a defensive stance, ready to fight, just in case. I turned back to the doorway and gasped to see the silhouette of a person there.

"*Glacia!*"

There was a jolt in my body, and then it felt like my muscles all knotted at once, like I had a thousand charley horses. I couldn't move or speak. It was like I was frozen solid.

"Oh, it is you!" the person said.

Then the pain, the twisted stiffness in my muscles was gone. I stumbled backward into Aunt Ruth's nightstand and knocked a lamp over, sending it crashing to the ground. It shattered on impact. I ignored it and spun to face the doorway.

"Lacy?" I exhaled in relief. "Wha—"

"There is no time. Listen to me. You need to act quickly. We must retrieve your magic now," Lacy interrupted. Her face was stern and serious, more so than I had ever seen.

"What? Lacy, what are you talking about?" I asked, looking her up and down.

Lacy didn't answer; instead, she grabbed my wrist and pulled me out of the room. I yanked my arm away from her but followed anyway.

"Lacy?"

"There is no time," she repeated.

"No, what did you say when you walked in the room? What was that?"

Lacy ignored me and walked down the hall to the Ruth's office.

"Lacy, it's locked, it's always…"

Lacy closed her eyes and said something so softly that I couldn't quite make it out. Then the door popped open.

She moved with determination into the room, still ignoring me. I stayed in the hallway, my mouth hanging open as I tried to rationalize what was happening around me.

"What are you doing?" I pressed.

Lacy knelt down on the floor and pulled the rug back.

"Lacy, answer me!" I demanded.

She ripped up a floorboard and tossed it on the floor beside her. I watched as she reached down beneath the floor, pulled out a small box, and lifted the lid. In it was a small piece of paper that she appeared to be reading. She set that aside too and reached in to grab something long and slender from beneath the floor. She carefully put the little box back and put the plank back in the floor, stood, and turned to face me.

In her hand was a sword. And not one of the wooden swords from the gym or the sparring foils. A real, actual, legit sword.

"Lacy?"

Lacy walked toward me. "Take it."

I stepped back and hit the wall behind me.

"Jason?" I turned my head toward the stairs and called out.

"Take it. It is yours." Lacy looked firmly at me, turning the hilt of the sword toward me. "I know what to do now, but we have to hurry."

"Lacy, put that thing away!" I blurted. My skin prickled and sweat beaded on my forehead. "Crap." I wiped my forehead. The hot flash was happening again.

My skin tingled, then felt like it was on fire. My vision went black for a moment as my heart beat rapidly, faster than it ever had. My limbs shook and I felt almost weightless for a moment, like that feeling you get right before the elevator stops on your floor.

I blinked a few times as the hot spell began to fade.

"Are you finished?" I heard Lacy ask behind me.

"Huh? What's happening to me? What's wrong with me?" I asked as I clasped my trembling hands together and bowed my head. "I keep getting this really weird th—"

"I know," Lacy interrupted. "Just breathe."

"Lacy? What is this? What is all of this? And what do you mean, you know?" My words came out more like a whimper.

"I know what you are feeling," Lacy said sympathetically.

"No, you don't understand. I keep getting this thing where my skin is burning and..." I paused and took a deep breath.

"It feels like you are going to explode, and your skin tingles and feels like tiny needles are darting at it, right?" Lacy said, looking bored.

"How did you know that?" I started to feel angry with her. It was almost as if she was toying with me or something, and I didn't like not being in the know. I sank to the floor of the hallway.

Lacy sighed and joined me on the wooden floor. "I just know, dear girl. That is the protection spell wearing off. You are completely yourself now."

Lacy placed the sword on the ground and took my hand.

"There are so many things that they should have told you. But right now, there is no time. I am going to need you to do as I say and keep your mouth shut, or I will shut it for you."

I squinted at her in the dim light of the hall. The outside light was nearly gone now, casting very little light through the windows of the house.

"Why are you acting like this?"

Lacy didn't answer.

"Jason?" I called down the hall again.

"They took my mother," Lacy said.

"Who did?" I stared at her. "What in the hell are you talking about?" I was breathing loudly now.

She held up her hand to silence me and turned her ear toward the stairs. A shudder of unease hit my chest and radiated throughout my entire body. I rose to my feet. My knees felt shaky and my whole body was trembling.

There was movement downstairs. "It's Jason," I said.

I could not stop shivering.

Another clamor, only this time it sounded like it was coming from farther away. Outside, maybe? Then we heard a woman scream.

"That is not Jason." Lacy stood.

My stomach was twisting in a giant knot. I was nauseous, faint, and obnoxiously hot again. Beads of sweat gathered between the goosebumps on my skin. Terror. What I was feeling was sheer, unadulterated terror.

"Take the sword," Lacy urged me, gesturing to the weapon lying on the floor.

My thoughts immediately went to Jason. What if he was in trouble?

I stared down at the sword. The grip was covered with a dark swirled pattern. The rounded cross guard was a dark metal. This was the real deal, and it was making me a little hesitant.

Lacy's face didn't echo what I was feeling at all. No apprehension, no worry, no panic. She just looked calm and maybe even a little annoyed.

I curled my hand around the grip, and blue light burst from it as my fingers tightened around it. Startled, I dropped the sword with a gasp.

Lacy didn't look fazed at all by the sword's touch-activated light. "It is all right. Just pick it up."

I reached out and gripped the handle again, and again the grip lit up in a brilliant blue under my hand, but this time, I held on. Tiny beams of blue light escaped between my uneasy fingers, and a prickling sensation shot up my arm like it had fallen asleep, but only for a moment. It was like an electric shock that caused no pain. Then the glow dimmed.

"Why is it doing that?" I asked her.

"It is okay. It is meant to," Lacy answered.

I pushed past her and headed down the hall. I hurried down the stairs, the light of the sword's grip casting a blue glow around me.

I held up the sword to light the kitchen. The house was completely dark now.

"Maddy?" I heard Jason's voice call out. I turned to see him just as the back door slammed behind him.

"Who's there?" Lacy asked as she came down the stairs behind me.

"It's Jason." I looked at her out of the corner of my eye. Why was she acting so strange?

"Looks like that energy crisis rally was pretty legit, Lacy," Jason said.

Lacy didn't respond. Instead, she grabbed my arm and pulled me out into the backyard. Jason followed. I flinched as the ringing sound erupted from the same cluster of trees in the backyard.

"That noise. It has something to do with all of this, doesn't it?" I asked.

"What's going on?" Jason asked, following closely behind me.

"Wait!" Lacy ducked behind a row of trash cans. Jason and I followed her lead.

"What's going on? Did you hear that scream?" Jason looked distraught. His face was covered in sweat, and so was his gray T-shirt. I held the sword up higher to see him better.

He jumped back, knocking into one of the metal garbage cans. "Whoa! Why do you have a sword?"

Before I could answer him, Lacy clamped her hand over his mouth. "Quiet!"

He looked back at her, confused. Lacy lowered her hand and traced her finger along Jason's chin before she turned her focus back to me.

Jason looked at me inquisitively and pointed at Lacy when she was no longer focused on him. He looked just as bewildered as I felt.

"What do you feel now?" Lacy asked me.

"Huh? I feel the same," I whispered to her.

Lacy shook her head and scrunched her face up, like she did when she was thinking hard. "That cannot be right," she said.

Then I saw something move in the backyard. I shifted over to get a better look. I squinted hard into the dark. It looked like a campfire—no, like a torch.

"Do you see that?" Jason whispered to me. We were both leaning over, looking out around the garbage cans.

I nodded.

There was a small group of people walking toward the trees at the edge of Ruth's yard.

What were they doing?

I focused on the torch and gasped as it lit up one of the people in the group, bound and being carried.

Jason patted my arm. "Is that—"

"It's Aunt Ruth."

CHAPTER 8

"Aunt Ruth!" I called out, but before I could stand and run to her, Lacy grabbed my wrists with both of her hands.

"You cannot go over there," she said, her eyes wide. "You are not ready. Just let them go."

"What? Let them go?" I shook my head, baffled. "Are you out of your frickin' mind?"

I looked to Jason for some backup. He was biting his fingernail and not speaking, hunched over as he peered around the silver garbage can. No help there.

"Lacy, go get help," I pleaded. Maybe she was in shock, but her behavior was beyond frustrating.

I took off toward my aunt and her captors, leaving Lacy and Jason by the cans. They seemed to be in the same spot that I had wandered into earlier today. This all felt like a really screwed-up dream.

The sun had completely set now. The moon gave me some light, but not enough. With the power out and the street lights dark, the only real light that I had to guide me was the blue light coming from my sword's grip.

I lost sight of the people, but the light of the torch they carried was unmistakable, even through the trees. Getting to them would be no problem, but then what? I knew how to fight and I was good at it, so that part didn't worry me, but the intensity of the situation was growing with every step I took. What did they want with Aunt Ruth? I didn't even want to think about why they were taking her into the woods. I would stop them before they hurt her.

As I entered the wooded area, I could see them. The group had stopped. I ducked behind the tree trunks. My cheek scraped against the bark as I peeked around the side of the oak. I saw three people with Aunt Ruth, and they were all wearing long hooded cloaks. One held a torch, and the other two each held one of her arms.

By the light of their torch, I could see a gag covering Aunt Ruth's mouth. Her hands and feet were tied together, but she kept thrashing back and forth until we locked eyes. For just a moment, we both were perfectly still. She looked relieved.

If *she* saw me, it would be seconds before the cloak-wearing jerks noticed too, as they were all facing in my direction. I stepped out from behind the tree and called out, "Let her go!"

Ruth yelled something from under her gag, but it was muffled and I couldn't understand.

Within seconds, the two men holding Ruth's arms threw her to the ground and charged at me. They hadn't even reached me before she started working at her ropes. They clearly had no idea who they were messing with. There was no way that these idiots would beat Ruth and me together. No way.

I tossed the sword to the ground and did a somersault to my left as the blue light vanished. Aunt Ruth always said the darkness could be a weapon if you used it right.

The two goons stopped, looking for me, as I jumped to my feet. The first guy got my foot in his manly parts and buckled over. I grabbed the other one's shoulders and threw my head into his face with all the force I could muster.

I spun and grabbed my sword from the base of the tree where I had tossed it. The man holding the torch was fixated on me, too busy to notice that Ruth had successfully gotten out of her foot bindings. She was working on her hands now.

There you go, Aunt Ruth. I smiled at her, knowing that this would be over soon. Nobody could take down Aunt Ruth—not even me. Everything was going to be okay now.

I lifted my sword to see the downed guys in cloaks still writhing in pain. One was holding his junk, the other holding his blood-soaked face.

"You broke my nose!" he said, his speech muffled by his hands cupped over his face.

"And not the first one of the day, either!" I shot back. I turned back to the guy with the torch and held my sword out in front of me. His eyes weren't on me; they were focused on the blue glow of its grip.

"Well, well, well. You are a Witch, too," the hooded man holding the torch started. "You must be the daughter of this betrayer. You can die right next to your mother, you filthy snake."

"I don't know what the hell you're talking about. I called the cops," I lied. "So let her go right now."

I looked back at my aunt. "Don't worry, Aunt Ruth, help is on the way."

"Your aunt?" He looked utterly shocked, then squinted at me. "No, it cannot be."

He shook his head. "You? Is she that brazen to keep you here, right next to the portal?" He shook his head again in disbelief. Then he dropped to one knee and bowed his head.

"Huh?" I squinted at him.

"More of you?" The man raised his head and leaned over to look behind me. I turned to see Jason standing there.

"What are you doing here?" I waved him away. "Run!"

And in that moment of distraction, the man with the broken nose knocked me down and rolled on top of me.

"Jason, help Ruth!" I yelled, just as the bloody-faced man wrapped his hands around my neck. I struggled to breathe and my sword slipped out of my hand.

Things went hazy as I heard yelling, scuffling. The man's fingers squeezed tighter and I couldn't distinguish the voices. I only heard random words. Leaves crunched and sticks snapped as feet shuffled around me.

"Stop!"

"No!"

"Help her!"

Someone fell on top of the bloody-faced man. He let go of my throat and left me there, coughing and trying to take in air.

A huge roar, a gust of wind, and then it was quiet.

"Jason? Ruth?" I sat up and looked around. I was alone.

My entire body tensed as my stomach churned.

What just happened?

"Aunt Ruth!" I screamed, but the trees stayed silent.

I felt along the ground and picked up my sword. All I could hear was my own heartbeat now as my eyes darted around the wooded area.

"Maddy?" Jason stumbled out from behind that tree, rubbing the side of his head.

"Oh, thank god." I ran to him. "Where did they go? Where's Ruth?"

Jason didn't answer; instead, he motioned to the tree. He wrapped his hand around mine and pulled me to the other side of the giant oak.

The tree.

"Don't touch it," I warned Jason, but he laid his hand on the trunk of the familiar oak tree. I had stood in this spot earlier today. I looked up at the top of the motionless tree.

"No, Maddy. It's like they went inside of it," Jason whispered, not taking his eyes off the tree. "I think I got knocked out for a minute, but I swear that's what I saw. I swear it."

Before I could question the insanity of that sentence, something moved behind Jason. I pushed him behind me and held up my sword.

"Who's there?" I called, and lifted my sword to cast light toward the shadowy trees.

Out of the dark stepped a young man dressed in all black. He stepped into the blue glow of my sword, casting a strange shadow on his strong jaw. His hair was short and sort of swept back away from his forehead. And then, even in the blue light, I saw them: the unmistakable green eyes. The same eyes that had looked down at me earlier today in the pool house at school.

"You. Who are you?" I asked, pointing my sword toward him.

He angled his face, casting soft shadows on his pronounced cheekbones.

"Ren Raker," he replied, simply and seriously.

"Ren?" I asked. "Where is my aunt?"

Ren held his hand out. "You must come with me, princess. This is no place for you."

"Princess?" Jason repeated, looking at me. I shrugged at Jason, just as confused as he was.

"Nicely done, Porter." Jason and I jumped at the sound of another voice. It was Lacy.

She walked over to us and stopped next to Ren. She didn't look scared or worried. Her face was relaxed, and her pace was no longer rushed. I felt like I was on a prank show, but a really unfunny, annoying one. Nobody was giving me any answers and my aunt was gone.

"Where is Aunt Ruth?" I looked up at Ren. He and Lacy were staring at each other now, not speaking.

Jason wasn't looking at the strange interaction of my cousin and this random dude. His stare was fixed on the oak tree. He ran his hand up the trunk, but it didn't seem to affect him the same way it affected me.

"You will not find her here," Lacy said calmly, raising her chin.

"Lacy, what is going on?" I demanded.

Lacy scoffed and her eyes narrowed. "You want the truth? Fine. You are from the realm of Everly, an adjacent dimension."

I squinted. "Pardon?"

"Ruthana kept you here to protect you because the king decreed that all Magics must be destroyed."

I blinked a few times and opened my mouth to speak.

"No!" Lacy shouted in my face, her nose an inch from mine. "There is no time! I am sorry that she did not tell you, but you can wallow in that later. I need you to go through that portal and get my mother."

Ren crossed his arms.

Before Ren could reply, Lacy raised her hand at him. *"Glacia."*

Ren froze.

I jumped. "How are you doing this? What is that you keep saying?"

She looked at me like I was an idiot. "He is frozen. I froze his muscles with magic."

Confused, I shook my head. "What?"

"I just—I need him not to talk for a minute so I can get this out." Lacy laid her finger on her lips for a moment. "Mother has been keeping your true identity a secret from you. Just through that portal is Everly. That is where you were born. You are the daughter of the leader of the Rosewood Coven. My mother, Ruthana, is her sister. To save you, my mother brought you here. That is the truth."

I took a step back and didn't speak. Holding the bridge of my nose with my eyes squeezed shut, I tried to comprehend what she was saying. "Everly? And my mother was the leader of the Rosewood Coven? My *mother*? Lacy, have you gone mental?"

"I realize this is a lot to process, but all will be explained, I promise. Right now, I am asking you to trust me. Can you trust me, your cousin, whom you have known your entire life? Please?" Lacy's big blue eyes were earnest as she spoke.

I looked at Jason.

Lacy leaned closer. "If you seek the truth about your mother, you will find it in Everly. Every answer you seek is there, I promise."

Jason started pacing behind me, mumbling to himself.

"Yes, but..." I sighed. She looked so certain. "That's where Aunt Ruth is?"

Lacy nodded, her blue eyes practically twinkling.

"A portal?" My mind still hadn't wrapped itself around that part.

"Maddy, I'm going to go call the cops. This is nuts," Jason interrupted.

"It will not help. You need to leave right now. Time is running out. They are taking her to the temple, and then it will not be long before she meets her end. The king likes to keep a tight schedule."

"But I—yeah. Okay. What do I have to do?" I dropped my hand to my side.

"Ren, can you take her through as we discussed?" Lacy waved her hand at him. Ren took a deep breath and was moving again. He sighed loudly but seemed strangely unfazed at being frozen and unfrozen. He nodded at Lacy.

"We have to go now. Something is not right. They should not have known she was here." Ren crossed his arms, looking at Lacy sternly. "There is something you are not telling me, I know it."

"Close your lips or I will rip them off, Porter," Lacy said calmly, with a slight smile.

"Lacy?" I took a deep breath. This was all so unlike her. She was Lacy— sweet, kind Lacy.

"How did *they* know where to find her? That was never a part of this. You are working with them, are you not?" Ren asked, looking very upset with Lacy.

"Maddy?" Jason whispered behind me, pulling my arm.

"Stop!" I shouted. "All of you, stop. I will help Ruth. Just stop. Just stop whatever the hell you are doing. Where is she?" I asked, looking back and forth between Ren and Lacy. I had never been more confused in my life, but one glaring fact remained: Ruth was in trouble.

"I will meet you in Everly, where the water curves to the mountain range, near the tallest trees in the grove. Do you know it?" Lacy said to Ren.

"Of course I know it," Ren shot back. This mystery man clearly did not like my cousin. And I couldn't say I blamed him at the moment.

"Be steadfast and watch the moon. If they get Ruthana to the temple, it won't be long until it's too late. I do not have to tell you to keep her hidden from the Cloaked?"

Ren squinted at her for a moment. "I know what to do."

Lacy turned to me. "Guard that sword. It is yours and only yours, understand?" Lacy's tone was sharp and serious as she spoke.

"Okay, but…" I started to say, then just nodded.

"Listen. Every strange feeling you have had, every time in your short life here that your soul told you that you did not belong, that you were destined for more—it was right. And every single answer you seek about who you are, who your parents are, where you came from…it all lies in Everly. Do not be scared. I must go." Lacy nodded at Ren, and without speaking, he placed his hand on the tree. A burst of light flashed so brightly I could hardly see, and as it faded, Lacy was gone.

"Lacy?" I called after her. I looked over to Jason. He looked as dumbfounded as I felt.

I was intensely confused, which of course just fueled my anger. Ren looked annoyed, staring at me as I tried to make sense of all this. I tensed my jaw and watched his impossibly green eyes looking back at me.

"Not to interrupt this clearly epic staring contest, but we need to do something besides stand here," Jason insisted. "I vote that we call the cops."

Ren and I continued to look at each other, not breaking our stare. I adjusted my hand on the grip of my sword, hoping he wouldn't see that my hands were shaking.

"Ready?" Ren asked. "I will explain it all once we arrive. But I was not lying. Something is wrong here. Very wrong. We need to leave."

"No, nope. We need to call the authorities," Jason said, shaking his head.

"Every answer I seek. Is that true?" I asked Ren, ignoring Jason. "About my parents?"

"Yes," Ren confirmed. "Now. We must go." Ren walked to the tree next to Jason. I turned to follow.

"Maddy, I don't like this." Jason whispered.

I couldn't look at him. I knew how ridiculous this all sounded, and I knew that if I let him, Jason would snap me back to reality.

"And where did you get a sword?" Jason continued. "Do you have any idea how dangerous that is?"

I pressed my lips together and tried to come up with something sensible to say. But the weird thing was that even though I should be, I wasn't freaked out. I felt a strange ease. Logically, my mind raced to rationalize and understand what had just happened, but I felt a calm that I couldn't explain to Jason. So I didn't try.

"You can't possibly trust this stalker dude," Jason said. "Don't you think it's a little weird that he showed up at the pool house and is here now, when all of this is going down?"

"He said he is going to help me," I replied, breaking my silence, not turning toward him. "You heard Lacy. We need him to find Aunt Ruth."

"You don't know this guy. Just because he says he can help you, that doesn't mean he's a good guy. What do you think? You think that the bad guys all wear black hats and curled mustaches? This guy is hiding something," Jason whispered in my ear.

Giving in, I turned to face him and met his glare. I hoped he would see that I was scared. I hoped he would see it in my eyes so that I wouldn't have to say it out loud.

Jason gave a defeated sigh.

"Tell me this isn't just about finding your parents," he said softly.

"Ruth is my aunt. If I can help her, I'm going to," I said, sidestepping his question. He nodded.

"You don't have to come," I said softly, eyeing the tree. Ren stood with his back to it, facing us.

"Have I ever let you do anything reckless alone?" Jason replied. "There's no chance I am letting you go with this guy without me."

"I'm glad," I admitted wholeheartedly.

Ren was standing still, watching us and clearly listening, even if he wasn't chiming in.

"You never have to go at it alone, Mads." Jason rested his hand on my shoulder. "What's on your shoulder? Is this blood? Are you hurt?" he said, looking at his hand and then showing me.

"Oh, it's just that guy's blood, not mine."

Jason cringed. "Um, eww."

"I am not really worried about that right now, Jason." I rolled my eyes a little.

"Hepatitis. Hepatitis doesn't worry you?"

I chuckled.

"Ready?" Ren asked, gesturing to the tree.

"Ready for what?" I looked up at the oak with unease. "I am not going near that thing."

"If you want to go to Everly, you are."

I scrunched my nose. "Isn't there another way to get there?"

"No," Ren answered. He reached out and grabbed my wrist with one hand and Jason's with the other.

"Let go," I demanded, trying to pull my arm from his grasp. "That thing's dangerous!"

"Home," Ren whispered.

And just like that, he closed his eyes and threw himself backward toward the tree trunk, pulling Jason and me with him. Just as Ren's back hit the bark, a brilliant flash of light erupted from the tree's center. Then we fell through the trunk, and I felt as though we were spinning wildly in circles. There was a deafening roar all around us. The light was so bright, I couldn't see a thing, and then I hit the ground hard.

CHAPTER 9

I blinked frantically, still disoriented from the fall. My eyes began to focus. Lying flat on my back, I saw only trees. Infinite deep green leaves poking out of curving branches blocked the sunlight.

The sun? Was it daytime now?

I sat up slowly and rubbed a dull ache in my lower back. The ground felt wet under my hand as I propped myself up to sitting. Jason was next to me, picking leaves off his arm.

"What the frickin' hell was that?" Jason demanded.

Ren hopped up quickly but didn't answer.

"Jason, are you okay?" I asked him.

"You are both fine," Ren responded as Jason nodded to me.

"I wasn't talking to you, dick!" I said through my teeth.

Ren loomed over us, his arms bent, hands resting on his hips like an overgrown Peter Pan. My eyes were still shocked by the sudden light. It was a jarring switch from the pitch black of Ruth's yard to here.

But where was here?

Jason rubbed his eyes, too, clearly having the same trouble as me.

I could see Ren better now. He had sandy brown hair that swept back and off his forehead. The stubble on his jawline was thicker than I thought, but he still had a boyish quality to his face, making him look my age or maybe a few years older. He had dark eyelashes that drew even more attention to his eyes. They weren't as distinct here and certainly didn't look as luminous as they did when I had encountered him earlier, but they were still a striking green. I brushed my hands together, shaking off the bits of leaves and dirt that clung to my empty palms. Empty?

The sword! Where is the sword?

My hands flew over the ground, searching through the clumps of dirt and broken leaves around me on the moist ground.

"Relax," Ren said. I looked up to see him holding the sword. I slid my hand over the grip and sighed in relief. The now-familiar blue that I had come to expect still glowed under my hand. I didn't know why, but it was a comfort to me.

"Oh, wow! That thing really glows. I thought it was my eyes playing tricks on me," Jason said. I turned to face him. He looked a little calmer than he was a few minutes ago.

The light went off and then on again as I passed the sword to my other hand. "No, it really does that."

"But how?" Jason asked. The blue light hung in the thick, hazy air of the forest.

I looked down at the sword, turning it over and back, not really sure how to answer. "I don't know. It just does that." I shrugged, examining it further.

"You got this from the Witch, right?" Ren asked, raising an eyebrow as he looked at the blade.

"A what? No, I got it from Lacy."

Ren gave me a little nod and he half smiled. "We need to get moving." He turned from Jason and me and started toward a little path where the ground was more worn.

"Whoa there, Skippy. Hang on. How is it daytime?" I called after him. "Did we get knocked out?"

He turned back to look at us, cocking his head to the side a touch. "No. Different dimension. Pay attention."

Jason and I exchanged confused glances before looking back at Ren.

"I really don't like you. Where is Aunt Ruth?" I replied, pushing myself off the ground.

"The temple is this way. Follow me." He pointed up the path.

"I don't see anything!" Jason angrily protested as I pulled him to his feet. We were both a little wobbly.

"Then walk faster," Ren replied.

"Wait, Ren. What—what is all of this? Seriously? Where are we?" I demanded.

I placed my hand on the towering tree trunk next to me. The trees were massively tall. Taller than any tree I had ever seen. The trunks were impossibly wide, and their bark was so dark, they looked black. "This doesn't look like Greenrock," I said as I turned in a circle.

"That is because it is Everly. You are not in Greenrock anymore," Ren explained, sounding annoyed.

The tops of the massive trees seemed to curve together down the path in front of us, making a long, lush archway. The ground was covered in giant green leaves and twigs that snapped and crunched beneath our feet. Dew had collected on almost everything and glistened in the beams of sunlight that shone through breaks in the tree cover like hazy spotlights. The air was damp and clung to my skin.

"How is it daylight?" I asked again.

"Time moves a little differently here, you will find," Ren answered. "Too much to explain right now. We need to get moving. You will want to do this quickly."

Jason looked awestruck as he stepped around a cluster of stones on the ground at the base of one of the trees and started to follow Ren. I hooked a finger in Jason's shirt to stop him.

"Stay by me. I don't trust him," I whispered in Jason's ear. We followed Ren but stayed about ten feet behind, just to be on the safe side. I still wasn't sure where we were exactly. Or maybe I was dreaming and this was just a really crappy nightmare.

I pinched myself. Nothing happened.

I reached over and pinched Jason.

"Ouch! Quit it." He swatted my hand away.

Nope. Not a dream.

"Your aunt is a Witch, so they are taking her to the Temple of the Ember Isle. That is where they take all the Magics," Ren explained. "We need to get to her before she gets to the temple and they put her with the other Magics."

I balled my fist and shook it out nervously as I spoke. "Magics?"

"Yes, Magics. Witches, trolls, fairies, Merfolk, Readers and the like." He nodded. "I think we can cut them off on the Temple Road, but we must go now. Getting to her before she is taken into the temple will be best because, like the Witch said, the king keeps a tight schedule."

"Um, okay." I shook my head, not fully sure that I understood anything that came out of Ren's mouth, other than that we needed to get to Aunt Ruth.

Jason looped his arm through mine. He was still looking around at the trees that surrounded us. They seemed to get bigger as we kept following Ren, and our path became more and more cluttered with branches and large rocks as we walked. Jason leaned close to my ear. "Why do you think he's helping us?"

I shrugged. "Let's find out."

"Ren? Question. What do you get out of this? Why are you helping us?" I asked him. Ren turned his head to glance at me but kept walking.

"Just be happy that I am helping you, or you would have been right there with your aunt in that roundup." He laughed a little.

I swallowed hard. "Oh, yes, this is all sooooo funny," I said sarcastically. "What is it you need from us, exactly?"

This time, Ren stopped and turned around. I stepped in front of Jason and kept my focus on Ren. I lifted my sword up just enough to remind him I had it.

"What is the problem?" Ren asked. "You should be grateful, not suspicious."

"Why?" I put my hand on my hip. "You sucked me through a tree and have given us zero information. I just met you like five seconds ago, so, yeah, suspicious."

"That is not true. It was at least thirty minutes ago," Ren replied, but not in a joking way. He looked one hundred percent serious, and I wasn't sure how to respond. I rolled my eyes.

"Look, where I come from, people don't just help people for no reason," I stated firmly.

"You do not know where you come from," Ren replied with a cold, blank stare.

Jason's hand was on my shoulder before I could react to Ren. I squeezed the grip of the sword so tightly, my fingertips began to go numb.

"Chill out, guys," Jason said behind me.

I could feel my face burning like it did when I was mortified or angry. I couldn't really tell which I was now—maybe a mix of both—but I didn't take my eyes off Ren.

"Let's just go find my aunt," I said through my teeth, still locked in a stare with Ren. He didn't seem to like me, which made absolutely no sense.

Ren sighed a lengthy, annoyed sigh, then turned and started down the path once more.

"I'm going to find out more about this place," Jason said, hurrying past me to Ren's side before I could object. My sword and I trudged along behind them while Jason probed Ren for information. I didn't like Jason so close to Ren, but so far, Ren didn't seem like he had any intention of hurting us, so I didn't freak out. But I kept a watchful eye on their every move.

"So, Magics, trolls, and fairies?" Jason asked Ren. "You're telling me that those things are real?"

"I am." Ren nodded. "And Strongbloods."

"What is a Strongblood, exactly?" Jason asked.

"It is a race of superior humans. They are faster, stronger, and incredible fighters. They keep order here in Everly. I am a Strongblood," Ren answered.

"What does Aunt Ruth have to do with any of this?" I called to them, a foot or two in front of me.

"Everything." Ren slowed until he was next to me, but we still kept up a brisk pace.

"Meaning what?" I asked.

"Well, all Magics are to be executed under the king's Magus Decree, but your aunt is the reason the Magus Decree exists."

"Huh?"

"She is a Witch, so she is subject to the Magus Decree on that alone. She also took you from your parents and raised you in a different world," Ren explained, running a hand through his hair. "She is also the most wanted fugitive in Everly."

"Ruth, a fugitive?" Jason scoffed.

"Wait, so you're saying I was born here?" I pointed at the ground.

Ren nodded. "On the Ember Isle."

"What's the Ember Isle?" Jason asked.

"The Ember Isle is where the Strongbloods live. The king of the Ember Isle lives in the temple there, ruling over the other Strongbloods and non-Magics."

"What about this?" I held out the sword.

"Your sword? That is Witch magic. Do not wave that around when you see anyone out here, or they will haul you right off, too."

"So all that stuff—fairy tales, magic stuff—it's all real?" Jason asked, sounding shrill.

"In Everly, yes," Ren replied.

I chewed my lip and nodded. Jason's eyes were wide, and his pace had slowed. "You okay, Jason?" I cut behind Ren and walked with Jason at his new snail-like pace.

"I just—does anyone else feel dizzy?" Jason put his hands on that back of his neck and dropped his head down a bit. His voice was higher than normal. "I smell toast. That's bad, right?"

"Deep breath." I rubbed his back. Jason nodded and took in a long deep breath. "Let's just stick together, okay? This is a lot, but we have to stay calm, okay?"

Jason nodded. "Now you sound like me," he said with a smile.

"Well, someone has to be the Jason of the group." I smiled back as we reached a fork in the path. One path curved to the left and the other stayed mostly straight.

"This way will be the quickest to get to the Ember Isle." Ren pointed to the straight path. We turned and walked with Ren.

"But we have to meet Lacy first, right?" Jason asked. He seemed a bit more relaxed now.

"Try to walk faster, if you can," Ren said, not answering Jason.

"So Lacy gets to know about all of this. Why keep it from me?" I asked Jason quietly.

"It is of little importance what your family squabble entails," Ren snapped.

"I wasn't talking to you, dick." I rolled my eyes, already exhausted by Ren. I stayed next to Jason as Ren walked ahead of us. Jason reached over and grabbed my hand just as a little light fluttered past my head. It buzzed right past my ear, and I swatted at it.

"Stop!" Ren spun around and raised his hand. We watched as the little twinkling light descended onto his palm, like a feather floating down from the sky.

Ren leaned closer to it. "I thank you kindly for this favor."

The light grew brighter for a moment. And then a voice spoke from it: "Four more Magics were brought down the Temple Road. You must hurry. The moon is growing."

The little light dimmed and flew up and off into the trees.

"Um, what the French was that?" Jason asked as I stood with my mouth open.

"A fairy. Cypher Fae deliver messages here in Everly, but only the intended person can retrieve them," Ren said casually. "That message was from a friend. Ara in the Jade Village. She is Empress of the Fae and the keeper of the Cypher Fae."

"Holy crap, that was a fairy?" Jason asked, excited, as the fairy flew up and out of sight into the heavy tree cover above us.

"You have a friend?" I snickered.

Ren looked to the ground quickly and looked embarrassed for a moment. "Ara was my mother's friend. I do not have—I do not know her beyond that, really."

"Ren, I—I didn't mean—I was joking," I stammered, feeling guilty now.

Ren cleared his throat and straightened himself, but he avoided my eyes now.

"We should hurry," he said. He turned and kept walking.

It wasn't the first time I had put my foot in my mouth and for sure wouldn't be the last. Ren walked away from us. Jason elbowed me in the side, hitting my arm and shook his head.

"Ow." I pulled my arm away, waiting for the pain to hit.

"Oh, I'm so sorry!" Jason lightly touched the bandage on my elbow. "I didn't mean to hit your cut."

"No, it's fine." I turned my arm to get a look at the bandage. "I actually forgot it was there."

"Eww, you probably should have changed this. It's pretty gross."

"What's wrong with it?" I tried to get a good look at my arm, but the angle was too awkward.

"It's soaked through. I hope it didn't reopen it or something," Jason muttered as he peeked under the blood-soaked bandage.

Just then, Ren turned and stopped in front of me, grabbed the bandage on my arm, and ripped it off in one swift swipe. As if by instinct, I balled my fist and swung, making contact with his lower jaw. Ren stumbled back.

I rubbed the spot just above my elbow where the glass shard had cut me earlier. "What the hell was that?"

"You are not hurt, Madison. You are fine," he said, holding his jaw with one hand and rubbing where I had hit him. "Look!" He gestured at my arm. "You do not believe me? Look!"

"Um, he's right, Maddy. I mean, seriously. There's no cut or anything. It's like...it's like you healed already." Jason examined it again.

"Wait, what? There's no way it's already healed. I just did that this morning!"

Ren sighed. "You healed."

I looked back up at Ren, who was standing in front of us, arms crossed over his muscular chest. He had a slight smile, seeming amused at my current fluster. So few people would find this much delight in being a knowledge hoarder, but Ren seemed to revel in knowing more about me than I did.

That was it. I couldn't keep calm a second longer. I stepped forward. Jason slid his hands onto my shoulders as if he sensed my mounting anger.

"I *healed*. I healed, and you don't feel the need to offer even the slightest of explanations, you smug jerk?" I blurted out.

"It is the sword," Ren said, raising his eyebrow. "You are a Witch. Ruthana must have put your magic in the sword. The sooner you accept this, the better. Just be glad you have found your magic and let us keep walking, girl."

"Don't call me 'girl,'" I shot back, annoyed.

"Very well." He shifted his weight impatiently. "But I must point out that you *are* a girl."

"Well, thanks. I guess that explains the boobs, then," I mocked, pointing to my chest.

Ren looked up to the sky quickly, his cheeks red.

I smiled to myself, happy to have wiped the smug look off Ren's face, but I was still as antsy as ever. My skin prickled. I needed to run or fight or scream. Something to get this energy out. I felt unruly.

"Maddy, try to stay calm," Jason said quietly.

"I just, like, healed myself, so can everyone stop telling me to be calm? Me freaking out seems to be the only reasonable reaction. So, actually, it seems that I am the only rational person here right now." I was squeaking, my voice was so high.

Jason rested a hand on the side of my head and dropped his chin. "Whoa. Relax! It's crazy, but let's just focus on the bigger crazy right now. I'm having a hard enough time with the rest of this."

"You—you... I'm a Witch? Nobody thinks that's crazy?" My exasperation at the situation turned my words into a mangled mess of high-pitched noises punctuated by hand gestures.

Jason smiled. "Yes, well...I didn't get any of that, so let's just put a pin in it for now, okay?"

Still baffled, I twisted my arm as much as I could to see my elbow, and this time, Jason assisted.

"See, no cut," he said, smoothing my hair back as I dropped my arm.

"It was a deep cut, Jay."

He shrugged. "Maybe it wasn't as bad as you thought?"

I nodded. "Yeah, maybe." Jason's logic was easier to swallow because it was too hard to wrap my head around Ren's reasoning.

Could I actually heal myself?

"We need to be quiet and move quickly. Do you understand? Am I not saying it right?" Ren paused, looking from me to Jason. "Is there another phrase that you use in your world to imply urgency?"

"No, we're just processing, Ren," Jason said. "Come on. We should go."

"The sooner we meet Lacy, the better," I agreed. "I have some new questions for my sweet little cousin."

Ren didn't say anything but gave me a nod.

We continued in silence. The path was lined with more large trees, making me feel tiny. It really was quite breathtaking. I tried to think about the trees in Greenrock, but I couldn't really picture them in detail beyond their height. It was like everything was clearer to me here. Walking closer to the edge of the path, I reached out and ran my fingers over the bark. It wasn't as rough as it looked. Like it had a little touch of fuzz on it. The lines of the bark swirled in a million different directions, and parts of it jutted out like it was ready to break right off.

Did all trees look like this and I just never stopped to notice?

"Okay," Ren started, making me jump.

I shifted my focus back to the path and to Ren.

Ren cleared his throat. "We need to get to the Temple of the Ember Isle before your father knows you are here. Surprise is our best approach, but if they have your aunt, then they might break her before they kill her."

"Whoa, whoa. Back it up. My *what?*" I said, feeling like I had just been punched in the stomach.

"Your father. He will send a party out for you if he thinks you are here, so we need to stay hidden as best we can."

I stumbled back into the trunk of tree and caught my balance.

Jason rushed over to my side. "Careful, Maddy." His eyes were just as wide as mine felt.

I spoke the words out loud: "My father…is alive."

CHAPTER 10

"Did you say her father?" Jason spoke softly. "Like her actual, real father?"

Ren looked at each of us, genuinely confused.

I felt sick. I was going to be sick. I covered my mouth with my hand.

"Yes. You need to pay attention," Ren replied.

"Sense the tone, Ren!" Jason shot back, pointing at his own face.

I felt like I was free-falling from the top of a building, but in a good way. In a wonderful way. I tried to catch my breath to speak as the smile overtook my face.

"My…father?" I managed to mumble through my grin. "My father is alive. He is here, and he is alive?"

Jason and Ren stood in front of me.

"Maddy, are you okay?" Jason asked.

Ren's usual grimace and smug demeanor were replaced with a more human look of concern now. "I am sorry," he said meekly.

"Oh, no, don't stop being a great big jerk on my account, buddy. I'm fine. I just…it's not every day that the little orphan girl is told her parents are dead and then finds out that her father is actually alive!" I exhaled loudly and fanned my face with my hand.

Ren nodded. "I do not understand. What is happening?"

"And you're sure he's my father?" I asked softly, focusing on Ren's slightly chapped lips. I watched them as he spoke, waiting for him to say that he was kidding or that he was mistaken.

Ren nodded. "Yes."

"Right, so that makes me…"

"His daughter?" Ren answered quietly.

"Wooowww. Ha! Okay. I, um—I am going to just take a quick—I need to go for a run. Or—yeah. Can we just take a quick pause? I just—I need, like, a minute or ten." I turned away from them as tears rolled down my cheeks.

"Maddy, why don't you sit down?" Jason asked behind me.

"No, no. I'm—I'm okay. Just, wow." I jumped up and down in place and shook my hand—the one that wasn't holding a sword.

"I thought she knew that," Ren said delicately.

"Don't tell me, tell her!" Jason replied.

"Madison, I am sorry. I did not know," I heard Ren say.

I didn't turn around to face Jason or Ren. I couldn't do anything but smile, but the joy quickly turned to anger. Anger that I didn't know about this. Why didn't I know this? Why was this kept from me? This couldn't be real. None of this could be real. All the anger, fear, confusion, and sadness that I had buried so deep exploded within me.

And then a burst of uncontrollable energy surged through me. I dropped the sword and sprinted away from them, pushing my legs faster and faster. Running had always been my go-to when things got stressful, not because I wanted to run in races but because it was the only way I could feel normal again after I got this upset. Running was never fun. Running was therapy. It was what I did when I fought with Aunt Ruth and when Lacy annoyed me.

I ran.

I darted through the trees. I couldn't breathe, couldn't think…all I could do was run. All my emotions intensified, and I pushed my legs faster and faster, racing through the trees, running faster than I ever had.

Every reasonable, rational thread that had been holding me together suddenly seemed frayed and broken. I felt out of control, crazed, and panicked. Everything that Lacy had said replayed in my head. I felt betrayed by her. I felt betrayed by Aunt Ruth.

She lied.

She knew about this and she had lied.

I jumped over a fallen log and kept going.

Ruth had lied, and that bothered me, but Lacy—that made me ache. Did she know? I shook my head. It felt like my lungs were tearing open with each rapid breath as I pushed myself farther, running as fast as my legs would take me through this unfamiliar, endless forest. I felt open, raw, and exposed, like I was no longer in control of myself.

I clenched my teeth so hard that a molar might have cracked. My thoughts ran faster than I did.

I didn't belong in Greenrock.

I am from another world.

My world.

Aunt Ruth lied.

My father was here and he never came for me.

He never came for me.

A father.

I have a father.

Suddenly, two firm arms wrapped around my shoulders and jolted me to a stop. My legs swung forward, like I had slammed the force of my body into a giant metal rod.

A hand clamped over my mouth, and I was pulled over to an enormous tree trunk. I struggled violently, swinging my legs and throwing my head back.

"Shh," Ren whispered, his lip resting on my ear. "It is just me. It is Ren."

My body relaxed with relief. I stopped fighting Ren's grip on me and my protests came out as a few pathetic whimpers. He slowly lowered his hand from my mouth.

"I can't, I can't. It's all been a lie." My voice shook as I spoke. Beneath me, my knees buckled, and I felt the pain in my throat begging my eyes to cry, to let the emotion out. I leaned my head back against him, holding it in. His arm was still wrapped around me, just under my chin. We stood silently as I hung there against him like a grief-stricken child.

"You have to be quiet. We are not alone here. You have to be quiet if I am to keep you safe," he urged softly.

Feeling dizzy, I grabbed his arm with both of my hands to steady myself. We were still and silent again. The only noise was the rustling of leaves in the trees around us.

"I thought you knew about your father. I am so sorry," he said, even quieter.

I squeezed my eyes shut. "I think I always knew that I didn't belong there. I always knew." I shook my head and leaned it back on Ren.

"I am sorry, Madison," Ren said softly, in a gentler tone than he had used in the entire time I had known him. Ren's arms stayed firmly wrapped around me, and I could tell by his voice that he meant his apology. But it didn't change the facts.

I then realized I was digging my nails into Ren's arm, and I loosened my grip, which seemed to prompt him to hold onto me tighter. In any other capacity, I would have protested that he was holding me like this. But in that moment, I didn't care. I felt like I needed him to hold on to me or I would explode into a million tiny bits.

My racing mind began to slow, and my heartbeat felt closer to normal again. Aunt Ruth. How could she keep this from me?

We need to find Aunt Ruth.

Of course, I wanted to find her to make sure she was safe, but I also needed answers. More desperately than I wanted anything, I wanted answers.

Ren shifted, his arm muscles trembling a bit. I realized that I was still putting all my weight on him.

I pulled away and stood on my own. "Where's Jason?" I asked with urgency. I must have run farther than I realized, because as I looked back, he was nowhere in sight.

"Wher—"

"He is way back there. You are really a fast runner. You have a moment to get yourself together," Ren said, looking around and not at me.

I turned sharply to him, studying his face. There was such a simple honesty to him, but his blunt observations made me feel defensive, even if they were true. I wanted to mess up his stupidly perfect James Dean hair just to see the unruffled look on his face disappear. But I didn't. I stood still, composing myself—for Jason, not Ren.

This wasn't Ren's fault, and it wouldn't be fair to take it out on him. Fun, but not fair. It wasn't his fault that I had been habitually lied to my whole life.

This was Aunt Ruth's fault, and we needed to find her.

I wiped the remaining tears from my face, took a long breath in, and let it out with a whooshing noise. Now was not the time to fall to pieces.

Jason needs me to be strong.

"Ready?" Ren adjusted a pair of daggers in his boot.

"Yeah." I wiped my shirt over my face, collecting the sweat and the tears.

"Your racket surely attracted someone, so we must get moving." Ren's eyes darted over the trees around us, studying our surroundings.

I shook my head. "My god, just when I start to think you are a semi-decent human being—"

"Quiet," Ren said, cutting me off. There was a rustling sound and the crunch of sticks.

"Jay!" I called out as he came into view.

Jason stopped a few feet from us and put his hands on his knees, panting loudly. He was holding my sword.

"We will slow down so you can keep up, Jason." Ren waved a hand at him.

"Yeah, okay…yeah, great," Jason said breathlessly. "Or, you know, maybe a heads-up that we would be sprinting through the woods would have been nice."

I chuckled.

"Hey, Mads. You good?" Jason asked, holding his side, sweat dripping down his temple.

"Yeah, I'm okay now." I gave Jason a half smile. I glanced at Ren out of the corner of my eye before walking over to Jason.

"Here," Jason said and handed me my sword. "It's so heavy."

"Let's find you some water." I took the sword and wiped his sweaty forehead with my other hand.

"Gross, Maddy." Jason sneered.

"Oh, shut it."

Ren cleared his throat. "Keep your footing and watch for movement. This is not a hostile area, but things are not always as predictable as one would like," he said, starting ahead of us.

"Onward." Jason pointed at Ren.

"Onward," I echoed with a nod.

We shadowed Ren closely through the labyrinth of trees and brush for what felt like hours. Ren moved effortlessly, as if he had traveled this way frequently. The trees thinned out and the clammy, moist air of the thick forest gave way to the heat of the sun as we continued. Bushes and flowers dominated this part of the path as the trees spread out, offering very little shade.

Ren hopped onto a fallen tree trunk and slipped off the other side, falling to the forest floor in a spectacularly clumsy move. Quickly, he jumped up and brushed his clothes off, then turned to offer me his hand to help me over. I ignored him.

Seriously?

"No, no. I'm good," I responded, declining the aid of the guy who had just wiped out.

I thought I caught a glimpse of his smile when I hurdled over the trunk without his help. At times, I felt like Ren was watching me from the corner of his eye.

Jason jumped over without help, too. Back home, he was a top athlete: the captain of our school's baseball team and the best hitter by far.

We kept pace with Ren, who showed no sign of slowing down.

"What's his story, huh?" I leaned over and asked Jason as we continued.

"Mysterious, hunky stranger?" Jason replied.

"And a jerk," I added.

"A very attractive jerk." Jason laughed.

"Perhaps."

"Where did you guys run off to before?"

I shot him a smile and winked. "Are you jealous, Mr. Vega?"

"Puh-lease. If anyone were to steal you away from me, they'd bring you right back," he snickered. "There aren't many who know how to handle my Maddy like I do."

I nodded. "True story."

"Maddy, did you see his eyes back in Greenrock? They were almost glowing," Jason continued softly. "They aren't here, but they're still so green. Like fanfiction green."

"Yeah, I don't know what that means."

Jason scoffed. "Yes, you do."

I smirked. "Okay, fine, I do, but I'm not proud of it."

"Maddy?" Jason's tone was serious now. I looked over at him.

"Yeah?"

"If you want to talk about it, your family stuff, you know I'm here."

"I know. I just…not now."

I passed my sword from hand to hand, and the blue light went on and off like a light switch. The sword was starting to feel heavier and heavier as we walked, and my hands were starting to ache.

Suddenly, Ren stopped. "Hide, quick!" he ordered.

Jason and I followed Ren off the path. The three of us ducked down behind a large bush full of sharp thorns that pricked and poked at me.

"What is it, guys?" Jason asked nervously. I bit my lip as the panicked look returned to his face.

"The Cloaked," Ren said pointing to the right of us.

"The what now?" I looked around.

"Maddy, your sword," Jason nudged me.

"Right." I set the sword down on the ground and the blue light disappeared.

"The Cloaked," Ren said again, in a disgusted sort of way. "They patrol the villages, looking for Magics. They work for a bounty from the king. They should not be here. They do not usually frequent this stretch of forest."

Moving the thorny branches of the bush we were hiding behind, I was able to see them. They were wearing ankle-length cloaks, some dark, some light-colored, all with giant hoods. Each of them wore a different shirt beneath their cloak. Various weapons dangled from their belts.

"The people who took Aunt Ruth had cloaks on," I whispered to Ren.

"Those were not the Cloaked. That was the King's Guard. They wear cloaks when they leave the Ember Isle so that they can blend into Everly. It is not too often that Strongbloods mingle with the people," he clarified.

The Cloaked stopped. They were closer to us now, so I tried not to make a sound as I reached my hand through the bramble and moved another branch to see them better. Sitting on a rock was a giant man. My jaw dropped slightly. He was a foot or two taller than the standing people, and he was seated. He was shackled at the wrists, and his ankles were bound with a large rope.

"That man—" I started.

"That is no man. He is a mountain troll," Ren whispered.

"A mountain troll?" Jason asked.

I peered at the giant again. He had an out-of-control beard that covered a little too much of his face to be a normal man's. His frame was huge, his shoulders wider than the shoulders of any person I had ever seen. And on the top of his forehead, within a tangled mess of white hair, were two horns.

I gasped.

"What is it?" Jason whispered as he leaned over to look through the bush with me. "Holy crap."

I held my hand over my mouth as Jason and I gawked at the mountain troll. He clearly wasn't human, but he also wasn't an animal. He was something you would see in a movie. Yet here he was, right in front of us, and I still couldn't believe it.

"How—"

"The Cloaked take them from the mountains as workers to carry the carts and for protection in the woods," Ren explained. The way he said it made it clear that giant furry men like this were common and nothing out of the ordinary for Everly.

"He's a slave?" Jason asked.

Ren shifted and pulled a slender-bladed dagger from his boot and spun its handle in his hand.

"Yes. Stay down and let them pass. They outnumber us greatly. It is best if we just—"

"Porter!" a voice growled behind us.

Before we could turn around, Ren was knocked to the ground, away from the protection of the bush that hid us. I looked back to see one of the Cloaked towering over us. He jabbed his boot into Ren's back, pinning him to the ground.

We had been spotted.

CHAPTER 11

"Hey!" I yelled in a deep, growling voice.

The Cloaked raised his dagger in the air, but before he had a chance to lower his weapon to strike Ren, I lunged toward him with a grunt.

I knocked the Cloaked off Ren and we struggled, rolling around on the ground. His dagger grazed my jaw, missing my throat, which seemed to be his target. I cracked his cheekbone with my fist repeatedly as my body heat rose. I did not stop hitting the Cloaked until I heard Ren yell my name.

The Cloaked slumped over on the ground. I had done more damage than I intended. His cheek was already puffy, and blood dripped from a cut above his eyebrow.

I stood up. "Sorry, I—" I stopped when I saw Ren and Jason out of the corner of my eye. Ren was fighting with another one of them. Jason, too. It seemed that all the defense classes that he had attended just to hang out with me were being put to good use.

I turned back to my Cloaked attacker, but he was no longer a threat to me or anyone in his current state. My sword was still on the ground. Grabbing it, I backed away from the man I had beaten to a pulp as the blue light on my sword glowed bright.

Just then, I felt someone grab my arm.

"It's me," Jason said breathlessly. I turned to see two more Cloaked down and writhing on the ground. Neither was as badly injured as the man I had just finished with.

Jason wasn't looking at me. He was staring at the bloodied Cloaked a few feet in front of us. He looked back at me and didn't say anything, but I could see the worry hidden deep in his brown eyes.

"We need to get out of here," Ren said, jogging over. He quickly looked me over as he panted loudly, sweat collecting on his forehead. "They will have seen Madison's sword by now and will be sending for backup. Witches are not easily taken."

"Obviously." Jason motioned to the man I had beat up. Ren peered at the man and then back at me, but he didn't look surprised or even worried like Jason had. He simply gave me a nod.

"What now?" Jason asked.

I looked back at the only Cloaked still standing and the mountain troll next to him. The Cloaked wasn't looking at his fallen men; he was looking at me. No, he was looking at my sword. Then he raised his hand and pointed at Jason, Ren, and me.

"Run!" Ren commanded in a low, gruff voice. Seconds later, the mountain troll charged at us, bellowing. The other Cloaked that Jason and Ren had taken on managed to get to their feet again, and they ran at us now, too, weapons in hand.

"Stop, Witch!" one of them hollered.

"Um, yes. Running. Running sounds good," I sputtered.

Jason, Ren, and I turned and bolted. I quickly outpaced them. As I sped through the trees, I whipped my head back. Ren was coming up right behind me now. He was fast, too, but I remained slightly faster. My eyes flitted over the brush and trees, looking for Jason. He was farther back now, still ahead of the Cloaked and the mountain troll, but too far back from Ren and me for my comfort. I stopped suddenly, sliding on the slick leaves beneath my feet.

"What are you doing?" Ren yelled as he stopped and sprinted back to where I was standing. He pulled my arm. "Madison, run!"

"Jason!" I shouted, ignoring Ren's pull at my arm.

Ren grunted and sprinted away, leaving me to retrieve Jason alone.

"Hey! Ren!" I called after him in frustration. No time to plot his murder. I needed to get Jason out of danger. These guys weren't messing around.

"Holy shiz…" Jason exclaimed as he reached me. I grabbed his hand and kept his pace.

"Don't stop!" I ordered.

I pulled Jason along with me and held my sword out in front of me as we ran. Ren was nowhere in sight. I could hear the Cloaked and the thunderous stomps of the mountain troll behind us. We weren't moving fast enough. I felt my heart beat frantically, but I ran with focused determination. I scanned the area for something to hide in or behind, but the rows of bushes had given way to more trees that were spread too far apart to provide any type of coverage for us. The path we ran on was getting wider, making us even more visible to the Cloaked. We were coming up on a giant rock formation near where a few large willow trees were mixed in with the dark-barked oak trees.

Another fork in the path. I pulled Jason to the right, with me. The new path cut around the rocky formation, blocking us from our pursuers' view for the moment.

Just then, without warning, someone bashed into my shoulder, knocking Jason and me through thick layers of low-hanging, vinelike branches to my right. The branches whipped me in the face.

Jason stumbled and fell a few feet away, within the shielding cover of the willow's crown. I spun around and swung the sword in my hand at whomever had pushed me.

It was Ren. He ducked, just narrowly missing being struck with my blade. He dove forward to put his hand over my mouth, and then I realized why. Out of the corner of my eye, I saw the giant shadow just outside the thick layer of wispy willow branches.

The ground trembled slightly. The mountain troll. I shuddered, and my eyes darted to Jason. He hadn't moved.

Ren took his hand off my mouth and held his finger to his lips. He slowly reached down and grabbed my sword by the blade, pulling it from my hand with a wince, and the blue glow faded immediately.

We stood motionless, our faces inches apart. I swallowed hard, loudly. My heart raced as the voices grew in volume and quantity just on the other side of the branches. I could hear the troll panting loudly.

"Check by the spring. They could not have gone far. It was Ren Raker, I am sure of it. Find him!" the low, gruff voice said firmly.

I watched Ren as they spoke.

"He will fetch no bounty," another voice said. "We just need the Witch."

Ren looked at me when they said this, and my eyes widened. Surely they were talking about me.

"Did you see what she did to Monty? That was no Witch. She was a Strongblood," a lower voice answered.

"A Strongblood would never keep company with a Porter. She must be a Witch with a strong punch. Her sword was glowing," the voice said. The man said *Porter* as if it were a slur, or something so disgusting that he couldn't possibly say it any other way. Ren's gaze dropped to the ground, and he bit his bottom lip.

"Just find the Porter and kill him," another voice responded. "Take the Witch if you can."

I shivered. I heard more mumbles and shuffling, and then it got quiet. Ren walked to the thick wall of sagging willow branches and looked out.

"They are gone," Ren whispered, and ran his hands through his hair. He didn't look me in the eye but stood there for a moment, making the silence feel incredibly awkward.

"Jay?"

"I'm fine. Just catching my breath." He held up his thumb as he laid sprawled on his back next to the trunk of the willow tree.

I looked back to Ren. "Why do they want to kill you?" I asked him softly.

Ren didn't answer me. "Ow," he said instead, and looked at his hand.

"What? What's wrong with you?" I asked.

"I cut my hand grabbing your sword." He clutched his hand into a fist and held it to his abdomen.

"Let me see it." I held my hand out to him. He hesitated for a second, then placed his hand onto mine and flattened it. Squinting in the dim shadows of the tree, I saw that he had a thin red cut in the middle of his palm and another three on the base of his first three fingers.

"It's not that bad," he said. I raised an eyebrow at him. I ripped the sleeve off the left arm of my black T-shirt.

Ren shifted like an impatient toddler. "You do not have—"

"Shut up." I didn't look up at him as I wrapped the cloth around his hand and tied it in a knot on the back.

"There you go. All set," I said, my tone dry.

I met his gaze. He looked almost surprised, but he was gracious as he opened and closed his hand. "Nicely done," he said delicately.

I nodded as I reached down and grabbed my sword

Inside the cover of the willow tree, I felt a little safer for the first time since we got to Everly. I stepped over Jason and slumped down to the ground, leaning against the trunk. I turned to rest my cheek on the rough bark, which felt oddly comforting.

Jason sat up slowly and groaned like he was doing a really strenuous sit-up.

The glowing blue grip of the sword offered additional light now that the gently swaying branches had blocked out most of the sunlight. Jason placed a hand on my knee.

"You okay, Maddy?" His voice was raspy, the way it always got when he was really tired.

I nodded. "Are you?"

Beads of sweat collected above Jason's lip and on his brow. It was much cooler here under the willow tree, but we had been moving quickly through the woods. Both of us needed water.

The ground felt almost fuzzy beneath my hands. I heard a noise above my head—Ren lit a red lantern that hung from a nail in the willow's trunk. The little flickering flame of the lantern cast a soft light in the area beneath the tree as I looked around. The ground wasn't fuzzy after all. I was sitting on a rug on the ground. I ran my fingers over the worn patterns of maroon and beige swirls.

"Have a seat," Ren said, gesturing to the oriental-style area rug. Jason scooted over onto the rug next to me. I leaned over to see Ren rummaging through a large brown chest on the ground on the other side of the willow's trunk. I looked back at the lantern.

"Where did this stuff come from?"

"Greenrock. The rug was quite a pain to lug back," Ren replied.

"It's nice. What is this place?" Jason asked.

"This is my home of sorts, I guess," Ren answered as he closed the lid of the chest.

"Home? You live here?" Jason asked, sounding unintentionally judgmental.

Ren looked to his feet and rubbed his hand on the back of his neck. "I am not very welcome in the villages."

"Um, water. Do you have any water, Ren?" I interrupted him in an effort to switch the subject.

Ren met my eyes, and the corners of his mouth turned up briefly. He reached back into the chest and pulled out a satchel and three canteens. He tossed two canteens toward us and plopped the brown satchel on top of the wooden chest. I started chugging my water immediately.

"They might be a little warm," Ren said. "I filled these up a while back."

"Thanks, dude," Jason replied.

While drinking, I watched Ren walked back over to us. He met my curious stare. I did not look away as he lifted the lantern from the nail on the trunk of the willow and set it on the rug between himself and me.

Who is this guy?

He seemed so confident and powerful when he first brought us here, but the Cloaked hated him enough to want to kill him. And he lived under a willow tree?

"Rest up, and we will head back out," Ren said softly. He, too, sounded wiped out from that chase.

Jason put the cap back on his canteen and set it on the rug in front of him. "What in the hell was that all about?" he asked, looking up at Ren.

Ren fiddled with the makeshift bandage I had wrapped on his hand. "My admirers, you mean?" He chuckled to himself before drinking from his canteen.

He caught me staring, so I quickly turned my head away from him and looked down at the round, faded black canteen. The water was more warm than chilled but still refreshing. My limbs tingled with exhaustion as I repositioned myself.

Ren put the cap back on his bottle. "That was the Cloaked and their mountain troll trying to kill me," he said, a little too calmly.

"I'm sorry, is that a normal occurrence for you?" Jason asked.

"I am not as well liked as most around here at the moment," Ren said, bowing his head a little.

I scoffed.

Jason raised an eyebrow at me.

"Why is that?" he asked Ren.

Ren sighed. "People think I am not a true Everlian because I can walk between the worlds. I am not really a Magic, but my father was a Strongblood." He cleared his throat and repositioned himself on the rug next to me. "Right. Yes, well, as I have said, I am Ren Raker, Strongblood and Porter to Everly."

"Damn, try fitting that on a business card!" Jason quipped.

"Right." Ren looked at Jason, clearly perplexed, before continuing. With his bandaged hand, Ren ran his fingers through his hair, biting his lower lip, looking very deep in thought. "I can access your world through portals. If they can find the portal, anyone from Everly can enter your world, but they can only get back with a Porter. It keeps random Floridians from wandering these lands. Portals are also hidden and almost impossible to find."

"Portals?" I asked, raising an eyebrow.

"Yes, portals. The tree behind your aunt's home was a portal," Ren replied matter-of-factly, but he paused to look at me.

The tree.

"I touched that tree and my nose bled," I said. "I heard that ringing noise. It was coming from the tree, and it was like I had to touch it. Like I *had* to touch the tree."

Jason nodded, raising his eyebrows. "Um, sorry, what? Trees—trees talk to you?"

"Whenever an Everlian uses a portal without a Porter, an alarm goes off," Ren explained. "That's what you heard. It was the same sound you heard at the pool. That's how I knew."

"Knew what?" I asked.

"That it really was you."

"Oh."

Ren fixed the strap of his boot, and I let my eyes linger on him a few moments after he looked away.

"But why did my nose bleed when I touched the tree?" I finally asked.

"You touched a portal while the alarm was going off," Ren answered, eyebrows raised. "What did you expect?"

I rolled my eyes at him.

"So you get here by going through the magical alarm tree?" Jason asked.

Ren looked up. "Yes, sort of."

"Okay, and so this place…" Jason continued his assessment. "It's kind of like Wonderland. And Ren, you're the white rabbit!" He chuckled.

"White rabbit?" Ren sat up straight, his eyes a little wide. "I prefer the cat."

Jason nodded. "Do you know that movie?"

"It's a book, you goon," I corrected him. "How do you know it, Ren?"

"It is one of my favorites. A bit exaggerated, but a great work." Ren replied.

"What do you mean, exaggerated?" Jason took another swig of his water.

"Well, I was never able to figure out if the author was truly an Everlian, but the setting in the book always felt oddly familiar," Ren answered. "We have no talking cats or smoking caterpillars here, but that book makes me think of Everly whenever I read it." He put his hands on the rug and leaned back.

Jason and I looked at each other, dumbfounded, for a moment. Then Jason dropped his jaw dramatically.

"Curiouser and curiouser." I shook my head.

"Indeed," Jason added.

"I still can't believe this is happening," I admitted. "It's just so unreal."

"Oh my god, what if it isn't real? What if someone slipped something in the food I got us at the restaurant? We've been drugged," Jason said. "This can't be real. Maddy, we are Alice. No wonder that movie was so trippy."

"Jay, we weren't drugged!" I said, smiling at him. He looked a little bewildered, and I wasn't quite sure if he was serious or joking. It looked like a mix of both.

"You can't prove that," Jason replied.

"I have a question," I said, folding my arms in front of me.

"You have so many questions," Ren said before I could ask it.

"I'm sorry, but do the people you usually zap through trees just follow you around like puppy dogs?"

Ren raised his eyebrows at me.

Jason clapped. "Okay, I'm going to jump on the crazy train for a minute here. So, Aunt Ruth is at the temple, and that's where we are going. But if they think Maddy is a Witch, like those Cloaked guys did, and the king has that Magus Decree thingy, then should we really be walking into that temple?" Jason looked at me skeptically.

"I know for a fact that the king will not kill Madison." Ren rubbed the stubble on his chin as he spoke.

"How can you be sure of that?" Jason asked.

"Because he is Madison's father."

CHAPTER 12

"Oh, that's why you called Maddy 'princess' back in Greenrock," Jason said to Ren.

"Well, yes. Why else?" Ren looked perplexed.

"She *can* be demanding and bitchy sometimes," he said to Ren, but Jason was looking at me.

I flared my nostrils at Jason.

"You okay?" Jason asked me. "This is big."

I shrugged.

"So the king who's having all the Magic peeps killed, that's my daddy-o?" I shook my head. "I knew it. I knew the other shoe had to drop. Him being alive was too good to be true. Of course he's a raging psycho!"

"Yes," Ren said.

I huffed and laid flat on my back on the woven rug, draping my arms above my head.

"Mads?" Jason laid next to me. "You seem to be handling this portion of your history a little better. No sprinting, so that's good."

"Well, I guess I am past emotionally rocked," I replied, staring up into the top of the willow tree. "Let's go with comfortably perplexed for the moment." I closed my eyes.

"How did any of you know where to find Maddy and Ruth?" Jason asked Ren. "It's been like, what, seventeen, sixteen years."

I opened my eyes and turned to see Ren stand up.

"The King's Guard never stopped looking. The princess' abduction is still a rather fresh wound here. And I *had* to find you. It's a good thing I did," Ren replied in a complacent sort of way. "You seem to attract trouble."

"Oh, shut up, you pompous jerk!" I sat straight up. I was not even sure why I was suddenly angry with Ren.

Ren sneered. "I am putting my neck on the line to help you. Some respect would be nice."

"From the looks of it, your neck being on the line has nothing to do with helping me!"

"Oh, really?" Ren shot back.

"Yeah, really! It also seems like you did something to piss everyone off long before I came along! Those Cloaked guys wanted to kill you!" I jumped to my feet.

Ren huffed loudly. "You know nothing."

"Don't talk to her like that, dude." Jason stood and walked between us, focused solely on Ren.

I took a deep breath. Maybe attacking Ren wasn't the wisest endeavor, but he just got under my skin. I avoided looking back at him in an attempt to move on, for Jason's sake as well as my own.

"It's fine, Jay." I sighed. Jason turned his back to Ren and gave me a wink.

"How about instead of fighting, we go over the plan," Jason suggested. "We have to meet Lacy, right?"

"Um, yes," Ren said, standing. He ran his hand up the trunk of the tree and lowered his head. "We really need to get moving. The king's right-hand man, Captain Asher, has started using the Cloaked to round up the Magics, and there are so many of them at the temple already. And the moon will be full in four days."

"Meaning what?" Jason asked.

I stepped forward. "Meaning, if we don't get to Ruth before she gets to the temple, it's bad, and if we don't get to her before the full moon, they will kill her. Right, Ren?"

Ren turned to face us and leaned against the tree trunk. "Right."

"We just have to get Aunt Ruth before they reach the temple," Jason said. "And then we can go home."

"No, we have to help those people. The people in the temple that my—that the king is going to have killed. We can't leave them there," I said, picking up my sword.

Ren looked at me, surprised.

"Don't look so shocked," I scoffed. "I'm a lovely person."

Ren sniffed. "Sure."

I held up my middle finger.

"Okay, moving on," Jason intervened. "We get Ruth and we bust out the locked-up people. What's the danger level on that? You know the temple, right? Just a quick in-and-out?"

Ren shook his head and cleared his throat. "Not exactly. Back before any of this, before Strongbloods took over, the temple was home to the Witch Queen and her non-Magic wife. Back in that time, there was very little crime, but when it did occur, the queen felt that it was the crown's duty to keep the prisoners right there in the temple so that they could not harm the people of Everly. Some of the prisoners were Magics so, clearly, they could not be imprisoned by conventional tactics. The queen put a spell on the courtyard of the temple that would hold the Magics, preventing them from escaping."

"Um, okay. So, the king is using magic to keep Magic people prisoner so that he can kill them for being Magics because he thinks that all magic is evil? Yeah, that's not a contradiction or anything," Jason summarized.

Ren's eyes darted back and forth. "Yes, that is correct."

I scoffed. "Daddy sounds like a peach."

A gust of wind from outside the willow tree made its long branches sway gently back and forth.

Jason nodded. "Yeah, okay. But if that's the case, how will we get them out?"

"You would be willing to do that? To help the Magics?" Ren looked to me, ignoring Jason's question.

"You told me that my real father isn't just alive, but that he had my aunt kidnapped, and that he is now rounding people up to kill them on the full moon. If there is a way we can help them, then hell yes," I answered.

Ren walked quickly to the rug and moved the lantern back up to the nail on the willow tree's trunk, making his face much more visible.

He furrowed his brow. "There is a counterspell to break the former queen's original spell. My father..." Ren's eyes closed for a moment. He took a deep breath but remained silent.

I shifted my weight from foot to the other. I looked over at Jason and widened my eyes, willing him to speak so I didn't have to. Jason nodded and walked over to stand between Ren and me. I let out a sigh.

"Your father? Is he gone?" Jason questioned, his hand firm on Ren's shoulder. Ren nodded.

"Yes, my father is gone," Ren replied slowly and softly. I could feel the ache in his words.

"We are so sorry for your loss," Jason said sweetly, gesturing back to me.

"You started to explain about the counterspell," I added.

Jason spun his head and glared at me. "Madison!"

"No, it is fine," Ren continued. "My father was the royal record keeper and served as one of the king's most trusted confidants—he and Captain Asher. It was my father's research that uncovered the magical spell on the courtyard. He was not happy with the king's abuse of it, so he spent all his time looking for a way to break the courtyard's spell," Ren told us slowly as he fixed his eyes on the lantern. Even through his calm, steady stare, I could see his jaw tensing.

"What happened to your father?" Jason asked sympathetically. He was so great in these situations. I, on the other hand, contemplated flagging down the Cloaked just to escape this conversation.

Ren looked at me for a few seconds before answering. "He did it. He found a way to free the Magics by breaking the spell on the courtyard. The night he shared it with me, there was this storm in the village. Prestin, just north of the Ember Isle. It was not like a rainstorm, but it was like the air caught fire. It got very hot, and it was so bright you could not see. I ran, but when the storm was over, the entire village was gone, and my father with it." Ren kept his head down.

"What do you mean, gone?" Jason prodded, emphasizing the word *gone*.

"I mean it is no longer there. Only the land remains. The homes, the trees and"—Ren hesitated—"the people. Just gone."

Ren met my inquisitive stare. I lingered in his gaze for a moment. There was so much pain in his eyes; so much sadness.

"What kind of storm would do that?" Jason asked.

Ren nodded and did not break his stare. "That was no regular storm. And I do not believe it was a coincidence that my father perished in it. It was the king's doing, I am sure of it." He said *king* like it pained him to even speak the word.

I coughed loudly and fidgeted with my sword's handle.

"You think the king did it to get rid of him before he tried to do the spell on the courtyard," Jason stated.

"I know he did," Ren said with a sneer.

Great.

At last, Ren shifted his focus to Jason. "But what the king did not know was that I had the book with the ritual in it. My father gave it to me that night so I could free the Magics and end the terror once and for all. Bring peace to Everly."

"And Aunt Ruth. She is a, uh…a Witch?" I fumbled over the words. "And that would make her a Magic." My stomach twisted with worry as I imagined her. "Will they even wait until the full moon?"

"I do not know the answer to that," Ren answered. "We had better get moving. Jason, can you help me with this?" He motioned to the chest behind the tree trunk, and Jason hurried over to assist him.

Ruth kidnapped me. She wasn't just another Magic. She was a criminal in their eyes.

I didn't move as Ren hurried past me to grab the canteens on the ground and prop his satchel against the willow trunk.

"What will they do to her, Ren?" I begged of him quietly. He stopped walking abruptly, but he did not speak. He pressed his lips together and the corners of his mouth turned down in a frown.

I laughed absently. "That bad?"

Ren dipped his head down and then looked back at me without speaking.

I traced a half circle in the dirt with my foot.

"Ren, will they kill her?" I inquired directly. "Before the full moon. Can we actually save her?"

"The king usually sticks to his schedule," Ren said. "That's all we can hope for."

"My father is going to kill them." I bobbed my head up and realized I hadn't blinked. I exhaled loudly. "My father is going to kill my aunt, and we may not be able to save her."

Ren didn't answer.

"How?" I asked bluntly.

"How what?"

"How will he kill them?"

"Maddy, what kind of question is that?" Jason walked over to me. "Ignore her, Ren. She tends to say the most inappropriate things when she gets uncomfortable."

"It is alright," Ren replied. "She should know."

"I mean, really. How can he kill a Witch? I just—I always thought it was hard," I said, feeling the tears fill my eyes.

"Maddy." Jason tugged at my hand and stared at me with his eyebrows scrunched. "Let's just get going, guys. This is just about the weirdest conversation I have ever been a part of, and that includes the time Maddy kept spouting off Jody Foster facts to my grieving father at the memorial dinner for my Aunt Clarice."

"I choked." I shrugged at Jason, trying to laugh away my worry for Ruth.

Jason leaned his shoulder into mine. "Ready?"

"Yeah, we should go," I agreed. Jason and I started to walk out from under the willow tree's branches.

"Wait," Ren said. "We are not going that way."

Jason and I stopped and turned around to see Ren standing on the far side of the willow tree. He reached over and pulled aside a cluster of long branches to reveal an opening in the side of the large rock formation that I had seen when we were running from those jerks.

"We will be going through here. It is a cavern that will lead us to the Jade Village and we can cut the Cloaked off there, before they reach the Temple of the Ember Isle," Ren explained, letting the branches fall back as he walked toward me and Jason.

"Cool." Jason smiled. "Is that where we'll meet Lacy?"

Ren gave a nod. "I am going to go grab us some more water, and we will head out. Stay here," he said to Jason, and collected the other canteen.

"Hurry up," I told Ren as he walked past me to leave the safe cover of the willow tree.

"Their hands and their heads," Ren muttered behind me. I pivoted back to face him.

"Huh?" I asked.

Ren took a deep breath but didn't look at me.

"Their hands and their heads. That is where a Witch's power is emitted. So, they are removed. That is how they are killed."

"Oh." I blinked a few times. "Right."

"Whoa," Jason said. "Man, Maddy. We shouldn't be here."

I stood motionless for a moment, my mouth agape. "Their heads and their hands. That's horrible."

"Okay, wait, Ren. You never explained what Maddy has to do with this. I get that her dad is the king and all, but it doesn't explain why you were looking for her," Jason pointed out. "I mean, you didn't know that Ruth was going to be taken when you came to Greenrock, did you?"

Ren shook his head. "No. I was there for Madison."

Jason and I exchanged looks.

"The ritual to free the Magics. It uses three people: one with the blood of the royal line, one with the blood of a Strongblood, and one with the blood of a Magic. All three are needed to break the binds. The royal must say the words and do the ritual. It will drop the spell from the temple's courtyard and free the Magics. They can use their powers to escape," Ren explained.

"You just said that the Strongbloods and the Magics hated each other," Jason said. "And the king is so not going to be down with this plan. How are you going to get their blood for this spell and get them all to participate? Maddy is great, but she isn't exactly a snake charmer. If your plan is to get her to make the two sides get along to do this ritual just because the king is her dad, you might want to go back to the drawing board."

"He's not wrong," I added. "I don't do people." I fiddled with the grip of my sword as Ren looked from Jason back to me.

"My father found a loophole in the ritual," Ren said, looking back to Jason.

"A loophole?" Jason raised an eyebrow.

"Great, those never fail!" I grumbled sarcastically as I turned away from them, took a few steps toward the cave opening, and stopped.

Then it hit me. I spun around to face Ren again.

"Wait. My mother was a Witch, and my father is the king of the Ember Isle and a Strongblood." I shook my head. "That makes me all of the above."

"Yes, Madison. It is you," Ren confirmed with a nod, his emerald eyes piercing mine.

"I'm the loophole," I whispered.

CHAPTER 13

My heart was pounding in my chest as I stared blankly at Ren. It all made sense now.

"Whoa," Jason muttered.

"Your mother, a Witch, and your father, a royal and a Strongblood, and they made you." Ren folded his hands together in front of him and watched me with the concern that a doctor would after telling his patient she was going to give birth to unicorn triplets.

"Mads?" Jason walked over to me.

"No, I'm okay." I smiled, still wide-eyed.

This is a good thing.

"This could be good," I said aloud.

I was important here. My father was a monster, but I could right the wrong.

"My blood," I said. "My blood is a part of this counterspell to free them? To free the Magics? Are you sure?"

"Madison, I would not lie to you, I swear it. My father did extensive research on the matter," Ren insisted.

"Why all the secrecy? Why didn't you just tell me this when we met? Why are you keeping things from me? I am here. I am doing what you asked. I deserve to know! What else don't I know?" I asked. I felt the heat in my cheeks.

"Would you have believed it then, Madison? If I had walked up to you in the pool house and told you this, would you have believed me?" Ren's face was stern though I pointed my sword at him.

And then a single thought overwhelmed me: Aunt Ruth.

"How did they know where to find Ruth, Ren?" I asked, gripping my sword tightly.

Ren glanced down at his boots. I saw the handle of a dagger showing on the side of his calf.

"Huh? Ren, how did they know where to find her?"

"Madison, I promise I do not know why the King's Guard was able to find her. But I promise we can get her back." Ren held his hands up defensively.

"Mads, put the sword down," Jason urged me.

The willow branches rustled loudly in the wind.

"You were there, at the pool! You were following me," I accused Ren. "You led them to her. You must have."

"Honestly, I do not know how anyone found Ruth. People do not follow me. People do not care what I do or where I go. Ruth was never in the equation for me. But it was clear that something was happening to Ruth after I got there—that, I will not deny. That is why the spell on you faded. It was as if another Witch was targeting Ruth, but I cannot be sure."

I tried to breathe normally, but I was nauseated and with every breath I took in, I felt dizzy. He made sense. I hated that he was making sense. It shouldn't make sense.

"Just stop talking," I mumbled, lowering my sword to my side. I heard Jason sigh as the tip of my sword touched the ground. We stood in a loose triangle near the cave opening.

"What about my mother? Lacy said she was the leader of the Rosewood Coven. Is she—is she—" I cleared my throat.

"Alive?" Jason jumped in. I watched Ren and waited for his answer, not blinking.

"That, I do not know. The Magics all went into hiding when King Dax signed the Magus Decree. And your mother has not been seen since you were taken from the temple," Ren said. "But I know she was mighty. The most powerful Witch in all of Everly."

"Really?" I paused for a moment, thinking about my mother as a Witch, casting spells and doing magic. It was a far cry from the way I had always imagined her—as a quiet woman with a sharp mind and knack for baking. "And my father's name is Dax." I knew he was doing terrible things, but learning his name still made me smile.

Ren cleared his throat. "I am sorry I do not know much more than that."

"No, it's fine, but I hate to burst your father's bubble. I don't have magical powers. The Strongblood thing, sure, fine. Whatever. I am fast and I can fight, but that's because Ruth trained me. She taught me to fight, but I am not a Witch." I dropped my sword to my side.

"Yes, you are a Strongblood. And you are a Witch. Part Witch, at least," Ren argued.

"Don't you think that's something I would have noticed?" I shook my head.

"I do not know how it works, but, Madison, I know it is true. It is the reason that Ruth took you. People here are not of more than one bloodline—it is unheard of. Until you."

"And you are sure it is me?" I asked.

"My father assured me," Ren replied, sounding almost shocked that I would question his faith in his father.

"Guess what, Ren? Grown-ups lie all the time. All of them!" I said. "And from what I gather, everyone in Everly lies. I can't be the person you think I am. A Witch. A loophole. I'm just me."

"What of the ringing alarm of the tree, then?" Ren asked, annoyed now. "You would not hear it if you were not a Witch, Madison. I hear it only because I am a Porter. You hear it because it is a magical spell. You are a Witch."

"The tree," I said softly to myself, and nodded. "So what am I, like, the chosen one?"

"Not exactly. You are the one who could upset the structure. The anomaly," Ren clarified.

"And my parents are alive. Or at least one of them is," I stated.

Ren nodded.

I felt defeated. I had lived for eighteen years without knowing who I really was. Knowing the truth about my parents was supposed to be great. Why did it feel like I was suddenly the mayor of Suck Town, USA?

Jason rested his hand on my shoulder. "Maddy?"

"It's just…girls like me don't get a happy ending. Girls like me don't find their parents in some magic land with trolls and fairies…girls like me…"

"You better not be screwing with her," Jason said pointedly to Ren.

"I swear, I would never," Ren replied.

Jason nodded. "Okay. Get the water and we'll go," Jason said before turning back to me. I wasn't used to seeing Jason be so firm with people.

"Maddy, I did n—" Ren started. I held up my hand with my palm facing him.

"Madison. Only he gets to call me Maddy," I corrected Ren. I could feel my irritation getting the better of me, but I didn't care. "I will do your ritual after we get Aunt Ruth. Getting her to go to the temple after we rescue her might take some convincing, but I am in. Let's just go."

"That's great, Madison," Ren answered in an almost professional tone.

"I am not doing it for you, Ren. I am doing it for them," I said, cold-eyed and stone-faced.

He narrowed his eyes, staring back at me for a few moments. "If that is how it has to be, then so be it."

"So be it," I echoed.

Ren looked at the ground, took a deep breath, and exhaled it slowly. He held up the canteens in one hand. "I will be back in five minutes. Be ready to leave when

I return." With that, Ren darted out from under the weeping willow, leaving Jason and I alone.

The willow branches swayed gently, offering moments of hazy light that faded as quickly as they came.

"Jay?"

"Yes, darling?"

"Darling?" I laughed weakly.

"Sweetums?"

I shook my head. "Nope."

"Sugar plum."

"Not even a little bit." I smiled. "Let's sit," I suggested, and we sank to the ground and settled onto the plush rug.

"Mads?" Jason started. I curled my hand in his.

"Hmm?" I replied.

"You okay?"

"Me? Sure." I tried to sound plucky.

Jason sighed.

"Maddy, Princess of Everly. Savior of the Magics!" he joked.

"Daughter of the vanished coven leader and a mass-murdering king. Yep. I am peachy keen," I said sarcastically, doing jazz hands next to my face. "Worst birthday ever."

Jason's face lit with enthusiasm. "Aw, Maddy, I know this is insane, but you could make a real difference here. All that crap you're always babbling about, having something that you care about. Something that matters to you. You could make a difference here. Here in Everly."

I met Jason's eyes and let myself enjoy the idea for a moment. "Yeah, only I meant that I didn't want to run races my entire life. I wanted to be known for something other than my speed. I wanted to change the world. This is all...just crazy."

Jason raised his eyebrows. "Well, lady, here's your chance. This may not be the world you meant to change, but it's the world that needs you."

I dropped my head down as that concept hit me in all its truth. "Yeah, I will save the Magics, but I am more worried about Ruth. I don't even want to think about everything else he just dropped on me. Getting her back is priority one."

"Ruth is a tough chick. But yeah, priority one. We'll get her back." Jason patted my knee. "And then we will all live Everly ever after."

I turned my head slowly, and Jason was smiling widely at me.

"Wow, that was awful!" I chuckled. "How long have you been waiting to say that?"

"Way too long!" Jason laughed loudly. "After we find Ruth—which we will—if you're ready, we'll acknowledge the other things that we aren't going to focus on right now," he said with authority.

I nodded.

"I mean it, Maddy."

"I know you do. You always do."

"Mads, you are Witch and a Strongblood. And a frickin' princess!" Jason exclaimed.

I looked down at the long metal blade, pressing my lips together. "Yeah, I guess I am." I turned the sword over, looking at the handle's glow.

"Crazy." Jason squinted at the sword. "So, your magic is stuck in there, huh?"

"I guess? And I can't explain it, but I feel weird when I don't have it in my hand now. Is that strange?"

"Um, this is all strange. Does it glow in my hand, too?" Jason asked. I handed it to him, and the light went dim. "Damn, I was hoping I was a something, too. I guess I'm just a dude." He sighed.

"The best dude," I corrected.

"Jason Vega, the intensely attractive, Puerto Rican-Italian, simple dude," he said, and lifted the sword up. He waved it around, knocking over Ren's satchel that was leaning against the tree. The contents fell out.

"Oh crap," Jason said.

"Clearly, you haven't held a sword before, Jason Vega, the simple dude!" I laughed.

"Gah, yeah. I'll leave the swords to you, Maddy." Jason smiled, setting it on the ground. "You have skills."

"Ruth made me a fighter. That's all her."

"Or it could be Everly. You're half Strongblood and half Witch. You're Princess Madison." Jason nudged me. "How crazy is that?"

"That is crazy."

"But calling it crazy doesn't mean it isn't true," he added.

I raised my eyebrows. "Maybe if I say it three times?"

Jason and I locked eyes and whispered "Crazy, crazy, crazy," in unison, with only the slightest of hope that it would actually work.

I looked around. No change. I shrugged as I leaned over to replace the scattered contents of Ren's bag: a small knife in a brown leather case, a book, and a small rectangular box that looked like a glasses case.

I grabbed my sword and the book. It was a hardcover, and on the ground next to it was the book jacket for *The Catcher in the Rye*.

"Oh, I love this book!" I said excitedly.

"Nerd alert." Jason picked up the last of the scattered items and stuck them back in the satchel.

I flipped the book open to the middle. On the almond-colored pages was handwriting in rich swirls of cursive. This wasn't a just a book. I slammed it closed.

I took in a sharp breath and slowly started to open the book again before dropping it on the rug beneath us. "It's his journal!"

"Should we read it?" Jason pondered.

I nodded. "It could totally just be a spell book or something."

"What if it's the book with that ritual that Ren was talking about?" Jason raised his thick black eyebrows. "We've got to check it out."

Could I really be that invasive?

Yes, and I needed to be. I needed some clarity on *something* here in Everly. I sat cross-legged and flipped through the pages. There was a name on the inside cover, and I read it aloud: "Lawrence Raker."

"Lawrence?" Jason repeated. "Was that Ren's dad's name?"

"Maybe this is his journal." I couldn't really feel guilty for reading it. Ren knew everything about my life. I was just evening the playing field. I started to flip through, page by page, but paused midway through the book as another name caught my eye: Madison.

"This dude has girl handwriting," Jason muttered.

"Jason, look at this," I said, pointing to my name on the page.

He reached out, grabbed the book from my hand, and began to read the passage out loud. He cleared his throat. "'The girl goes by the name Madison now. She has the same auburn hair as her kin but far surpasses them with her quick wit. She is seventeen years of age, which matches the Otherworld timeline, according to the research. My skepticism on her identity was silenced today when I witnessed her athletic skill. It is clear that she is a Strongblood. She is incredibly fast, beating everyone here. She is matched to others of the Ember Isle in her skill.'"

I sat back and dropped my chin to my chest. "Holy crap."

"What? What is it?" Jason asked urgently.

"I'm an alien."

Jason leaned back away from me and squinted like he was nearsighted and trying to read small print. "Come again?"

"I am like an alien superhero," I repeated.

"Oh, lordy. I think I know where this is going, but go on. Explain."

"I'm super-duper fast, right?"

"Yeah, but why does that make you an alien?" Jason said, still not following me.

"It's like I'm an alien who goes to another planet of lesser beings and the only reason I'm super-fast, is because everyone is just slow. And that makes me look like a superhero to the regular folks, just like in the comics," I explained.

"Oh, good lord, why couldn't you just play with Barbies like the other girls?" Jason dropped his head all the way back.

"Shut it. I'm serious. If I had stayed here, I would be just be another person. The Strongbloods are all fast and strong and stuff here. Ren caught up to me, no problem. I am not super."

"Maddy, you are super, even if you are from Everly," Jason said, his tone more serious now, and leaned forward.

"No, don't you get it? If I had stayed here, I would just be average—maybe even less than average because I am only half Strongblood or whatever. I wouldn't be known for my speed. I would just be Madison. The only reason everyone thinks I'm so fast on Greenrock Island is because everyone there is naturally slower than me. I am a fraud."

Jason laughed and shook his head. "Let's just keep reading." He flipped a few pages back and kept skimming, running his finger over the written words.

I chuckled. "I don't think you understand how upsetting that is to me." I stared at him, wide-eyed.

Jason laughed and continued to thumb through the book. It wasn't hard to get Jason to laugh, but that never made it less gratifying, especially now. I looked around the willow tree as the long branches gently swayed. It would be quite relaxing here if things were different. If I were here for a visit and not a rescue mission.

Aunt Ruth was strong. Nobody could hurt her. I knew that was the truth, but that still didn't stop the nagging worry in the back of my mind that refused to let up. That worry only seemed to get worse with each passing second.

"Where is Ren? We need to go." I set the sword down next to me and retied the laces on my red sneakers—not because they were untied, but because I needed something to do with my hands.

"Maddy, he was, like, *studying* you. Looks like old man Raker was hot for you." Jason shook his head, turning the page. I elbowed his rib, and he winced with a laugh.

"No, the handwriting is totally different back here. The beginning pages are drawings and a bunch of crap that makes no sense," I said, flipping to the second half of the book. "The part we just read is in someone else's writing. I think it's Ren's. Ren's dad didn't go to Greenrock. Ren did."

"Well done, Veronica Mars!" Jason said.

I nodded, happy with my deduction. "Do you think this is the book Ren was talking about? The one with the ritual in it?"

Jason traced his finger over the words, skimming through a passage. "Hmm…here. This might…no," he muttered as he paged through the small book. "Here! This might be something."

"What is it?" I pressed, scooting closer.

"Not the ritual. Seems like our Mr. Tough Guy Ren Raker is actually just a big ol' softy! Look at this." Jason turned the journal toward me. On the page was a drawing. It was me. It was a drawing of me sitting on the branch of the oak tree that stood just outside my window back home. I studied the picture. It was drawn in such great detail. The drawing was so meticulous that I even recognized the shirt in the sketch.

"It's my Led Zeppelin shirt that Lacy found at the secondhand store," I said aloud as I read the words written beneath the drawing: *Her tree.*

I imagined Ren drawing this. His strong features softened in my mind as I pictured this scruffy, hard-nosed guy drawing carefully, his hand swooping over the page with each pencil stroke. I also felt exposed. "He was following me. I get why. I get that he needed to make sure, but it's creepy, right? Like, what if I had been picking my nose or something truly embarrassing? So creepy."

"Yeah. He's on the low end of the creep spectrum, but still, this is weird."

"Why couldn't he just go to Ruth or to me?"

Jason scoffed. "Well, think about it. Ruth wanted to keep you hidden. She would have kicked Ren's ass. And you—you for sure would have kicked his ass. I sort of get it. He needed to be sure."

"I guess," I said. "Do you think—does it say things about my parents?"

"Let's check it out," Jason said. "Has any of this actually sunk in? It still feels like a dream to me. I can't imagine how you're feeling right now."

"Confused." With each page turn, subtle mustiness hit my nostrils.

"At least it's answers. That's something."

"True story," I replied, and moved my sword's grip closer to the book to see better. The lantern above us provided a fair amount of light, but some of the writing was still hard to see.

"In the page before that, he goes on and on about taking you to safety but fearing your reaction," Jason continued. "Maybe he isn't so bad. He was just worried about you. And I know you're into him. I can see it all over your face, little miss. I think Ren could be the Angel to your Buffy, the Jess Mariano to your Rory Gilmore, the Ron to your Hermione, the—"

"Enough!" I held up my hand. "How dare you! You know I'm Team Spike."

"My apologies." Jason laughed. "But my observation still stands."

I rolled my eyes. Anyone could see how attractive Ren was, but that really was the last thing on my mind. "Oh my god, no way! The dude is a nut job and pompous and so, so arrogant," I protested.

"But hot," Jason added.

"He's not horrid," I replied.

"I miss my Caleb. Everyone must be so worried back home." Jason said, changing the subject, and leaned his head on me. "We were going to dinner with his parents tomorrow. I guess that's out the window."

"I will try to get you back in time for your dinner, Jay," I said.

"It's okay. This is where I need to be. You and me, kid. Always." He nuzzled his head on me like a puppy.

"Stop!" I laughed and pushed his head away.

"I ruv roo, Princess Maddy. I ruv roo!" Jason said in his best Scooby-Doo voice.

I laughed even louder as I wrestled him off me.

"I think our valiant knight Ren has the hots for you, too, Princess Maddy." Jason raised his eyebrows obnoxiously and poked me with his elbow a few times.

"No way, José." I shook my head.

"Well, he clearly has a thing for you. On the one page—"

I held up my hand to cut him off just as we heard a rustle from beyond the cover of the willow. Startled, I jumped up, grasping the sword tightly. Jason slowly climbed to his feet as well.

"Uh, Jay, we need to go."

I turned to scan the area. For the first time since this madness had started, I really did wish Ren were here. I felt the hairs on my arms raise with genuine fear.

"Uh, I actually wish our valiant knight was here now," Jason said, his tone uneasy.

"Me too. A lot, actually," I seconded, looking for movement beyond the willow tree branches.

"Ren, where are you?" I whispered to myself.

CHAPTER 14

"Ren?" I whispered, holding Jason's hand in my left and my sword in my right.

Nothing.

I kept my eyes on the perimeter of the tree. I couldn't help but feel a little betrayed by Ren leaving us alone as I saw the tension on Jason's face.

"Maddy?" Jason whispered. My stomach twisted at the worry in his voice. *I hate this. I hate that he is in a position to be afraid.*

"Damn it, Ren," I said, my teeth clenched.

Just as I said his name, Ren burst through the willow branches. Jason and I screamed in unison like we were watching a horror movie.

Ren stopped in his tracks. "Quiet! Why are you screaming?" he asked, annoyed.

"I thought it was a Cloaky, or Cloaked guy, whatever you call them," I said angrily. "You said five minutes. That was longer than five minutes."

I looked back up at Ren; he was already looking at me. My tired eyes traced his jaw, following the dark stubble of the mustache and beard that speckled the bottom half of his face. His hair hadn't moved an inch, like he had just stepped out of an overpriced salon, making me want to punch him in the face a little bit more than I already wanted to.

I turned away from him quickly.

Ren cleared his throat. "All right, are you ready to go? It is only a two-hour march through the cavern, but I have water and shelter if we need it. Also, Jason, I think it wise for you to be armed."

He pulled out a crossbow out of the chest next to the willow's trunk. "Jason, here you go."

Jason grabbed it and immediately pointed it to the side and pretended to shoot it. "Yes! Pew! Pew, pew!" he exclaimed with joy.

Rummaging through the chest again, Ren pulled out a quiver full of small arrows. He handed Jason the little quiver and a rope.

"Here, tie this around your waist. Do you know how to use one of these?" Ren asked, pointing to the crossbow.

Jason shook his head.

"It is easy, and you will not have to come too close to inflict a bit of damage. You just put the arrow here, pull this back, aim, and fire at your target," Ren explained. Jason nodded, looking a little more nervous now. "It is old and does not pack as much punch as it used to, but it will sting them enough to scare them off.

"Now, here. You can hook the bow onto the belt as well. Always have it at the ready." Ren clapped his hand on Jason's shoulder, knocking Jason forward a bit.

"No prob, Bob," Jason acknowledged.

Ren cocked his head to the side, a confused look on his face. "My name is Ren."

Jason looked at me over Ren's shoulder, his eyebrows raised dramatically. He snickered. "Sorry, Ren. That was just a saying. It just—it means that I understand."

"Right. Okay." Ren nodded, turning back toward me and holding out another slender black rope. This one had a scabbard attached to it.

"Here, this is for your sword," he said. "It may be a little big for your blade, but it should work."

Ren reached around me to tie the black rope around my waist. His cheek grazed my earlobe.

"I've got it." I pulled the rope from his hands and took a step back, tying the black cord in a knot at my hip. I slid my sword into the scabbard.

Ren nodded in approval, then started to place both hands on my shoulders before changing his mind. "Now you look like a true warrior," he said.

Jason burst out laughing. "Bah! No, she doesn't! She looks like a lunatic with a sword, and I look like a deranged cowboy."

Finally, the insanity of this entire day peaked with both of us bursting into laughter. We did look ridiculous. Jason was right—with the crossbow on one side and the quiver on his other hip, he had a bit of a cowboy gunslinger quality about him.

Jason continued, "It's like we're in an action movie, but someone forgot to give us our costumes." He laughed, doubling over. "Wardrobe! We need wardrobe over here!" He mocked snapping his fingers over his head.

Our laughs subsided as I reached up to lower Jason's snapping fingers. Ren surely wouldn't understand that reference, and I certainly didn't want to waste another second. We need to get moving.

Jason tilted his head. "It's good to see you smile, kid," he said.

"Okay, I have the canteens," Ren said, closing the lid of the chest. He put the satchel over his head so that the thick leather strap crossed his chest diagonally and held an unlit torch in one hand. "Ready?"

No. But there was no other way.

Jason put his arms around me. "Okay, I know you hate hugs, but I don't care," he said, pulling me close. I didn't stop him, but I did groan loudly.

We stood there for a second or two as it struck me: This could be hard. Ren felt the need to make sure we had weapons. That had to mean something. I wrapped an arm around Jason and squeezed him tightly.

Jason let go first and stepped back, resting a hand on each of my shoulders.

"Jay, this may be dangerous and it may suck." I frowned.

"Maddy, I promise that I won't let you go alone, not ever."

"And I love you for that, but I…" Tears filled my eyes, and I took a deep breath before continuing. "You don't have to do this."

"Ren, lead the way," Jason said, never taking his eyes off mine.

"Okay. Let's go." I nodded, wrapping my hand around the grip of my sword for light. "We aren't going to find anyone standing still in here."

With a nod, Ren lit the torch from the lantern and it burst into flame with a roar and a crackle. Ren walked to the cavern entrance and pulled the willow branches back. The torch flared up.

"Whoa, a torch? Isn't that a bit much?" Jason asked and took a step back.

"Yeah, can't we just take the lantern?" I pointed back to the lantern hanging from its nail in the trunk of the willow tree.

"Goblins hate fire. Always bring a torch in the caverns. The lantern would not be enough to scare them. Remember that," Ren instructed us.

I rolled my eyes but nodded.

Ren walked into the cavern and Jason and I followed.

The cave was much cooler, and the air was damp and smelled musty, like the basement of Aunt Ruth's house in the spring. Above our head, the cavern ceiling was high—too high to see with the light of the torch. The ground was fairly smooth and even. The walls seemed to be getting farther apart as we walked.

"Watch out on your right," Ren stated. "Don't step on them."

I looked over to see a half dozen stacks of books, each piled ten or eleven books high.

"Are all of these yours?" I asked, looking down at the collection.

"Yes. I enjoy the written word," Ren answered.

"Maddy, too," Jason chimed in behind me.

"Really?" Ren replied, turning his head only a bit, never taking his eyes off the path ahead of him. "I figured you more for an athlete."

"I can be as many things as I want to be," I replied.

"They didn't have a TV when Maddy was a kid. Just books. Right, Mads?" Jason added.

I stopped and whipped my head around to whisper "Shut up." I wasn't embarrassed or anything like that, but Ren already knew enough about me—more than I did. He didn't need to know every detail of my childhood in Greenrock, too.

Ren didn't respond, thankfully.

I squinted to see the titles on the tops of the piles. "These look like the books back home. Like, the actual covers and everything." I squinted, recognizing the classic, unmistakable blue cover of *The Great Gatsby*.

"I prefer the writers from your world. I like the magic-free stories," Ren replied, still walking. I trotted a little faster to catch up to him, and Jason followed.

"Really? What is your favorite?" I asked, curious.

"A favorite? I would have to think about that."

Ren held the torch to the side of him, lighting the path as we walked. The cavern curved as we continued on, and the musty smell only grew stronger. Soon our path had widened so that the wall to our left was no longer lit by Ren's torch. Jason's hand was hooked into the thin black rope around my waist, and as the cavern grew wider, Jason moved closer.

"This is sort of spooky," he said softly.

My sword in its scabbard swung at my side, hitting the top of my calf every few steps. I kept a hand on the sword's grip. Like Ren had said, my sword was a little too small for this scabbard, so holding it also stopped it from rattling around as I walked.

"How much longer?" I asked Ren, who I was following almost as closely as Jason was following me.

Ren sighed loudly and stopped to face me, making me stumble as I halted in order to avoid colliding with him. "Madison, you said you deserve to know everything, right? Well, this information is not a conversation that one has while walking like this."

"Whoa, hey. Can we stop *after* we exit the super-creepy dark cave?" Jason asked, his voice echoing off the cavern walls.

"Shouldn't we keep walking?" I asked Ren while hooking my arm around Jason, who was standing at my side.

"Yes, you are right. We should not stop." Ren, caught in a thought, ran his hand through his hair. I started walking again with Jason on my left and Ren and his torch on my right.

"Ren, just talk. It's okay. I am the princess of the evil Ember Isle empire hell-bent on killing all the Magics, which is further complicated by me being half Witch. What else could there be?" My voice echoed slightly in the in the silence of the cave.

He didn't say anything.

"Just tell me," I urged him, apprehensively.

"I was not sure I should say anything, but I feel that I must share what I recently learned," Ren stated.

"Okay." I nodded.

"It is about your cousin."

"What do you mean?" I asked, nervous to hear the answer.

"I do not think that the guards of the Ember Isle came upon your aunt on their own. I think they were aided." Ren lowered his chin, making the torch cast an ominous shadow on his face.

"Okay, we knew that," I said.

"By Lacy," he said flatly.

"What?" I shook my head at the idiot idea.

"When I went to fill our canteens, I intercepted a Cypher Fairy that was headed to deliver a message to your father, King Dax of the Ember Isle...the message was from your cousin, Lacy."

I stopped walking and crossed my arms. "Lacy is sending a message to my father?"

"Yes."

"What?" Jason asked. "Are you sure it was her?"

"It was her voice, yes." Ren nodded.

"What was the message? You said that only the intended person could receive the Cypher Fairy's message," Jason added.

"I have my ways with the fae," Ren retorted.

"I don't understand. Why would she do that?" I asked. I felt my body sway a little, like I was standing on the deck of a rocking boat. "You think Lacy led the guard to her mom? And that Lacy is sending my father a message? My father, the man who is rounding up Magics to kill them, including her mother?" I asked softly, like a confused child. "But why? What was the message?"

Ren didn't answer.

How bad is it?

I glared at my feet, unable to look at either of them in the eye. I crossed my arms in front of me, wanting to continue on our path but unable to make my feet move beneath me.

"What was the message?" Jason asked.

Ren looked at me and back to Jason. The torch flared brighter for a moment.

"What was the message?" I repeated urgently.

"It was a warning. Lacy was warning your father that we are on our way to the Ember Isle," Ren stated. "She was betraying us."

CHAPTER 15

"You're lying. Why are you still lying to me?" I asked, taking a step back from Ren. Jason put his arm firmly around my shoulder.

"Madison, I speak only the truth to you, I promise," Ren insisted. "When I was in Greenrock, it was Lacy who found me. She told me about Ruthana, about you. I did not understand it then, but it was what I wanted, so I did not question it. She seemed to want me to protect you, so I did not see any malice in her actions…until now."

"I don't believe it!" I growled.

"Something is wrong…with all of this. I had a strange feeling about her then, but I did not know exactly why. She knew who I was, and it was almost as if she knew why I was there. I think she was involved in Ruthana's capture." Ren ruffled his hair in thought.

"That's her mother! She'd never do it!" I yelled, my voice resonating from the stone walls. "You don't know her. She's the sweetest girl on the planet. She's so…"

"Madison, please—" Ren put his hand on my shoulder. I knocked it off, pushed my hands into his chest, and flung him back into the wall.

The torch fell to the ground, and Jason swooped down to pick it up. I glared at Ren for another second. "This can't be true."

I turned sharply and placed my hand on my sword's grip again as I walked ahead of them. No amount of tantrum that I threw at Ren would change the facts. Lacy had been acting strange when Aunt Ruth was taken. Something wasn't right.

"Why would Lacy warn him? I don't get it," Jason said behind me to Ren.

Before Ren could answer, I turned back around. "You were never going to take us to meet her, were you?"

"No." Ren looked at his feet. "The spot where Lacy asked us to meet her is in the other direction."

I scoffed.

Ren chewed his lip for a second. "We are going to the Jade Village to get supplies and to cut your aunt off at the Temple Road. I had my doubts about Lacy before this, and now I cannot rationalize what she has attempted to do. We cannot trust her."

"I don't understand. She's...she's the good one," I mumbled to myself, turning back around.

"She's right. You don't know her like we do, Ren. Something's wrong," Jason said.

Could it really be true? Could Lacy have fooled me all this time? Maybe I didn't really know my cousin after all.

"No," I whispered painfully, and shook my head. Just because I knew it wasn't true, that didn't make it hurt less.

We walked in silence for what felt like forever. The cavern was long, and the ceiling was still high enough that it didn't make me feel claustrophobic. Ren had said that it would take two hours to get to the Jade Village, but I didn't want to ask him again how much longer. The walls had narrowed enough that I could see them by the light of my sword's grip, though. I preferred that to the big, open, too-wide part of the cavern a ways back. I lifted my sword out of the scabbard to look at the wall. Squinting, I could see lines—no, scratches, perhaps? There were similar markings on the other wall. I ran my fingers over the etched grooves. They didn't look like natural lines on the stone surface.

What did this? An animal? Or was it the goblins Ren had mentioned earlier? I slowed my pace so that I was a little closer to Ren's torch. Jason and Ren talked behind me about random topics, but I ignored them. Jason had a knack for conversation—something I envied.

I broke my silence with a cough, cleared my throat, and stopped walking abruptly. Jason laid his hand on my back. "Madison, are you all right?"

"She was involved. She was a part of this whole thing," I said. "She was so calm and almost cold. And then that fairy. She did this. But why?" I asked, staring at the ground.

"That is the question," Ren said quietly. "I am sorry, Madison. I did not wish this."

"It's not your fault," I replied without looking at him. He didn't respond, and I started walking again.

"Um, hey, guys..." Jason said. "Do you see that?"

I lifted my head and squinted to focus ahead of us. Just yards in front of us, the cavern pathway was lit in a glowing bluish green.

"Is that the Jade Village?" I asked hopefully.

"Sort of. It is the grotto," Ren said. "There is fresh water within. Follow me."

I scrunched my nose. "The grotto?"

"It is a sight to be seen. Come on." Ren waved us along as he took the lead, torch in hand.

"Hey, Ren?" I hurried to his side, Jason following right behind me.

"Yes, Madison?"

"Is there anything else?"

"What do you mean?"

"Is there anything else you need to tell me?" I clarified.

Ren shook his head.

"If you are lying to me, I will break your nose," I said with a withering stare.

Ren looked at me and then back at Jason.

"She will," Jason confirmed.

Ren smiled and shook his head again. "There is nothing else."

We kept walking as the bluish green glow grew brighter and the sound of flowing water grew louder. Just as we reached the opening, the cavern narrowed, forcing us to walk single file. Ren ducked into the opening first, and I followed. The cavern opened into a fairly large circular area. There was a small waterfall on the far side of the grotto, a steady stream pouring down from a crevice in the cave wall into a swirling pool below. Off to the right, there was another opening a bit larger than the one we had just passed through.

Ren walked around to four torches that hung on the wall, lit three that had burned out, and replaced the fourth with his own. He tossed the unlit torch on the ground.

"Wow..." Jason's voice bounced off the walls of the cavern over the soft sound of rushing water. He stepped out from behind me and stared at the ceiling, the source of the green glow.

My mouth fell open as I lifted my own eyes to the ceiling of the cave. Above us, the cavern was dotted with thousands of tiny bluish green specks glowing like stars in the night sky. They pulsated with light, growing brighter and dimmer in no particular pattern. It was without a doubt the most beautiful place I had ever been.

"Whoa."

So many little lights, some brighter than others, beamed above us. They were the source of the glow that we had seen in the cavern tunnel.

"Can I drink this?" Jason asked Ren, who had pulled the canteens out of his satchel. Ren nodded.

Jason slid his hands into the water of the pool at the center of the grotto, and started drinking.

"This is amazing!" Jason exclaimed. "Maddy, come over here!"

I stood hesitantly, looking at the water glowing beneath the gorgeous twinkling turquoise lights and at the slick, rocky path that I would have to walk to get to the pool. Jason had made his way over there with ease, but then again, he wouldn't have any trouble if he fell into the swirling pool of water—not like me. I could feel the anxiety bubbling within me as I cracked each knuckle on each hand in quick succession.

"I'm good," I replied, playing it cool.

Ren stood next to me as I returned to gazing at the walls and ceiling of the grotto. Reflections from the water danced on the walls in glowing ripples of light.

"I like your lightning bolts," he remarked quietly.

"Oh, um, thanks," I replied, and touched one small silver earring. "They were a gift…from Lacy."

Lacy. She must have had good intentions. She must have, or she wouldn't have sent that Cypher Fairy. I knew her. But my optimistic attitude didn't stop my stomach from hurting when I thought about her possible betrayal. It felt like I had been punched in the gut.

"What is that up there?" I pointed to the ceiling of the cave.

"Those are infant fae. They stay within the caves until they mature, and then they join their clan in the forests. They are in just about every cave near the Jade Village," Ren answered.

"Baby fairies?" I smiled widely and looked up. "That is the cutest thing I have ever heard."

"Are you going in?" Ren motioned to the water. He looked very *Rebel Without a Cause*, minus the red jacket and cancer stick.

"No, I'm good. You go ahead." I shook my head and folded my arms over my abdomen, trying to gauge Ren's intentions.

Why is he being so nice all of a sudden?

Ren smirked. "Are you sure? I do not mind saving you again."

"Ha. Ha. Ha," I replied sarcastically.

Ren stepped closer to me and chuckled. "I liked that you punched that boy. That was amusing."

"You liked that, huh?" I smirked, thinking of how good it felt to punch Shawn Milton.

"He deserved it. He was a pig."

"Oh, I remember." I rocked back on my heels. "Kicked off my birthday with a splash, that's for sure!"

"It is your birthday?" Ren asked curiously.

"Yeah, or it was. I don't even know what day it is now. But yes, a very eventful day, to say the least."

"Why were you even near the water? It is a known fact that Witches do not float."

"She's a Witch!" Jason yelled in his best Monty Python villager voice, and splashed some water at me. By now, he was sitting on the edge of the pool with his feet dangling in the water.

"Knock it off!" I shot back.

My smile fell as I watched Jason splash his legs around. My whole life was explainable. All of it. The thing I was great at and the thing that scared me to death—there were legit reasons for both. Valid reasons that would have made them easier to accept. I was fast because I was a Strongblood, and I couldn't swim because I was a Witch.

Everything I had always wondered about myself now had a simple answer, but it came at a cost greater than I could have fathomed. And I could never go back.

"Are you okay?" Ren asked.

I narrowed my eyes at him. "Yeah. It's just—I don't understand. Why would she tell the king that we're going there?" I rubbed my temples, then quickly pulled my hands back and huffed loudly.

"What is it?" Ren uncrossed his arms, looking alert.

"Nothing, I just—my Aunt Ruth does that all the time." I smiled. "Whenever she gets stressed, she rubs her temples like that."

"Um…I will be right back, guys. I have to use the little boys' room." Jason climbed out of the pool.

"Take a torch," Ren said, hurrying over to Jason and pulling a torch from a slanted holder on the wall. "And don't go too far."

"Do you want me to go with you?" I asked Jason. He promptly wrinkled his nose and shook his head.

"Well, be careful."

"You will miss me, but know that I shall return." Jason bowed like he was closing out a show or something.

I laughed as he trotted out of the grotto the way we came in, leaving just Ren and me in the magical little cove. I looked up at the fae.

"Can they hear us?" I asked.

"I am not sure. Legend says that the fae can hear for miles and that they can speak to each other without words, just in the way they fly." Ren followed my gaze up to the curves of the rock, which was covered with little lights. The cluster of fae right above us seemed to glow a little brighter as he looked up.

"Looks like they like you."

"I keep the torches lit to keep the goblins out. The fae have always been good to me, and I offer my protection," Ren replied.

"Ah, the Cypher Fairy from before. That's why it gave you the message. They all love you."

Ren nodded.

"Will Jason be okay out there?" I looked toward the passage out of the grotto.

"I did not see any threat on our way here, so he should be fine," Ren said, then paused. "You really care for him. Are the two of you…" Ren waved his hand in a circle as if waiting for me to finish his thought.

"Are we together?" I raised my eyebrows and said carefully, "Jason and I have a love that no other could match."

"I see." Ren looked to the ground quickly and ran his hand through his hair.

"Why do you care, Ren?" I shot back, looking at him as he fidgeted.

"I do not. I do not care. I was merely making conversation," Ren replied quickly, still looking down.

"Really?" I snorted.

"There is nothing that I could possibly consider a more irrelevant subject, honestly," Ren continued. "I just want to make sure that when it comes time to engage in battle, you have your mind in the right place and y—"

"Ren. Chill."

Ren stopped picking at the corner of his thumbnail and looked at me from the side of his eye before reluctantly turning back to me.

"Jason and I are not together. And I can assure you that we never will be. He is like my brother. He is the most important person in the universe to me," I explained.

Ren clarified. "He is your family."

"Well, no. He is *like* my brother, but I don't have any real blood relatives other than Lacy and Ruth—or at least, that's how it used to be." I stared at my feet.

We were silent for a moment. It felt like I was suddenly trapped on the world's longest elevator ride. I sucked at small talk, and Ren seemed to be no better. I looked at the cavern opening, willing Jason to return and save me from this awkward silence.

I can't stand here in silence anymore.

Staring at the slick walk around the edge of the water, I decided to brave it. Taking the tiniest steps possible, I walked over to the pooling water in the center of the grotto and sat on one of the flatter rock forms that lined the twinkling water. I pulled my shoes and socks off before sliding my feet in.

"Careful!" Ren said, and walked over to join me by the water. "It can b—ahh!" he bellowed as he slipped. He fell on his back and landed with a clunk as his dagger fell out of his boot and hit the ground. I reached for him, but it was too late. I pressed my lips together and slapped my hand over my mouth to keep from laughing.

Ren sat up and put his arms on his knees, but his tense face suddenly gave way to a slow smile as he shook his head. "So it goes, right?"

I smiled back at him.

"So it goes," I replied softly.

I let my eyes linger on him after he looked away. He fixed the sheath that held his dagger on his calf, then stood. Ever so cautiously, he walked over to where I was sitting and held out a canteen. I accepted it and took a quick drink.

"Why are you only nice when we are alone?" I prodded.

"Oh, I—I did not mean to be."

I raised my eyebrows.

"I meant that I do not mean to be harsh with you." Ren sat on the rock next to mine, almost as if he were intentionally distancing himself from me. "I am out of practice when it comes to real people, I suppose. I prefer to read about people, not to actually interact with them."

"I'm with you there," I laughed. "I tend to get lost in my shows."

Ren looked confused for a moment.

"TV shows. Television and movies." I raised my eyebrows waiting for him to catch on, which he didn't. "Oh my god. When this is all over, we are watching like thirty straight hours of television!" I exclaimed as all the titles of my favorites scrolled in my head. "But what to start with? Hmm. I am going to need to really ponder on that." I tapped my chin.

"When this is over, you would still want to be around me?" Ren asked innocently.

"I guess." I gave him a quick glance. "It might not be terrible. Would you want to be around me? Me and Jason?"

"Sure," Ren replied

"Cool." I moved my legs back and forth in the water and watched the changing reflections on the walls of the grotto.

"Madison, I am truly sorry for the way I told you about your father and about all of this with Lacy." Ren's voice was lower now as he turned the conversation to a more serious place. "I know how vital she is to you. I could see it the moment I found you. I do not have anyone who I can depend on, but if I did, I would be upset, too."

"It's okay." I screwed the cap back on the canteen. "I, um…I thought something was wrong back at my house with Lacy. I guess I just didn't really want to think about it. But I know her. This is just a misunderstanding. She would never do anything like that on purpose."

Ren looked at me sympathetically. He ran his hand through his hair and then rubbed his jaw with his palm. "Yes, you are right; it may just be a misunderstanding. Maybe she is ju—"

"No, it's okay. You don't have to defend her actions." I forced a smile back at him. "I just don't really want to think about that right now. But thanks for trying."

Ren shot me a quick half smile.

I let my gaze go back to the ceiling, to the tiny little lights. "I can't believe this is real. It's extraordinary in here."

"I come here to relax often. It is said that the fae can have a calming effect on a person." Ren sighed.

"Now that you mention it, I do feel really calm. If you knew me a little better, that would surprise you. I am not generally very patient." I closed my eyes for a moment.

"Here." Ren stood and held his hand out to me. "Give me your hand."

"I can't say that I want to rely on you for balance," I replied, only half joking.

"Just come here." Ren laughed quietly. I put my hand in his. His palms were rougher than I thought they would be. I stood and followed him away from the water.

"Okay, stand here," he said as he stopped me and moved to stand behind me. He put his hand on my shoulder and lifted my arm with his other hand.

"What are y—"

"Shh, be still," he whispered.

Ren's hand cradled my wrist so that my arm was out to the side and above my head.

"Do not move."

Without moving my head, I looked up as the fae began to stir. Little lights slowly started to flutter and dance away from the ceiling down toward Ren and me. The tiny little lights spun and swayed back and forth above me. I angled my face up to watch.

A few lights dashed in a loop around us as we stood still. I let out a small laugh, in awe of what I was seeing.

"This is amazing," I whispered.

"Shh," Ren insisted. I could hear the delight in his voice.

Then two of the fae descended a little farther. I made my palm flat and they landed on my open hand. They felt warm, and I could only feel the slightest tickle as the fae moved around on my skin.

"*The Adventures of Huckleberry Finn*," Ren said softly in my ear.

"Huh?"

"You asked me what my favorite book was," he replied. "*Huckleberry Finn.*"

I smiled. "That's a good book."

"Happy birthday, Madison."

I smiled but did not respond. We were quiet again as we watched the fairies.

"Ren?"

"Hmm?"

Two more lights floated down and landed on my hand.

"Before, you said you didn't have anyone to depend on."

"I did."

"You can depend on me...if you want to," I whispered, to avoid disrupting the fae.

For that moment in the cave, I didn't think about Lacy, Ruth, or my father and his decree. We didn't speak. In that moment, it was just Ren and me in the most beautiful place in the world.

And I didn't want it to end.

CHAPTER 16

The fae fluttered back up to the ceiling one by one, as if done with their visit. I slowly turned to face Ren. He half smiled at me

I grinned back at him. "Th—"

"Run!" A voice boomed into the grotto. "Run!"

I jumped, startled. Ren pushed me behind him and grabbed his dagger. I echoed his defensive reaction, pulling out my sword.

"Jason!" I screamed when I saw him. He stumbled in from the grotto's entrance, breathlessly pointing behind him as he sank to the ground near the pile of our belongings. His torch was gone.

"What happened?" I yelled, running to him. "Are you okay?"

"What happened, Jason?" Ren asked.

Jason lifted a shaky hand, pointing to the cave opening through which we had entered the grotto. "Two of them…I kicked the crap out of the one, but there are more and they're coming."

"Who is? Who is coming?" I pressed as I held Jason's arm.

"Goblins. They call them Soul Suckers," Ren said with a half smile.

"Huh? That sounds like a not-good thing, like a not-smiling thing. Why are you smiling? Why is he smiling?" I asked, looking from Ren to Jason.

As I did, three pairs of glowing red eyes appeared in the cave entrance.

"Glowing red eyes never mean anything good. Like, ever," I said flatly.

"Ruthana trained you to fight, right?" Ren asked, not taking his eyes off the oncoming creatures.

"Yeah, people. Not goblins."

"Okay, well, this is Everly fight training," Ren said, twirling his daggers in his hands. "Ready, Madison?"

"Do I really have a choice?" I said as two of the little creatures jumped onto Ren, biting and snarling at him as he swung his daggers at them.

"Hey!" I barked as a goblin jumped down from the ceiling onto me, knocking my sword to the floor of the grotto. "Crap."

The goblin was on me, scratching and clawing like a rabid little animal. It smelled like moldy food and was no taller than a small child, but its face was demonic and jarring. Its hair was tan and coarse, covered in green moss.

"Get off of me, you little psycho!" I muttered as we struggled.

It spit and hissed as I wrestled it. The goblin clawed my arm from my shoulder to my elbow, sending shooting pain up my arm as the four lines turned red with blood. I screamed and fell back as the little creature turned toward Jason.

"Madison!" I heard Ren yell, but there was no time to answer. The goblin was heading toward Jason.

I dove onto the goblin, pinning it to the ground. It flipped to face me and I wrapped my hands around its neck and squeezed with all my strength. My skin prickled as the heat rose inside my body.

It was happening again.

I stared into its cold, red eyes as its fingernails clawed at my hands and arms and it thrashed its legs wildly. I clenched my teeth and its eyes began to bulge as it slowly stopped its struggle.

"What am I doing?" I let go, stumbling backward. The little creature slumped over on the ground, its chest heaving. I watched as its bewildered eyes darted around the cave. It backed out of the grotto and disappeared into the dark tunnel. It looked as scared as I felt.

Jason fired an arrow at it as it escaped.

"Help Ren!" Jason pointed.

I turned to see Ren fighting off the two goblins on the other side of the grotto. He moved with great agility, but the goblins were quick and climbed all over him, thrashing and biting. He grabbed one and whipped it at the wall of the cave, where it landed with a sickening crack. The one remaining goblin shrieked loudly, piercing the silence of the cave and echoing through the cavern tunnel.

Jason moved the crossbow toward it, aimed, fired, and missed as the creature rolled to the side. Ren slipped and fell onto his back.

"Ren!" I yelled, grabbing a torch from the wall. The goblin climbed onto Ren, tearing at the skin on his chest as Ren fell to the ground. I ran to them and waved the torch at the goblin, taking care not to light Ren on fire. The goblin retreated from the grotto.

"Are you okay?" I asked Ren.

Ren laid on his back, panting. "You remembered what I said about fire." Ren's shirt was torn; his chest was scratched deeply and bleeding through the holes in the black shirt.

"I did." I nodded. "Your chest. That looks bad."

Ren shook his head. "It looks worse than it feels, really."

Or you're in shock. "That's good." I nodded, humoring him. "Jay? How about you? Are you okay?"

"Oh, yeah, yeah…this is totally normal." Jason lowered the crossbow to his side. "This is totally not insane. Totally normal."

I nodded slightly, studying his face. Jason looked flustered, his eyes wide, and he wasn't really blinking. As I stood slowly, Ren got up and retrieved my sword.

"Thanks." I nodded as he handed it to me, but I didn't take my eyes off Jason, who was pacing on the other side of the grotto now.

The light of my sword's grip glowed brightly. I felt the tingle creep down my arm. Ren and I stood there in silence, and then I gasped as I watched the slices on my arm begin to mend. I had a sudden feeling of wooziness as the blood disappeared. I reached for Ren's arm in an effort to steady myself. As I did, the sword's light burst out even brighter, sending a beam of blue down through my arm as if it ran in my veins. Ren's cuts began to heal before our eyes as well.

Ren lifted his hands to his face, feeling for the wounds, and then to the bite marks and scratches on his chest. Nothing. I released his arm, and he looked astonished.

"Amazing!" he exclaimed.

"Whoa, did you know I could do that?" I asked, shocked by what had just happened.

"No." He looked at his now-healed arms and then back to me. "My hand, too." Ren pulled the strip of my black shirt from his hand. He opened his palm, and there was nothing there.

"Wow," I said.

"Awesome!" Jason yelled, getting both Ren's and my attention. "Great, great, great. Can we keep moving? Those things were creepy, and I don't really want to see more, like, ever." He attempted to attach his reloaded crossbow to the makeshift belt, but his hands were trembling badly now.

"Jay, are you all right?" I asked, walking over to him as he fidgeted with the rope.

"Oh, yeah, yeah, yeah. I'm fine…I just can't get this knot out," he replied. "This rope needs to be tighter."

I reached over and untied it with ease. Jason rubbed his face with his hands. His eyes were bloodshot, and he looked exhausted

"Jay, it's okay to be ruffled. This has been a crazy day," I assured him as I slipped the rope around his waist, tying it into a knot. He grabbed my shoulders.

"Maddy!" He was much louder now, his fingers digging into my shoulder blades. "This is *the* crazy day. The craziest of them all. I don't know, Maddy, but you aren't frazzled by all this? You aren't even freaking out! You just choked out a little goblin thing." Jason's voice boomed through the grotto as he pointed at Ren.

"And him! This dude—we know nothing about him but, hey, let's follow him around like two little puppy dogs! Yeah! That is a *great* idea." Jason's voice was shrill now.

I looked at Ren and back to Jason.

"Great frickin' plan!" Jason yelped, backing away from me. "Don't get me wrong, Ren. I'm sure you're lovely, and under different circumstances I may have even tolerated you, but I would have been fan-frickin'-tastic had I never met you!"

"Jay, calm down." I stepped toward him.

"I miss my Caleb. My very hot and very normal boyfriend, who I left behind to get chased down by trolls and insane little goblins!"

His eyes were even wider as he walked back and forth, mumbling incoherently. I had never seen him like this.

"*No!* No, no, no. This is just all in my head. This isn't happening. I'm going to wake up in my nice warm bed, and this will all have been just a dream. And I'm going to be back in Greenrock with my boyfriend and my non-goblin-containing life. This isn't real. Nope, nope, nope, not real." Jason stopped walking and turned to face me.

"Jay, calm down, I just—"

"No, I am not going to calm down! This is…this is crazy, and I'm the only one who seems to notice! This can't be your life. It can't be. It's too dangerous. This can't be your real life, Maddy." He waved the crossbow wildly in his hand.

"Jason, I have never seen you like this. You are freaking out." I tried to sound calm—actually, I tried to sound like him in the many calming speeches he had given me over the years.

"I *am* freaking out! Join me, won't you?"

Ren moved past me and walked toward Jason. "Jason, let us continue to Ara's. There we can rest and replenish." He raised his hand and set it on Jason's shoulder.

"You…this is all your fault! We were fine before you came along. Mister grand Magic-saving schemer guy! Don't think I don't see it. I see how you look at her! I see it. You, you…home wrecker!" Jason shrieked.

Jason swung his arm to knock Ren's hand away, and then I heard a pop and a whistling sound. I stumbled back as something smacked me in the face. My right eye went dark, and all I could feel was a warm tingling sensation there.

"That's strange…" I mumbled as Jason and Ren looked back at me, horrified.

I lifted my hand to my eye and froze when I realized that it wasn't my eye I was touching. It was the feathery end of a crossbow bolt. I gasped and felt myself fall back.

Ren caught me and held me tight before I fell to the ground. "I have you, Madison. I have you."

And then all I saw was the dancing little lights of the fae on the ceiling before it faded to black.

CHAPTER 17

Groggily, I opened my eyes, my right eye still dark. I could hear what sounded like waves crashing just on the other side of a wall. I lifted my head up.

I heard a mumbling sound to my left, which startled me. It was Jason. He was lying on a cot a few feet away. My own cot was just a couple inches from the ground, I realized as I slid my trembling hand down to touch the floor.

Is that sand?

Jason mumbled as if he was talking in his sleep. He now wore a sleeveless, cream-colored linen shirt and light gray linen pants with boots that went up to his knees. His calm, sleeping face was much different than the last time I saw him.

"Jay?" I whispered. He didn't answer.

I used all my strength to push myself up onto my elbows. I pulled my arms back to prop myself up when my hand grazed something soft. It was Ren's hair. He lay on the ground next to me, his head on a mat near my stomach.

A dream. This must be a dream, I thought as I laid my head back down. Maybe all the craziness that had happened was just a dream and this was the part right before I woke up. I closed my eyes—eye, I corrected myself. My eye. I felt the dull, throbbing pain. This was not a dream.

I slowly raised my free hand to my right eye. I ran my fingers over something ridged and smooth covering my eye and a string that ran down to my ear.

An eye patch. I had an eye patch, but what was it made of? It felt cool and polished. I pulled my hand away. It felt like my eye was open, but I didn't have the courage to lift the patch to feel my eye beneath it. But I had the sword, right? The sword would have healed me. This must just be a precaution.

Blinking some more, I turned my head to look around. It looked like we were in a tent of some sort, I deduced as the walls billowed slightly in the breeze. The walls went straight up to the ceiling in the circular room, but the middle of the ceiling was raised into a point. It reminded me of one of those old military tents. A little table on the other side of Jason held various bottles and jars. Next to that, a cloth door let in a beam of sunlight every few seconds as it moved with the wind.

Outside the little room, I could hear birds cawing. I remained still as a tear rolled down the side of my face. I clamped my hand over my mouth to hold back my sob.

I reached down to grab my shirt to wipe my face. The fabric was not the soft jersey of my black T-shirt, but rougher. I ran my hands over my stomach and down my leg. My shorts were gone and replaced with pants made of the same fabric.

Why wasn't I wearing my own clothes?

"Madison?" I heard a low, gruff whisper. Ren sat up, his hair wild, his eyes bloodshot and wide. Quickly, I wiped my cheeks with the back of my hand.

"Madison? How do you—are you..." His voice was rough and scratchy.

"I have been better." I looked around. "Where are we?"

"We are..." Ren dropped his head and rubbed his eyes with his hand. "Sorry, I..." He lifted his head, sat back on his legs, and cleared his throat. His expression changed to serious and still, but it seemed forced.

"I apologize, Madison. I never should have given Jason a weapon. He was not trained." He looked down, avoiding my face.

I reached my hand out toward him. Ren took my hand in his and cradled it carefully.

"Are you okay?" he asked, helping me brace myself.

"No, I..." I swallowed loudly. My mouth felt dry and sort of sticky. I lowered my gaze away from his. "Just—can you help me up?"

Ren put his arms around my waist, pulling me closer to him with gentle ease. He held me very carefully and lifted me up slowly. I felt like a baby deer. My muscles were sore, almost like I had just worked out.

"Careful," Ren whispered as I attempted to balance myself.

"I'm okay," I reassured him, but I winced as I sank into him, losing my balance completely. Ren lowered me back down to the cot.

"How do you feel?" he asked sweetly.

"Your loophole is still alive." I gave him a thumbs-up and smiled. He looked away, seemingly annoyed.

There's the Ren I know.

I nervously chewed on the side of my thumb. "How is Jason?" I asked, turning my head to check on him. He hadn't moved.

"He was quite distraught when we arrived, but Ara counseled him and he finally agreed to eat and rest. We are in the Jade Village now."

"Wait, how did we get here?"

"You passed out when the bolt hit you. I carried you the rest of the way. It was not far to get here." Ren was looking at the patch on my eye now.

"How bad was it? My eye?" I asked quietly, looking away from his face, afraid to hear the answer.

"Luckily, it ricocheted off the cave wall, but it still went straight through your eye. Ara said it didn't go far enough in to kill you. We were able to heal you with the sword, and we stopped the bleeding at least, but your eye..." He paused. "Your eye has a hole."

"My sword didn't heal me?"

"We could not get the arrow out without some tearing. Ara did what she could to help, but there is a large hole in your eye. Ara says she thinks the hole is getting smaller, so that is good news. She fashioned the cover for your eye to protect it."

"Well, good. That is good, right? I guess being a Witch doesn't solve everything, then." I paused. "It's good that I learn about my powers. It's good."

I pressed my lips together, trying to stop thinking about it.

"We need to get back out there. We need to get to the temple. We have to help those people and get Ruth." I tried to stand again. My legs felt weak and unstable, and I fell back to the mat. Ren reached out to catch me as I did.

"No, Madison..."

"I have one eye, and I am not dead," I huffed. "God, what is wrong with my legs? Did I fall hard or something?"

"You have been asleep for nearly two days. You need to build your strength, eat—"

"Two?!" I yelled, before remembering Jason was asleep next to me. I lowered my voice. "Two days? So there are only two days until the full moon now?"

Ren nodded.

"Did you talk to Ara about Ruth? Did anyone see her? Have there been any more Cypher Fae?" The words flew quickly from my mouth, and I started to feel a twist in my stomach.

"A fairy came to Ara to tell her that the party accompanying Ruth had arrived at the temple. Beyond that, we do not know."

I braced myself on Ren and stood, ignoring my legs' weakness as I did.

"We need some supplies, and we can keep going. I can do it, I know I can," I insisted.

Ren didn't respond. He just looked concerned, like he was thinking very heavily about it before replying.

"Ren?"

He still didn't answer, pensively staring almost through me.

"Ren! Let's go!" I urged him impatiently. "I am not giving up! We are so close!"

"Madison—"

"Fine, you stay here and think. I'm goin' to the temple." I tried to steady myself on my wobbling feet.

"You are impossible, you know that?"

"That's what they tell me," I replied.

"You have been unconscious for two days, Madison. Just hold on a minute." He reached out to help me as I shakily stood there. "You cannot just jump out of bed—"

"I have to, Ren. You said it yourself. If we didn't get Ruth before she got to the temple, the king might kill her. It's my real father up there killing people. I need to stop this. I have to save my aunt. You have no idea how it feels, knowing there is nothing I can do to help her right now. We need to get there." I grunted as I took a step.

"Trust me, I understand," he said with a twinge of anger.

"You are awake!" a cheerful voice called from the doorway behind me.

"Madison, this is Ara," Ren stated.

I whipped my head around to face her. In the light of the doorway, she was a picturesque silhouette.

"Sit and be still! Your legs need rest, little acorn," Ara ordered as she came into the room. "Ren, go on and get this sweet girl some food. She must be starved."

She was right. I was starving. I felt like I hadn't eaten in a week.

I watched Ara as she moved within the small room. She couldn't have been much older than me. Her honey-yellow hair was long and wavy and nearly white around her face, like it had been bleached by the sun. She wore it tied in a ponytail just under her right ear, and tiny sea shells were tied into the ponytail at different lengths. Her dress was seafoam green and looked like one super-long scarf draped and tied around her, crossing like an X over her chest, wrapping around her waist, and tying at her hip. She crossed over to sit at the foot of my cot.

"Greetings, Princess. I am Ara, Empress of the Fae." She bowed her head, and the shells in her hair began to clink. Now that she was closer, I could see her more clearly. She had incredibly long eyelashes that curled up perfectly. Her eyes were an amazing shade of violet, and they popped against her dark brown skin. She had a few freckles on the bridge of her nose and on her cheeks.

"Hello, Empress." I said and bowed my head, not really sure what to do.

"I am only royal to the Fae. No need for all of that. Just call me Ara."

I nodded. "Got it. It's nice to meet you, Ara. I'd love to chat more but we really need to get to the temple, but I thank you for your hospitality," I said quickly, staring at her and then looking back at Ren.

"Certainly." She beamed at me. Her voice was smooth and calm.

"Ara, can you check her eye again? Maybe if she held the sword again, it would—"

Ara raised a hand to signal Ren to stop speaking. "Ren, please go and get her something to eat."

"Coffee? Do you have coffee here?" I asked.

"What is that?" Ren responded.

I turned my head to the ceiling and squeezed my eyes shut. "Oh my god, I hate this place." I frowned as I plopped back down on the cot.

Ara smiled brightly, placing her delicate hand on my forearm. She shook her head, making the shells clink a bit. "Worry not, little acorn. We will make your body well enough to finish your journey."

She turned back to Ren, her expression a bit sterner now. "Off you go now, Ren!" Ara moved closer to me, her eyes still on Ren. He seemed hesitant, looking back to me as ran his hands through his hair.

"Are you all right?" Ren asked me with a furrowed brow.

"Ren, I will not leave her side," Ara assured him.

Ren stared at me a few moments longer, then nodded and exited the room, limping as he went. He turned back to me once more before passing through the glaringly bright doorway.

"Wait! Ren!" I called loudly.

He charged back through the door with wide eyes. "What? What is it?"

"Food. Get me as much as you would get for yourself, okay? Don't skimp," I said. He nodded and smiled as he turned back to the opening of the little tentlike cottage.

"Wait, Ren!" I called. He poked his head back in.

"I don't know if you're really getting me here. I want you to get the portion you would normally eat, okay? No, double that. Okay?" I requested.

Ren grinned and left. I heard him yell "Okay!" from outside the room.

"He has not done a thing since he brought you here, aside from worry," Ara said. "He had been in that spot nearly all day."

"Really?" My mouth fell to a frown as I pictured Ren at my bedside. "He didn't try to go save Ruth from the road without me?"

"He did," Ara said, laying her hands on her lap. "But I am afraid he failed."

"Oh." I sighed. "So she is there? My aunt is at the Temple of the Ember Isle?"

Ara nodded. "Truly. But know that Ren did all he could to save her. He was beside himself with guilt when they got away with her. He would not even speak after that. He just sat with you, silently, not even looking up when I entered the tent." Ara twirled a lock of her long wavy hair around her fingers.

"Wow...I..." I paused. "Well, I am the key to this whole plan—his plan to save the Magics. Or my blood is, I guess."

"Yes, that too," she said, smiling. "Let me open this shade. You need sunshine."

Ara went to the wall next to the little doorway and rolled up a window-sized flap that hung in the cottage tent. Sunlight flooded the entire tent as she tied up the fabric with perfectly knotted bows. I squinted as my eye adjusted to the brightness. Ara sat on the edge of my cot again.

"Your mind is heavy. I have been told that I am excellent to speak with, if you would like to pass the time with me. I feel as if I know you. Jason has spoken of nothing else but you. Water?" Ara held out a cup.

"Um, sure." I paused, letting it all sink in. It was hard to keep up with everything she was saying. "So, um, did you say you are the Empress of the Fae?"

"I did." Ara nodded.

"Are you a fairy?" I cringed, feeling stupid for asking.

"The world of the fae is quite complex. I am their empress simply because the former empress was killed and I took her place, but I am not one of them," Ara explained.

"Gotcha. I have another question." I took a long drink of water from the wooden cup, then spoke softly and with caution. "Ren intercepted a Cypher Fairy that my cousin Lacy was sending. She was sending it to the Temple of the Ember Isle that we were on our way to."

"Ren told me so, yes." Ara nodded.

"Is it possible that the fairy got the message wrong?"

"I wish I had an answer that would ease your troubled mind."

I forced a smile. "Right, right. Of course." I swallowed hard.

Just then, a little ball of light entered and landed on Ara's shoulder.

"Is that a—"

Ara raised her finger to her mouth to quiet me. She kept her eyes on me and calmly nodded as if listening to a story.

I leaned in but heard nothing. If the fairy was making noise, it was so low that it was impossible to decipher.

The little light rose up and zipped out of the tent.

"My fairy just informed me of some news from the Ember Isle. Six more Magics were delivered to the temple today," Ara said.

I gasped, dropping my water cup. "Six? We need to get there now! How long until we can reach the temple?"

Ara pursed her rose-colored lips. "You could get there in a day's walk."

She waved her hand, and another little light zipped out of the tent. "I have sent for Ren. I will go with you to the temple."

"Is—is that safe? Aren't you a Magic, too?" I asked.

"I am. But I am the Empress of the Fae. If the king intends to harm me, he knows right where to find me. The fae are small, but they are mighty. Not even the king would take them on," Ara replied elegantly. She seemed so calm, so collected, given what she had just said. Somehow, it made me feel calmer, too.

"Ren said that the king would kill them during the full moon."

"That's in two days," Ara confirmed.

I shivered as I remembered what Ren had said about how they killed Witches. "Why the full moon?"

Ara's smile fell. "You mean, why does King Dax only kill the Magics on the full moon?"

I nodded.

"It's what keeps the spell on the courtyard so strong," Ara said, not meeting my eyes. "The sacrifice of the Magics keeps the courtyard spell powerful. And everyone knows the king will do anything for power."

I looked away. "Oh."

It got quiet for a moment. I felt a twinge of guilt. Like my father's actions were somehow linked to me, even though I had never met him.

Change the subject.

"Uh, I like your shells"—I pointed at her hair—"in your ponytail."

Ara shook her head, and the shells jingled in her ponytail as they knocked together. "I like to hear the sea singing when I move," she said, and as she moved, I caught a glimpse of something on her neck, just under her ponytail. "And this way, the sea is always with me."

"What is that, there on your neck?" I gestured. "If you don't mind my asking."

Ara lifted her ponytail. "It's a gill. My father was a Merman. See?" Ara lifted the side of her dress to show green and purple shimmering scales covering all of her thigh.

"Very cool." I stared in awe. "Mermaids? That's crazy."

Ara stared at me with a smile, but did not speak.

I shifted and moved the strings on my seashell eye patch. "Um, so did you make this?" I asked.

"Oh, yes. Truly. It is from my personal shell collection. It was always a favorite of mine, so I thought it'd be perfect for a face as lovely as yours." She twisted her hair again in her long, slender fingers. She had rings on each finger. Some were small silver bands that looked more like springs coiling from the knuckle to the nail bed.

It was silent as I leaned over and looked toward the doorway, anxious for Ren to return. The ocean was breathtaking. There was a cliff and what looked like more forest farther down.

"It is pretty here," I murmured, unsure of what to say. I bit my lips together. "This place just feels so unreal."

She nodded slowly with a warm smile. "You have seen it, and you still do not believe this is real? As real as you and I?" she asked.

"I believe I'm here, sure. But it's like I'm dreaming. I must be. It's all a little hard to take in." I avoided her stare.

"It is not this place that troubles you. No, it is that you have a home in this land. That you are the Scion of Everly gives you doubts?" She moved closer to me. Her violet eyes seemed to gleam in the light.

"The Scion?" I raised my eyebrows at the word.

"The heir to Everly," Ara proclaimed. "My fae and I remain loyal to your coven, as we have for decades."

"My coven?"

Ara nodded, proudly. "Yes, the Rosewood Coven. They have led the Magics' side of this battle, and we believe the coven will save Everly. And then there is you. The girl who is the rightful inheritor of the Rosewood Coven and the heir to the Ember Isle. Strongblood and Witch. The Scion. Not ever has there been a person with two different Everly lineages. You are every bit as special as I imagined."

"So it's true that I am only supposed to be one or the other?" I asked quietly, looking away, toward the door.

I looked over to Jason, who hadn't moved.

"You are the first of your kind, yes," Ara stated. "As far back as our history goes, there has never been a child born of a Witch and a Strongblood who has retained traits of both bloodlines. Strongbloods and Witches have had children before, but over time, the traits of one will trump the other."

"What do you mean?" I asked as the waves crashed even louder outside the cottage.

"A child may be born with Witch blood and Strongblood, but as they grow, one always gives way to the other. Either the Witch powers fade completely and the child is a Strongblood or vice versa."

I nodded. "Okay, then how am I both?"

"Ren said that your magic is your sword. Your dueling bloodlines were never given a chance to see which would dominate. You grew up as a Strongblood, it seems. Now that you are grown and your magic is seeping back into you through your sword, you have traits of both the Strongblood line and the Witch line."

"But I sank in the pool. Wouldn't that make me a Witch?"

Ara paused to think. "That is curious. See? You are the first, so I am not sure of the rules. When we sort out this mess with your father, I would love to bring you to a Reader."

I sniffed. "My father. Still strange to hear."

Ara nodded. "It would be stranger if it wasn't."

"I know I should hate him. I should hate him for what everyone has told me he has done. He is evil. He has to be. He is a murderer. Right?" I begged, more desperately than I had intended to.

"It is fine to want to know. It is fine to want to know him, to be curious about where you come from. Do not feel guilt for that desire," Ara reassured me.

"I wish I was in Greenrock. I wish this wasn't real," I said, barely audibly. "I just want to be home."

"No matter how soon you return, it will not feel like the home you knew. The place will be the same, but you never will be." Ara smiled sympathetically.

"They say you can never go home again." I fiddled with the hem of my new linen shirt.

"Truly. You will never be the girl you were yesterday. Every day will change you. You long to be the person who you once were in that house. That's the home you miss, not the house itself. Home is always a memory, no matter how long you are away," Ara said.

I nodded.

"That is not all that troubles you," Ara said, shaking her head, making the shells click together like a tiny wind chime.

I shifted on the cot. "No, I suppose not. But it doesn't matter now, does it?"

Ara didn't respond. Instead, she lowered her head as if waiting for me to continue.

"It's just—it is so much to take in. Ruth was always super evasive, but I shared a room with Lacy. I lived in the same room as her, and I had no idea she was a Witch. How is that possible? You should have seen how she acted that night. She was like a completely different person. She wasn't my sweet, spunky little cousin. She was cold and determined. It was like she was someone else. I don't know. I have always been able to trust her. Should that change now? I don't know. I just..." I paused. "And my mother is lost here somewhere. And then, not only is my father alive, but he is hell-bent on wiping out a chunk of the beings in this world. No matter how many times I think it or say it, it still sounds made up." I shook my head.

"And here I was thinking you'd be shy," Ara said sweetly. "Jason said you weren't much of a talker."

I'm not.

"Sorry, you really are easy to talk to," I agreed with a smile. I wiped my face. "Well, even if my eye isn't working, the tears work just dandy!"

"It pains me to see you sad." Ara reached out to rest her hand on my foot. I moved my foot quickly and tucked my legs under me on the cot.

"I don't get it." I put my hand to my forehead, feeling angry at everything now. "Ren. Why is he helping me? Why is he being so nice to me?" My eyes fell, as did the volume of my words. I wasn't sure if I had meant to say that last part aloud.

"That I cannot answer for certain, but I have always known Ren to be kind. I do not know him well as a grown man. I knew his mother, and I knew him as a child." Ara paused. "He has lived alone for so long, poor boy."

"He lived alone? For how long?" I asked. "It sounded like he and his dad were super close."

"They were. But Ren has lived in the forest alone since he was fourteen," Ara replied.

"What?" I shook my head. "Fourteen? Why so young?"

"Has he told you what he is?" Ara looked down and smoothed the fabric of her dress.

"Yeah, a Porter."

Ara nodded and looked to the doorway of the cottage. "Yes, but did he tell you that Porters are seen as a danger here?"

I shook my head. "Ren's annoying, but he's not a danger."

Ara leaned closer to me, her face turning very stern. She looked back over her shoulder at the door again. "There is a reason Ren is not welcome in the villages. A reason he stays on his own." She paused. "Did he tell you about the storms?"

I nodded my head, listening intently. "The one that killed his dad."

"Yes, the energy storms." Ara checked the door again.

"What does that have to do with Ren?"

"Ren's father was the royal record keeper. He delivered the news to the Rosewood Coven that their lands were being seized by King Dax. In retaliation, the Rosewood Coven cursed Ren to be a Porter. Ren's mother fought the Witch who inflicted the curse, but she lost the battle."

I gasped. "She died?"

Ara nodded. "Yes, and that's when the storms started. They only happen when Ren is near, and we haven't been able to figure out why. After the first few, Ren's father moved him to the woods and had Ren cut ties with his life in the temple to protect him from the angry villagers. And to protect them from Ren."

"He was all alone?"

"He was all alone."

CHAPTER 18

"All of that happened to him because of my family. He should hate me," I said to Ara. "My mother's coven killed his mom and cursed him, all because of an order my father gave. He should hate me."

Ara leaned closer to me. "You are more than your mother and father's daughter, Madison."

"We need to get to that temple. I need to stop him. I have to. My father needs to be stopped. I won't let him hurt Aunt Ruth, too."

Poor Ren.

I thought about the storms and got a nervous twinge in my stomach. "Ara, what causes them?" I looked to doorway again. "The storms. I mean, are we safe with Ren?"

"I wish I had an answer. I really do," Ara replied softly.

Jason stirred next to me but still looked fast asleep, which didn't surprise me. That kid slept through everything when he slept on my floor. Once, I kicked him in the face accidentally and he didn't even budge.

I cleared my throat, shifting on the cot and getting increasingly annoyed at Jason's heavy sleeping. I pushed myself to standing. My feet felt hot, like the blood was going to cause them to burst. I felt faint but stayed on my feet, determined to walk out of this tent on my own. But first, I needed Jason. I wouldn't go anywhere without him. I walked around his cot to the window Ara had opened.

"Sit, dear, please. Ren will return in a moment and he—"

"No," I said calmly and loudly. "I am okay."

Ara smiled at me apologetically.

"Of course." She stood.

I placed both of my palms flat on the small table that sat under the open window. My head bobbed forward as I focused on keeping my knees from shaking. The sand felt cool beneath my feet.

"Ara, thank you for everything, but we need to get going. I won't let him ruin anyone else's life." My voice was louder now—shrill, even. I was overwhelmed by a determination to run out of the tent, but my limbs were not cooperating. I turned around.

"Jay!" I yelled.

He flailed awake. "Oh, hey, Maddy! You're awake!" Jason exclaimed, jumping up.

"Finally!" I said, trying to stay focused on standing without wobbling. Jason wrapped me in a hug and I let him, happy to see him calm.

"The path to the temple is not long," Ara said serenely as a dozen little flickering fae wafted into the tent and danced around above her head. She stood near the doorway and fiddled with the shells hanging from her side ponytail.

"Maddy, are you okay?" Jason asked, placing his hands on my face. "Oh, Maddy, I am so sorry. Your eye." He pulled me close for another hug. The fabric of his shirt was scratchy on my cheek.

"We are leaving," I informed him quietly, pushing him back. "I have to stop him. I have to."

Ara smiled and held out a pair of boots. "For you, Madison."

Smiling, I grabbed the black suede boots. They were floppy and tall and looked like the ones that Jason had on that went up to his knees.

"Thank you, Ara. You are very kind," Jason replied.

"Madison?" Ren burst into the room carrying two giant plates of food. He set the plates on the small table behind me and grabbed my arm to hold me up.

"Stop." I turned my head toward him.

"Are you okay?" Ren blurted.

"Maddy?" Jason said timidly as he held my other arm.

My knees buckled. Ren and Jason caught me and helped me stand. It was clear that I was not fully recovered.

"Ara, what happened? What did you do?" Ren whipped his head to Ara, sounding livid.

"She didn't do anything." I said. "We are leaving. I need to get to that temple."

"Madison, we are not leaving until you have rested." Ren turned his gaze back to me.

"*We* as in Jason and me. Not you, Ren. You have lost enough because of him."

"What?" Ren lowered his voice, looking only at my good eye as he spoke. "What did she tell you?"

"Nothing. I just don't want you to keep wasting your time with me and my problems."

Ren shot Ara an angry look.

"Jason, are you ready?" I asked, shifting my weight onto Ren.

As he walked away, I caught a glimpse of Jason's face. He looked upset. In this entire shuffle, I didn't even think to see if he was okay after everything that went down.

"Jay? I am fine. My eye will be fine. Get the bags so we can leave." I steadied myself enough to turn and grab a piece of bread that rested on top of the mound of food that Ren had piled on one plate.

"My sword—can you get my sword?" I asked Ren with a giant wad of bread in my mouth.

"Huh?" Ren looked at me like I was crazy.

"I got it." Jason replied softly. He walked to the other side of the tent and grabbed the bags and my sword. It was in a new scabbard, but the familiar handle still poked out at the top. Jason quickly walked over to me and put the sash over my head, avoiding my eyes.

"Thanks." I smiled, but he didn't look at me.

I ran my hand over the deep brown sash that crossed my new orange shirt, holding my new scabbard to my back. It was much more comfortable than the black cord from before.

"Jason?" I took another bite of bread. "I am okay, I promise."

He finally met my stare. His deep brown eyes were so sad.

Jason sighed. "I am so sorry."

"It was an accident, Jay." I smiled with a lump of bread in my cheek. "It will heal."

"Take the handle," Jason said softly, gesturing to my sword. I reached back and pulled the sword from the scabbard. I much preferred having my sword strapped to my back like this. A familiar tingle shot through my arm as the blue glow burst outward.

"Better?" Jason asked. I lifted my legs, bending them, rolling my ankles around. I nodded.

"Ara?" a voice called from outside the tent.

"Come in," Ara responded.

A young man entered. He was dressed in a sleeveless white shirt and dark pants with boots that laced up his calves, like the ones Ara had handed me. His tousled brown hair fell to his shoulders. He looked like the guys from that Trojan horse movie we watched in Mrs. Carter's English class.

"Five of them, on the western hill on the Temple Road. The Cloaked. They look like they have a prisoner," the young man said, motioning outside the tent.

"Thank you," Ara answered. "I will handle it. Ren, can you grab some rope for their capture?"

Ren nodded but looked flustered, switching his focus from me to Ara and then back to me. "Madison, we must go deal with the Cloaked out there. Can you stay here? I need to speak with you alone, please." Ren ran his hand through his hair.

"No, we're leaving. Thank you for everything, Ren. Really," I said, not looking at him.

"The Cloaked are on the Temple Road. We need to deal with them before anyone can continue," he said.

"Isn't there another way to the temple?" Jason asked Ren.

Ren shook his head slightly. "The woods can be dangerous, and there is water on the other side of the road. Unless we plan to swim there, the Temple Road is the only way to the temple."

"Maddy, you aren't in any shape to fight. Let's just stay here. We can come up with a different plan to get to the temple. There must be a reasonable approach," Jason said more quietly now.

"No! The plan is, fight bad guys, save Aunt Ruth, and defeat the king. And if I have to do it by myself, then that is what I will do. Reasonable approaches left the building a long time ago, guys, about the time the mountain troll showed up to chase us. Or maybe even a little further back, like when I was given a magical glow sword in my house. I am not staying behind. I will never give up on finding Aunt Ruth and bringing her back to Greenrock or bringing justice to those who deserve it. Even if I have to crawl there, I am going." I attempted a slow steady breath. I could feel my hands trembling with my nerves.

Jason smiled a reluctant smile. "Well, that was dramatic. It's just so dangerous."

"I know, Jay." I looked down, poking the tip of my sword into the sand.

"You don't suppose that our charm and clever, witty antics will persuade them to move aside without any violence at all, do you?" Jason said with a big fake grin, holding both thumbs up.

"No, I do not think that would be very effective," Ara chimed in, letting me know that it wasn't just Ren who was slow to catch on when it came to sarcasm.

Jason smiled at Ara.

"Maddy, I want to find Aunt Ruth, too. I just—I just don't want you to get hurt more than you already are." Jason pursed his lips. "Why are you hell-bent on you and me going alone all of a sudden?"

"Because my family has taken enough of Everly. I need to put an end to it. Alone." I held the sword tighter, and I felt my muscles steady themselves. I bent my knees a little as I met Ren's stare. "I will help you clear the road, and then Jason and

I will head out from there. Thank you, Ara, and thank you, Ren, but I don't think we will be needing your help. We have disrupted your lives enough."

Ren looked so hurt for a moment. I didn't mean to treat him differently, but I also couldn't ignore what Ara had just told me. I felt like I might crumble into a thousand tiny pieces if I stared into his eyes a second longer.

The room was silent for a moment. I slid the sword into the scabbard on my back and sat to put my new boots on.

Ara held her hand out, something clutched in it. "Madison, here you are," she said, handing me a pair of fingerless black gloves.

"What are these for?" I questioned.

"So that people don't know that you are a Magic," Ara replied. "Otherwise, they might try to capture you, too."

I slid the gloves on.

"Very Madonna, love them," Jason whispered. I half smiled back at him. "Thank you, Ara."

I walked past Ara and didn't look back at Ren as I picked up a plate of food and exited the tent, followed by Jason. I shoved another chunk of bread in my mouth. Finally, I could eat in peace. My legs were still a touch on the shaky side. I kept going. I heard Ren and Ara speaking to each other behind me, but they did not follow.

Wow.

I stopped chewing when I stepped outside. Nothing could have prepared me for the beauty of the Jade Village of Everly. The colors were brighter, the air smelled sweet, and the breeze was warm but not hot. The sand was more white than beige. It was beautiful.

"This is incredible," I said.

In front of us was a sea of perfectly blue glittering water, with waves lightly crashing into the sandy shore. The sky was a lovely shade of pink as the sun beamed through the perfect white clouds. We were standing on a wooden boardwalk that stretched along the entire span of the shoreline as far as I could see. To our right was a large rock formation. That must be where the cavern let out, and I noted a few different openings on the side of the mountain. Next to that was an endless white sand beach. Along the boardwalk, there were other cottage tents much like Ara's.

On the sand a little farther down the breakwater, a topless woman stood facing the sea, her arms resting on the top of her head. She looked more like a French painting than a real person as she slowly swayed to the rhythm of the waves.

It seemed like clothing was not high on the list of essentials for anyone here in the Jade Village. I averted my eyes from the topless lady only to come upon a man and woman lying on the sand a few feet from us. They were kissing passionately, covered only by the sand that clung to their skin. I quickly looked up to the sky.

"Oh, wow."

Jason chuckled. "Yeah, they're pretty…uh, free here in Jade."

I turned to Jason, expecting him to be equally awestruck, but he was just looking at me, grinning.

"That's right. I forgot we've been here a couple days," I said.

Behind the tent was more sand, then larger houselike structures farther from the boardwalk on a street made of pebbles, and then bright green trees as far as the eye could see.

"Maddy?" he started. "Did something happen between you and Ren? Why don't you want him to come with?"

I didn't answer, just sighed a little and continued to eat little red fruits that looked like cherries but tasted like sweet lemons.

"We really need him. You have to see that."

I still didn't reply. Telling him about the energy storms would only make Jason worry, and he didn't need to be doing any more of that on this journey.

"Maddy?" Jason walked in front of me and grabbed my shoulders. He bent his knees to drop himself to my eye level.

I looked back at him for a few moments and decided to tell him at least part of the reason why Ren shouldn't go with us. "My parents killed his parents and cursed him to be a Porter," I spat out. "He has lived alone in the woods ever since a Witch from the Rosewood Coven killed his mother and cursed him. And it was all because of an order that my father handed down to take control of the coven's lands. My mother and father are the reason he lives alone in the woods and everyone hates him. He is a Porter because of them."

"Oh, Maddy. This isn't your fault, though. You know that. And we need Ren. If he isn't mad about that stuff, then you shouldn't force that on him."

"These people, who I have yearned to find my whole life, are just monsters. They ruined Ren's life and they killed his parents."

"Dude, that sucks." Jason paused. "Eat something. You'll feel better." Jason nudged my plate toward me.

"Okay." I chewed for a moment. "You sound like your grandmother."

Jason took a piece of reddish meat from my plate and examined it. "Which one? Italian or Puerto Rican?"

I smiled. "Both."

"True." Jason laughed. "Should we be asking what the heck it is we're eating?"

"Nope. It tastes good, who cares? And it's helping. My legs don't feel so wobbly." I took another bite of a bread that tasted like sourdough and had a really crunchy crust.

"Um, hey, so, Ren asked me if we were a thing. You and me," I mentioned.

"Oh, ha, well." Jason smiled. "Did you tell him I was gay?"

I stopped eating for a moment. "Oh, no. I didn't really think of that. I just said that we are like siblings."

Jason laughed. "Yeah, even if you were a dude, we would only ever be this."

I nodded. "This is better."

"Yeah, it is."

We both looked back out at the sea again as the waves crashed against the shore.

"How are your sea legs?" he asked.

"Better, actually. I think I just need to move around a bit." I bent my knees a few times.

"And the eye?" Jason asked hesitantly.

"It will be fine," I assured him with a smile, setting the nearly empty plate down on the ground behind me. "They said that the Cloaked guys are on the path. Do you have your crossbow?"

Jason chuckled. "Um, no. I think my crossbowing days are over." He pulled a long, slender club out of a holder on his back.

"Looks like a baseball bat! Perfect!"

"Hell yeah. A bat is much more my speed." Jason nodded, putting the bat back in the holder on his back.

"Come on!" I motioned for him to follow me.

"Mads, I meant what I said. We need Ren. I know you're upset, but we should wait for him, and Ara, too. We don't even know where we are or where to go!" Jason argued.

"No need, amigo. The Temple Road will lead us there, and it's up that way somewhere. We have our weapons. Let's just go. We don't need him," I insisted, and began to quickly walk down the boardwalk, careful not to look at the couple on the sand. Jason did not follow, but I didn't turn to confront him. I knew I was being stupid, and I didn't need him to tell me that.

"Madison?" I heard Ren call behind me, but I did not stop.

I sighed to myself, walking faster down the boardwalk as the wooden planks creaked beneath my feet.

"Madison, please!" I heard more footsteps on the boardwalk behind me as I pressed on.

I quickened my pace as the footsteps grew louder and faster until they were right behind me. Ren took hold of my wrist. I pulled it away quickly and reluctantly turned to face him.

Ren looked concerned. "Madison, Ara told me that she told you about my parents."

I stepped back and nodded.

"Madison," Ren said softly.

"Is it true?" I met his gaze. "Did my parents do all of this to you?"

Ren ruffled his hair but did not answer me.

"Is it true?" I asked again.

"Yes," he said. "But that should not change anything. We still have a mission. We need to free the Magics. That is all I care about."

I nodded, then spun around and kept walking away from him.

"Madison, you are going to need to offer me some sort of guidance here," he said loudly. "Why are you so upset?"

I didn't answer him.

"So what, then? This is the end? After all of this, you are just going to leave for the temple alone, and what? You do not know the way, and even if you find it, what are you going to do when you get there, huh?" Ren moved in front of me.

I pushed past him, and I did not hear his footsteps this time.

"I thought we were in this together now," he called after me. "You said I could depend on you."

I stopped, feeling like my insides had just been ripped out. "But you shouldn't." I turned around. He walked to where I stood and I lowered my head. "I understand that you want to save the Magics for your father, and it's the right thing to do, but why would you want to help the people who ruined your life? Aunt Ruth is part of the Rosewood Coven. Why would you want to help her? You can lie to me and say this is just about the ritual and the mission, but Ara told me what you tried to do while I was out."

Ren looked anguished but didn't speak.

"Ren, I can't let you help me, knowing what they did to you." I looked down. "It feels wrong."

I turned and kept walking, even more eager to find the Cloaked. I needed a fight. I needed to punch something, and I needed to do it now.

Ren trotted behind me. "Madison."

I slowed my pace and came to a stop. Ren crossed in front of me again. "Hey, stop." He looked exhausted. His green irises were even brighter against the bloodshot whites of his eyes, and his once-sparse beard was starting to fill in more, like he hadn't shaved in days. Turning my head toward the steep hill to the left of the boardwalk, I let out a sigh.

"Ren, I can't even look at you now. I just can't do this with you. Everything they did, it changed the entire course of your life. You lost everything because of my family."

Ren dropped his hand from my shoulder. "So did you," he said quietly.

CHAPTER 19

"Is everything okay?" Ara said in a cheerful voice behind me.

I didn't answer as Ren walked to Ara and I crossed my arms.

More footsteps.

Jason stopped and stood next to me but didn't speak. I closed my eye and listened to the water crash loudly onto the shore to the right of the boardwalk. The sea was louder here, maybe because of the wind, or maybe because I wanted it to be. Either way, I tried to let the sound drown out Ren's and Ara's voices.

Sounds of people's laughter caught my attention and I opened my eye. I turned toward the source. On the other side of the hill, there were more little buildings. Wooden carts lined the path between the buildings, like the farmer's markets they held in Palm City back home. The people weren't close enough that I could hear their conversations, but they smiled and laughed like there wasn't a magical war raging in Everly.

"Madison?" Ara asked behind me. Jason and I spun around to face her and Ren.

"Yes?" I replied, trying not to show my frustration.

"The Cloaked are just up that hill," Ara informed us. "Ren, Madison? Care to join me in this fight?"

"She can't fight now," Jason interjected. "She's been out for days. Right, Mads?"

"Madison can decide how she feels." Ara smiled at me. "It's just a capture, not a kill."

Ren didn't say anything. His eyes were fixed on the hilltop.

"She can't fight now. Ren, don't you have anything to add?" a frustrated Jason asked Ren, taking a step closer to him so that we were standing in a loose circle on the boardwalk.

Ren looked right at me and answered, "I would never tell her where she can or cannot go."

I rolled my eyes—or eye. "This is stupid," I said, then turned and started up the hill, ignoring Jason's protest. It was sand for about ten feet and then the hill started to fill in with patches of grass, making it easier to climb up the slope. Walking with one eye blacked out made me feel like the ground was closer to my foot than it was, and I stumbled to the side a little.

I adjusted my steps and reached the top. Then I saw them: a few of the Cloaked and a mountain troll pulling a four-wheeled wooden cart behind him by a rope connected to his waist. Seated on the bench of the cart was a captive, their hands bound, a burlap bag over their head. Surely another Magic for my father's twisted full moon execution party.

I cracked my knuckles and shook my hands out. Ren was at my side now. Refreshingly, he didn't tell me to stop or ask me to rest. We exchanged a look and kept low as we moved closer, staying out of view of the Cloaked.

A low roar rumbled through the air as the hairy mountain troll threw his head back. He looked like the one we had seen the other day, but his frame was smaller. His wrists were bound together in front of him with what looked like a rope. Unlike the troll we had encountered in the forest, this one's ankles were also bound, making his steps smaller. Just then, the group stopped walking and the troll yelled again. One of the Cloaked walked up and kicked the back of the troll's knee, buckling his leg.

"Jerks," I growled under my breath and tightened my jaw as another one of the Cloaked knocked the troll in the head.

"Get up! We must keep moving!" the Cloaked yelled.

Ren held a coil of rope in one hand, and with his other, he held up his fingers and counted: one, two, three. On three we ran at them.

They saw us and turned quickly to brace themselves. I ran toward the tallest one of the group and threw a punch at his jaw, narrowly missing him as he lunged to the side and fell.

My opponent rolled away and pulled a long baton-looking thing from his belt as he jumped to his feet. I backed away, scanning the area for more attackers.

Out of the corner of my good eye, I saw Ara flying through the air like a bird, striking with fierce accuracy and grace. Jason had reached us, too. I gave him a nod as he swung his club into the back of the Cloaked about to strike Ren.

"Thank you, Jason!" Ren ducked and charged another Cloaked.

Ren was smiling as he battled with one of the Cloaked about his size. He loved a fight as much as I did, it seemed.

I ducked to avoid a baton as the Cloaked swung for my head. It was like the world slowed down but I didn't. An unfathomable feeling.

I felt a surge of adrenaline as I swung my fist at the Cloaked guy's face again, this time making contact. My blood raced as I pounced on him, knocking him on his back just as his baton made contact with my cheekbone. I heard the crack and felt pain shoot through my face. My head swung to the right. I grunted and started punching, alternating both hands. Over and over.

I felt more heat in my body than in my previous hot flashes. Something felt different. Sharper. It was as if someone else had taken control of my arms, making me punch faster and harder than I ever thought I could. I heard no other noises—just my breathing, my racing heartbeat, and the thumping sound my fists made when they hit his face.

"Madison!" A muffled voice broke through my fog. I didn't stop punching until someone's arms wrapped around my waist and pulled me off the Cloaked. I fell onto my back, blinking, my head spinning.

Everything came back into focus: all the noises of the people, the rustling trees, the distant crashing waves. The heat in my body started to dissipate, too.

Jason stood off to the side, staring at me with wide eyes, panting. Ara and the Cloaked she was tying up were looking at me, too. I took a deep breath and saw that Ren was standing over me, holding his hand out to help me up.

It was only when I put my hand in his that I saw the blood covering my hands. I gasped.

Madison, what did you do? I looked over at the Cloaked and my mouth fell open. His face was bloodied beyond recognition, and his eyes were already puffed and bruised. He moaned and rolled onto his side.

Ren grabbed my arm and pulled up. He spoke softly, like he didn't want Ara and Jason to hear him. "It is okay, Madison. It is not your fault. That is the Strongblood side of you. You will feel the urges to fight and to kill, but you must hold back."

"I did that?"

Ren nodded. Ara finished tying up two more of the Cloaked that were lying on the ground, and Jason helped. All of the Cloaked were bound and defeated. The one I had fought didn't need any ropes to keep him from escaping.

"It's over?" I asked, wiping my hands on my dark pants.

"Yes, we just need to deal with their captive and the troll," Ren replied, and stepped away to go help Ara with the captured Cloaked.

The Magic's head was still covered as they sat in the cart.

"Don't worry, I will help you," I said.

The mountain troll was on his knees, groaning. The troll looked bigger and bigger the closer I got, making me slow my pace. He turned his head toward me but didn't move his large body.

"Well, hello there," I said nervously, taking a step so that I was in front of him.

The mountain troll opened his mouth but didn't speak. His teeth were a muted yellow with spots of brown near the gumline. He tilted his head to the side, studying me. His hair was curly and coarse, with orange hairs sprouting from his face like a sparse lion's mane. His right horn curled like a spiral gray shell, but his left horn was broken, only an inch or so long. He wore tattered, ripped gray pants and a loose-fitting muted brown shirt. Blood speckled the shirt, although he had no visible injuries, and he had a burlap sack on his back.

On his knees, he was still about a foot taller than me and twice as wide. I kept my eyes locked on his, studying him. He didn't seem vicious. He seemed frustrated. I imagined I would be, too, if I were kept like a prisoner.

"I won't hurt you, I promise," I said, noticing that the rope wound around his wrists was a faded pink. Blood, perhaps.

His face softened and he relaxed his stance, rolling his shoulders back.

"You can understand me, right?" I lifted the corner of my mouth in a smile.

The mountain troll grunted.

"Are you hurt?" I asked softly.

He did not speak, but he looked at his wrists and back to me.

"I am Madison," I said, stepping toward him. There was a soft gentleness in his eyes as he opened his mouth, letting a small noise escape. I reached back and pulled my sword from the scabbard. The troll's eyebrows furrowed and he bellowed something I didn't understand.

I heard someone, either Jason or Ren, calling my name from the bottom of the hill. I disregarded them.

"No, no, listen, I am just going to cut these ropes. And then I am going to need you to not kill me, okay?" I said to the troll. He relaxed his face again.

I slowly rested my hand on the troll's wrist. He jumped and leaned forward to yell into my face, blowing my hair back and spattering my forehead with his saliva. I closed my eyes and mouth tightly.

When he stopped, I opened my eye, and I did not move as a droplet of his spit dripped from my nose. I felt my pulse quicken in anger, though, and I started breathing faster.

Without thinking, I screamed back in his face in the lowest growling tone I could manage.

And then I stood still, stunned at my own impulsive reaction.

I had just screamed in a mountain troll's face. I screamed at a troll who was like twice my size and then some.

He stayed unmoving for a second and blinked. I braced for his reaction. For him to rip my head off or to throw me off the top of this hill.

Then the troll threw his head back with a roar. I jumped and lifted my sword up. He was laughing.

Holy crap.

I wiped my face and let out a quick laugh, relaxing my posture. He lifted his bound wrists and I carefully sawed through the ropes until they slid off, falling to the ground. The skin beneath was raw and bloody.

"Gullway." The troll pounded a fist on his chest.

"Madison," I repeated, putting a hand on my chest. I gave him a nod. "Gullway?"

He repeated his gesture and said his name again. I walked around him and cut the rope between his ankles and the one attached to the cart. The Magic in the cart struggled and yelled, but it was muffled by the hood.

"I will be right with you," I said to the Magic.

Gullway climbed to his feet and pulled the remaining rope off his ankles. He ripped the rope from his waist with a grunt as he turned to face me, towering over me, at least seven or eight feet tall.

"Ma'son," Gullway said. The way he said my name made it sound like he wasn't using his tongue when he spoke. Like when you would talk while holding onto your tongue as a kid.

I smiled and nodded.

Gullway grinned at me, revealing his large crooked teeth. My worry faded as I looked at his face. This was not a monster. He was just grateful to be free. I slid my sword back into the scabbard.

"Go! Be free, Gullway!"

Gullway tilted his head to the side like he didn't understand.

"Go on," I said.

Gullway nodded and smiled widely before bowing his upper body down. He stood, turned toward the trees behind him, and walked away. As he reached the tree line, he turned back.

I waved. "Go, be free!" I repeated.

"Did you just fight a mountain troll?" Ren asked and I jumped. Jason and Ren were right behind me, next to the cart.

I looked back, but Gullway was already gone. "Nope. I freed him," I said.

Jason chuckled. "Of course you did."

I looked at Ren out of the corner of my eye, then met his gaze. He didn't seem to care that I had caught him staring at me.

"You okay, Maddy?" Jason asked.

"Yeah, I'm fine."

"I am going to help Ara get those Cloaked down to the village." Ren motioned back to Ara and the Cloaked that she had seated and tied up a little farther down the hill. "We need this cart."

"Oh, okay." I walked to the side of the cart and helped the Magic out.

"Careful," Ren warned me as the Magic stood on the ground next to me. Jason held up his club.

"It's fine." I shook my head at Jason. He lowered the bat.

Ren's jaw was clenched and his eyes narrowed. I reached over and pulled the burlap bag from the Magic's head, and I gasped.

"Lacy?"

CHAPTER 20

"Cousin!" Lacy smiled brightly, her blue eyes twinkling. She didn't look stressed or worried. "Hello, Jason."

"Oh my god, Lacy!" Jason pushed between us and hugged her tightly. Her hands still bound, she simply leaned into him.

I felt relieved, but now a thousand questions swirled in my head.

"Why are you here?" I asked sternly. *More Cypher Fae to send to my father?*

"I will be back," Ren said quietly, narrowing his eyes at Lacy. I nodded at him as he lifted the rope and began to guide the cart over to Ara.

"A little help?" Lacy held up her tied wrists. I pulled my sword again and cut her ropes. Jason beamed at Lacy and I chewed my lip, awaiting her explanation.

Lacy swung her arms around me. "I had to come and find you!" she exclaimed, still clinging to me tightly. "You did not meet me at the designated spot. But it is okay now. I have found you."

"Lacy, stop." I pushed her back. She didn't seem to care that I was unhappy and didn't even inquire as to why. "What's going on?"

"I came to find you. We need to go. Quickly!" Lacy insisted, grabbing my arm.

"Go where?" I shot back. "You need to explain yourself."

"Maddy," Jason said. "Don't be so harsh."

"Harsh? You know what she did!"

Jason took a deep breath. "We don't really know what's going on, Mads."

"You cannot be here. They are coming for you." Lacy ignored Jason and me. She was so serious now, and her general chipper nature was replaced with that same hard stare that she had from before.

"I can't just leave. I need—" I started.

"We are going back to Greenrock." Lacy crossed her arms.

"What?" I was beyond confused now. "We have to go get your mom."

"No, we have to go," she said. Her eyes welled up with tears. She spun away from us, sobbing dramatically now.

"We have to get to the temple. That's where your mom is, Lacy," Jason said as he put an arm around her, trying to comfort her.

"No, my mother is home. We must get back!" Lacy cried.

I shook my head. "What? How is she back home? Ruth is in Greenrock?"

Lacy nodded vigorously and kept her eyes wide. "Yes, she escaped! She sent me to find you and bring you home as well."

"She escaped?" I smiled. *That's the Aunt Ruth I know.* "Why didn't she come with you to find us?"

"She was being hunted," she answered, tears streaming down her rosy cheeks. Lacy was acting so erratic, it was hard to be angry. All I could do was stand there, baffled by her quick, intense mood swings.

"Are you ready?" Lacy asked.

I shook my head.

"What about the Magics? We need to go help them, too," I said.

"Yeah, they're all still trapped up there," Jason added.

"Mom already did it," Lacy replied. "She helped them all."

"Oh," I replied.

"You are free to go home now," Lacy said to Jason, and then turned to look at me. "You don't have to stay here."

Jason raised his eyebrows, "Oh, well, that's great, right, Mads?"

I nodded, but I still felt odd about all of it. "Yeah, great."

"But we must hurry. The Cloaked are looking for Witches. It is best if we get to the caves. It is over, Madison," Lacy said. She started down the hill with Jason following closely behind.

But it doesn't feel over. I slid my sword into my scabbard and followed them.

As I walked, I could see Ren and Ara down in the village. They were standing close together, talking. They didn't look up as I waved my arm.

"Wait! I have to say good-bye." I stopped at the bottom of the hill as Lacy and Jason continued toward Ara's tent—or maybe toward the caves. They were both in that direction.

"Jason, wait!" I called again.

He stopped and turned, but Lacy grabbed his arm and kept pulling him along. Jason shrugged and kept walking. "We'll meet you by the caves!" Jason shouted. Lacy smiled at me and continued blabbing away about something.

Something feels wrong here.

Standing halfway between the bottom of the hill and Ara's tent, I pulled my gloves off and wiped them on the back of my pants. They were covered in blood and troll spit. Gross. I was stalling, but I didn't have any other choice. I couldn't just leave and not tell Ren and Ara.

Oh, crap. What would I even say to Ren?

"Madison, we must go!" Lacy called. I put my disgusting gloves back on and looked over to where Lacy and Jason were standing, just outside Ara's tent.

"Madison?"

It was Ren. I turned around.

"Is everything okay?" He already looked concerned.

Ara passed us and smiled as she kept walking toward Jason and Lacy. I smiled back and pushed the tip of my black suede boot into the sand.

"Ren, I have to go," I said abruptly.

"What?" Ren's eye brows furrowed. "What do you mean?"

I motioned to Lacy. "My cousin said that Ruth is home and that she freed the Magics."

He raised an eyebrow. "If the Magics were freed, we would have heard by now. Ara!"

Ren started to walk past me, and I grabbed his wrist. "Ren. Lacy wouldn't lie." He turned back to me, and I let his arm go as he took a step closer.

"Madison, let me look into this. Something does not feel right."

"No, Ren. She said it was over," I replied softly. I didn't want to tell him that I felt like something was wrong, too. It just didn't make sense for Lacy to lie to me. She may have kept this secret from me, but she had never outright lied to me before. Even if she was being weird, she was still Lacy.

I started walking to Ara's tent, where Lacy, Ara, and Jason stood waiting.

Ara smiled at me. "I hear your journey is at an end. I am sad to see you go."

"Thank you, Ara," I answered. "I hope to see you again someday."

"Good-bye, Ara." Jason wrapped her in a prolonged hug. "Thank you for everything. You are the coolest."

"It was a pleasure to have you, Jason. Give my regards to your boyfriend." Ara kissed Jason on the cheek.

"You got it," Jason answered, and smiled glowingly. "He is going to be so happy to see me!"

Ara smiled at me, then narrowed her eyes at Lacy before turning and retreating to her tent.

"Who told you that the Magics were freed?" Ren walked up to Lacy and stood a little too close to her for my liking.

"Chill, Ren." Jason held up his hand.

"Do not speak to me, Porter," Lacy sneered. "Madison, we must go. Now." Lacy turned and started walking toward the cave openings.

"Ren, thanks for everything, man. I'll meet you by the cave, Mads," Jason said, then followed after Lacy.

"This is the end then? You are leaving?" Ren spun to face me and lowered his voice. "What about your parents? Is that not reason enough to stay?"

I took a deep breath. "I need to have a long talk with my aunt about all of that." I swallowed loudly. "I can't stay here."

"What about the courtyard and the spell? You said you would help me." He clenched his jaw.

I paused. He was right, but I needed to get Lacy and Jason back to Greenrock, and I really needed to talk to my aunt.

"I don't know what you want me to say," I replied, growing frustrated with his lack of understanding. "I have to go home."

"This is your home!" he erupted. His face was red and his eyes wide.

"No, it isn't! This is the land of crazy, and I need to get my cousin and my best friend out of it."

"What about the spell? Are you just going to bail on that plan?" Ren shouted.

Ara walked cautiously out of her tent.

"I will come back. I just…" I looked toward Lacy and Jason. "I need to get some answers."

Ren opened his mouth to speak, but I cut him off.

"I am leaving. Get over it!" I threw my hands in the air.

"Fine!"

"Fine!" I yelled and stomped toward the cave opening, where Jason and Lacy waited for me.

The two of them looked tattered and tired, but they grinned as I got closer. They stood next to the cave, under the trees. The wind had kicked up, causing the trees to sway heavily in the warm breeze.

Aunt Ruth was safe at home. It's what I had hoped for since this journey started. And no matter how mad I was at her, it was good to see Lacy—and, of course, my Jason. My two best friends. Two of the only people I had ever cared for being safe and sound and knowing that Aunt Ruth was far from my vengeful father should have made this a truly happy moment. I hadn't finished what I had started in Everly, but I had found out more about my parents. I knew more about them than I had ever known in my whole life.

But for reasons I couldn't explain, I had never been more heartbroken.

CHAPTER 21

Lifting one of the lit torches from the wall, I walked silently ahead of Jason and Lacy into the cavern. It was very narrow, and we could only walk single file. I had been unconscious for the last leg of our travels to the Jade Village, but it was pretty easy to navigate once we started walking.

"You okay, Maddy?" Jason asked from behind me.

"No," I said without turning around. I adjusted the eye patch on my face.

"This whole thing has been absolutely crazy. Lacy, I can't believe you never told us about all of this," Jason said as the cavern opened up into a wider space, making walking the path much less cramped.

"What do you mean?" Lacy asked.

"What do *you* mean, what do I mean?" Jason shot back. "Everly, Maddy's parents, everything."

"Right," Lacy answered.

I stopped. Jason bumped into my back, but I didn't budge.

I turned around to face him and Lacy.

"Maddy?" Jason asked.

"I have to come back here. I have to finish what I started with Ren, and then I need to find my parents. And I can't wait until Ren just shows up again. What if he never shows up again?" I turned around, but Lacy was blocking my way. "Ren needs to come with us so he can bring me back after I talk to Aunt Ruth."

Lacy looked concerned. "No, he cannot."

"I need Ren to bring me back after we get you and Jason back home safe." I took a step to the left, but Lacy stepped over to block me.

"You cannot get him, Madison," Lacy said. "You must trust me."

"No, I do. But I have spent my whole life wanting something to matter to me the way that winning all those races should have mattered. For so long, I have wanted something to make me feel something…this is it. I can't leave for good. I have to free the Magics and face my father." I took a deep breath and smiled. "I need to go get Ren."

"No, you should come with me to the portal. We will send Jason back, and we will start a new mission to find your mother. There are things that you have not seen. Magic that you could not have dreamed of!" Lacy exclaimed.

I looked her over again. Her blonde hair flipped wildly around her face. Her eyes were different.

And then it hit me.

I felt like my heart jumped into my throat.

"Lacy is on the swim team," I said.

Jason narrowed his eyes at me but looked to Lacy for her response, taking the torch from my hand.

"Yeah," Lacy nodded. "Of course."

"Lacy is on the swim team," I said again.

I straightened my posture, feeling my lip curl. I reached back and pulled my sword out of its sheath.

"You guys are being so strange." Lacy tried to push past us, no longer trying to stop me

I shoved my hand sharply into her chest, and she stumbled back into the stone wall behind her.

"Stop it!" Lacy shrieked.

"Lacy is on the frickin' swim team," I barked. My voice boomed off the gray rock walls of the cavern.

"I heard you!" Lacy yelled back. Her nostrils flared in her anger.

"Witches sink in water," Jason said with authority behind me.

"Lacy can swim. Lacy is not a Witch. What are you?" I demanded.

"Or who are you?" Jason added.

"What do you mean? It is me, Lacy!"

"Stop lying!" I said through my teeth.

Lacy's face fell from a terrified protest to a cool smile. "Oh, fine. Being a teenager is exhausting," she said with a sigh, and raised her hands up above her head. Before I could take action, she yelled something in a language I couldn't understand.

Beams of light shot from her fingertips, and her eyes turned to a hazy gray.

"*Glacia*," she hissed.

I tried to move, but I was frozen. Jason stood unmoving to my left.

I forced out a sound, but without being able to move my lips or anything, it was just a spurt of useless noise. It was like only the outside of me was frozen. I could move my tongue and I could breathe, but that was it. The rest of my body was a statue.

Lacy stepped back in front of me and placed her finger on my lips, shaking her head back and forth. "No, no. Do not make me take away your ability to breathe, too. I just needed to get you away from the bad people. You are safe now, little bubbies. Do not worry. Auntie Sinder will protect you." She spun to face Jason, pointed her long finger at him, and twirled it in the air.

"You do not belong here, but I am pleased you came along, too. I have wanted you since I first saw you. A treat for me, indeed," she said softly.

Again, I forced sound out of my barely parted lips.

She spun and slapped me hard on the cheek. "Quiet! Aunt Sinder is talking. Do not worry. I meant what I said. We will return him home. I am not that cruel."

I could not move to wince in pain, but my cheek burned from the slap.

She walked over to Jason, who was standing with his hands on hips and his head tilted back slightly.

"Just a few minutes and we will be on our way again." She traced Jason's lips with her finger, ran her hand down his neck past his chest, and grabbed his belt. The sight of her all over Jason was jarring, and even though I knew it wasn't Lacy, it still looked like her.

"Mm. You make a fine statue. I wish I had frozen you in my quarters. We would have a fine time." She leaned into Jason and kissed his neck, moaning.

I made more sound, this time louder, and I held it for longer.

"Enough!" she screamed. She held her palm to her face and shook her head. Lacy's blonde hair turned to thick black curls that fell past the plunging neckline of her long green dress. She had cool gray skin that matched the color her eyes were now. Blue veins were visible beneath her thin skin. Her face was long. She had a small nose that swooped up a little at the end like mine and a sharp jawline. Even with her gray skin, her face looked somewhat youthful.

"That's better." Her voice was low and smooth. "Where were we, lovey?" She pressed her body against Jason's and laid her head on his chest. She looped her arms through his and hugged him.

"Sinder?" a voice called out. "Is that you? Sinder?"

Sinder spun around and rested her hand on her hip. She was very narrow, and her arms were quite thin. Brushing her hair back from her face, she let out an exasperated sigh.

"In here!" she called out. "I have her and her handsome companion. We are just waiting on you, sister."

She focused back on Jason. I saw a tear roll down his cheek. Sinder leaned close to him and licked the tear from his cheek.

"Oh my, puppy, I forgot to let you blink!" Sinder twirled her finger in the air and Jason blinked rapidly, sending another tear down his cheek.

My mind exploded with rage and frustrated anger.

"Oh, Sinder. You did not get far, now, did you?" the same voice laughed from behind me. The voice was higher than Sinder's. "I told you this would happen, did I not?"

"You are so wise, sister. I could not fool them for long," Sinder sung out.

"Oh, is this her? The one who will save them? We must not harm her," the voice stated. I felt a cool-skinned hand resting on my neck. "Oh, yes. I can smell the power in her blood. She is a Strongblood, all right." I felt a face press into my arm. "It is intoxicating! So much power surging inside of her, unlike any I have ever met. And she really does have magic, how curious!"

"Well, of course she does. She is the daughter of the Great One, the greatest Witch of our time!" Sinder said, sounding almost sarcastic.

"Do you think the Great One knows she is here?" the sister asked.

"Of course," Sinder said, caressing Jason's face. "The girl's energy screams to me. The Great One must hear it as well."

"Oh, Sinder, free them. What are you doing? They are not our prisoners," the sister said, still out of my view.

"Kaya, she threatened me," Sinder protested.

"Sinder, we are to work together," Kaya answered. "This is no way to begin a journey! It was your fault for not going with her when they crossed in the first place."

"But wait, sister, I want to play with this one a bit longer. He is so sweet. And this hair." Sinder was on Jason again, running her hands through his hair. She kissed his neck again.

"Sinder!" Kaya said with a little airy chuckle.

Sinder tore Jason's shirt open, revealing his tanned, muscular chest and abs. Sinder squealed in delight.

"Oh, just a few minutes, sister. Look at him! He is perfection! I have been starved for touch. All we do is hide and plot and hide. I desire contact." Sinder began kissing Jason's chest.

I closed my eyes and concentrated on my sword hand. I focused all my energy on moving it. This was just magic or something. It wasn't real. I needed to move.

Focus!

And just then, my hand tilted up, lifting my sword slightly.

Yes! I screamed in my head.

"Did you see that?" Kaya shrieked, still out of my view.

Sinder was completely wrapped around Jason now, kissing his face and neck, her arms twisted around his neck.

"Sinder!" the voice yelled again.

"Hmm? Yes, Kaya?" Sinder turned abruptly. "What is it?"

"The girl. I think she just moved her hand!" Kaya said.

"Impossible. Her strength is no match for my magic," Sinder said dismissively. "Have you been into the troll swill again?"

"Well, yes, but I saw it! I know I did!" Kaya protested. "She is the daughter of the Great One!"

I tilted my hand up again.

"Oh!" Sinder exclaimed. "But no! It cannot be!"

Kaya laughed gleefully. "Incredible!"

Sinder raised her hands again in the same way she had before and called out something else I didn't understand. Light shot from her fingertips, and a bright burst of white briefly lit the cave.

I stumbled forward with a rush of soreness, like I had just worked out for hours. Apparently, that was the aftereffect of trying to move while magically frozen.

Jason yelled and stepped backward, knocking himself against the rocky wall behind him.

I charged at Sinder, my sword out, and passed right through her. She had vanished. I ran into the cave wall and fell backward a bit. Pain shot through my forehead where it had smacked into the wall.

"Oh, yes. Great power!" Sinder sneered.

She was now on the other side of the cave, next to Kaya. Kaya was shorter, with the same black hair, only hers was swept up into a tight bun on her head; her skin reflected the same gray tone with visible blue veins. Her eyes were a bit darker gray.

I moved myself in front of Jason.

"You okay?" I asked him.

Jason nodded, pulling his ripped shirt closed. His hands were shaking.

"Maddy, your head is bleeding," he pointed out.

I rubbed my forehead where I had hit the wall. Blood on my hand. Great. I still had my black gloves on. Healing myself in front of these two seemed all too risky. I could deal with another bump on the head.

"Perfect," I groaned, and wiped the warm blood away from my eyebrow.

Sinder giggled. "Such grace!"

I clenched my jaw. "Who are you? Where is Lacy?"

"Sinder. Why are you toying with these children?" Kaya asked. "We have a mission to start."

"Getting them to do what I wanted was much easier and quicker as little Lacy." She chuckled. "Such fun."

"You are bold, sister. Never let them never say otherwise."

"Who says I am not bold? I am nothing if not bold!" Sinder lifted her chin.

"Did you see Ruthana?" Kaya asked. They stood like two women gossiping at an office water cooler, complete with dramatic hand gestures.

Sinder nodded. "Oh, yes. For a moment."

"What did you do with Lacy?" I yelled, my voice echoing through the cave tunnel. I could feel myself filling with anger like a climbing thermometer.

Sinder and Kaya both jumped, startled by my volume. Kaya placed her hand on her chest. "My heavens, child. There is no need to roar. We may be old and timeworn, but we can hear you just fine."

I bit my lip and sighed in frustration. "What did you do to Lacy?" I said through my teeth, lowering my volume slightly.

"She is home in your world, I would assume," Sinder replied. "She was not there when I came for you. Now, we must start our mission."

"I was already on a mission. I was on my way to the Temple of the Ember Isle, you lunatic! Ren was—"

Sinder and Kaya exchanged glances. "Ren Raker, the Porter, son of Lawrence Raker, the Strongblood? You were willingly working with such filth?" Kaya asked.

"He is helping us get to the temple. He helped us cross into Everly," I said. "And he is not filth."

"Yes, that was all I needed him for, the crossing. But we are not going to the temple. You were not meant to be with the Porter, girl. You are the Scion of Everly, the savior of the Magics, not a travel companion to the world walker, son of such scum. I apologize for us getting separated, but I had to find my sister," Sinder replied.

"So at the house...that wasn't Lacy. That was you?" I asked.

"It was." Sinder nodded.

"But how did you know where to find the sword?" I blinked rapidly, trying to process.

"I have my ways."

"So, wait...if you aren't Lacy, does that mean Ruth isn't home?" Jason asked softly.

"Oh, no. Ruth is still at the temple."

"What?" I shouted.

"Oh, yes. She is a part of this mission, whether she wanted to be or not. I did not plan to be followed by the guard, but I was. The chips fell and I played the hand I was dealt. We needed a way to get you and Ruthana here. I improvised. After all, we needed someone inside the temple if our plan is to work. Ruthana would never agree to come back here, no matter what the cost. So, you see, it is all for the best."

"Ruth is in danger because of you! Don't you care at all?" I asked.

"Ruthana was never going to tell you who you are. She was going to let you live out your days as a simpleton, never realizing your true power. I set you free. I have seen you then, and I see you now. There is a change in you, girl. Do not pretend that you have no passion for this cause. I have seen it within you—and you said it yourself." Sinder tapped a finger on her chin.

"You don't know anything about me," I said.

"I know you were following that Porter blindly. Oh, sorry, poor choice of words." Sinder gestured to my eye. "And I know you should be praising me and showering me with kindness for rescuing you!"

Sinder took a step closer, and I shifted to keep myself firmly between her and Jason. "We have to go. I need to save my aunt."

"There is time for that, but we must think bigger than releasing a prisoner. We must put an end to King Dax and his guards, the Strongbloods, and even the worthless Cloaked. Take them all down once and for all."

I exhaled loudly in frustration. "We were going to break the spell on the courtyard that holds the Magics prisoner there. I had this all covered. I need to go get Aunt Ruth, so whatever grand plan you have, it's too late. I am going with Ren to the temple."

"No, no. We will not merely release the prisoners and kick Dax out of the temple. We are going to kill all of the Strongbloods, and you are going to help."

"Kill them?" Jason asked. I looked back at him. His eyes were wide and full of worry. I took his hand and held it tight. *I will get you out of here.* Jason forced a smile.

I turned back to Sinder. "I am not going to help you kill anyone, you lunatic. I am going to save my aunt."

"Listen, girl," Sinder started.

"No, you listen," I interrupted. "I don't care what you thought would happen, but let me make this perfectly clear. You lied to us, you put my aunt in danger, and I just watched you grope my best friend. I will never, ever help you. I am going to go get my aunt now." I turned to walk away, back out of the cavern, with Jason's hand tightly in mine.

"Wait. Your mother would never agree to your plan," Sinder said.

I stopped.

"Ruth is in the temple, and we will make sure she is freed, but first we need to put an end to the rule of the tyrant who started this mess. We will begin our plan to prevent it from ever happening again," Sinder said. I turned back, making sure to keep Jason behind me. Kaya nodded as she started to walk over to where Jason and I stood. I tightened my hand around his, and he took a step closer to me.

"No. I am not going with you. Ren will take me," I insisted, raising my sword.

"And we'll do it without hurting people," Jason added.

"Ren? He speaks nothing but lies, dear. Did your handsome knight tell you how it is that he found you?" Kaya inquired.

I didn't answer.

"That boy was lost with rage when he came to find me," Sinder explained. "He was broken and grief-stricken and full of vengeance. His family had been wronged and he wished to seek vengeance, but all he had was anger and nowhere to look. And the most perfect arms I have ever seen—but that is beside the point."

"What was he looking for?" I asked.

"Well, you, of course. He wanted to find you and avenge his family's demise. He sought to kill you. It was then that I realized I could use the boy's ambition for our coven's rebirth!"

"What? Ren? No, you're wrong," Jason stated. "Ren would never try to hurt Maddy. He loves her."

I blinked slowly. *He wanted to kill me?*

"Ren told us everything," I said. "He told me about my father and about what my father was doing to the Magics. I know about his family. He told me everything."

"He may have ended up choosing a noble way, but it does not change his intention. He meant for you to die," Kaya said. "And how do you know he still does not plan to kill you?"

I opened my mouth but did not speak.

Sinder moved closer to me. "Because maybe he does not intend to do it himself. Did your Porter tell you that your existence threatens the powers in Everly? That if your father sees what you truly are, *he* will kill you? You are Magic and Strongblood. You are the only link between the two, so he will seek to sever you. I wager that the Porter failed to explain the threat you face while you are here. You must stay with us. Stay with your kind. We will free Ruth, kill the Strongbloods, and find your mother. It is the only way to end this."

I didn't answer. I just tried to take it all in.

"And when I was little Lacy Rosewood, I sent a Cypher Fairy to your dear daddy to let him know you are in Everly. He is already looking for you, so you have little choice. You must stay with your coven, girl," Sinder said.

I let out a sigh and looked at Jason out of the corner of my eye. He squeezed my hand. The fairy—the fairy Ren had intercepted from Lacy. *My father has no idea I am here.* That was a welcome revelation.

"Sinder, do not be so harsh," Kaya said, and then she turned to me. "Your cause was sweet and well intentioned, but now it is no longer needed. We are thinking bigger in this war on the Magics. And after Dax falls, we are going to find your mother and fix all this. Reunite the coven. We need four. Since Ruthana is otherwise engaged for now, we have you."

"She is not otherwise engaged! Sinder got her captured to force her back into all of this!" I yelled.

Sinder groaned and stomped her foot. "Ruthana deserves what she gets. It is because of her that we are in this mess. Our coven fell because of her—because we did not have the four. First she followed your mother to the temple, which weakened us, but then she left Everly and we crumbled. Without the four in Everly, the coven cannot stand. She doomed us. Doomed your mother and doomed you."

Sinder spun and walked back to her sister's side, laying her hand on her head like a dramatic actress after a lengthy scene.

"Do you know where Madison's mother is?" Jason asked, letting go of my hand.

"Who is Madison?" Kaya asked.

I raised my hand. "That would be me."

"I forgot, yes. Yes, that is right." Kaya nodded.

"No, we don't know where Madison's mother is just yet. I imagine she is looking for you, too. Ruthana used her powers to keep Madison hidden from the coven. She was one of the most powerful Witches in Everly before she left with you. To be your guard," Sinder stated bitterly. "Haven't you heard all this before?"

I shook my head.

"She left to guard me? Guard me from what?" I asked.

Kaya and Sinder exchanged confused looks and turned back to me.

"You really do not know. Ruthana left Everly to protect you from yourself, dear," Kaya said. "You have evil inside of you."

CHAPTER 22

"Evil inside of her? What does that mean, exactly?" Jason asked.

"Her father is a Strongblood. They are all that is evil and wrong in Everly. But the king is the worst of them. He is of the Ember family, the most ruthless of the Strongbloods. When Dax took the crown, he went mad with power. Ruthana gave up her life, her coven, and her power and fled from this place to protect you from it all. It was the best way to ensure your safety," Kaya said, concern showing in her eyes.

I looked to my feet and tried to mask my emotions.

Sinder crossed her arms. "Are you sure you do not know the story? It is very popu—"

"No, Sinder! I do not know the story, okay! I do not know the story," I yelled.

Sinder turned up her nose. "I don't see how. It is very well known."

"Sinder, shut up!" Jason shouted.

"I know one way to keep me occupied," Sinder said, and made a kissy face at Jason.

"Sooooo not going to happen, hagatha."

Sinder jutted her lip out in a pout and put her hands on her hips.

"Everly was led by Magics. It was ruled by our coven, not Strongbloods. But now Witches are few in number. This was our land, and we intend to take it back," Kaya explained further.

"If Maddy is half Witch, then why doesn't she have powers like you do?" Jason asked.

Kaya took a step toward me, looked me up and down, and smiled, making her gray eyes gleam. "She does. She draws out a little every moment she touches the handle."

The blue light is my magic? "It's in the sword," I said.

"Yes, girl. Ruthana stored your power in it so that you could live an impossibly boring, simple life," Sinder said. "And she put a spell on you to hinder your Strongblood side and hide you."

"Then how did you find me?" I slid my sword back into its sheath.

"You are in your eighteenth year now. You can no longer conceal your powers, and neither could Ruthana. Your beacon grew brighter. I did not even need much magic to break Ruthana's protection spell," Sinder explained.

I bit my lip. Ruth was protecting me. She gave up her life here for me. I shook my head, thinking about the last time I spoke to her. "She didn't want any of this life for me," I said.

"Ruthana was such a talent. This is not the first time she had put others before the coven. She wanted to renounce us and marry that soldier who is always following King Dax around. 'Tis a pity. Our little sister was by far the most gifted of the four of us," Sinder said.

"Sister! Bite your tongue. Vilda is the mightiest of us," Kaya exclaimed.

"Who is Vilda?" Jason asked.

Kaya and Sinder exchanged looks.

"Ruth's sister and our sister. The youngest of the four of us," Sinder answered, her tone even. "Your mother, dear."

I took in a sharp breath. My mother's name. *I know her name.*

"Sweet Ruthana! What would she say if she knew you were working with the son of Lawrence Raker, putrid Record Keeper of King Dax? What would she say if she knew that you trusted him more than your own blood?" Kaya asked.

Before I could speak, Sinder waved her hand at me, and it was like a clamp slammed my lips together. I could not speak. I screamed inside my closed mouth, but all it did was puff my cheeks out.

"Stop it!" Jason yelled, stepping out from behind me. "Like, seriously, come on! That's your niece! I guess I can't be too shocked, everything here is so frickin' screwed up! There are trolls and goblins and then you two! I think, hey, I'm almost home, and instead I get groped by one of the ugly stepsisters!"

He turned to Sinder. I tried open my sealed lips to speak, but Sinder's magic was too strong.

Jason continued, "No offense, lady, but what the hell is wrong with you?" He was borderline hysterical now, waving the torch as he spoke.

"I can't help it. I simply adore young men of your world," Sinder replied.

"So do I!" Jason yelled back. "So do I!" He smacked his hand on the wall as he said each word. "But I would never treat people the way you have. What was the point of messing with our minds like that, by pretending to be Lacy? Huh?" Jason was edging on shrill now. "What is wrong with you people?"

I reached for Jason's hand, but he pulled away and kept ranting.

"And Ren! That dude is great. He really is. He may have this whole awkward, weird vibe and his hair is unnaturally perfect at all times, but he's a good dude. Maddy, you didn't see it, but when you were out, he was so worried about you. We were going to save Ruth, and then these evil hagzillas messed it all up." He stopped pacing and pointed at Sinder. "This is your fault!"

Sinder was clearly a bit startled. She put her hand on her chest and turned her shoulders as if she were a proper lady at a French court being officially offended.

I rolled my eyes, still unable to open my mouth.

Kaya let out a soft chuckle. I felt myself smiling at Jason somewhat proudly, but worry was still at the forefront of my mind. Sinder was unpredictable. There was no telling what she would do.

She lifted her chin and looked away from Jason like she had hurt feelings.

Jason raised his eyebrow. "Whoa, Sinder. Your neck—what is that, a neck tattoo? That's terrifying! Who does that?" He squinted at her. "You people are insane!"

Sinder covered it with her hand and looked away. Even with her hand there, I could see that she had a deep red scar that ran all the way around the gray flesh of her neck.

Kaya nodded. "Oh, that? Yes, Sinder was the Witch who helped King Dax figure out that you need to remove the head *and* the hands of a Witch, or they will heal themselves. Sinder was one of his first Witch executions."

I cringed.

"Wait." Jason's shoulders lowered and his eyes darted back and forth. He stepped toward the women. "So you can heal yourself?"

"And others, if we desire. It is a gift of the coven. Most of us can, after years of practice," Sinder answered, still looking away.

"Sinder, we have explained what we want. Let us let the girl decide," Kaya said. "And I think you need to give our niece her words back."

Sinder pursed her lips to the side and rolled her eyes.

"She does not get to decide. She comes with us. That is all." Sinder sighed. "Dax will not turn away his sweet daughter, and then we will strike."

I held up my middle finger.

Sinder grumbled something and sneered. "The one you call Ren—he has no loyalties! He cannot be trusted."

"Sinder, dearest. We will go to find Vilda. No need for all this muck. Conflict gives you wrinkles, sister," Kaya said.

"I will not let her win. She is a ghastly, unkempt barbarian, niece or not," Sinder said.

"Sinder, she is the child of our sister Vilda, the Great One," Kaya said. "You know what will happen to us if you harm her. Vilda will seek her vengeance and then some. We must not let our pride muddle our judgment. And now I see why she was hidden."

I furrowed my brow at Kaya.

"What does that mean, exactly?" Jason asked.

"Madison will be great. Sinder has seen it," Kaya said. "Madison's power is greater than I could have known. Being a Strongblood and a Witch is a true anomaly. Your friend must pick a side, and I need you to aid us by helping her choose the correct side: the Magics. The Strongbloods can't stay in power, or we will all suffer. If Madison joins us, the Magics of this land will rule again. If she goes with Ren Raker to the Temple of the Ember Isle, Everly will crumble. He may be a Porter, but at his core, he is a Strongblood, just like his father. Madison must rejoin the coven if Magics are to reign over Everly once more."

"Kaya, you mistake yourself. You have not seen what I have seen. Her story is not a happy one. It *will* end in blood. She will trust the wrong people, she will deny destiny, and Everly will perish in blood and fire," Sinder said harshly.

"Okay, pause," Jason interrupted. "Kaya, you say that Maddy's blood is full of power and that she will save Everly or whatever, right?" Jason asked.

"Yes." Kaya nodded slowly, and a soft, gentle smile spread across her face. "Her past tells a great deal about her future."

My past? What does Kaya know about my past?

I felt my heartbeat quicken. I didn't believe a word either of them were saying. My lips were still tightly sealed, so I couldn't interject.

"And, Sinder, you say that Maddy's story is not a happy one and all the stuff that Kaya said is crap?" Jason asked.

"Oh, sweet boy. Your mouth moves with elegance when you speak. It is enchanting," Sinder said with a devilish smirk.

I rolled my eyes.

"Okay, gross." Jason cringed. "Answer the question."

"Only because it is you who asks. But yes, I speak the truth. If this beast of a girl puts her trust in the Porter and walks into that temple, she will not walk out. That leads to the end of it all. The nightmares that plague the minds of babes will pale in comparison to the destruction and terror that will fill each speck of life in Everly," Sinder said.

"Yikes, okay. Yeesh," Jason said. "You may be able to work your Witchy magic and make predictions, but I know Maddy better than anyone. She won't go with you to find her mom unless you save Ruth, and she really won't kill people."

Jason turned and winked at me.

Oh, no. What is he getting at? I cleared my throat loudly.

"Sinder..." Kaya said in an urging sort of way.

"Oh, right." Sinder shifted her weight, annoyed. She gave an exasperated sigh and twirled her finger in the air, muttering something under her breath.

My lips tingled. I opened my mouth and closed it a few times.

"Jay!" I whispered loudly in protest and searched Kaya and Sinder's faces for any sign of aggression. "I know what you are trying to do, but you have to stop." I waved to him from where I stood, by the cavern wall. Jason had walked toward the Witches and was now standing between them.

Jason looked at me and then back at Kaya. He pulled himself up, looking more confident than ever. "Can you heal Madison? She was shot—"

"No, Jason! No!" I grabbed his arm.

He shrugged off my touch and disregarded me altogether. "Kaya, please?" he asked, ignoring my pleas. His eyes were wide and desperate. "Do that, and we will work something out with you."

"Jason, stop it! I don't want their help!"

"You still ponder trusting the Porter and going to the temple, do you, dear girl?" Sinder asked, her tone suspicious and heated.

"Just fix her, please. We can sort all of that out," Jason said with authority.

Jason's new assertiveness toward these dangerous women surprised me. Yes, on paper they were my aunts, but in reality they were strangers, and one was for sure a teenager-groping psychopath.

"My eye is fine. I told you that. I don't want her to do anything. I don't want any magic or Witch healing. I am fine. I will heal on my own." I felt flustered and spoke quickly.

"Maddy, I shot you in the eye with an arrow. If your aunts can fix that, then let them," Jason said calmly.

"If you come with us, I will heal you. I give you my word," Kaya said as I grabbed Jason's wrist and pulled him behind me, away from the Witches. "And for the good of the coven, I will help you extract all of your magic from the sword."

"Give us a minute," I said, and pulled Jason to the other side of the cavern.

Kaya nodded and even stopped a disgruntled Sinder from following us. "Take a moment to discuss," Kaya said.

"What are you doing?" I asked Jason. "I told you my eye was fine."

"Is it, though?" Jason ran his fingers through his hair. "I just want to get out of here with you in one piece. They're your aunts. They can help."

"What? Jason, no. No, we can't trust them. You were just screaming at them for being crazy, and now you want to work with them? You saw what Sinder did. She was screwing with us. Kaya might be telling the truth, but Sinder can't be a white hat. And there is no way we could be certain she is on our side," I said.

"We could ask." Jason shrugged.

"What? No," I said, miffed.

Jason looked over at Sinder and Kaya.

"Um, hey, are you hags good or bad?" Jason asked.

I rolled my eyes and couldn't help but smile.

"Come over here and I will show you a little of both, puppy," Sinder replied and rolled her hips.

Jason shivered dramatically. "I'm pretty sure that lady just made me gayer," he whispered.

I let out a single chuckle.

"What if they come with us to the temple to help save Aunt Ruth? We might be safer with them rather than against them, and then after Ruth is safe and sound, you can go with them to find your mom," Jason suggested.

I sighed, and he kissed the top of my head, then mockingly spit. "Your hair smells like feet, you little dirtball."

I snickered.

Kaya let out a roaring laugh at something Sinder said.

I looked back to the exit. "We could leave. They aren't even looking."

Jason looked at them and then at me. "It's your call, Mads."

"What if they are telling the truth about Ren? What if this was all just to get me to the temple so my father would kill me?" I chewed my lip.

"What is the chosen word, children?" Kaya interrupted.

We ignored her, and Jason shook his head at me. "You didn't see what I saw when you were out after the grotto. There's no way Ren wants you dead. Trust me."

"I don't know who to believe. I don't trust any of them." I shook my head as Sinder narrowed her eyes at us and lifted an eyebrow. I cleared my throat. "We are just figuring out the plan," I said as her eyes pierced me.

Sinder exhaled loudly. "Okay, enough chatter, kiddies." She held her hands out. "You want sure sight, niece? I will give you the sight you seek!"

"No!" I yelped. As if I were being tied up in ropes, my arms were pinned at my sides, and Sinder flicked her wrists. I slid across the cave floor to her. She placed her hand on my forehead and began chanting something.

I let out a sharp scream.

CHAPTER 23

It felt like someone was piercing my temples with thousands of hot, tiny sewing needles. I could smell burning hair and what had to be my own burning flesh.

I fell to my knees and screamed in pain, but I could not hear my own cries. I felt the pokes and pains in my temple intensify. I could see nothing but a jarring white light now, and I was weightless, like I was floating.

And then I hit the ground with a thud, the pain in my temple gone. I blinked rapidly and put my hand to my injured eye. It was there. The shell was gone. I laughed a bit, relieved.

Looking up, I stood, taking in a quick breath. I was not in the cave. Jason and the sisters were gone.

I was in a large empty room. The ceiling was higher than a two-story house, and the walls were a peach stone with markings and images carved into them. There were four large white columns toward the center of the room, and in the very center was a black circle on the silvery marble floor. The room was covered in a sort of haze, like I was looking through fogged-up glasses.

"Hello?" I called out. My voice sounded far away, even though it was my own and had come from me.

I heard a laugh. Sinder.

I reached for my sword on my back. Nothing. I looked down at my clothes. I was wearing a dark robe.

"Sinder!" I yelled. "What is this?"

She laughed again but was nowhere to be seen. It was like her laughing was inside my head.

"What is this? Where am I?" I demanded.

"You wanted sight. Here it is. This is what will become of you if you trust the Porter, continue on this path, and go with him to the temple." Her voice echoed in my thoughts.

Fading in like a memory, four chairs appeared next to the pillars. In each chair was the slumped body of a person. Blood from each of them dripped to the floor. I stepped toward them. The floor was slanted to the center of the room so that the blood pooled in the black circle.

And then it was clear I was no longer in control of my limbs but more like a passenger in my own body. My movements were not my doing.

Who are these people?

"Who do you think?" Sinder spoke in my thoughts.

I moved toward the first one. She was dressed all in white, her head resting on the back of the chair. Her throat had been slit.

"One," Sinder whispered.

I walked to the next chair. The occupant's body was covered in chain mail, a shiny glove on one hand and forearm.

"Two."

My heart beat more rapidly.

The next was a young man all in white, like the one at Ara's tent today.

"Three."

No, what is this? Stop this.

Sinder made no response.

The body I was trapped inside pivoted toward the last chair. It was a woman. Her hair was cut in patches, some so short that I could see her scalp. Her shoulders and head were completely slumped forward. A dark red splotch soaked the front of her cream shirt. I walked to her, dread building in me.

"And four," Sinder said ominously.

It was Lacy. My sweet cousin Lacy.

My dream body was just as crushed by this as I was. We fell to the ground, crying. We sobbed, lying on the marble floor.

"Shh," Sinder said. "Watch."

Stop this! Stop it!

The hard marble floor trembled. I did not move. I saw feet walking toward me. Dark shoes. I blinked and more tears fell from my eyes.

"No, no, none of this. No crying. Crying is for the weak. Say it. Say it," the man's voice called down to me.

My body rose and straightened out the robe. The man's hand lifted my chin, but my eyes stayed downcast.

"Say it," he said. I could hear voices, murmurs in a room off in the distance.

"Crying is for the weak," I said monotonously.

172

"That is right. Fix your hair," the man said disapprovingly. "Does it always look like that?" He reached up and moved my hair around. I did not look up to see his face. He smelled like stale tobacco. He was breathing loudly. My eyes stayed focused on the ground.

"We are tough. We must never show emotion, or they will think us weak, and we cannot have that, now, can we? It is important that our power is fixed in the minds of the lesser folk of Everly. Now fix your robe. They will be here any minute. Go, take your place," he told me, and I watched his feet move to the side. "Go on. Do not make us wait for you."

I walked over and stood at the center of the black circle. Blood from the four victims was now a few inches deep. It covered my bare toes. I shifted my weight on my feet.

I knew this wasn't really happening. But feeling like a visitor in my own body in some sort of dream created by Sinder did not change the realness of it all. I felt another tear roll down my cheek as the doors behind the man swung open.

"Stop crying now!" the man growled at me again. "Everything you do now reflects on me, and if you make me look bad or embarrass me in any way, you know the cost. I will burn them all."

What is he talking about?

Sinder did not answer.

I wiped the tear from my face and did not look at the four dead people around me.

"Stand up straight," he ordered. My head turned away from him.

My dream body obediently pulled up and rolled back her shoulders. I felt our fear. I felt the anguish that churned inside. I also felt the determination to keep control. The tears stopped.

"Don't ruin this, or I will kill the rest. Understand?" he said. Then, "Welcome, welcome!" he bellowed, not waiting for my response.

I looked up enough to see a group of about fifteen people in their forties or fifties. They were all wearing gray, similar to the clothes worn by people we had encountered since our crossing into Everly. But this group was older; their robes were pressed and clean with long, billowing sleeves. Their eyes were emotionless, but their faces held big, beaming smiles as they approached us.

They formed a circle and joined hands just outside the four pillars, with me and the victims at the center.

A short-haired woman to my left met my stare as she bowed. She smiled at me, but this time her eyes echoed her smile. It was genuine, which made me shudder.

How could anyone smile in a room that held four dead people? I felt sick. The smell of the room made me feel even sicker.

So much death.

I shifted my feet in the pool of blood as two young men about my age walked over, one on each side of me.

One of them untied the robe, but I did not stop him. The other boy pulled the robe from my body and draped it over his arm.

What is this?

No answer.

I looked down to see that I was completely naked. One of the boys cradled my robe as if he were carrying a person. The circle parted for him to cross through it. Tiny drops of blood dripped from the bottom of the robe and left a trail as he walked away from us. The circle closed again.

My eyes stayed fixed on the ground, but I could see both feet of the man from before as he entered my dream body's sight line. He bent down and dipped a thumb into the pooling blood at my feet. He stood slowly and smeared the blood on my forehead. My gaze stayed fixed on the blood. I did not move. I did not speak.

The blood ran in a slow drip down the bridge of my nose and fell from the tip into the pool below. I wanted to wipe it away. I wanted to run out of there, but I had no control. I was just watching. A stranger in my own body.

The circle parted again, and I watched the man's feet as he walked out. The people of the circle began to hum one long note in unison. I sunk to my knees in the blood of the four people. I extended my arms out to my sides.

The young man who remained in the circle knelt in front of me. His hair was short and dark, and he had a certain softness to his face that the others in the room did not. I met his eyes for a moment and could see the sadness in them. He wasn't like the others with their strange looks. He dipped his hands in the blood and ran them down one of my arms, then the other, covering my skin in red. He put his blood-soaked hands on my neck, smearing it down over my breasts and then my stomach.

The circle's humming grew louder.

My eyes closed as I began to shake. *This can't be real. This can't be real.*

The humming stopped.

I opened my eyes and was back in the cave. Jason was holding my head to his chest, rocking me back and forth. The fabric of his shirt covered my face, and I breathed in and out deeply as I wove my fingers onto the back of his shirt, holding so tight that I felt the fabric begin to tear a bit.

I was back with my Jason. I was okay, or as okay as I could be after what I had just seen. And then the shock faded as a nervous fury gripped my body and the familiar heat coursed through me.

"It's okay, Maddy. It wasn't real. Whatever she did, it wasn't real," Jason assured me as I sat up, every muscle tensing as I tried to calm down, but it was no use.

I frantically wiped my face with the gloves. My breath was shaky and unsteady. I looked at my hands, turning them from the front to the back.

"She is fine. Now she knows," Sinder said.

Sinder's voice. But this time, she was right in front of me. Kaya and Sinder were arguing. It was as if they were swaying back and forth, but I couldn't tell if they really were or if my eye was jumping around.

My body felt like it was on fire, and I could not stop shaking.

"Maddy, it's okay," Jason soothed me, holding my hand in his hands.

I pulled my hand away quickly. Somehow, his touch made me uneasy now.

"There! She is just fine. I just felt that she should know the truth about what her future could hold," Sinder said to Kaya. "And now you can heal her. She will be fine."

"That is not a certain future, Sinder. You meant to hurt the girl. You toy too much with the hearts of others," Kaya said. Then she turned to me. "Are you all right, dear?"

But I didn't answer. I was trembling uncontrollably. The images of the dead. The blood, and the young man covering me with it. His touch. The man's stare. And the humming. All my muscles tensed, making it difficult to walk, but I forced my steps.

"Maddy?" Jason sounded apprehensive as I approached my aunts.

I reached behind me and flicked back the holder that kept my sword in its scabbard. With one fluid motion, I pulled the blade from my back and swung it with a grunt, hitting the back of Sinder's neck and slicing through to her throat. Blood sprayed my face, Kaya's, and the cave walls as Sinder's head fell at my feet.

Kaya screamed as she fell to ground, staring at her sister's decapitated body. She turned up her pale face to look at me. The kindness that she had once worn on her peculiar face vanished. She looked shocked, bewildered at my actions. I didn't need to look at Jason to know that he would have the same look.

I pointed the tip of my sword at her.

"If that is what magic is about, I want nothing to do with it or you. Never, ever come for me again, or I will do the same to you," I said as blood dripped from my chin.

Kaya shook her head slightly. "You were meant to be different," she whispered sadly.

"Madison?" Jason muttered.

I reluctantly turned to look back at him and adjusted my eye patch. Jason's mouth was open in shock, his eyes wide with terror and fear as he stared back at me. He started to say something, but I didn't want to know what it was. I walked past him, back toward the Jade Village.

"It was nice to meet you, Aunt Kaya. Tell my mother I said hello."

CHAPTER 24

The sun was brighter than I remembered it ever being when we reached the Jade Village. Jason and I walked in silence. We weren't strangers to silence. We were pretty comfortable sitting in silence most days, but this particular silence was somehow louder than any conversation we had ever had.

I had nothing to say. I felt nothing. I could only think about the image of Lacy and the people in the chairs and my blood-soaked feet. It replayed in my thoughts like a movie that I didn't want to watch.

At last, we reached Ara's sand-colored tent. I pulled back the cloth opening of the tent to walk in. It was empty. No Ren. No Ara.

I walked to the cot I had slept on and sat down. Taking a deep breath, I cradled my head in hands.

"Mads?" Jason sat next to me.

"I don't want to talk about it," I replied, not lifting my head. I still could not look at him. I still felt hot and my heart was racing faster.

"It's okay, Mads." He put his hand on my back.

I stood and backed away. "I don't deserve comfort, okay? I just need to find Ren. We need to get to the temple. Time is running out."

Jason stood slowly. His eyes brimmed with tears, and he was wringing his hands, something he only did when he was truly worried.

I did this. I made him feel like this.

Even though I felt bad that Jason was upset, I didn't feel guilt for what I did to Sinder. Not at all.

"Oh, hello," Ara said as she entered the tent. "I thought you had left for home."

"Where is Ren?" I asked.

"Madison, your face. Are you all right?" Ara asked, concerned, looking at me and then at Jason. Jason didn't respond. He just stared down at the sandy floor of the tent.

"The blood isn't mine. I'm fine."

Ara was silent for a moment, but I saw sorrow in her eyes as she looked at me. Not disappointment, but not something I wanted to dwell on.

"Oh. I see," she replied softly. "Come here, Madison." She held out her hand, but I didn't take it.

Jason moved next to the doorway of the tent and crossed his arms.

"Where is Ren?" I repeated, walking toward Ara.

"He went to ask others if the Magics have been freed," she replied.

"They weren't," Jason said.

I sighed. "It was all a lie. My aunt is still there, and I need to get there, like, now."

Ara grabbed a basin of water and sat it on the table next to me. "I see," she replied. I could tell she was putting the story together on her own, or at least parts of it. The sun beamed through the tent flap and it was as if the skin on her high cheekbones sparkled purple for a moment.

"Jason, what happened to her?" Ara asked as she grabbed a cloth, dipped it in the water, and started wiping my face with it. I pulled away when she put her hand on my chin.

"It's okay," Ara said softly. She wiped my face but didn't hold my chin this time. She wrung it out, and the basin of water turned pink.

"We ran into some Witches, but Maddy took care of it," Jason answered softly.

"I see. You are the messiest girl I have encountered in all my years, Madison. Just look at you," Ara said, shaking her head and examining my fingers. "I have another shirt that might fit you."

I nodded.

Ara looked from my good eye to the eye patch. "What have we done to you, Madison? Your heart is so heavy with dread."

I swallowed hard and looked away from her studying eyes.

Ara thankfully didn't press the matter. I didn't want to talk about it. Cutting Sinder's head off was rash, but really, it was her own fault. Or maybe it was the hot flash. Either way, I couldn't feel guilty about it.

"Let's get moving. We need to get to the temple," I stated. "Where can we find Ren?"

Before anyone could answer, I heard a voice outside the tent. "Madison!"

I jumped and so did Jason, startled by the sudden shout. *Ren.* I stood and walked out of the tent into the immense sunlight, following his voice. A blinding gleam shone from the water. I glanced back at the tent, but Jason wasn't following.

And then I saw him a few yards away. I didn't yell back as I watched him. Ren was breathing heavily, scanning the area for me. He held both daggers in his hands. Even at this distance, I could see his panic. He yelled my name again. But why did he look so worried?

Was Sinder right about him and his intentions? I needed to know.

"Ren," I called out without moving.

Ren spun quickly, and I could see the relief hit him when he saw me.

"Madison!" His heart was racing so loud I could hear it as he came close.

"I saw the blood in the cavern," Ren said breathlessly. "I thought something happened to you."

"No, it's okay now. I'm okay." I looked down at my feet.

Ren bent to meet my stare. My gaze followed him back up as he stood tall again. "You do not even believe that. What happened to you? There is blood all over you."

"It wasn't Lacy," I said, feeling a sudden seething anger toward him. "It was Sinder, and she told me what you did." I pushed my hands into his stomach and knocked him to the ground.

"Madison, what are you doing?" Ren stumbled backward in the sand.

"I told you I wanted the truth. You said you told me everything, but you didn't. Now, I need the truth. I want all of the truth."

Ren's confused expression turned serious. "Okay," he replied. "What do you want to know?"

"Did you use Witches to find me?"

Ren nodded. "Yes."

"You were going to kill me," I stated, seriously and even-toned.

"Yes." He ran his hand over his chin and rubbed the back of his neck. "But that was before all of this. I swear. After I found the ritual, I came to find you. I did not enter Greenrock with ill intentions."

I studied his face for a few moments.

Then I swallowed and looked away. "That is what they said, too."

"Whose blood is on your face?" Ren asked, wiping my eyebrow.

"The last person who lied to me."

"Madison, we are in this together now. You must understand that," Ren said, and set his hand on my face. I stared back into his eyes for a moment before turning my head sharply.

I took a step back. "Did you know that Sinder was pretending to be Lacy back on Greenrock Island?"

"Your cousin, the Witch? That was Sinder?" he said, genuinely surprised. "Did you know?"

"No."

"But she was telling the truth about the part where you wanted to kill me," I muttered.

"What?" Ren took a step closer to me.

"They lied about the Magics being freed and about my aunt. We have to go."

Ren nodded. "Here come Ara and Jason. Let's get some supplies, and we will go."

"Wait, Ren."

He stopped but didn't say anything as he stared back at me. I undid one of my lightning bolt earrings and took a step closer to him.

"What are you doing?" Ren asked. I grabbed the top of his shirt, just under his chin.

"This way, I will always know it's you and not a Witch. Just show me this, and I will show you the other half." I stuck the earring through the fabric of his shirt and secured it with the earring back. "That's how we will be sure."

Ren looked down at it and nodded. "Okay."

"Hey, guys." Jason stopped and stood next to me. He gave me a half smile.

Ara smiled sweetly at me and tilted her head to the side. "Jason told me what happened to you in the cavern. How are you?"

"It wasn't real, whatever she did to you," Jason reminded me.

"Wait, what happened in the cavern?" Ren asked.

"Look, I just want to go to the temple and set the Magics free. I want to get Aunt Ruth out safely," I said to Ara. "I don't want to talk about it."

Ara nodded, and the shells on her necklace chimed as she swung her hair back. "Let's go then. Ren, come and help me with the supplies."

Ren turned to look at me twice before slipping into the tent behind Ara.

"Maddy," Jason started. "I just—I—what happened to you?"

I chewed on my lip and didn't reply.

"Madison, you cut off someone's head!" Jason whispered, like someone might hear even though we were all alone. "I know she hurt you, but…wow."

"It needed to be done." I sighed.

"Kaya was kind to us. She would have helped you," he said.

"You don't know that. And Kaya is fine. If she wasn't able to heal Sinder, she would have been much angrier than that. You heard them. Sinder healed herself when my father cut off her head." I dropped my stare to the ground.

Jason stepped closer to me. "Just like you did."

"Just like I did."

He shook his head. "Madison, you are starting to scare me." And he turned to walk toward the tent.

"That makes two of us," I said softly to myself as I followed him.

CHAPTER 25

Ren walked alone ahead of us on the Temple Road. He had both daggers out and was scouting our path. We hadn't spoken a word since our talk on the beach, but Ara and Jason chatted behind me. It was late afternoon, so the sun wasn't as hot as we climbed the slight hill on the Temple Road, and the trees that lined the road on the left provided some shade. We were much more prepared on this leg of the journey. Ara had packed a satchel for each of us with food and water. I had a new scabbard with my sword firmly on my back instead of hitting my leg while I walked.

I reached into my satchel and began munching on one of the cookies that Ara had wrapped up. Since we had arrived in Everly, I hadn't had a normal meal, a normal shower...or a normal moment.

I couldn't shake that vision Sinder gave me or the feeling of rage that I felt afterward. And if I was being honest with myself, I hadn't really thought about whether Kaya could heal Sinder, but it hadn't stopped me from swinging my sword through Sinder's neck.

I opened a canteen that I had grabbed from the table at Ara's. I took a swig and began to cough. It wasn't water; it tasted like mouthwash and smelled like paint thinner. I coughed again. The stuff completely cleared my nasal passages.

"It is a touch early for the troll swill, Madison," Ara said behind me. I didn't turn around as she and Jason laughed.

I spit what I hadn't accidentally swallowed onto the sandy dirt path.

Ren slowed to walk next to me. He held out his canteen, and I hoped it was water. I smelled it before taking a drink.

"We will be at the temple before midday tomorrow," he said in a rather chipper tone.

I nodded.

"We will have to set up camp in a couple of hours and walk all morning tomorrow, but we will get there, Madison," he said.

I nodded.

"Madison, are you ever going to speak to me?" Ren asked, shifting the large sack he carried over his shoulder.

I adjusted the new black shirt Ara had given me to change into.

"So, whatever they told you, whatever they said to make you upset, trust that it is simply that—to upset you," he said, more harshly now. "You can trust me, Madison."

I kicked a rock as we continued to walk, and I adjusted the strap on the bag that hung from my shoulder. It wasn't lying properly because of the strap of my scabbard, and it pinched the skin at the crook of my neck.

"Hey, Madison." Ren stopped walking right in front of me.

I sighed. "What, Ren? What do you want from me?"

Ren sighed, too, setting his large bag on the ground in front of him. "I get that you are angry that I did not tell you about my first plan, but I have told you nothing but the truth now."

I did not answer him.

"Fine. Forget it." He clenched his jaw and reached into the bag. "Here, put this on and hand out the others." Ren shoved three dingy gray cloaks at me and slid his cloak over his head.

"Cloaks?" I looked mine over.

Ren nodded and adjusted his cloak. It looked a little short on him. He lifted the large hood over his head.

"Wolves in sheepskin," I said with a nervous smile, trying to break the tension that I had one hundred percent caused.

Ren nodded. "Wolves in sheepskin."

He took his canteen out of my hand and kept walking on the path to the temple. I stood there for a few moments until Ara bumped into me. She looped her arm around my elbow, and we walked with linked arms. Jason fell into step on the other side of me.

"Here you go." I handed the cloaks to Jason and Ara. They put them on quickly. I clutched mine to my chest as we started to walk again.

"Jay, about before…" I started, smiling at him. Ara trotted up to Ren, and the scabbard on her back bounced as she jogged.

"Jay, I am—"

"Mads, it's okay. I—"

"No, Jason!" I stopped walking. "Let me talk." I held his hand and squeezed my eyes shut. "Just…just let me tell you how I feel."

I felt a tug on my hand. I opened my eyes to see Jason fall to the ground, nearly pulling me down with him.

"What the hell? Jason, what are you doing?" I said, baffled, as I examined him. He didn't look injured or anything.

Jason lay on his back with his eyes closed. He dropped his hand from mine and put it on his chest. His tongue fell out the side of his mouth.

"You said you wanted to talk about your feelings! I just died of shock," Jason exclaimed, then let his tongue fall out the side of his mouth again.

"Shut it." I kicked his foot, making his boot flop up and then back down again.

"Must be all that troll swill, booze hound!" Jason widened his eyes, shook his finger up at me, and laughed.

I snickered. It felt good to laugh.

"Come on, get up, you loon. We need to keep moving," I said seriously, but still with a smile.

I looked up to see Ren trotting toward us, a concerned look on his face, but before I could tell them everything was fine, Jason pulled me down to the ground with a sharp yank at my hand. I fell on top of him and screamed as Jason locked his arms around me in a bear hug.

I pretended to struggle a bit, laughing and play-fighting him off, but then I stopped. I relaxed. I slid my arms around Jason and I simply hugged him. I rested my forehead on his cheek as our laughter ceased.

"I am sorry, Jason," I whispered.

"I know."

"I'm glad you're here with me."

"I know." Jason held me tighter. He took a long, slow breath. "She was showing you something, wasn't she? The future, right?" he asked softly.

I nodded my head against his collarbone.

"Bad?" He sounded worried.

I nodded again. "Real bad." It was so vivid, and when I closed my eyes for too long, I saw it all again. The vision. I shuddered.

"What is going on? Are you all right?" I heard Ren's voice above me, but I didn't look up.

I started to sit up when I heard the growling and rustling. The ground shook. My palm rested on the road, and tiny pebbles jumped and danced around it. "What the hell?"

Just as I lifted my head to assess the noise, a huge, hairy arm knocked Ren a few feet away, and he landed hard on his back.

"Ren!" Ara screamed.

I started to reach for my sword but was thwarted as two massive arms reached out and pulled me up off the ground. I flipped my head back in my struggle.

I began to kick my legs wildly as Jason climbed to his feet and pulled out his bat. Ara helped Ren to his feet. Ren shook his head, seeming a little dazed, but he quickly focused as our eyes met.

"Let her go!" I heard Jason yell.

I was being held around my waist with my back to the creature, my arms pinned to my sides by its incredibly muscular arms. The bag loosely hung on its back kept hitting my shins, making me wince. I hit it hard with my heels and swung my head back again, catching it in the chin. The creature groaned.

"No!" it grumbled in a loud, gravelly rumble. "No, garl!"

It was speaking?

It smelled like wet dog. Ren, Jason, and Ara charged the creature, each yelling. Ara did some acrobatic flips and jumped high, kicking the creature in the face. She moved quickly and elegantly, like a graceful ninja. She wasn't delicate, though. Her kick jarred the creature and it took a few steps back.

"Whoa," I murmured.

She flew through the air like a bird of prey, a combo of lethally precise energy and grace. She was striking the creature before it even knew she was there, while Ren kept its focus on him with his daggers and Jason hit it with his bat.

"Troll, I mean it—if you hurt a single hair on her head, I will rip your flesh from your bones!" Ren roared. He ducked the troll's fist once again.

"Let...her...go!" he grunted as he ducked and rolled away from the troll's swings. His cheeks were red, and his face shone with sweat.

"Troll!" Ren screamed.

But the troll bellowed loudly and caught both Ara and Ren with a low swing of its arm. They fell to the ground.

It turned toward Jason.

"Jason, run!" I yelled, muffled beneath the troll's shirt draped over my face.

Ara jumped onto the troll's back. It grunted loudly. It loosened its grip enough for me to pull my arms out and start hitting it.

Jason hit the troll in the legs with the bat, and the troll yelped in pain. Then it kicked its leg out, throwing Jason to the ground, knocking his bat from his hands.

"No!" I dug my fingernails into the sweaty, hairy skin of its armpit.

The troll grunted, picked up a boulder that was at least three feet wide, and hurled it through the air—right at Jason.

"Jason!" I screamed. He was reaching for his bat and did not see the rock flying at him. My entire body tensed.

Oh god...

But before the boulder could touch him, Ren dove onto Jason. The two slammed onto the ground, Ren covering Jason like a blanket.

"No!" I screamed. I crushed my knuckles into the troll's gut and bit its side as hard as I could.

Ren's screams cut through the air as the giant rock smashed onto his arm. Jason slid out from under Ren and tried to push the rock off as Ren moaned.

"Ren!" I punched the troll again. "Put me down!"

The troll winced. "No, garl!" it scolded me.

I bit it again, and grabbed a clump of its hair and pulled as hard as I could.

The troll groaned and dropped me to the ground. I rolled to the side and jumped to my feet.

"Ren!"

I bolted to Ren's side. He was writhing in pain, his forehead pressed to the ground. Ara and Jason were on one side of the boulder, ready to push it. They started, and Ren screamed again.

I put my hand on the back of his head. "It's okay, Ren."

Ren yelled in agony.

"Wait, we need to lift it up and off, don't slide it!" I commanded. I circled around Ren and wrapped my arms around the boulder to move it. Jason and Ara stood on the other sides and tried to lift with me.

"Run, garl!" The troll yelled. I looked up to catch a glimpse. It was standing a few yards away, looking incredibly confused.

Then it hit me. "Gullway?" I grunted as I struggled to lift the boulder.

Gullway nodded.

I lifted the boulder slightly but couldn't get my arms around it enough to move it. I screamed in frustration.

"Hold on, Ren," Jason yelled.

"Gullway!" I shouted. "Help me!"

I tried a different position to lift. "It's okay, Ren. It's going to be okay," I said, my voice strained. Ara looked panicked as she and Jason tried to help, but even with my strength, I couldn't get a good grip on it.

"Gullway, help me! Please!" I cried.

The mountain troll finally trotted over, meeting my eyes.

"Gullway!" I screamed desperately at him, tears streaming on my face as Ren continued to writhe in pain.

Gullway narrowed his large eyes and nodded. Jason and Ara moved away from the boulder as he bent down.

"Aye, garl," Gullway said. He lifted the boulder and easily tossed it into the trees with a booming crash.

Ren rolled onto his back. His blood-covered arm was shredded. A bone stuck out from the skin, and his face was pale, sweaty, and covered in sand. The rocks and sand of the road were soaked with blood. So much blood. Too much blood.

"Oh, stars, there is so much blood." I heard Ara say behind me.

I dropped to my knees, pressing on what looked like the source of most of the bleeding. My hands were shaking terribly.

"Perfect, Madison. Keep the pressure right there." Ara said.

"Do you want to do it?" I asked.

"No, your strength is needed here." Ara replied.

"Should I go get help?" Jason asked.

Ren grimaced.

"I've got you. I've got you," I whispered, and plucked my black gloves off with my teeth, then pulled my sword. The grip shone blue. The tingle in my hand wasn't transferring to Ren fast enough, and the blood circle grew larger.

"Just like in the cave. Remember, Ren? Remember the time in the cave?" I mumbled, shaking as I spoke.

Ara moved to Ren's side in the sand, facing me. "Is it working?" I asked.

"Not fast enough," Ara said. "Concentrate!"

"What?" I said, confused. "I'm trying!"

"The power comes from you. Concentrate," Ara instructed me. I squeezed the sword's grip tighter and pressed Ren's shredded arm firmly with my other hand.

"Come on, Ren," I whispered in his ear. Ren whimpered a bit.

I felt my arm tingle even more. Ren's skin began to fuse around the edges of his injury, but it was happening too slowly for how fast the blood was coming out of his mangled arm. The pulse of blood flowing from his artery continued. The bleeding wasn't slowing, and that was all that mattered now.

A thought struck me: I had been hurt when my magic healed us before!

"Gullway, put your hand here." I gestured to Ren's artery and the mountain troll obeyed by pushing Ara aside, slumping to his knees and dropping his sack to the ground. He pressed Ren's arm with his hand, keeping pressure on it. His hand wrapped around Ren's bicep with ease.

I sat back and quickly pulled the blade of my sword across my hand, cutting my palm, and then touched Ren's arm with my bloody hand. The blue of my grip glowed brightly under my other hand.

"It's working, Maddy," Jason said.

"The bleeding is stopping!" Ara exclaimed.

"It's working, Ren!" I leaned over his face, looking into his green eyes. He wasn't blinking.

"No!" Ara cried.

"Ren?" Jason rested a hand on his chest.

"No, Ren! No!" I buried my face into his neck and sobbed, not loosening my grip on him. I lifted my head to look at his face.

He was gone.

CHAPTER 26

No, no, no!

"Ren, please!" I pulled the sword across my palm again, cutting the freshly healed slice wide open. When I put my hand back on his arm, the blue light grew brighter again. "Please?"

I watched his eyes. Not blinking. No change. I pulled the blade over my palm and put it back on his arm a third time, not even feeling the pain anymore.

"Maddy, you have to stop," Jason begged me, crying. I ignored him.

"Ren," I managed to say. My voice broke. "I'm so sorry."

"Maddy." He gently laid a hand on my back. I shrugged his hand away and gripped Ren firmly with my cut hand, still holding my sword in the other.

Refusing to budge, I pressed my hand into Ren's arm.

"Ren," I whispered. "Please, Ren. I'm so sorry for before. I'm sorry that I got mad. I trust you, I do. It doesn't matter how you got me here. I'm here. I need to be here." My voice broke again as I began to sob. "So do you. Please, Ren."

Ara and Jason stood on either side of us. Gullway stayed hunched over on the ground next to me, his giant hand on Ren's arm. We didn't speak. The only sounds that filled the silence were our muffled sobs as we surrounded Ren's lifeless body. I laid my head on his chest.

"I'll do better, Ren," I said into the fabric of his shirt. "Please."

His chest moved. Startled, I sat up. "Ren?"

He blinked and took a deep breath.

"Ren!" I began to laugh and cry at the same time, somewhat hysterically. I hugged him tightly. His eyes were only partially open.

"Ren?!" Ara shrieked. She dropped to her knees above him and cradled his face in her hands, kissing his forehead.

Jason grabbed Ren's hand, still crying.

I can't believe it.

Ren looked at each of us, and a smile crept over his face as his eyes filled with tears.

"You're going to be okay, Ren," Jason said.

Ren nodded, looking at Jason and grinning widely before looking up at Ara, who was stroking his hair. And then his eyes stopped on me.

"Hi," I said softly, tilting my head to the side.

"Hello," Ren replied, still beaming.

Ren looked over at his injured arm as Gullway lifted his hand. Ren's artery had stopped gushing, most of the shreds of skin had healed, and the bone was no longer visible.

"Whoa!" Ren's eyes went wide when he realized the mountain troll was looming over him. Gullway jumped back and grunted a little.

"It's okay," I assured Ren. "He helped me move the boulder."

I looked Ren over. His face was still very pale and his eyes were still half closed, but he was alive. I put my hand on his chest and felt his heart beating strong.

Ren smirked.

"I have never been so happy to see that stupid smirk." I shook my head and smiled.

Ren smiled widely and let out a laugh. It was the happiest I had ever seen him.

"Jason, are you okay?" he asked, his voice raspy.

"Dude." Jason nodded. "You saved my life!"

"What just happened?" Ren narrowed his eyes, sounding woozy.

"I think you died." I tried to take a few deep breaths to calm down as I wiped my face with my arm. He was awake and talking, but his blood still covered the road beneath him.

"I am okay. It is okay," Ren said softly, still smiling. "Thank you. All of you." He beamed, but it was clear he wasn't at one hundred percent just yet.

Ren started to sit up.

"Wait," I said, lifting the blade of my sword to my palm again.

"Madison, what are you doing?" He grabbed my open hand.

"Healing myself was the only way to heal you too," I replied, pulling my hand back and cutting my palm. Everyone stood quietly as I laid my bloody hand on Ren's shoulder. I closed my eye and focused on Ren. I imagined his wounds healing and his energy coming back. My arm tingled. I exhaled loudly and opened my eye.

"Wow, Maddy, look at this," Jason said, pointing to Ren's wound. His arm wasn't even gashed anymore. It was continuing to mend and heal. My finger traced the longest of the raised pink scars.

I smiled. "It's healing." I followed Ren's eyes as they went to my ear. I grabbed the earring and smiled. "Still me."

He touched the little silver lightning bolt earring on the collar of his shirt. "Me, too," he replied.

"How do you feel, Ren?" Jason touched Ren's mended arm. "Can you move it?"

Ren looked over at his arm. He opened and shut his hand, then lifted the arm from the blood-soaked ground. Both Jason and Ren looked at me as I put the sword back in my scabbard. Jason's mouth hung open, but it still turned up in a smile. Ren grasped my hand and examined it. It had healed, too.

"Help me up." Ren lifted his good arm.

Jason braced his back as he sat up. "Careful," he said as Ren steadied himself. I felt a dull pain shoot up my arm, and then it went away when Ren stopped moving his arm.

"Wait, don't move your arm. Let it rest," I said, startled. I rubbed my own arm.

"You okay?" Jason narrowed his eyes.

"Yeah. Sympathy pains." I snickered, standing up, and wiped my face. "Um, Ren...before, when you were out, I said some things that I should have told you when you were awake."

"I heard you. I heard what you said," he whispered. I turned away.

"Are you okay?" I asked Ara, who had still not said a word.

"Thank you, Madison," Ara said. "That was amazing."

I half smiled. It *was* kind of amazing.

"Can you stand?" I asked Ren. He nodded, so I reached down and lifted him with his good arm. Jason stood, too.

Ren faltered a bit. "Ahh!" he yelped.

I put a hand on his chest and his back. He toddled forward. "Whoa, take it easy. You okay?"

"Yeah, I think so." He sighed, looking at Gullway, who was still standing near us. "Hey, troll?"

"That's Gullway," I said. Gullway grunted at Ren.

Ren looked at me. "The one from the hilltop?"

"Yeah."

Ren nodded. "I see. You set him free. That explains it." He looked back at Gullway. "Gullway, you thought she was in danger, which is why you grabbed her, right?" Ren asked him. "You thought we were the Cloaked and she was in danger."

Gullway nodded.

191

"She set you free, so you tried to protect her?" Ren asked.

Again, Gullway nodded.

"Garl save Gullway. Gullway hers," the troll said in his low, grumbly voice.

Ren nodded. "Then you will come with us."

"Ren, no! He just tried to kill you guys!" I argued.

"He thought he was protecting you, Madison. He is in your service now. That is how the troll code works. You saved him. Now he owes you a life debt," Ren explained.

I chewed my lip, shaking my head. "Technically, he owes me two life debts," I said with authority. "He killed you."

"He will protect you. We need him. Look at how much damage he can inflict."

"Ren is right, Madison." Ara stepped forward. "He will be very helpful to us."

Gullway nodded.

"And no boulders. Got that, Gullway?" Jason pointed his index finger at Gullway.

"Aye," Gullway nodded again.

A mountain troll on our side certainly wouldn't hurt, I hoped. I kept my arm around Ren's waist.

I studied Gullway again. "Aye. Gullway, you can join us, but I am watching you."

Gullway nodded.

"Gullway, can you take my bag?" I lifted it from my shoulder and held out the small satchel. He took it.

"Let's keep moving. The sun will be down soon," I stated. Ren and I pivoted on the path to continue on the Temple Road.

Ren walked pretty well, considering he had just died and come back to life, but he still seemed to be straining as Ara and Jason walked ahead.

"Do you want Gullway to carry you?" I asked as we took a few steps. Ren had his arm around my shoulders. I held his hand with mine and kept my other arm around his waist.

"No, I am okay," Ren said, and shifted his weight, leaning on me less as we walked. "To the temple?"

"To the temple," I agreed.

CHAPTER 27

We walked relatively quietly on the Temple Road for the next hour or so. It wasn't really a road; it was a dirt path about as wide as a compact car. My calves started to ache even though the road's upward slope was gradual.

The forest to the left of the Temple Road was denser than the wooded area near the portal, and the trees were much smaller here. Their trunks were thinner and their bark was white, but they were still massively tall. Their roots rose up past the dirt and lay twisted on top of the ground.

To my right, I could hear the crashing of the sea against the rocks. There was a steep drop-off to the sea below, making me stay as far left as I could on the path. I took a deep breath and the air smelled like Greenrock. That salty smell gave me a certain comfort I hadn't expected.

Ren was walking on his own now, but he stayed by my side after two more healing sessions with my cut hand and my sword. Even though he reassured me he was okay, I watched him out of the corner of my good eye.

Jason and Ara walked in front of us. Gullway walked behind me. I could hear his breathing getting heavier as we continued.

"You okay back there, Gullway?" I said aloud. He just grunted back.

I started to feel tired, too.

Ren looked over at me, and our eyes met.

"Doing okay?" I asked.

He nodded.

We all had the gray cloaks on now, me included. The material was itchy and mine smelled worse than me after a boxing class at Ruth's Gym, but it was a necessary evil. If we wanted to get into the temple undetected, we needed to play the part. And having a troll with us only made it more believable.

Just then, Ara stopped and raised her hand. We all came to a stop.

"What is it?" I asked.

"Shh," Ren whispered.

I turned, canvasing the area. The sounds around us were the same as they had been for the entire walk. The trees rustled in the breeze. The ocean gently roared as the water crashed against the shoreline. I opened my mouth to question Ara again, and then I heard it: a gentle rumbling sound.

"To the trees!" Ara pointed at the wooded area to our left. Jason, Ara, Ren, and I ran into it.

"What is it?" I asked Ren as we ran together, farther into the thick of the trees. Gullway stomped behind me.

"Someone is coming. We need to get off the path," Ren answered.

"Come on, Gullway!" I urged him as I waved him along. He was panting loudly. "Gullway, are you okay?"

The troll nodded. His face was wet with sweat, as was his shirt.

Ara pulled Jason to the ground and they laid flat on their stomachs.

"Get down!" Ren insisted. He rested his head on the ground next to Jason. I couldn't tell if he was hiding or just exhausted.

I stood until Gullway reached me. Then I lay on the ground next to Ren and watched the road. We were far enough back from the path and behind some brush; hopefully, we would not be seen. The same couldn't be said for the giant mountain troll with our group.

"Down, Gullway!" I instructed him.

He crashed to the ground, falling forward like a giant tree. I rolled to the side as he landed on his stomach between Ren and me. Then Gullway farted. Long and loud.

Jason snorted and started laughing.

"Shh!" Ren insisted, although he had started to laugh, too.

I clamped my hand over my mouth and buried my face into the ground to suppress my laughter.

"What? Are you all children?" Ara said to Ren, Jason, and me, but it only made us laugh harder.

"Sorry, but are farts not funny in Everly, like they are in our world?" Jason asked, laughing.

The noise from the road grew louder. I regained my composure, looked up at the path, and saw about a half dozen of the Cloaked. A horse was pulling a large wooden carriage that was painted blue. It reminded me of those old-timey carriages you see in western movies.

The carriage had large, open windows, allowing me to see inside. The passengers were also wearing cloaks, but they were a deep blue color, and their hoods were down.

"More Magics," I heard Ren whisper.

"Headed to the temple," Ara chimed in.

I lifted my head to get a better look. The passengers on one side of the carriage had bags on their heads, just like Sinder did before I rescued her. I moved a branch over to peek at the driver. He was dressed nicer than the other Cloaked we had encountered. He wasn't even looking around as the carriage passed us; his face remained forward, and he looked almost bored.

"Aren't they worried that someone will attack them?" I asked. "Don't the other Magics fight back? That guy wasn't even checking for danger."

The cart continued up the slope and soon was out of sight.

"Doubtful," Ren replied. "The Cloaked haven't been opposed. They are too feared."

Ren sat up. I stood and extended a hand to help him up, then brushed the dirt and leaves from my shirt and pants. Jason and Ara walked over to us.

Gullway hadn't moved. I nudged him with my foot.

"Gullway?"

Nothing.

I laid my hand on his back and rocked him a little. He let out a rattling snore.

"He's asleep." Ara laughed.

"Couldn't you have found a fully functional mountain troll to put in your debt, Maddy?" Jason snickered. "You know, maybe one that doesn't try to kill us, fart, and then pass out?"

We all laughed.

"The sun is going down. I guess we set up camp for the night and head to the temple at dawn," I said, looking at Ren and Ara. "This area is pretty clear."

There weren't many bushes, and the trees were spread a little farther apart right here but still dense enough that we wouldn't be visible from the Temple Road. It was an ideal spot for resting. Ren set his stuff down and slumped to the ground against a tree.

Ara sighed. "Truly. It is best to travel by the light of day. I guess this spot is as good as any."

I nodded. "Gullway thinks so."

"Don't have to tell me twice." Jason dropped his bag on the ground and plopped down next to Ren. "Hills are the worst."

"You should relax, Madison. Tomorrow's tasks will not fall lightly on you," Ara said. I turned to face her, and I smiled when I saw that she was holding a sword smaller than mine. She twirled it in her hand, showing off her skill.

"Cool sword."

"Thanks." She slid it in her scabbard and pulled her long, silky hair into a ponytail. Her dress fluttered in the wind, and her skin shimmered in the glinting sunlight.

I looked down at my own clothes. Unlike Ara, I was disgusting. My arms were splattered with dried blood, and my black shirt was damp with sweat. To top it off, my seashell eye patch kept slipping down my face, making it a constant annoyance. I groaned as I tried to get it to sit right on the back of my head.

"Madison, if you braid the string into your hair, it won't move," Ara said. "May I?"

"Sure." I nodded and turned around.

Ara made quick work of my hair, pulling my ponytail out and combing through my tangled knots with her fingers. I kept my head straight, staring at the peeling white bark of the trees in front of me.

"Oh, cool," Jason said behind me. "What kind of braid is that?"

"Fishtail," Ara replied.

"A half-Mermaid is giving me a fishtail braid." I sighed. "That's kind of awesome."

"There. Now your string will stay put," Ara said cheerfully. I reached back and ran my hand over the thin plaits of the braid.

"Thanks." I smiled. "I don't think my hair has ever been braided like this before. Super cool."

"Thank you. My mother taught me."

I felt a little twinge of jealousy but forced a smile. "That's really nice."

"That's cool," Jason said, crossing his legs and leaning against a tree. "Is that a Mermaid thing?"

"Mermaids don't have much need for hairstyling, but my mother loved to braid and tie knots. Her family made ropes and nets for fishing in the Jade Village," Ara said.

"Aww, is that how your parents met? Fishing?" Jason asked as the wind picked up again, making the leaves roar as they rustled above us.

Ara nodded. "Truly. Now, come help me gather some sticks, Jason. The sun is setting and we will need a fire."

Jason groaned and climbed to his feet, following Ara around the little clearing that we occupied. They walked around Gullway, who still hadn't budged.

"How do you feel?" I stood in front of Ren and tapped his foot with my own.

He rubbed his hand through his hair. His emerald eyes were bloodshot, and his eyelids drooped. "I have been better. But then again, that is the first time I have ever died and been brought back to life, so maybe this is how you are supposed to feel." He looked up at me and smiled.

"Do you want me to heal you again?" I asked, reaching back to grab my sword.

"No, no." Ren held his hand up. "No, you have done enough."

I half smiled. "Okay."

Ren dropped his head back against the tree. "You look concerned."

"Yeah. Just thinking about Lacy." I sighed. "I know she must be a worried mess in Greenrock."

"You will see her again. I did not realize that it was not her back at your house. I am relieved, though," Ren said.

"Relieved?"

"Yes. I really disliked Lacy when I met her in Greenrock. But it was not her. It was Sinder." Ren looked away as he spoke.

"I hate Sinder." I clenched my jaw.

Ren leaned back, looking deep in thought. "Me, too."

"Don't worry. She got what was coming to her," Jason chimed in as he and Ara walked past us, holding a few sticks of varying sizes.

"How so?" Ara asked, clearly intrigued.

"Jason, wait," I cautioned.

"Maddy took her head off in the cave. Literally," Jason replied absently, reaching down to pick up a stick.

I winced and looked down at the ground, not wanting to see Ren's or Ara's reaction.

"The blood. The blood that was covering you before." Ara stopped. "Was that Sinder's?"

"I didn't touch her hands. She can heal. We just needed to get away, and she messed with my mind," I said, louder than I intended to. "I had to. She was in my head."

"Oh, yeah, no, Mads!" Jason spun around. "I didn't mean it like that."

"I am sure you did what you had to do, Madison," Ren said.

I smiled at him gratefully. Ara was already looking at me when I turned around. She dropped her sticks into a pile near the middle of the clearing, away from the bushes and trees.

"I wish you had taken her hands off, too," Ara asserted with an icy stare.

I didn't respond, not at all sure what to say. Ara stayed there, just staring at me. Her usual smile was replaced with a scowl.

"Uh, Ara," Jason stammered, walking to her. "Can you braid my hair, too?"

Ara looked away from me and nodded.

"Make me look like Katniss," Jason said, closing his eyes as Ara ran her fingers through his hair to begin braiding it.

I shook my head and turned back around to face Ren.

"Don't mind her. She and Sinder have a past," Ren whispered. "How are you?" he asked softly, shifting around to get comfortable.

I raised an eyebrow. "I have no idea." I sank to the ground next to Ren. My legs tingled, and I realized how tired they really were.

"We will get Ruth back, Madison. And we will set the Magics free. My father would be very proud if he could see what we are planning to do."

I smiled uncomfortably. "Your father."

"Hey, it was not you. You know that. Everything that happened with my parents—that was not you," Ren reassured me.

I sighed. "I would hate you. If it were me, I mean. I wouldn't be able to help myself," I replied, not looking at him. "How can you forgive me so easily?"

"I guess we just come from different worlds," he answered and chuckled.

"Oh my god, Ren Raker!" I laughed. "Did you just attempt humor?"

He smiled widely. "The key word is *attempt*, I suppose."

I laughed again as my stomach growled. "Any chance they will feed us some real food at the temple before they try to kill us all?"

"No, it is unlikely," Ren said, smiling.

Jason and Ara returned to where we sat against the white trees. Jason slumped down on the ground. His hair was in three French braids running down the back of his head and then all tied together at the nape of his neck.

He put his hand on my knee.

"Madison, you are hungry," Ara said. It was more of a statement than a question, but I nodded anyway.

"Like the wolf," I agreed.

Jason shot his arm up. "Jason is hungry, too!"

Ara turned. "Gullway," she said rather loudly. "Gullway!"

"Gullway!" Ara yelled again.

This time the troll woke. He rolled on his back and grunted.

"Gullway, are you hungry?" Ara asked.

At that, he sat up and yawned. "Eaaaat."

Ara walked over to where he sat. "Gullway, I will be needing your help," she said slowly to our new troll companion.

Gullway nodded.

Ara stood up and placed her hands on his shoulders. Gullway gazed up at her with a gaping smile.

"Follow me, Gullway."

The two of them walked out of the wooded cover. I stood to watch them. As Ara walked, she unwrapped the chiffon-like fabric that she had wrapped around herself, set it on the ground, and continued, naked, out of the forest.

"Where is she going?" I asked.

Ara jumped onto Gullway's back as they crossed the path to the cliff's edge that overlooked the water below. I squinted in the dimming sunlight and could only see their silhouettes. Ara climbed and stood up on Gullway's shoulders. I gulped as she sprang from his back, and I heard her splash into the water below. Then Gullway walked to the edge and climbed down to follow her.

"Whoa!" I gasped.

"Do not worry. Ara is an amazing swimmer. She will come back with fish, no doubt. We had better start a fire," Ren said as he started to get up.

"I got this, pal. Rest up." Jason stood quickly. "Want to help, Mads?"

I nodded with a smile.

Jason and I walked over to the edge of our little area and started collecting more sticks and twigs. He began handing them to me, and I cradled them in a stack.

"How you doing, Maddy?" Jason asked.

"I honestly don't even know anymore. This has been such a frickin' crapstorm," I said. "Nothing has been going our way. I'm just trying to keep it together."

Jason plopped another branch in my arms and stopped to look at me. "Nobody could handle this as well as you, Maddy. You're stronger than you give yourself credit for. You're doing great."

"I have no clue what I'm doing, actually. A week ago, my biggest issues were which show I was going to start binge watching this summer and how much I hated running track. And now...now I find out my real dad is the tyrannical Strongblood leader of the Ember Isle, which is at war with the Magics formerly led by my Witch of a mother—who is missing, by the way. Oh! And my aunt that I used to complain about is actually my good aunt but she's missing and my cousin actually *wasn't* in cahoots with my estranged evil father who plans to kill all the magical folk in what is actually my native land that I am the heir to. That was just something cooked up by my evil aunt, who I beheaded in a cave," I said in one breath.

"Well...yeah. That too." Jason shrugged.

I sighed. "Do we have enough sticks?" I asked, looking down at the cluster in my arms.

Jason eyed the pile. "Yeah, should be. Now it's time to see if I can start a fire." He clapped his hands and rubbed them together.

I dropped the wood in the pile that Ara and Jason had started. Ren was already there, on his knees, digging a hole in the ground. He started arranging the sticks in just the right way.

"All right, now, lighting it might be the tricky part, but I think I can do it," Jason said with enthusiasm. "We better get started. It's getting pretty dark out here."

Ren looked at Jason, pulled something out of a pocket, and tossed it to him.

A lighter.

"Cheater," Jason said under his breath. He bent and ignited some dried leaves, and the fire started immediately.

We all sat down around the fire and silently watched it spread, crackling, over the sticks. As I stared at the longest stick, an ember landed on it. It started to glow, followed by an orange flame. The flame soon climbed the stick, leaving nothing but blackness in its wake.

My mind wandered to the very spot that I had been avoiding: my parents. I had a father and a mother. And I had spent countless hours of my childhood dreaming that this was true. So many daydreams of the perfect family that I wanted so badly.

I missed the versions of my parents who existed in my mind. I had held onto them for so long, it felt wrong to replace them with the actual people.

My heart beat faster. *Did my mother send me away? Did she send me away with Aunt Ruth to live in another dimension?* I searched my mind desperately for any memory of a woman coming to visit—someone that Ruth called a family friend, or something like that. But my racing mind was searching for something that didn't exist. My mother had never come for me.

I clenched my jaw as I thought about my real father. Not the baseball team coach and grill master who I had imagined in my mind. Nope. My dad was a madman, hell-bent on killing the Magics.

I thought of him hurting Ruth. Sinder. The Magics.

Me?

How could my father be a monster? I sighed. *He can't be.*

What if everyone's wrong? Or maybe they're lying to me? I balled my fists. *Why would they lie? Why?*

"Oh, wow," Jason said, breaking my trance. "Maddy!" He shook my shoulder.

I blinked rapidly as the flames in front of me flared up. My skin felt prickly. The fire had swelled up so high, it was taller than a mountain troll, and it licked at the lower-hanging branches above us.

"Back up, Madison. You have to back up," I heard Ren call to me.

"I am not..." And that's when I realized. "Wait...is it me? I'm doing that?"

"It's getting too high!" Jason yelled.

Oh god.

I closed my eyes and took a deep, calming breath. I cracked open my good eye. The fire had gone down a little, but not to the manageable level it had been.

"Grab a cloak!" I heard Ren yell.

I stepped around the fire to see them scrambling. Ren threw a cloak onto the fire to smother it. Flames shot up through the fabric as holes burned into it immediately.

"No, wait," I said frantically, shifting my stare to the flames that danced in front of me.

Focus, Madison, I could almost hear Aunt Ruth saying.

I held my hands out, palms down, and imagined the flames lowering and calming. I inhaled and exhaled slowly and thought of Aunt Ruth. I pictured her standing in front of me, going over that stupid breathing technique that she made me do for relaxation at the gym. Breathing in and out slowly.

Calmly and slowly.

I opened my eye to see that the fire had died down to a mini version of the threatening campfire it had been. And standing there with their mouths open were Ren and Jason.

"Well…that's new," Jason stammered.

And I grinned widely back at them.

CHAPTER 28

"Maddy, how on...how did you do that? You just controlled fire!" Jason yelped as he and Ren rushed over to me.

"Are you okay?" Ren asked, looking me over.

I met Ren's concerned stare. "I'm fine. I feel great, actually." I smiled, feeling exhilarated.

"*Fire*, Maddy! How did you do that?" Jason pressed.

"I don't know. I was staring at the fire and I started to think about—I started to get upset, and then the flames just grew," I explained.

"That is amazing. It must be the Witch thing!" Jason exclaimed.

"How did you get it to go down again?" Ren asked.

They stood around me, shocked and excited.

"I cleared my mind and did some of those dumbass breathing techniques that Aunt Ruth used to make me do. She always said that it was important to learn how to calm myself." I smirked, remembering how insistent she was about it all.

"Huh. Do you think she knew?" Jason asked softly.

I looked back to the fire.

"I don't know," I muttered.

Jason shook his head. "Amazing! My best friend controls fire. Just amazing."

"Let's just get you away from the fire, to be on the safe side, Madison." Ren grabbed my elbow walked me into the trees. "Jason, can you mind the fire?"

"Yep."

I turned back to look at Jason, who promptly waved me away with a wide grin on his face. I winked at him, then realized I had winked with the eye that was covered with the shell patch. *Nice going, Madison.*

I followed Ren as we wove through some trees. Lucky for us, the moon was near full and bright, making the forest easy to navigate. Ren stopped at a small clearing and turned to face me.

"That's better," Ren said warmly. "Do you feel calmer now?"

I nodded.

Sinder and Kaya were wrong about him. They had to be. They just shared the same view of him as every other bitter Everlian.

"That was pretty cool, but next time, try not to burn the forest down." Ren smirked. "You had me worried."

"Don't worry about me, Ren," I replied. "I won't let you down. I will get to that temple to do the ritual and set the Magics free and get Ruth out. I won't let anything get in the way."

He almost grimaced at my comment. He didn't speak, but I could see that he was troubled as he scrunched his eyebrows in thought.

"Madison, you mean more than just the ritual. The ritual is important, yes, but so are you," he said.

"Ren?" I asked, looking into his eyes. "I'm not good at this stuff."

Ren tilted his head to the side. "What stuff?"

"People." I shook my head and laughed nervously. "I do—what I mean to say is, um…" I stopped and chewed on my lip.

Ren took a step back and nodded. "I am not very good with people either."

"It's just, I don't have many friends, and now I…" I growled in frustration at myself. "I'm really glad you aren't dead."

Ren grinned, clearly amused by my flustered state.

"I mean—never mind." I smacked my forehead with my palm.

Ren leaned forward. "Thank you, again."

"Oh, yes. Um, for what?" I asked, feeling bumbling and awkward.

"For saving my life. You are pretty amazing," Ren said. He pointed to my earring pinned into his shirt and smiled. "Don't worry. It's still me. That shouldn't have been the first time I thanked you."

I laughed nervously. "You're welcome."

"Here." Ren reached into his pocket, pulled out a canvas-wrapped book, and handed it to me.

His journal.

I took the small hardcover book and flipped it open. "What is this?" I asked, pretending I hadn't already seen it. This time, the fake book jacket was gone.

"It has the ritual in it. In case we are separated at the temple. It is on the first page."

I nodded. "Thank you for this. And thank you for having faith in me." I paused, then went on. "And for not killing me like you had planned. Although you might have regretted that one a time or two on this trip." I smiled at him.

"'I have found out that there ain't no surer way to find out whether you like people or you hate them than to travel with them.'" Ren winked at me.

"Oh yeah?" I raised my eyebrows.

"Mark Twain wrote that." Ren gave me a proud nod. "In the book *Tom Sawyer Abroad.*"

"I guess I should give that a read." I smiled back.

"Yes, you should. I picked it up the last time I stopped into your world," Ren said, not meeting my eyes at first. "I can lend it to you when this is over, if you would like?"

"Let's just focus on getting to the temple and getting out alive," I said. "Then we will talk books."

"Maddy! Ren!" I heard Jason call, interrupting us. "Come on."

Ren and I made our way back just as Ara and Gullway approached. Ara wrapped her dress around herself as she walked. Gullway carried a cluster of fish.

"Thank you, Gullway. I can take those now." Ara reached her hand out.

"Gullway cook."

"You want to cook?" Ara raised her eyebrows. "Gullway, that would be lovely. Thank you. I have a knife in my bag if you'd like to use that."

Gullway shook his head and pointed at the burlap bag the size of a potato sack that he had been carrying. Ara took her seat by the fire as we all turned to watch Gullway.

Needing the light of our fire, Gullway picked up a small boulder and moved it over by us. Out of the corner of my good eye, I saw the group collectively tense at the sight of Gullway with a boulder, and I smiled.

To my surprise, Gullway pulled a pot and a handful of vegetables out of his bag. He cleared his throat as he unrolled a cloth on top of the boulder. The cloth contained several small paring knives. He then pulled out what looked like a small grate with legs, and he placed it over the fire.

He moved with authority, unlike the clumsy oaf of a troll that I'd had him pegged for. He was skilled and worked diligently.

Without a word, he began preparing the fish, slicing the meat into pieces and putting them into the pot. Gullway's large hands moved swiftly as he sliced the vegetables and added them to the pot with some water. He stirred his concoction with a wooden spoon, and he threw in pinches of what looked like herbs.

"Wow, Gullway," I said, breaking the silence.

"Dude, you just made a fish stew in like ten minutes. That was cooking show-level stuff. You are, like, the Gordon Ramsay of trolls, Gullway," Jason said, also impressed.

Gullway leaned over and set the pot on the metal grate, then laid a few pieces of the fish right on the metal. The fish cooked quickly, and the smell made my mouth water.

"We should go over the plan," Ara announced.

Ren nodded. "Well, we will get to the temple gates and pretend that Jason is a Magic and we are the Cloaked bringing him in."

"Pardon?" Jason scoffed. "Why am I the decoy Magic?"

"Because you will be able to get out of the courtyard, being that you are non-Magic." Ren pointed at Jason. "Annnnnd...because I used your cloak to get the fire under control."

"Right." Jason gave a defeated sigh and frowned.

"And what about my—my father?" I asked. "Will I..."

"No, Madison. You will not be able to see him. If he knows you are there, your safety will be comprised. He cannot know who you are. It is too dangerous," Ren answered, knowing what I was about to ask.

I crossed my arms and sniffed. "Then what happens?" I narrowed my eyes.

"Well, according to my father's research, you will go to the center of the courtyard and do the ritual. That will end the prison spell keeping the Magics there, and we will be able to escape," Ren said looking at me.

"I will call on the fae to help get everyone out. The Magics may be weak if they haven't been fed for days," Ara added.

I nodded.

"Madison, the spell on the courtyard may weaken you, but the spell should not affect me or Jason, so we will help you," Ren continued.

"But aren't you a Magic?" Jason asked.

"No. I am a Porter. My father was a Strongblood, and the Porter curse does not make me a true Magic. It just makes me less of an Everlian."

I frowned. "That isn't true."

"Could one of you do the spell, then?" Ara inquired.

Ren met my gaze. "It must be Madison."

"And you are sure that all this will work the way you have planned? Truly?" Ara asked Ren. "And that the ritual will work with Madison's blood?"

"It was my father's research. I do not doubt him," Ren replied confidently.

I leaned over. "Then neither do we."

I flipped open the book as Gullway handed me a wooden cup filled with stew. He looked so proud. I thanked him and started eating. The vegetables and fish in the stew were delicious. The carrot-looking pieces were still a little crunchy, and the broth warmed my throat. I tipped up the cup and poured more into my mouth, then went back to looking through the little book in my lap.

The fire crackled, and Gullway clanked around, passing out full cups to Ara, Jason, and Ren.

"Gullway, this is marvelous!" Jason said, his mouth full of stew.

Gullway's eyes were brimming with pride, and he almost looked surprised at such praise.

"Thank you, Gullway. We all really needed that," I said to him. Gullway nodded and took away my empty cup. He then poured his own cup, stood, and left the light of the campfire and our circle.

I looked around at Jason, Ara, and Ren. They didn't seem to notice Gullway walk over to a fallen tree trunk and sit down. He faced away from our group and began to drink the stew out of the cup. I watched him as he ate.

Jason turned to Ara. "But really, Ara, where did you learn to fight the way you do? You were like this tiny little crazy ninja lady!"

"One does not live in Everly and not learn to fight!" she responded. "I watch over a faction of the fae. Each relies on me to protect them and their way of life. It takes more than a tender word to do so."

"Especially if you are a Magic. The temple guard will kill you with ease if you cannot fight," Ren added.

"I can't even aim an arrow," Jason said glumly.

Ara jumped to her feet and took a fighting stance. "On your feet, Otherworlder! I will teach you!"

I looked back over to Gullway. He was still perched on the log. I stood, walked over to him, and laid my hand on his shoulder. He jumped at my touch.

Gullway fell to the ground on his knees and bowed his head, dropping the cup on the dirt.

"Oh, no, Gullway, I am so sorry." I reached down and picked up the now-empty cup. "I will go get you some more."

The troll looked up at me and stared for a moment.

"What is it, Gullway? Are you okay?"

His eyes searched my face. He rubbed his chin, rumpling the coarse red hairs that framed his face.

"Garl give Gullway food?" Gullway leaned closer to me, as if asking me a secret question.

"Yeah, of course I will, Gullway," I answered quickly, confused by his reaction.

"Here, let me." Ren was at my side now. He reached down and took the cup from my hand. Ren leaned close to me and whispered, "Trolls do not get served food. They must eat the scraps of a meal when they are in the service of the Cloaked."

I felt my cheeks warm with anger and took a step closer to our giant companion. "Gullway, listen to me. You are not in my service. You are one of us. Do you understand? If you fight beside us, it is because you want to. You are not a servant. You are my equal. Please, come and eat with us." I gestured to the circle around the campfire.

The giant mountain troll looked to Ren and then back to me. Gullway's bottom lip trembled, and his eyes filled with tears as he climbed to his feet.

Gullway laid his hands over his heart and bowed his head.

"*Molad an Banron,*" Gullway said, and looked back up at me. I bowed my head back. Gullway started back toward the fire, and Ren and I followed behind him.

"What did he say?" I asked.

"*Molad an Banron?* It is troll. It means 'Praise the queen,'" Ren said softly.

My mouth dropped open slightly. "Praise the queen?"

Ren winked at me. "Trolls may not say much, but they hear it all. And they understand it all. He knows who you are."

I watched as Gullway rejoined the group.

"But I am not a queen," I said under my breath.

"Yet." Ren raised his eyebrows and walked toward the fire to rejoin our small band of companions. He took a seat by the fire as Ara and Jason continued to spar.

"Okay, I give. Ara, you are the baddest babe in Everly. I need to sit down. I'm starting to see spots." Jason laughed.

I watched them all for a second. The stakes were so high, and we all knew it. But we didn't talk about it.

"Let's get some sleep, guys. Big day tomorrow," Jason said.

He was like our little troop leader all of a sudden.

"You need to get some rest, Mads." Jason unrolled a cloak so that it was flat on the ground. "We'll have to share."

"Sorry," Ren said as he laid his cloak out next to Jason's and, well, mine.

Sleep. Sleep sounds good. I laid down on the cloak and stretched out before rolling on my side as Jason curled up close next to me.

"Good night, Mads," he said, putting his arm around me.

"Good night, Jay." I settled into him, little spoon to his big spoon. I tucked the small book under my side.

"I will take first watch," Ara said, standing and walking out toward the Temple Road.

Ren lay down on his cloak and faced me and Jason. I watched him settle onto the ground. I could see the flicker of fire reflecting in his eyes and couldn't help but smile at him.

"Good night, Ren."

"Good night, Maddy," Ren said with his eyes closed.

He called me Maddy, and this time I didn't correct him.

CHAPTER 29

Jason fell asleep quickly, as did Ren. Ara was on the far side of our little circle, pacing back and forth. I watched Ara's silhouette as she navigated gracefully through the trees. She moved like a long-limbed fairy, almost like she was gliding over the brush.

I wished I had gotten to know her better. Her story was a curious one. Her dad was a Merman and she was now an Empress of the Fae, and she was a strong, skilled fighter.

The only sounds now were the crackle of the fire and the almost melodic sound of Gullway snoring. He had plopped down on the other side of Jason, no cloak or anything, and slept hard—like he was in a luxury bed at a fancy hotel.

I rested my cheek on my arm and closed my eye. The moment I did, I saw it again: the dead bodies. The blood. My god, the blood. I opened my eye quickly.

Well, that solved that. I guessed I wouldn't be sleeping...ever again. Could that vision really be my future? Or was Sinder was just messing with my mind?

Either way, I couldn't wipe the vision from my imagination long enough to rest. I rubbed my good eye with my the back of my hand. The leather fingerless gloves made a squishy sound against my eyelid, which made me smile. It was a sound that only Jason would find as amusing as I did.

Carefully, I lifted Jason's arm off of me and he rolled onto his back, half off of the cloak. Sitting up, I picked up the little book and flipped it open. The moon was bright enough that I could make out the words if I squinted hard enough at the yellowing pages.

Ren stirred. He looked so vulnerable when he slept. The hardness in his eyes was gone, and his mouth was in a slight pout, like a small child. He had a leaf in his hair. I reached over and gently pulled it out.

Ren's eyes flew open.

"What? What is it?" He looked around frantically.

"Nothing. Sorry. I, uh—you had a leaf."

Ren sat up and shook out his hair with his hand. "Did you sleep?" he whispered.

I nodded, even though I hadn't. "How do you feel?" I whispered back.

He let out a long sigh. "Like I died today." Ren pulled his legs up and rested his arms on his knees.

I bounced my legs and clicked my teeth together. I felt overly energized for someone running on a bucket of crazy and no sleep.

Ren was still looking at me. There was something unfamiliar about the way he looked at me. Like Jason looked at Caleb, but not exactly.

I smiled and stood. "Do you want to take a walk with me?" I asked.

Ren grabbed my outstretched hand. I pulled him up to his feet, and he let out a little grumble. I started to pull my hand back, but Ren kept a grip on it.

And I let him—but just for a moment as he steadied himself.

"You okay?" I asked.

He nodded, letting go. He took the lead.

Ara trotted into view on the far side of the dying fire. I waved, and she gave me a nod before jogging back toward the Temple Road.

We walked the path where Ren had taken me after I nearly burned the place down. I held my hands out, brushing the narrow tree trunks as we walked. My shoulder bumped into a tree on my blind side, but not enough to hurt.

Ren stopped in the same clearing from before. The tree tops hadn't grown together, so the moon seemed brighter here. I walked beneath the opening of the canopy toward a cluster of tiny purple flowers that shimmered under the light of the moon.

"Oh wow…" I bent down to touch the small, delicate petals. It was as if they were specked with glitter. "These flowers bloom at night?"

"Some flowers only open when they think nobody is watching." Ren reached down and picked one.

"Here." He laid the delicate flower in my open hand. I couldn't look away from his eyes as his hand grazed my palm. I felt a simple ease with him now.

"Thanks, Ren." I looked to the ground quickly, suddenly super unsure of what to say. "This whole thing has been crazy," I mumbled.

"Very."

I looked up at the star-covered sky that peeked through the trees above and took a deep breath, closing my eye.

"Madison, are you all right?"

"Ren, I—I just—I want to tell you that I—I really…" I turned and walked to the tree behind me. Its branches jutted out to the side, and I leaned on one.

I didn't need a mirror to tell me how red I was. My cheeks felt like they were on fire. Why was this so hard? I rubbed my temples.

"I really suck at this," I muttered.

I looked over at Ren. He was standing with his hands together behind his back, rocking back on his heels, eyebrows up.

I exhaled loudly. "Okay, I just—thank you. I want to thank you. My whole life might have been a lie, but it was great life so far. And the reason it was great was because of him. Jason and I have been together for as long as I can remember. I didn't have the cookie-cutter family like everyone else, and I never really felt like I missed out on anything. And I think that it's because... I was never lacking, because I had him. He was all the things that I needed him to be."

"You are welcome, Madison," Ren replied. "It is easy to see why you are so devoted to him. Jason is great."

"Why? Why did you do it?" I narrowed my eyes at him. "When you pushed him out of the way, you couldn't have known that you would be okay."

"I did not, but I knew without a doubt that if that boulder had hit Jason, *you* would not be okay." Ren rubbed the back of his neck with his hand. "So I chose you."

I felt a lump in my throat at his answer. "Thank you."

"I guess I am not as bad as they say, right?" Ren forced a smile as he walked over to where I leaned against the tree.

I shook my head. "Of course not."

He shrugged.

"Why is it a curse?" I asked softly.

"Being a Porter?"

I nodded.

He looked to the ground quickly. "I am not like them. I do not get to have a normal life, a family, a home. I have a job. I cross through the portals, and I bring people back to Everly. It's not like the other groups here. There are only a couple of my kind. The people here do not understand, so they fear it. They fear me and what I am capable of."

"It sounds like a gift," I said with uncharacteristic optimism. "Being able to travel through the worlds like that."

"It takes a toll. Trust me, it is a curse," Ren answered quickly, staring back at me. I studied him for a moment longer, and his bright, round eyes softened.

"I just don't get it." I reached up and hooked my hand on the tree branch above me. "Why doesn't everyone in Everly see what I see in you?" I cleared my throat. "What Jason and I have seen since we have been here."

"Because I do not let them." He shrugged.

I looked back at his eyes. I could see it in his face: something had changed for him, too. I didn't want to yell at him and fight him. I was happy to have him here with us, helping us.

"I think this is the beginning of a beautiful friendship." I smiled.

He chuckled.

And then all at once it hit me. This wasn't the beginning.

This was the end.

Tomorrow would be hard. It would be dangerous. I could lose him again. I could lose them all. We were marching into a temple where they were slaughtering people. Magic people. Anything could happen, and here I was strolling the woods like my aunt wasn't in crazy amounts of danger.

My heart sank. *What if I fail?* My eyes welled with tears as I covered my nose and mouth with both hands.

"I have to go," I blurted out.

Ren looked confused. "Madison, wh—"

"I—we should get back." I started walking as a tear escaped my eye.

"Okay," Ren said softly, clearly confused, and rightfully so.

"Let's just get some sleep, okay?" I said over my shoulder, and walked back through the trees. Everyone was still there, right where we had left them, only Ara was now sitting on the boulder by the fire.

"Right, good idea," Ren answered from behind me.

I felt a twinge of guilt for abruptly ending my walk with him, but what on earth could I possibly say to him now? I laid on the cloak facing Jason and closed my eyes. Burying my face in my arm, I quietly cried myself to sleep.

CHAPTER 30

"She cut her head off," Ara said softly. My eyes fluttered open, the one still dark beneath the seashell eye patch.

Jason responded in a whisper, "Yes, but she deserved it. She was using her powers on Maddy's mind."

"Even so, perhaps she and her father have more in common than we thought," Ara answered. "It is just all very surprising. I did not think Madison had that in her. I know Sinder deserved it."

I didn't move. They thought I was asleep.

"You don't know Maddy, Ara. She's a good person, but she has an edge to her."

"I know she has a good heart, but the Temple of the Ember Isle corrupts. That is what worries me. Her father was once a just man. He loved her mother dearly, but he fell under the spell of the darkness that Strongblood power can bring. He and Vilda began to fight about how Magics should be governed or whether they should at all. Vilda's sisters from the Rosewood Coven grew apprehensive when they heard of King Dax's growing influence over Vilda, so they used magic to break into the Temple of the Ember Isle and take Madison and her mother. After they disappeared, the king's hate for the Magics grew to the level that it is now," Ara explained.

"So, nobody knows where Maddy's mom is?" Jason asked.

"No, sadly," Ara confirmed.

They were silent for a few moments, and I heard Ren's breathing behind me. He was asleep and, judging by the snores, so was Gullway.

"She wants to know him, which is the saddest part." Ara broke the silence. "I can see it in the way she speaks of him."

"She's wanted to find her parents her whole life," Jason informed her. "She doesn't talk about it much, but I know it hurts her."

They were silent again. Jason coughed.

"Ara?"

"Yes?"

"What happens to King Dax after Maddy lifts the spell?"

"He must be killed. But Ren is too close to her now. I could not let him shoulder that burden. He cares for her and would not want to hurt her that way—that much is clear. This is why I decided to come along. I must kill King Dax. It is the only way this can end," Ara said coolly.

I swallowed hard and looked over my shoulder slowly. Jason and Ara were facing away from me, toward the fire.

Ara is going to kill him?

I couldn't let that happen. I couldn't. And I knew what I had to do.

Careful not to make any noise, I sat up slowly and picked up my scabbard, the little canvas book, and the cloak.

I looked down at Ren for a moment. "Thanks again," I whispered.

I stayed low on the ground and made my way toward the Temple Road. I moved slowly and as quietly as possible to avoid being caught. The trees were thicker near the Temple Road, so I rolled on the ground to my left, ducked behind a bush, and listened. I stood to peer over the bush, but Ara and Jason were still deep in conversation. Putting my scabbard on, I slowly walked away from the group into the thick of the forest.

There was only one way I could do this: alone.

I made my way to the Temple Road by the light of the moon and continued on the path climbing up the slight hill. Looking behind me, to make sure I wasn't followed, I started running. To my right, the moonlight glittered on the water. Everly truly was the most magical place I had ever seen.

I ran until I could no longer see the spot from which I had just emerged—or so I thought. The Temple Forest sort of looked like a copy of the same tree made over and over again. Then I slowed to a fast walk and flipped open the book. I held it against me to keep it steady as I read the words of the ritual that would break the spell on the courtyard.

Magic binds the Magics' line;
To mid' the temple doth confine.
A Strong, a royal, and Rosewood must bleed
Onto dagger or sword; 'tis the three that they need
To break the bind. Royal must they be
To plunge foil to soil so the Magics go free.

I studied the words again, repeating them over and over out loud.

"To plunge foil to soil so the Magics go free."

The "foil to soil"—*foil* was another word for sword. Blade in the soil?

I heard rustling behind me. I slammed the book closed and tucked it into the top of my pants, pulling my shirt over it. Looking around, I didn't see anything, but I pulled my sword just in case. I squinted into the dark woods to my left to see a pair of beady eyes looking at me. It was a rat, or something that looked pretty ratlike.

"Just you," I muttered. I slid my sword back into its scabbard and decided to start jogging again, just to be on the safe side. I thought of the spell, running over the words again.

To plunge foil to soil so the Magics go free.

Did I need to stick my sword in the ground? Where did my blood come into play? I shook my head. When did my life get so complicated?

Just then, my foot hit a rock on the road and my ankle buckled. I crashed to the ground, not able to brace myself. I winced in pain and looked down at my knee. My pant leg had ripped, and there was a cut about as long as a candy bar. It was bleeding pretty good, too.

"Genius plan, Madison." I sighed exhaustedly.

Ren had warned me that the woods could be dangerous, but it was the stealthy rocks on the Temple Road that I really needed to watch out for. I felt a knot in my stomach.

I hadn't even told them I was leaving. They were going to be worried. But I realized as I lay there, listening to Jason and Ara, that I had to go alone. I couldn't do the ritual if I was worrying about them. And I couldn't do what I had to do if I was worried that they were off killing the king.

I needed to go alone. But it didn't make me feel any less crummy.

Looking at the cut on my leg, I began to remove the fingerless black glove on my sword hand, but then I stopped.

"Not this time," I said aloud to myself as I climbed back to my feet. I limped along the rocky path that would lead me to the Temple of the Ember Isle. "I deserve this wound."

CHAPTER 31

I jogged along the path with my head down, frowning like a grumpy kid. I hadn't even faced my enemy, but I already felt defeated.

Alone was the way to travel. There was no way that the rest of the group could handle running this long. *My group.* I couldn't get Ara and Jason's conversation out of my mind. Ara admitting that she only came along to kill my father annoyed me, but knowing that Jason was sitting there discussing me hurt more.

As I reached the top of the hill, I lifted my head and gasped. I had been trudging along, staring at the ground, for so long that I hadn't even realized I was so close to the temple. I stopped, looking down the hill.

The Temple of the Ember Isle.

"There it is," I said. It was a legit castle. The entire temple was enclosed by tall, powdery white fortress walls on a massive, sprawling island. They were flat, not ornate, and the tops were straight. The temple itself was everything a castle should be: smooth white brick towers with arched windows and four wings all jutting out from the open center. The courtyard.

Home of the Strongbloods. Home of my father.

I made it. The moon still hung in the sky. I wished I had paid more attention to the time to be able to judge how long until dawn.

Light from the nearly full moon made the temple gleam even in the darkness. The island was set back in the water a little way, not too far off the shore. A single bridge connected the temple's entrance to the shoreline.

"Great. More water," I mumbled. I took the cloak from my bag and put it on. I ripped the neckline to make it wider, to allow for easy access to my sword, and started toward the bridge. It was long, about half the length of a football field. Something told me that a water entrance would be smarter than what I was about to attempt, but I was certain that me proving once again that I sink wouldn't do anyone any good.

And Witches sink, so they would know right away. My god, it's scary how normal all these things have become to me.

I may have only gotten my full gifts of strength when Ruth's protection spell was broken, and my magical abilities were slowly increasing, but I have had the gift of determination my whole life.

I wouldn't back down. I was getting into that temple.

There were two guards, a man and a woman, pacing at the end of the bridge. They were chatting as I approached.

"Evening," I said.

"Who are you?" the female guard asked.

Both were dressed like a modernized version of medieval soldiers. Instead of shiny silver armor, they had dark chest plates that looked sleeker and easier to move around in.

Neither wore their helmets, which were sitting near them on the wooden ledge of the bridge. The guards didn't seem to be threatened by me.

"Looks like you got roughed up. Are you all right?" the male guard asked.

"Got into it with some mountain trolls." I pointed behind me. "Woo-whee! A rough tumble."

"What are you doing out alone?" the female guard asked, looking suspicious. "Where is your Cloaked troop?"

"I, uh—lost my people. I just need to get some rest," I mumbled.

The male guard gestured for me to pass. The boards creaked beneath me as I stepped onto the bridge and began limping down its length.

"Wait, what is that on your eye?" The female guard put her hand on my chest. I met her eyes with my good one as she studied me.

I shrugged. "Fashion, you know?"

She looked me up and down. "What is your name?"

I kept my face calm and still. "Lorelai Victoria Gilmore of Stars Hollow."

"I have never heard of you." The female guard drew her sword. "What is your troop check-in name?"

"Troop Beverly Hills, ma'am," I answered.

The guards looked at each other and then back to me. My heart started to race as they seemed to have a silent conversation while I stood there like an idiot.

Then they both turned back to me, looking even more suspicious.

Plan B?

"Ah, screw it," I said, and punched the other guard square in the jaw, knocking him out cold. The female guard grabbed her sword and pointed it at me.

"Oh, whoops." I held my wrists out. "Sorry!"

The female guard rolled her eyes at the other guard, not seeming too concerned that I had just rendered him unconscious. She grabbed a piece of rope from her belt and coiled it around my wrists. "Don't even think of trying anything or this sword will go straight through you," she said. Then she pushed me down the bridge and began walking with the pointy end of her sword pressed to my back.

"I will be right back," the female guard called to the other guard, lying still.

She walked me down the length of the bridge to the massive wooden temple door. It was about twenty feet high.

"My god. How do you clean a door that tall? How?" I asked over my shoulder.

"Silence, rat." She pushed her hand into my back. "What's this?" She felt my sword under the cloak.

With my hands still bound, I spun around and, with a swift kick, knocked her sword from her hand. She charged at me with a grunt. I took her to the ground, throwing my bound wrists over her so that I had her in a bear hug. I tried to edge over to the side so I could throw her into the water. I didn't want to hurt her too badly, though she didn't seem to share that sentiment and tried to break free of me.

"Who are you?" she demanded as she kicked and thrashed.

"Still trying to figure that part out, actually," I said as we got close to the edge of the bridge.

"Give up now. They will never let you in like that! What is that on your eye? You look like a troll!" she said as she struggled. Her wild hair was in her face now. I looked down at her build.

"Hmm. What are you, about five-two, five-three?"

"What?" She looked at me like I was crazy, and I threw my head into hers, knocking her out. She went limp under me.

I blinked a few times and shook my head. "Ow."

I used my teeth to undo the knot binding my wrists.

"Okay, nighty-night. I am just going to borrow your armor," I said, and began taking the guard's armor off and putting it on over my clothes, moving quickly so that the guard I had rendered useless wouldn't notice. I strapped my sword and scabbard back on over the armor. The chest plate wasn't metal like I thought. It was more flexible than metal but sturdier than plastic.

I sprinted to the guard post, grabbed the female's helmet, and watched the male's chest move up and down for a moment. He stirred a bit, but his eyes stayed closed. I ran back to the female guard. She was still out. I slipped my cloak over her and smeared some of the dirt from the bottom of my boot on her face. Then I lifted her over my shoulder, walked down to the door of the temple, and knocked on it with three hard raps.

My heart raced as I waited.

"You got that one?" a voice called from behind me. I turned and waved a hand at the male guard who was at the other end of the bridge, rubbing his jaw.

He thought I was the female guard. Perfect.

I turned back to the door as it creaked open. Another guard dressed like me was standing in the doorway.

"What happened to you?" the guard asked sleepily. He sounded much older than the guard at the base of the bridge. He rubbed his eyes and yawned.

"Got into a scuffle with this one. Another Magic to lock up. I will take her down," I said, keeping my face angled down.

The guard waved me past without a second thought, sinking back into his chair. I exhaled slowly as I walked through the foyer of the Temple of the Ember Isle. It smelled a little like burnt leaves and sweat, and it was colder than the air outside.

The foyer of the temple was massive. The arch over the entryway to the building looked to be chiseled from marble. Every step I took seemed to echo. The walls were bare and endless. In front of me was one long hallway lined with torches mounted on the walls.

"Hey!" a voice from behind me called.

I flinched and turned slowly, still keeping my head down.

It was the guard who had let me in. "They want the Magic rats in the middle courtyard. They are setting up for the execution tomorrow. Just toss that one in," he said, pointing straight down the hall.

I nodded, my helmet shaking around on my head. I took a few steps away, and when I looked over my shoulder to see if the guard was still watching, he had already settled back into his chair. I looked back at the guard once more, but he looked like he had already fallen back asleep. I could hear him lightly snoring before I even made it to the doorway of the first room on my left. It was dark and empty; just a table and chair sat in the far corner.

Perfect. I dropped the female guard into the chair. Her head bobbed forward. I pulled a piece of fabric from the bottom of her shirt and stuffed it into her mouth and ripped a strip of the curtain to tie over it to gag her. I ripped two more to secure her hands and her ankles together.

I placed Ren's book on the window ledge, behind one of the curtains, and started toward the door when I heard more talking.

"Yes, that is right, sir. Eighty-two Magic folk for execution," a deep voice said.

"Lovely. I will be there at moonrise to do a few myself. Thank you, Asher," a second voice said.

I slammed my back into the wall as the echoing footsteps grew louder. Asher? As in Captain Asher from Ren's story? I pressed my cheek against the marble wall behind me, trying to slow my breathing.

"King Dax, sir, are you all right?" Captain Asher asked, concerned.

My heart felt like it was weighted down with stones. King? That would mean that the other man's voice...

The man on the other side of this wall was my father. *My father.*

"Sir? Sir, you look alarmed. Perhaps we sh—"

"No, no, I am fine. Let us keep going," King Dax responded.

I felt a hot tear roll down my cheek as I stayed pressed to the wall. I exhaled somewhat loudly and relaxed as the sound of the voices diminished.

My entire body shivered. My father. That was my father. I started to take small steps toward the doorway of my hideout room. I poked my head out as little as possible to try and see him.

All I saw was the end of a cape billow as someone rounded the corner. I jumped back into the room.

That was my father. I leaned against the wall again and took a shaky breath as I sunk to the floor. He was here. I had heard his voice.

Hugging my legs, I buried my face into my elbow and cried.

CHAPTER 32

I sat in the cold, dark room for a few minutes, trying to compose myself. Tears covered my face. I could only imagine what a mess I was, but I didn't care.

I wished with every ounce of my being for Jason. *I wish he was here with me. I can't do this alone. I can't handle it.*

Then I let out a long slow breath. "Okay, it's going to be okay. Focus."

Aunt Ruth. I needed to get to Aunt Ruth. That was what mattered now. Get to Ruth and set her free. Free the Magics.

I leaned on the wall and pushed myself off the ground. The female guard was still limp in the chair as I started toward the doorway and out into the hall.

"Guard!" a voice behind me yelled. I flinched and slowly turned. It was the same guard who had let me in. *Crap.*

"Yes?" I answered, making my voice lower and raspy.

"You are needed down at the south gate."

"Right." I gave him a nod.

I kept my head down, trying to cast as much shadow on my face as possible, turned, and started jogging down the hall.

"Guard?"

"Hmm?" I responded.

"That way." The man squinted at me and pointed down the hall behind me. "South gate."

I turned again and quickened my pace down the long hallway. Not knowing where I was going was making this really hard.

There was some shouting ahead of me. I hurried along, looking behind me as I entered a hallway lined with portraits, all oil paintings in massive gold frames. I slowed my walk and eyed each solemn face. Beneath every painting was a small plaque with the person's name. I stopped when I got to the last in the long row as a name caught my eye.

Echoing voices sounded through the hallway from both directions, but I didn't move. I studied the picture.

It was a man and woman, and the woman was holding a small child in her arms. The child looked to be about two years old. The woman's face looked as though it had been cut from the picture. The frayed pieces of canvas remained.

I stepped closer and ran my fingers over the names.

King Dax. Queen Vilda. Princess Lanora.

I lifted my hand to my mouth and took a few steps back. It was me. Me as a baby with my parents.

Lanora? My real name is Lanora?

This was a picture of my family. Someone had cut my mother's face out of it. I looked at my father in the portrait and squinted against the darkness of the hallway. His eyes. Even in the darkness, I could see that his eyes were the same amber color as mine. I chewed my lip.

I looked like him. I looked like my father.

He looked familiar in that the structure of his face was similar to mine. He had long, dark, wavy hair that fell to his shoulders. My mother's face was gone, but her hair draped over her blue dress in soft, loose curls. It was lighter than my father's, but it was hard to see the shade that well. I traced the flow of her curls with my hand.

I felt an ache in my chest as I looked at the child in the picture, a longing that I hadn't realized was already in me. I stared at my face. It was the only one of my baby pictures I had ever seen. Aunt Ruth always said she didn't have any, and now I knew why. I bit my lip to keep it from trembling.

I looked so innocent in my mother's arms. I had on a white dress with little flowers that were blue or black; I couldn't tell in the dim light. And, true to form, my hair was a mound of messy curls on top of my head. I looked exactly the same in the face. So calm and serene. A look that I don't think I had had since then. Not even at my age now, at seventeen—no, wait. I was eighteen. When this all started, it had been my eighteenth birthday.

Instead of a party, I had been dropped into the crapstorm that was my actual life. I tried to remember how long we had been here, but all the days of my journey seemed to blend together.

I looked back up at the portrait, kissed my fingers, and put them on my mother's hand.

"I am going to go find your sister, Mom. I am going to get your Ruthana back." My voice cracked as I spoke. This was something I had dreamed of my entire life: finding my parents. Finding where I had come from.

Here I stood, in the hallway of my father's house, and I felt even more alone.

Not in my wildest dreams could I have imagined who I really was: Princess Lanora, Witch of the Rosewood Coven and Strongblood of the Ember Isle, Scion of Everly.

This was it. This was what I had spent years dreaming I would find. Well, not this exactly, but I had wanted to find my parents and I had. I finally had.

I heard voices growing louder in the hallway that I had just walked down, so I jogged in the other direction. At the end of the hall, moonlight poured out of a brighter room onto the shiny marble hallway floor.

I jogged down the hall toward the room. As I drew closer, I heard sounds. Not voices, but the sickening sounds of those in pain. Moans and howls of agony. I stopped running and stepped slowly.

The courtyard.

I braced myself on the wall and looked inside, knowing that it could not be any sight I wished to see.

And I could not have been more right. I gasped.

I took a few steps back, unable to accept what I was seeing. The large, circular courtyard was filled with moonlight from above, casting deep shadows on the horror below. The green grass of the courtyard was littered with bodies. Some were moving; most were not.

Injured, bleeding, and broken Magics were all strewn about in a magical prison of death. I covered my mouth and nose as the smell hit my nostrils.

I searched the faces and the scattered motionless bodies for Aunt Ruth. I did not see her, but I could see a slab of black stone near the far edge of the courtyard. On the slab was a wooden table with three shackles sticking up—a large one in the middle of two smaller ones.

"Head and hands," I said aloud.

I started to take a step into the courtyard when a group of guards turned the corner, running hurriedly down the long hallway toward me. I hesitated. Should I run away, go into the courtyard and do the ritual now, or act like I belonged?

"Wait! We need to band together! There is an intruder in the temple! Here, guard, come here." One of them waved to me.

I nodded and slowed so that I was in the midst of the group of six or so guards. We jogged together down the hall back to the main foyer, where I had just come from.

I felt incredibly anxious as I tried to come up with a plan. What if the female guard woke up? Is that what this was?

"I am so screwed," I said through my teeth, dropping my head down.

We reached the giant door through which I had entered the temple. A clump of guards were already at the door, pushing into it with their bodies to hold it closed, and they waved us over.

"Hold the door! Hold the door!"

I was pressed into the door by the guard behind me. I leaned against it with the group of them, still in a haze from what I had just seen. There was so much chaos and yelling as something pounded on the other side of the massive wooden entrance.

I closed my eyes and tried to picture any movie or any TV show. Anything but the courtyard. I had to push the image from my mind.

"Hold the door!" another guard bellowed.

The door vibrated as something pounded on it. I heard a growling on the other side.

"What is that?" someone yelled.

"A troll!" the short guy next to me yelled.

"Did we lose a troll?" a guard in the back of the pack asked.

"Why was that not reported?" the woman on the other side of me boomed.

A troll?

"Gullway," I mouthed.

I felt panic course through me as I looked around at all the guards. There were too many of them. They would kill Gullway.

Damn it, Madison!

This was so stupid. Coming here alone, leaving them alone without knowing where I had gone. Of course they were going to come looking for me. It's what I would do if it were any one of them. I should have told them. I should have made them understand why I needed to do this.

"Hold it!" I ordered the guard on the door, and I rushed to the five guards in the back of the mob who were holding a door-width wooden plank.

I wrapped my arms around it, taking it by myself.

"Everybody down!" I screamed over my shoulder as I turned around and charged the door, holding the board.

With all my might, I lifted it into the two metal holders on either side of the door with a grunt and rested my palms on it, breathing loudly.

"There."

I turned to see the fifteen or so guards staring at me with wide eyes. The ones who had dropped to the ground when I ordered and the ones who I had knocked to the ground because they didn't listen when I yelled for them to duck were all climbing to their feet now.

I brushed my hands on my stomach. "That should keep him out."

"What, are you trying to be a Strongblood or something?" the tall one asked me defensively.

I shook my head. The woman next to me tilted her head to look at my face and then down to my leg.

"You better clean up. You know the king will not approve of you looking like that," she said.

"Right," I replied. "I should go do that." I began moving through the crowd with my head down.

"What is this? What is at the door?" a deep voiced boomed from the back of the crowd.

The guards parted, then lined up in a military fashion to reveal a tall man with short, dark hair and a long crimson cape hanging from his shoulders. He wore the same style of chest plate as the guards, but his was a deep red, not black.

My mouth fell open as I realized who it was.

It was the king. It was my father.

CHAPTER 33

"What are you doing standing around with an enemy at the door? To your stations! Now! I want them brought in alive. They have a troll with them, so take heed." King Dax's black-gloved hand pointed to the hallway next to him.

"You three stay here and help me hold the door. The rest of you, get to the south gate and await Captain Asher's orders. We need to stop the attack immediately," he instructed as he walked toward me.

I turned toward the door, hiding my face from him. Every muscle in my body tensed. I couldn't breathe. My hands shook.

I looked at him out of the corner of my eye. He was next to me. My father stood next to me, leaning his weight into the door that I had just barricaded.

The force on the other side of the door pounded wildly. I could hear deep voices yelling and a splash as something or someone hit the water.

"Stay on the door. Give it your weight! We do not want them to think it will give. Show them your strength." The king nudged me with his elbow as he leaned his shoulder into the middle of door.

"Your knee. When we are done here, go get that taken care of," he said. "Do not let your enemy see you bleed. Remember that."

His eyes were just like the portrait. They were the same light brown as mine, and he had long eyelashes that curled. I nodded, unable to speak to him. He looked younger than I would have thought.

I glanced back to the door and tried to breathe. I tried to calm my racing heart when he grabbed my arm and spun me to face him.

The door jutted in, splintering parts of it. Shards rained down on my head. I reached up and pushed my palms into the wood, setting it flush again with a dull, crackling pop.

"Great strength, guard. Have Strongblood in your line somewhere, do you?" the king asked me.

I nodded, keeping my face to the door. The pounding on the other side of the door stopped for a moment.

"Your eye—look at me." I turned my head slowly to face him.

Oh, no.

The king clutched my arm in one hand. With the other, he lifted the helmet from my head and sent it to the ground with a clank.

"Is that a shell on your...." The king's expression softened as he studied my face. His hand went to his mouth. "It cannot be," he said, his eyes pooling with tears. "Lanora?"

I said nothing as I stared back at him.

"Lanora, is that you?" King Dax put his hands on either side of my face. "What have they done to you?"

I looked up at him. Slight wrinkles were set around his eyes, but he did not look that old—not nearly old enough to have an eighteen-year-old daughter. He must have been in his thirties at the absolute oldest. His beard and mustache were black with no gray hairs. Could this really be him?

"Yes." My voice was more like a whimper.

He put his hand on his cheek. "What magic could have done this to you? I do not understand. How...?"

The king pulled me to his chest, and the hair of his beard rumpled against my forehead.

"I am your father, dear. Do you remember? Do you remember your father?"

I did not return his embrace as he held me. *My father.* I was in shock. Like I wasn't actually there but dreaming. This was all a dream. I squeezed my eyes shut. He pulled back and held me away from himself for a moment.

I didn't speak.

"What a day this is! My daughter has returned to me!" he exclaimed. "You there! Take my spot. I must take her to be treated. This is no place for the Princess of the Ember Isle."

He smoothed my hair and hugged me again.

"Say something, Lanora. Say something. Are you all right?"

I nodded. The other guards around me began to whisper. I felt sick and dizzy and more overwhelmed. He was right in front of me. My father was standing in front of me, and I couldn't speak. I wanted to hug him and ask a million questions, but all I could muster was silence, a wide-eyed stare, and shaking hands.

I need Jason.

I can't do this.

Jason should be here.

"I am so happy that you broke free of your captor! They brought her in. Don't worry, she will face justice for what she has done to you, my sweet Lanora."

"Ruth? No, please don't hu—"

"Yes, Ruthana of the Rosewood Coven," he said with disdain. "She will pay dearly for her crimes."

"But she thought she was protecting me," I said, staring through him, letting the weight of this moment press me into the ground. "You have to let her go. You have to let them all go."

"What have you been told? What has she told you about me? About your mother and her coven?" My father put his hands on my shoulders and looked down at me sympathetically.

"Nothing. She never told me," I answered, feeling like a small child. But before I could continue, he started talking again.

"Poor girl. Then let me. Your mother left her coven to be here with me, and that outraged her wicked sisters. The Witches declared war on me and my kind, the Strongbloods. They destroyed these lands with their magic and convinced the other Magics to join their cause. Those monsters stormed the temple with their sorcery and nearly killed your mother." He paused and tension twisted in his jaw. I could see the veins bulging just above his temple as he spoke.

"Even your Aunt Ruthana lived here, once. She came here with your mother and was to marry Captain Asher, as it were. But even the promise of marriage could not stop that snake from betraying us. She took you and fled the temple that night. And the Magics murdered thousands on the Ember Isle."

I blinked and tears rolled down my cheeks. "I—I didn't know that."

"That was the last time I saw you. And the last time I saw your mother—so, no. We will not be letting any of them go. They will pay for their crimes. Every single one of them. Until every ounce of magic is removed from Everly, none of us is safe."

I swallowed hard. "But I a—"

"How did you get this uniform?" He looked me up and down. "It does not matter. You are safe now. Do you understand? I will protect you."

I nodded absently and blinked quickly. He was a jittery man. He spoke quickly and seemed scattered, like his brain was jumping all over the place and his mouth couldn't keep up.

But he was my father. My dad had just said he would protect me. It was like I had wandered into one of my childhood daydreams.

This can't be real.

King Dax began walking me down the long corridor. I was in a foggy haze. I couldn't think. I couldn't act.

Could it be true? Was Aunt Ruth in the wrong? Was I wrong about my father?

He was speaking. He was rambling something at me, but I did not hear a word of it. It was like he was at the other end of the hall and I could just hear the echo of what he was telling me.

He'd looped his arm around me, hugging me to his side. I had him built up in my mind as this evil man. Ren and Ara made him sound like the devil, and yes, he was different than what I had expected. But not evil. Even after what I had seen in the courtyard, how could I believe that this man—my father—was evil? He seemed so normal. Well, as normal as any of this could be.

And then it hit me. The blinding reality masked by all this father-meeting haze.

My friends.

My friends were here at the gates, looking for me. They thought I was in trouble. I needed to tell them that I was okay, and I really needed to convince my father to let Ruth go. I could tell him that the Magics didn't kill me. I was fine. Maybe if I made him see that Ruth wasn't evil, he would still let me do the ritual.

I pushed back away from my father.

"What is it, dear? You do not need to be afraid now. You are home. I do not know what she has done to you, but we are going to fix it," he reassured me.

I took a few steps back and hit the wall behind me, causing me to jump.

"Sorry, um, my friends—my friends are out there," I stammered. "I need to speak to them. Can you take me there?"

King Dax folded his hands together and put his finger to his lip.

"They are not your friends. They are the enemy. From what I hear, one is a Porter—the son of another betrayer of the Crown. You must not consort with such people. I know what you must be feeling, but you need to trust me. I am your father, Lanora. You were taken from me, but now you are home. You are safe." King Dax spoke as if I were a small child.

I moved to the side to avoid his touch as he attempted to lay a hand on my shoulder.

"Lanora…" He furrowed his brow with worry.

"But if you just let me talk to them, they will leave, I promise. They are just worried about me." I tried to keep my voice from breaking as I spoke.

"They will be dealt with swiftly, I assure you," he replied, looking down the hall toward the temple door we had been holding shut.

"Sir!" Another man came running over to where we stood in the middle of the long hallway with all the torches. He was dressed like the other guards, but his chest plate had a design on it and his sword was longer. He removed his helmet, showing his sandy blonde hair. His baby face made him look not much older than me, but his deep brown eyes were hard and emotionless.

"We have them," he said. "We have the intruders."

"Excellent. Asher, it is she. Look." My father gestured to me.

Captain Asher. I couldn't help but look back at him with disdain.

He turned to look me over. "Who, sir?"

I watched as the realization hit him as he examined me. His shoulders fell a bit, and his studiously proper stance relaxed.

"It cannot be." Captain Asher took a step toward me, bowed his head, and tucked his arm in front of him. He looked back to my father. "Can this be fixed?"

My father shook his head. "I will not stop until I find a way."

I adjusted the shell on my eye, feeling self-conscious about it now.

"Princess…welcome home," Captain Asher said.

"Sir, the Porter and the Empress are with the troll," a guardsman yelled over to Captain Asher from the end of the long gray hallway.

A shudder ran through me. Ren, Ara, and Gullway were here. But where was Jason?

"I want them all questioned. I will meet you there," King Dax instructed Captain Asher with a nod.

"But, please, I need to see them. They're not dangerous. They're looking for me," I pleaded.

My father ignored me. "Asher, do you believe it? She has returned. And on her own, too," he said. "She has my instincts. Cancel your plans this evening. We will celebrate!"

"Your majesty, sir…please. I need to get to my friends," I said. My father continued to boast about me like I wasn't there.

"She looks like me, does she not? We will have to get her cleaned up and her wounds dressed, of course, but I want her by my side when we execute her captor tomorrow. And I want all of the Ember Isle there to witness it!" he exclaimed joyfully. "This is a great triumph."

I stepped away from my father. "Enough!" My voice echoed through the hall. My glance accidentally crossed over the torch that hung on the wall behind my father, and it flared with a soft roar. I immediately dropped my eyes to the floor of the hallway, hoping they didn't notice.

"What is it, Lanora?" the king asked.

I looked back up. Captain Asher's eyes narrowed. He studied me intently.

And...crap. He knew; he saw the fire flare up when I looked at it. He may have figured out I was a Magic, but it didn't matter. It was clear that my father had no interest in listening to my side of things.

Nope, I had to do this my way.

"Sorry...Dad, sir. I just—I do not feel well from the journey. And my eye hurts," I said nervously.

I mulled over the information I had. I needed to get to my friends. But could I get to them? And where was Jason?

"You there! Take my daughter to the infirmary. She has wounds," King Dax ordered a servant dressed in raggedy black clothing.

The servant hurried over to me. "Your daughter? The princess has returned?"

I couldn't stand to hear any more of this. "Ohh..." I put my hand on my head and acted as if I was losing my balance.

"Are you all right?" the servant asked, bracing me before I fell.

"Get the princess to the infirmary now!" Captain Asher pointed down the hall, but kept his calculating stare on me.

I leaned on the young man and stopped, looking back over my shoulder. King Dax was standing in the middle of the hallway. He gave me a smile. I could see in his eyes that it was truly genuine. It made my heart ache.

In a whirlwind of moments, I had met my father and found that he was nothing like I had thought. He wasn't an evil king perched high in his tower. He was an anxious, quick-talking man who seemed to care for me. And he was so pleased with my return.

But in the brief time I had been able to reunite with him, the reality had become painfully clear: He would kill everyone I loved, and he was going to do it whether I protested or not.

Every delusion I had let myself believe in order to get to this point faded. All the false hopes and the unjustified reassurances that I had given myself disappeared, too.

I know what I have to do.

I broke away from the young servant who was helping me and walked over to where my father was standing.

"What is it, Lanora?" he asked softly, still talking to me like I was a child.

"It was good to meet you," I answered.

"My dear girl. My dear girl," he said, and he hugged me.

Just a hug. Nothing spectacular about it. But it was one of those moments I had built up in my mind for so long that even though he was not the man I had hoped he would be, the moment was everything I had hoped for.

234

I broke down into tears—tears of what, I didn't know. I took a deep breath and I squeezed him tighter.

"You are strong, like your father," he said in my ear, lifting me off the ground.

"I am," I agreed as he lowered me back down.

"Wipe those tears," he said with warm eyes. "Remember, dear, our power is fixed in the minds of the lesser folk of Everly. We must not let them see our pain."

No.

A shudder went through my entire body, and my mouth fell open. Those words...that phrase. It all came flashing back through my mind.

The phrase was from my vision in the cave with Sinder. The man in the room with four pillars—it was him. The man in Sinder's vision was my father. I stared back at him, wide-eyed.

"I will see you after we sort this out, my dear," he said, patting me on the arm.

Captain Asher started down the hall, followed by my father. I watched until my father's dark red cape was out of sight.

"No, you won't," I whispered to myself.

CHAPTER 34

"My Lady, shall I take you to the infirmary now?" the servant asked.

I looked at my feet and spun around to face him, still reeling from my realization.

"Where are the intruders? The Porter, the Empress, and the troll?"

"They are being taken in now. Princess, if I may ask...what happened to you?" the young servant asked.

I touched the seashell on my eye. "Oh, I—uh—my friend accidentally shot me with a little arrow. But I am fine. Really."

"No, I meant—I apologize, it is not my place. Shall we go, then? Are you still feeling faint?" He held his hand out.

"The prisoners. Where are they, exactly? And I am going to need very specific directions because this place is a frickin' maze."

He didn't respond. I grabbed his hand and squeezed the pressure point between his thumb and index finger. A simple self-defense trick Aunt Ruth taught me. The young man yelled out in pain and buckled to the ground.

"One more time. Where are they?" I asked.

"Ahh!" he cried out. "Captain Asher is bringing them to be tortured now."

"Tortured? The king said they were being questioned," I said, alarmed.

"That is his way. He—he does not like to call it that. They are down that hall there, and take a left. You will run right into the courtyard."

My stomach churned. "The courtyard? They are being taken to the courtyard?" I asked, picturing the horror of the place. "I guess that works."

He nodded.

I released his hand slightly but still kept pressure on it. "Tell nobody. Understand?"

The young man nodded. I let go of his hand and he recoiled.

"What is your name?" I asked, pulling my sword out.

"Lang."

"Lang, do you have any family here in the temple?"

He nodded. "My wife works as a seamstress."

I leaned down. "Get your wife and run. Leave right now. Do you understand me?"

Lang nodded frantically and scooted back on the floor away from me. I pulled my sword and ran toward the courtyard.

"Down the hall and take a left," I said aloud to myself. Just as I was about to make the turn, a group of yelling guards rushed by me.

I let them pass, pressing my back to the wall. I needed to let the guard think that my friends were all secured in the courtyard, and then I would free them all with the ritual.

I leaned over and saw the courtyard at the end of the hall. "Let's do this," I said under my breath.

And just as I said it, someone grabbed my arm and pulled me into the room next to me. I spun to hit them with the sword handle when they grabbed my wrist. Then I saw the person's face.

"Jay!" I put my sword back in its scabbard on my back and hugged him so tightly I was certain I was hurting him.

"Maddy!"

Jason held me against his torn shirt. His hair was matted to his head, and his arms were scratched and dirty.

"Maddy, thank god! I was so worried. I was so worried," Jason rambled and kissed my forehead. He started to cry.

"No, I am sorry. I'm so sorry. I should have told you. I'm so sorry."

"Don't you ever do that to me again! Do you understand? Do you know what was going through my head?" Jason held me by the shoulders and shouted. A lump rose in my throat.

Keep it together, Madison.

"You have to be quiet," I whispered.

He clenched his jaw and shook his head. Each tear washed the dirt from his tan skin as it descended down his tense face, making a striped pattern under his eyes.

"Promise me that you will never do that again," he said through gritted teeth.

If he only knew what I had just been through. I crossed my arms and looked away. I didn't need this right now.

"Jason, stop. I need you to stop. Please, just be you. Please," I begged with a shaky voice.

"What?" Jason shook his head in confusion.

"Please, be you. I need you to be you. I am so sorry I left, I am, but I need you to be Jason. I need you to be you."

Jason exhaled loudly and wiped his tears. He dropped his head forward and put his hands on his hips.

"It's hard. This is all really hard," I said softly. *Please, just let it go.*

He glanced at me for a moment. "You're right. It's okay. I didn't mean to yell. Maddy, come here." Jason took me in his arms again and his tone softened. I felt his body relax around me.

Then he stepped back but held my arms with his large hands. "I am me," he said.

I nodded and took a deep breath as my eyes started to dry. "I can't get through this without falling apart if you aren't you. I need you to be you."

Jason nodded. "Okay. I'm right here. I've got you."

We hugged again, and I wiped my face vigorously. I took a long, slow, deep breath, just like Aunt Ruth taught me.

Jason looked me over. "Maddy, your leg. What happened?"

"Oh, that. No, I'm fine. I tripped," I said, dismissing his concern. "Where is Ren? And Ara and Gullway?"

"They were captured. I snuck in. It's okay, though. That was our plan. The guards didn't seem to care about me anyway. They just wanted the Magics," Jason explained.

"How is Ren?" I asked quietly.

"Terrible, Maddy. He's a wreck."

I rubbed my hand on the back of my neck. "I screwed up," I admitted, meeting Jason's eyes.

"Are you—are you okay?" Jason asked.

"No, but I want to be," I replied. "Let's go get our friends."

"Yes, let's go."

"We should try to stay hidden."

"Yeah, we don't want to run into your father," Jason agreed. "Did you see him at all?"

My lips parted to speak, and I froze for a moment. *Do I tell him?*

"No, I didn't," I said.

"Good. Let's get out of here before evil Daddy Dearest finds us." Jason threw his arm around me protectively.

I don't know what made me lie to Jason, but luckily, there wasn't time to dwell on it. We heard more yelling in the hallway.

"Madison! Madison!"

"That's Ren!" I whispered to Jason. I started for the door.

"Wait! We can't just run out there." Jason pulled my elbow.

"I have an idea."

Exhaling slowly, I slid my sword's blade across my forearm and winced. The cut started to bleed and, lifting my arm, I smeared the blood on Jason's forehead.

"Oh, gah! Gross, Maddy!" he yelped and swatted at me.

I ripped the collar of his shirt and put the point of my sword into his back.

"What are you—"

"Trust me?" I asked.

"Always," Jason said without turning around.

I pushed him out into the hallway behind a group of guards pulling Ren down the hall. It took twice as many to drag Ren as to drag Ara. Ren was kicking violently as they carried him backward toward the courtyard.

"Go!" I said in a low, gruff voice. Walking behind the group dragging Ren, I pushed Jason ahead of me. He raised his hands like a true prisoner as we walked down the marble-walled hall. Each noise echoed loudly around us.

The was so much anger in Ren's face. His eyes were wild and desperate, but he moved with such determination. It took like eight guards to drag him down the hall, and they were struggling to keep him from breaking away. His face went from bewildered to a relieved smile as he saw Jason and me. He stopped thrashing around and let the guards carry him down the hall.

I kept my stare locked on his. I couldn't breathe as I watched Ren stare back at me, smiling.

We entered the courtyard and my mouth fell open. I put my sword away. Lining the edge were nearly a hundred people, each more injured than the last. What I'd seen by standing in the doorway before hadn't even begun to crack the surface of the dreadfulness that lay within.

"Put them over there," a guard ordered.

I felt a wave of nausea hit me, and I felt weak. Was it the moaning bodies and the horror of the courtyard or the spell? I didn't have to decide. It was like I was being pulled to the ground. My muscles stopped functioning. Now I knew it was the spell. Even though I was only half Witch, I felt it.

"I might fall," I whispered to Jason. He braced me the best he could without looking too obvious as the guard threw Ren down near Ara.

Another guard struck Ren on the back, and Ren fell to his knees. Pain shot through my spine as he buckled forward. I could barely stand now.

"Are you okay? Maddy, you have to stand, they'll see you," Jason said with barely parted lips.

"I felt that. I felt Ren's pain. How…" I didn't finish my thought, but it didn't matter right now. Nothing else mattered as the horror of the courtyard crept over me. Each anguished, twisted face stared vacantly at nothing. There was blood everywhere.

"Come on! We are needed at the gate!" a guard shouted, and the group that had just brought in Ren filed out of the courtyard. Thankfully, they left me there. Just the Magics and my friends.

I dropped to my knees in the grass.

"Madison, I am so happy to see that you are all right," Ara whispered. She didn't seem affected. Not like me and Ren. I flopped to the ground. Across from me was a man with pale white hair. His face was covered in blisters, some broken and others crusted over. His lips were cracked and white like he had been baked in the sun.

"It's the spell, Madison. It is rendering you ill, just like the others, so you cannot move. We need to get you to the center of the courtyard to do the spell. I will go find your aunt," Ara said.

I nodded to her as best I could. But it wasn't the spell—not entirely. It was more than I could handle. So much death and suffering, all at the hands of the man who was my father.

"I need to talk to Ren," I said.

"What? Maddy, no. There's no time." Jason lifted me up, but I flopped like a wet noodle, unable to keep my legs locked.

"Jason, please," I said groggily. "Sinder's vision might be right. I might not get out of here."

"That's ridiculous. She was just messing with you. It's all crap."

"No, it isn't. It was him. The man from the vision. It was my father and the things he said."

"Maddy, you met him? You said you didn't," he said with narrowed eyes. "You lied?"

"I lied. I didn't know what to say. I met him and he was everything I wanted him to be, but at the same time he was nothing like I thought. But she was right. Sinder was right. I didn't believe her at first, but it was him—the man in the room filled with the blood of the four bodies. It was him. And I came here, just like she said not to, and she was right. She said that if I walked into the temple, I wouldn't walk out. I need to talk to Ren. Please, Jason, I just need to talk to Ren," I begged. "I need to say good-bye."

I scanned the faces of the fallen and broken Magics. Each more distressed than the last.

"My father did this. He did this," I said softly.

We reached Ren, who was only a few steps away. Ren didn't say a word as Jason knelt down—not until I spoke.

"Are you okay, Ren?" I asked. He was curled up on his side in the fetal position.

"Madison," he replied, lifting his head to see me. "Why is this happening? The spell—my father's research said it would not affect me. I should not feel like this."

"I don't think it's the spell, dude. You took a beating when we got in here, Ren. Just take it easy," Jason responded, gently laying a hand on Ren's back. Ren nodded back at him. I smiled at their exchange, because if Sinder was right and I didn't make it out of this temple, at least they would have each other. It was a morbid thought, but it gave me the comfort I needed to keep my composure for the time being.

"If it makes you feel better, I feel it, too. Everything you are feeling, Ren." I reached for his hand with mine. "I feel it, too."

A tear rolled down the side of his face. He closed his eyes and nodded.

I wiped the tear from his face. "I think you have some of my magic. I didn't mean to give it to you. I'm sorry. This is my fault. I bound us together somehow. I can feel things that you feel. It's my fault you feel this way now. I'm so sorry."

"No, do not be sorry. I am glad, Maddy." Ren opened his eyes.

I scoffed. "You can't be glad for this, Ren. Look at you. You can barely move because of me."

"True." He forced a smile. "But I am glad."

"I need to ask you about the spell," I said. "I put my blood on the sword?"

Ren nodded as another tear rolled down his face. "Yes, and you put the sword into the ground."

I touched my lightning bolt earring, still clipped to the collar of his shirt, and smiled.

"Guys, look!" Jason said. I turned to see Ara. She was seated about twenty feet away and holding someone in her arms.

"Aunt Ruth." I beamed.

"Do you have the book?" Ren asked. "If you do the ritual now, the binds on the Magics here will break and they can get out on their own."

"No. I left the book with the guard that I knocked out and whose clothes I took. First room on the left. It is safe," I replied. "Long story. But I don't need it. I memorized it."

"Of course you did, you little overachiever." Jason smiled. "Maddy, go. I'll stay with him."

"As soon as I do the ritual, you need to get Ruth, Ren, and Ara and get out. And find Gullway. Get them back to Greenrock, okay?"

Jason shifted. "What about you?" he asked. "Maddy, we're all leaving together."

"No, we can't, Jay. This place is crawling with guards. I am going to create a diversion. I will get the rest of the Magics out and I will—I will try to meet you in the caves. The grotto with the baby fae. But you heard Sinder. I won't walk out of here. I need you to save them. Please. Promise?"

"I am not leaving you here. You need me here, with you," Jason stated simply as tears welled in his eyes. "You can't even stand up."

I half smiled at him. "Do you know what the quickest way to get me to do something is?"

I took a slow, calm breath and focused all my energy on moving.

Then, slowly, I stood up.

Jason nodded and sighed. "Tell you that you can't."

I straightened my posture and took a few slow steps toward Ara. Every step got easier, but it was like I had just done a twelve-hour spin class. Ara was holding a ragged Ruth, who looked like a wreck. Her clothes were tattered, and her face was swollen and covered in blood.

"Aunt Ruth." Her name escaped my lips when I saw her. I wanted to go to her. I wanted to say a thousand things to her, tell her that all her training helped me and that she was the reason I made it this far, but there was no way I could. I didn't have the energy to do that and break the spell. I would have to tell her after. The moans of the Magics grew louder, and then, all at once, things grew quiet. The Magics started to turn to look at me—the ones that were able to move, anyway.

This ends now.

I took a deep breath and walked to the middle of the courtyard. I pushed the hair out of my face that had clung to my sweat. The spell made me feel like I was walking in mud with two broken legs. I pushed on, but my knee buckled with just a few steps to go and I fell to the ground.

Jason jumped to his feet. I held my hand up and shook my head, trying hard not to show that I was in pain. Jason sat back down slowly, keeping his concerned eyes on me as he did.

If Sinder was right, I wouldn't be walking out of here. No reason for Jason to risk helping me now. I mouthed "Love you" to him. He smiled brightly and mouthed back "Eww." We both smiled.

Deep breath.

"What are you doing? You know we are not to stay in the courtyard!" a guard yelled to me from the entryway as I knelt.

Pulling a glove off, I tossed it on the ground and I slid my sword over my hand, keeping my sword hand gloved. Not sure how much blood was needed, I smeared my blood on the tip and up both sides of the blade toward the hilt.

"Stop it!" The guard started to run to me. "You there! What are you doing?"

I took a few deep breaths and gathered my strength.

I carefully laid the blood-covered sword on the ground and stood as a guardsman charged me. Before he could even reach out to grab me, I swung my leg up and landed a kick, cracking right into his jaw. He flew to the side, dropped to the ground in a crumpled pile, and did not move.

I fell back to my knees on the green grass, having exhausted my energy. But out of the corner of my good eye, I could see her sitting up now. Ruth. Her mouth was open, and it was the first time I could remember seeing her look at me like that.

I pointed at her. "You. You taught me that," I said tearfully.

And I realized how much I loved her. Everything I was would be gone if I had grown up here. I owed Aunt Ruth everything. *And after we get home, I intend to tell her just that.*

"Stop!" another guard yelled, but he wisely did not approach me.

I picked up my sword. "Magic binds the Magics' line to 'mid the temple doth confine—"

"Stop!" another voice boomed. I ignored it.

"Lanora!"

I paused and looked up, my heart pounding now. In the doorway to the courtyard stood King Dax and Captain Asher. My father's face was not angry like the rest, but sad and destroyed.

"Lanora, what are you doing?"

"You can't keep killing these people! My friends, my aunt! You have to free them. Please!"

My father shook his head. "Lanora, these are no friends of yours. They are Magics. Do you not remember what I told you? The Magics murdered so many." He gestured to the prisoners around him.

"No," I said.

"Lanora, these monsters were the ones who took you away from me. Your mother and that evil rat took my sweet baby from me. And now—now, we will rule together, you and me. You will rule the Ember Isle. It is your heritage. Please, come over here, dear. Put that sword away."

"I am doing this with or without your blessing," I yelled back, lifting the sword.

"Asher, stop!" Jason screamed. I turned to see what he was yelling about.

It was Aunt Ruth. Captain Asher was holding her up by her neck, and he had a sword laid across her chest. Ara lay on the ground, holding her face.

"Stop it! What are you doing?" I yelled.

"Lay down that sword. Lay it down now," Captain Asher ordered. His eyes were cold, his voice robotic.

"Asher!" Jason yelled again.

"Do not hurt her!" I slid my sword into my scabbard. "Don't hurt her."

I stood slowly and raised my hands.

"Madison, no!" Ren screamed.

"Maddy, what are you doing?" Jason yelled behind me. "Keep going!"

"That's my girl," King Dax said. "Those two, there—seize them!" My father pointed to Jason and Ren.

"No!" I yelled as two guards grabbed Jason and Ren. "Dax, stop this, please!"

My father remained still and silent. He raised his chin.

"Let her go. Help her! She was going to be your wife!" I pleaded to Captain Asher.

"That was before. Before I knew what magic really was," he replied with a cold stare.

"Magics must die. All of them," my father called out to me as he stepped over another body.

"My mother was a Magic, and you loved her! What the hell happened to you?" I shouted angrily.

"Your mother was weak. She isn't even here to defend her people against me. She is nothing. She means nothing to us. Magic needs to be extinguished from Everly, Lanora. All of it, no matter the cost," my father spat back.

"My name is Madison." I narrowed my eyes at him.

"That is a name that criminal gave you. No, you are Princess Lanora of the Ember Isle, a Strongblood, like me."

"She is not a criminal! She raised me. And, funny thing about my bloodline, pops. I take after my mom, too," I stated angrily.

"What are you taking about?" my father asked.

"A Witch and a Strongblood," I replied. "I'm both."

"Impossible. You can't have her bloodline. One always beats the other. You are a Strongblood," he said dismissively.

"Well, something that you don't know about me is that I tend to be a bit of a rulebreaker." I rubbed my palms together and took a deep breath. Then I concentrated on the torch hanging on the wall near the courtyard's entrance. It flared up, nearly igniting the guard standing next to it.

"Stop it!" my father yelled.

I looked at the torch again. The flame grew even larger than before.

"Stop this, now!

"Afraid they will see? Afraid they will see what I am and think you are a Magic, too? How many did you tell, Dad? How many did you tell that I am your daughter? Enough that they will overthrow you, thinking you are Magic, too?" I had all the torches burning high by now.

"Stop this!" King Dax roared.

But I couldn't. Truth was, I wasn't sure what I was doing, and I had no idea how this newfound power worked.

"Release them or you will be sorry. I mean it!" I shrieked at my father, trying to maintain my confidence.

"I do not take threats, dear. Not even from you. Being my daughter is a gift, and this is what you do with it?" King Dax turned and nodded at Captain Asher.

And just then, just as I met Aunt Ruth's eyes, my entire world irrevocably changed. Captain Asher swung his sword into her bound wrists, severing her hands with one swift flick of his sword.

I sprinted to her, but I felt the weight of the spell in my steps. I ran as fast as I could to get to her. Terror filled her eyes as he lifted the sword up. I didn't look at the blood pouring from her handless arms. I ran, as fast and as hard as I could.

But for the first time in my life, I wasn't fast enough. Every meet, every practice, every sprint meant nothing now.

I wasn't fast enough to save her.

I screamed as Captain Asher's blade sliced through her neck and the life left her tear-filled eyes. Aunt Ruth's body convulsed as it fell to the ground like a crumbling piece of paper. Blood began to pool around her limp body on the sunburnt grass of the courtyard. Captain Asher left her there and returned to King Dax.

"Ruth!" I shrieked in panic.

She was dead.

The courtyard fell silent as I reached her. Her body had started to shrivel and turn gray.

Aunt Ruth was dead.

I dropped to my knees. My sobs echoed through the silent air as I laid my hand on Ruth's arm.

"Ruth," I said softly.

I heard a few gasps around me as a soft light fell over the ground. I wiped my tears and looked up. A massive swarm of tiny little lights descended, hovering above us, illuminating the entire courtyard in a soft yellow glow. Fae.

I looked back down at the body of my aunt and started to shiver, even though I was sweating. I touched her arm with the tip of my finger and traced the stiff lines that were forming in her hardening skin.

"Aunt Ruth, it's okay. It will be okay. I will fix this. I promise." I stroked her desiccated arm, unable to see through my tears. "Aunt Ruth. I know why you didn't tell me about my parents. I understand now. I needed to see it on my own."

"Madison?" I heard Ara's soft, gentle voice next to me. I didn't move, staying fixated on Aunt Ruth's corpse.

"I am so sorry. I am sorry I said I hated you. I didn't mean it. I hope you knew that I didn't mean it. Everything you did—the training, the workouts—you knew it would come to this. You knew I would be here someday, didn't you?" I paused as if waiting for an answer, but there was only silence.

"Lanora!" my father yelled, but I ignored him. "Lanora, come here now."

"I will make you proud. I will. I will help these people. I will be a leader, like you said. I will," I murmured, gently wiping my cheeks.

"Go, Madison," Ara urged me sympathetically, her eye puffy and bleeding from where Captain Asher must have struck her. "You need to hurry."

Three guards rushed toward me and Ara. I looked at Captain Asher and my father, who stood near the doorway of the courtyard.

"Ara, don't kill him," I said. "My father. You can't kill him."

Ara's mouth dropped open slightly.

"I heard you by the campfire. Promise you won't. I can't lose them both today." Ara tilted her head to the side. "Okay, I will not touch him. You have my word."

"Thank you, Ara." I wiped more tears from my face. "I can handle him."

"I will take care of the guard. Go!" Ara said, and took off toward the oncoming guards.

I stood up, gave Aunt Ruth's body one more look, and slowly walked back to the center of the courtyard. The sickness from the spell wasn't as strong as my adrenaline, and I powered through. At the center, I knelt and pulled my sword with a renewed strength, but I couldn't speak. I couldn't feel.

I failed. I couldn't do it. I had failed.

I could hear them all yelling. I could hear Ren yelling at Captain Asher. I could hear Jason yelling at me to do the spell, but I could not move.

I sank a little farther toward the damp grass-covered ground of the courtyard.

I had failed.

As I closed my eyes, ready to give up, I felt two arms wrap tightly around my waist and lift me up from the ground. I didn't need to look to know who was holding me so carefully.

"Jay?" I whimpered, barely able to speak.

"You aren't in this alone, Mads. I have you," Jason asserted. I could hear the pain in his voice as he spoke. He was crying, too.

"Say the words," he whispered.

"Magic binds the Magics' line to 'mid the temple doth confine," I recited. "A strong, a royal, and Rosewood must bleed…"

"Good. Keep going."

"Onto dagger or sword; 'tis the three that they need to break the bind. Royal must they be to plunge foil to soil so the Magics go free," I finished.

"Now the sword part." Jason said. "You're doing great, Mads."

I lifted my sword, then plunged the blood-soaked blade into the grassy ground.

A great flash of light blasted through the courtyard. The weakness that I had been fighting lifted from my body like a sigh of relief.

"No!" my father screamed as the Magics began to stir. Some stood immediately, while others rolled and shifted on the ground.

I turned and hugged Jason tightly.

"Thank you," I said.

"Anytime."

My father ran toward us.

Ara and Ren were fighting the guards who were trying to detain the freed Magics. "Go help them. I'll deal with my father," I said.

Jason nodded and went to join Ara.

"Help each other. Everyone out. Do not harm anyone. Leave the Ember Isle! Go!" Ara shouted.

I looked at Aunt Ruth's body, hoping the spell would undo what Captain Asher had done. But it hadn't. Why would it?

More guards started to pour in, and Magics began to attack them in defense. Screams rang out in the courtyard.

"Do you see what you have done?" Captain Asher yelled at me. Jason roared as he charged Captain Asher and punched him so hard in the side of his head that he knocked him out cold. But Jason didn't stop there. He stayed on Captain Asher, punching him over and over until Ren pulled him away.

I wanted to go to them. I wanted to, but I knew my mission wasn't over. I needed to distract the guard and the king long enough to get them out.

Ara waved her delicate hand, and the fae descended into the courtyard. They circled around the wounded and seemed to help lift them up and carry them out. My father stopped and swatted at the fae.

I looked at the chaos around me. Magics and guards locked in combat. Blood sprayed, screams rang out, and the horror just continued to grow. Bodies flew as the Magics regained their strength.

"Maddy?" It was Ren.

"You need to go!"

"Stop them!" I heard the king yell behind us as the courtyard emptied. The Magics were winning and escaping. We had won, but it didn't matter to me now. I had lost Aunt Ruth, and that was more crushing than I ever could have imagined.

"Go! I will distract him. Get them out of here!" I told Ren. "Find Gullway. Make sure he is safe!" My voice cracked. The noise of the scattered battles happening around us threatened to drown out my voice completely, but Ren knew exactly what I was saying, even if he couldn't hear me. I needed them to leave. I needed my friends to get to safety.

"We are not leaving you." Ren grabbed my arm.

"Listen to me! You have to take Jason. Promise me you will keep him safe. He won't go on his own, Ren. Promise me," I pleaded. I tried to maintain my authority of the situation as I looked back at him. I couldn't possibly say good-bye, so I didn't try. Jason was running toward us with Ara.

Tears filled Ren's emerald eyes as he ran his hand through his hair, nodding.

"Ren, promise to take him somewhere safe," I begged.

"I promise, Maddy. I promise," Ren said softly as I backed away.

"Maddy!" Jason pulled at my arm. "We have to go!"

"No." I pushed him away.

"Maddy, you did it. We can leave now," Jason pleaded as Ren and Ara grabbed his arms.

I watched as Ren and Ara pulled a violent and screaming Jason with them. Jason's wails carried over all the other noises in the courtyard. I looked away, unable to watch him as he realized I wasn't coming with them.

I couldn't go. I wasn't finished here yet.

"Lanora!" my father yelled at me. He looked panicked, stalking angrily toward me as his cape billowed behind him. His eyes darted around madly as the chaos spilled out of the courtyard into the temple halls and out of sight.

"Guards! Guards!" my father shouted, pointing them toward my friends. I needed to keep his focus on me. I needed my friends to escape, and I knew just what to do.

My father grabbed my elbow and shook me. "What have you done?"

"Sorry," I replied. I pulled the glove from my sword hand. "But wait...there's more."

"What are you doing now?" King Dax looked around, clear anxiety on his face.

"Better call your guard over. I call this the big finish," I yelled back over the growing roars of the few remaining Magics and guards fighting.

"I may only have a little Witch in me, but it's there. I hate to break it to you, but your daughter is a Magic, King Dax." I grasped the sword in my hand, and it lit with a bright flash of blue. I felt my wounds healing. Warmth ran over me and my skin tingled.

His mouth dropped open.

"I have spent so much time thinking about you, about what I would say to you if I ever met you. And here you are—big bad Dad. You killed Aunt Ruth. She gave up everything for me. I never..." I gripped the sword tightly and pressed my lips together.

"Why couldn't you just be wonderful? Why? Why couldn't you just be the dad I wanted you to be?" I begged as I felt my last wound heal. "Why?"

"Stop this! Stop this magic," my father demanded. His face was red, and his eyes narrowed.

"I can't. Don't you see that? I don't know how to control it. This is me. I am a Magic. I am everything you hate. You can hate me, but it won't change who I have become."

My father shook his head. His focus wasn't even on me now. He was scanning the area to see who else had seen me, who else knew what his daughter was. My first real act of rebellion against my real father, and he was more concerned about how it made him look, not about me. I studied the tension in his face; the way his eyes widened, his jaw clenched, and his nostrils flared when he exhaled. It was exactly what I looked like when I was angry.

I am my father's daughter.

"My father," I said shaking my head. "No matter how many times I say it, it will always sound weird. You are my father. I found you." My lip trembled beyond my control. "And you were supposed to be wonderful."

Some of the Magics and the guards were watching us now—the few who remained. They had all seen who I really was. My father turned to see them all staring at us.

"No," he said sharply.

I looked up at him, waiting for him to say something comforting. Maybe he would surprise everyone. I was his daughter. His hatred of Magics couldn't possibly be stronger than the look of joy on his face when he had seen me by the castle gate.

My father leaned his face toward mine and I smiled back at him. Maybe this would work out after all! Maybe...

His low, gruff voice was soft. "Lanora, you may have freed them today, but I will kill every last Magic. All of them. You cannot save them. You cannot beat me."

I met his eyes for a moment. The loving embrace and warm smile were distant memories now. I wasn't the daughter he longed for; that was glaringly clear. I was just a Magic in his eyes now. His eyes that looked like mine.

I opened my mouth to speak to him, but before I could, he grabbed my sword hand and spoke to the people in the courtyard, not to me.

"I would rather you die than live as a Magic!" he yelled loudly, so that everyone could hear.

And then, before I realized it was happening, King Dax, my father, plunged my sword straight into my gut.

I gasped loudly and buckled over. As I stumbled back, he looked down at me. His amber eyes filled with contempt as I started to fall.

What just happened?

I heard more screams as my head smacked into the grassy ground. Everything looked a little foggy in the night air of the temple courtyard. I tried to move my fingers along the browning blades of grass beneath me. It wasn't like the hard grass at home. It was soft and silky, even.

The grass couldn't distract me from the heat that was burning in my stomach. I coughed. Blood spurted from my mouth, and I rolled to my back as I smeared it away with my palm.

"Maddy!" a familiar voice screamed. Someone was there next to me. My gaze fell to the side as I saw my father running away, his cloak flapping as he ran.

And then someone knocked him to the ground in a crumple of bodies. Somebody was on him.

I saw Ara and heard the familiar sound of the seashells in her ponytail as her hands wrapped around mine. Her touch gave me more comfort than I thought possible.

"D—Did they get out?" I managed to ask.

Then Jason and Ren's faces were there, too.

"Madison, please stay. Please stay," Ren said quickly.

"It's okay. She's a Witch, it's the head and the hands, right...right?" Jason asked frantically.

251

"That is full Witches," Ara said. "I—I do not know about half Witches."

"I'm sorry," I tried to say, but I couldn't tell if the words actually left my lips or if I only thought them.

I felt lips on my forehead. It was Ren. They all looked so sad.

"Shh," I tried to say, but the blood on my lips made it a larger effort than I could handle. "It's okay... It's all going to be okay..."

Jason's face came into focus. He was yelling and holding my hand, I thought.

"My Jason," I slurred as I coughed out more blood. I wanted to comfort him, but I couldn't move anymore. The heat that radiated from my stomach had consumed me.

I felt them all around me—my friends. Even when I closed my good eye, I could feel them there.

And warmth. I felt warm.

Like I was sinking into a freshly drawn bath. Just warmth.

Then the voices went from an echo to a simple, tranquil quiet.

And then there was nothing.

Nothing. Endlessly peaceful nothing.

CHAPTER 35

I opened my eyes. Birds chirped loudly outside. I was in my own bed. In my own room.

I was back at Ruth's house.

"This is it?" I said softly.

I felt so different. I looked down at my skin, and it was paler than I remembered. I blinked slowly.

Death was peaceful. It was warmer than I thought it would be.

I stretched, not wanting to get out of bed. I didn't think death would be so comfortable. So calming. My heaven was Ruth's house? I wouldn't have called that, but I was happy to be here.

I swung my legs over the side of the bed. Everything was different. Different furniture. Even the walls were darker.

That's strange.

I felt anxious. Not the indescribable peace that I thought I would feel in death.

And then I thought of Aunt Ruth. They killed her. I wondered if she was here. Did you share a heaven with your family?

My anxiety switched to anger as I thought about what they did to Aunt Ruth. I ran the images through my mind and grabbed my side, remembering my own injuries. There was no wound under my shirt. No mark of any kind from my father plunging the sword into my gut.

My father killed me. The day I met him—he killed me.

Even in death, the notion stung. He had ended up being everything they said he was, no matter how hard I had tried to see him the way I wanted.

I stood, walked to the window, and lifted it open. A sunny, warm Florida day. I patted my comfy brown recliner with a smile. This wasn't different. This was right where I had left it.

With a pang of sadness, I sank into the chair. Jason. Ren. Lacy and Ara. And even Gullway. My friends. What would happen to them without me? I wasn't scared to be dead, but I wished I knew whether they were okay. I wished I was with them.

I started to cry loudly. I grabbed a tissue from my dresser and paused as I caught myself in the mirror.

In the place of the seashell eye patch, I had a standard drugstore-bought black eye patch. Very pirate-esque, of course.

I leaned closer to look under my eye patch. There was a hole in my eye that looked more like a slash. I let go and the eye patch flapped back into place. My hair was a frizzy mess.

"Even in death, my hair still sucks," I snickered. I saw my gloves on the dresser. *The* dresser—not my white dresser, but an unpainted one. Why did it all look so different?

I turned and looked around the room. Everything was different, actually.

"That's strange."

I saw my seashell eye patch lying on the dresser. I raised my hand to my eye and felt the smooth, satin texture of the black eye patch that had taken its place.

"How did this even get here?" I touched the pink grooves of the seashell just as the door to my bedroom swung open.

"Madison?"

And there, standing in my doorway, was Shawn Milton.

I dropped my shoulders forward. "Oh, crap. I'm in hell." I slid the seashell eye patch into my pocket.

Shawn looked confused. "Are you okay, Madison? May I get you some water?"

"I am dead and this is my hell," I said.

Shawn smiled. "You are not dead, Madison. Can I get you something?"

I squinted at him. He was dressed in a collared button-down shirt and a navy tie. His hair was short and tidy and he looked...refined.

"What? Why are you here? And why are you being nice to me?" I asked suspiciously.

Shawn looked even more concerned. "Madison, perhaps you should sit down. You seem a little out of it."

"Shawn, what are you doing in my house?" I demanded.

"Maddy?" said Jason from the doorway. A showered and rested Jason. Without words, I ran to him and hugged him tightly.

"Oh thank god! This is the best heaven ever!" I said after a few moments of embrace.

Jason pulled back. "What?"

"Of course I wouldn't have a heaven without you in it," I stated. "But why the hell is Shawn here? He's talking all proper, too, like a total creep. He is so gross."

"You know, I can hear you. You aren't even trying to whisper." Shawn raised an eyebrow.

"Whatever, I'm dead. I'll do what I want," I said back to him and held up my middle finger.

Jason furrowed his eyebrows. He reached out and poked my forehead with his index finger, pushing me back a little.

"Oww," I complained.

"No, you are not in heaven—you are very much alive, my dearest."

"Jason, do y—" Lacy came in from the hall. "Madison!" she exclaimed and ran to me, hugging me. I hugged her back tightly.

"Lacy!" I couldn't control my laughter mixed with happy tears. "I am so glad you're okay, Lacy."

I took a step back and looked at her. Her blonde hair was swept up into a bun, just like her mom used to wear, and she was wearing a pantsuit. She looked so different, too.

"Lacy...you look..." I started.

Lacy smoothed her hair on top of her head. "Oh, yeah, I had to meet with the CEO of a new company on the other side of the island. They may want to contract the gym for their employees."

I shook my head. "Huh?

"It's great to see you, Madison," Lacy said warmly as tears ran down her rosy cheeks.

"It is," Shawn agreed.

I scoffed. "Shut your frickin' face, Shawn."

"Maddy," Jason said. "Calm down."

"What happened? How am I alive?" I asked. Lacy looked a little baffled at my question.

"Lacy, Shawn...can you give us a minute?" Jason asked them and gave an awkward laugh.

"Of course. We'll be right downstairs if you need us," Lacy answered and smiled politely.

"I love you, Lacy!" I called out rather awkwardly.

"Love you too, Mad Dash," Lacy said with tears in her eyes.

Shawn and Lacy walked out of the room holding hands. Jason crossed the room and closed the door.

"How? How am I alive?" I asked, looking at Jason. "I died in the courtyard. I died, didn't I?"

"Your Witch power. It was in the sword," Jason said.

"My Witch power was in the sword? So, when he stabbed me…" I began.

"Your power was released back into you. It saved you."

My sword was leaning against the closet door in its scabbard. "See?" Jason said, handing it to me.

I wrapped my hand around the handle. Nothing. "Wow."

"Yeah. Ara said that's why your eye turned blue, too."

"Ara. Where are the others? Did they all get out?" I asked eagerly.

"Yes, they did. Ara, Ren, and Gullway are all in Everly, just through the portal. Ren keeps obsessively checking on us. It's pretty cute, actually."

"Everything is different." I chewed my lip. "Why is everything different?"

"Yes, that." Jason moved toward me. "Maddy, sit down."

Jason took my hands and we sat on the bed. Even the blanket was different.

"What is going on? Why is everything so different? What is wrong with Lacy? She looks so grown-up. She's seventeen and talking about meetings with a CEO? And Shawn—Shawn could almost pass for human."

"Maddy, they are different," Jason said, and cleared his throat. "They're two years older. Lacy took over her mom's gym. She's doing a great job, actually."

"Um, what?"

"Time passes differently in Everly. While we were in Everly, about two years passed here," Jason explained.

My mouth fell open.

"Shawn and Lacy live here now," he added. "After we…disappeared, she went to live with the Miltons. When she was eighteen, she moved back here. She said she didn't want your home to be gone when you came back. She doesn't know about Everly or any of it. They thought we—well, they didn't know what to think."

"No…no." I shook my head. "That is crazy." I darted to the door and swung it open. I stepped into the hallway, which used to be lined with pictures of Lacy and me as kids. Now it was painted a pale yellow with a thin chair rail about halfway up the wall. No pictures.

I walked down the hall to Aunt Ruth's room and pushed open the door. Her bed, which used to be covered in a ruffled white bedspread, was gone. There was no bed at all, actually. Just a large maple desk and a tall-backed office chair.

"What the hell is this?!" I yelled. Jason was in the hall now, too.

"Aunt Ruth hates when you touch her stuff! Why…" I started walking back to where Jason stood but stopped when I saw the office door. The door to Aunt Ruth's office, which she always kept locked, was ajar. I walked in.

Now the room was a master bedroom in navy and coral, straight out of a magazine.

"Lacy!" I yelled. "What did you do?"

"Maddy, calm down." Jason put his hands on my shoulders. "Just calm down."

"No! She hates when her stuff is moved. She hates it."

"Maddy, two years have passed. It's all moved. It's all different."

I tried to catch my breath as I folded my hands together and rested them on the top of my head. "Two years." I looked around the room. "This is unbelievable. So…graduation, our scholarships, college. Everything. We missed it," I concluded. "Two years?"

Jason nodded.

"Maddy?" Lacy hollered as she came running down the hallway toward me. She looked like Aunt Ruth when she had such a serious expression on her face. I turned away immediately. How could I look her in the eye, knowing that I couldn't save her mother? And if she asked me about Aunt Ruth, I couldn't lie to her. I turned away from her to focus on Jason.

"Maddy?" Jason asked before exchanging glances with Lacy. I had seen that look before. It was the look they exchanged when they thought I was about to flip out. In this case, it was justifiable.

"What did your parents say, Jason?" I asked him.

Jason looked down at his feet. "They moved away. Lacy is trying to track them down for me. After we disappeared, they searched and waited, but eventually they needed to get out of here. They live on the mainland somewhere. Too hard to be here."

"And I will keep trying," Lacy assured us from behind me. Even if she was older now, she still had the same voice with a certain amount of innocence still in it. She was still my sweet Lacy, untouched by the evils of Everly. I still couldn't bring myself to look at her.

"And Caleb?" I put my hands on Jason's.

"Moved on." He smiled. "Happy too."

"Lacy, can you get me something to drink and maybe something to eat? I'm starving," I asked without turning to look at her.

"Of course you are. You're always hungry," Lacy replied. I listened to her footsteps growing fainter as she walked back down the hall away from us.

"You okay?" Jason asked once she was gone.

"No, how could I be? It all happened without us."

Jason nodded.

I plopped down on Lacy's perfectly made bed. Jason sat down next to me.

"Two years—two years have passed. It's like we don't even exist here," I muttered.

"Yep. Depressing, isn't it?" Jason said. "You should have seen Lacy when I knocked on the door. She freaked out. Lacy and the town mourned us like we were dead and there I was at her door with her unconscious cousin who hadn't aged a day."

"Why did you come back here at all?" I asked, turning my head to look at him.

"There's a bit of a manhunt going on right now," Jason answered.

"Because I did the ritual in the courtyard," I said, picking at my thumbnail. There was a thin line of black under each of my fingernails. A little Everly memento.

Jason put his hand on mine. "Actually, they all think you're dead, Mads. They're looking for me."

I sat up abruptly. "Why?"

"Well, after your father tried to kill you, I sort of lost it. Well, not sort of. I lost it big time. I knocked him out. They have the Cloaked out looking for me, for crimes against the Crown. I am a wanted man."

"What? Jason, what's the matter with you? Why would you attack him?" I stood abruptly.

"Madison, he tried to kill you!" Jason shot back.

"So—so, why would you attack him? He's still my father. You could have hurt him!" I spun around as tears rushed to my eyes. I knew how irrational that sounded, but it was exactly what I was feeling. I just didn't understand why the thought of Jason hurting my psycho father made me so angry.

I blinked a few times and scanned the floor. I shoved the white woven rug out of the way. "The floorboard. When Sinder was Lacy, she ripped up a floorboard and found my sword. And there was a piece of paper," I told him as I felt around for the loose board.

"Maddy, don't rip up her floor!" Jason leaned back and peeked down the hall.

My finger slipped through a crack in the floor, allowing me to pull back the plank. "Yes! I can't believe I almost forgot!" I exclaimed as I set the piece of wood down next to me. Inside was a narrow little nook, and right in the middle was a book and a small box.

I grabbed both. I opened the box first as Jason sat down on the floor next to me.

Inside the box was a piece of paper—the same little paper that I had seen Sinder reading the night we went to Everly.

"Read it," Jason urged me.

I unfolded the stiff paper. Scribbled in curving black print were the words *"Molad an Banron* Vilda."

I read them aloud and dropped the paper.

Jason picked it up and read it. "Do you know what this means?"

"Gullway—Gullway said that to me. It's troll. It means 'Praise Queen Vilda,'" I said softly, and grabbed the paper back. "Vilda is my mother's name."

I tucked the paper and the book under my arm. With urgency, I replaced the loose floorboard. I ran back to my bedroom.

"What are you doing?" Jason asked, following me.

I didn't answer him. Instead, I put the scabbard on my back, slid my sword into it, and climbed out the window onto my tree. I maneuvered quickly down the tree and hit the ground.

"What are you doing?" Jason pressed as he followed me down the tree. "Maddy, stop. You're safe now. We're home. It's over. Just take a minute."

I shook my head. "No, it isn't." I walked to the backyard. "It will never be over. Ever. Jason, I can't stay here and pretend that Everly doesn't exist—not now. Not with everything we know. And what if they do come looking for you? I don't want Lacy to get hurt. We have to go back."

"Maddy," Jason protested.

"Greenrock went on without us, Jason. It's like we…" I stopped talking as I walked through the backyard. There at the edge of the property were three large stones surrounded by bright, colorful blooming flowers.

On each stone was a name: Madison. Ruth. Jason.

Jason was at my side. "We are dead here, Jason," I said softly.

Aunt Ruth. I started to cry as I crouched down and rested my hand on the stone with Ruth's name etched on it. The stone was warm under my shaky hand.

"Does she know? Does Lacy know?" I kept my eyes on Ruth's stone in the middle.

"She had already mourned her," Jason replied. "I didn't think it was fair to tell her what really happened. I said we weren't with her."

I took a slow, deep breath.

"Jay," I started, then stood, wiping the tears from my face and turned back. He put his hands on my shoulders and leaned his forehead against mine.

"Jason, you need to stay here."

"Hell no. No chance," he said, and backed up.

I stopped and examined him for a moment. He was different now. My Jason would never punch someone, and now he was wanted for punching my father, the king. I took a step back and looked up at his usually serene face. His bushy eyebrows made a hard angle as he pressed his lips together.

"I'm coming with you. I don't care what you say," Jason insisted.

"Are you sure?" I shook my head, more confused than anything else. "Why would you want to? You know what it's like there."

"I do," Jason said. "But I am not letting you go without me."

"I have to go back." I lowered my chin and narrowed my eyes at him.

"I watched you die, Maddy," Jason said with an ache in his voice. "I watched you die. I watched Ren carry you, flopping around like a lifeless fish, for two days. I can't do that again. I am going to be there to keep you safe."

I ran my tongue over my front teeth as I reached for the comforting grip of my trusty sword. "I won't be the one with a sword through my gut this time. Don't worry."

"What are you going to do?" Jason asked. I turned to look at the woods, at the tall swaying oaks that I spent my childhood sheltered by.

"I am going to fix the mess that my parents were too selfish to clean up on their own. Sinder was batshit crazy, but she was right. Lifting the spell on the courtyard is a small piece of the puzzle. We need to think bigger. Like, coven bigger," I explained.

"Reuniting the Rosewood Coven? That may be a little awkward now that you beheaded one of the lead members and all."

I held up the little piece of paper.

"This says 'Praise Queen Vilda' in troll. I need to find Gullway and talk to him. We need to find my mother before Sinder does." I folded the paper back up.

"Why? Do you think Sinder is looking for her, too?" Jason crossed his arms.

"Sinder is a jerk, but she's a smart jerk, and she saw this paper that night. If she figured out it's in troll, she has the jump on us. We need to go."

I chewed my lip for a moment.

"And Lacy?" Jason gestured to the house.

"She deserves a happy life. A normal life. Aunt Ruth wanted to keep it from her, and I am going to honor that. It's better this way. It is." I met his stare. "It is what Ruth wanted. If I say goodbye, she'll ask me to stay."

"She was proud of you, Maddy." Jason tilted his head. "You made Ruth proud. You don't have anything left to prove."

"How long have you known me?" I asked.

"Forever," Jason answered with a sigh. His dark hair fell around his face.

"Then you know that I have to do this."

Jason bit his bottom lip and nodded. "I know you do, I just—I can't lose you again. I can't."

"And you won't," I affirmed.

I looked back at the house and thought of Ruth and Lacy.

"Are you okay, Mads?" Jason stepped closer. The tension fell from his face, and he looked like my old Jason as he put his hand under my chin.

I was unable to speak for a moment as my tears welled in my eyes. I inhaled and exhaled slowly. The leaves rustled, and the sun warmed my face.

I kept my eyes on the house and nodded.

Jason rested a hand on my shoulder. "You know, we don't have to go back, Maddy. This is still your home. That hasn't changed."

"No, but I have." I smiled, thinking back to what Ara had said. "I can't stay here. I never belonged here."

"So, Aruba, then?" Jason squeezed my shoulder.

"Everly." I forced a smile. "Aunt Ruth spent my whole life getting me ready for Everly, and I never knew it. All the training and the workouts—all of it. She was getting me ready...and I couldn't save her."

I paused as Ruth's terror-filled eyes flashed in my mind.

"Jay, I couldn't save her," I managed to mutter through my choked sob as I pictured Aunt Ruth in the courtyard. "They all meant something to someone. They were all Aunt Ruth to someone. I have to help them—the Magics," I said, and took a deep breath.

"You aren't doing this alone. Ever." Jason held out his hand. "So whether you're telling me to stay or asking me to go, it doesn't matter."

I smiled gratefully at him and sighed. "Thank you, Jason. But what about the Cloaked?"

"I'll just aim for their eyes. I'm pretty good at that, apparently. Now, let's go kick some ass, doll face." He started toward the back of the yard.

"Doll face?" I scrunched my nose.

"Love muffin?"

I shook my head. "Eww."

"How about Madison Rosewood, Scion of Everly?" Jason laughed and bowed his head. I slapped my hand in his.

"Strongblood and Witch," I said with a snicker.

"Always such a rebel."

"Yeah, that's what they tell me."

"Good-bye, Greenrock," Jason said, looking back over his shoulder.

"And good-bye, Mad Dash," I whispered as we turned. We kept walking away from the house.

"I couldn't save her, but I will save them," I said under my breath. "I will save them."

We walked through Aunt Ruth's backyard, and there in the clearing was the tree that changed my life. Standing beside it was Ren.

A smile spread on my face as our eyes met. I quickened my pace and stopped just short of him.

"You—you have no idea..." Ren sputtered before throwing his arms around me and pulling me close to him. I took a breath and let my eyes close for a moment. I would forget my anger at everything for just this instant, and I would let this boy hug me. This boy who led me into the fire and carried me back out.

He squeezed a little tighter, and I felt a strange tug inside of me, like a feeling of relief to be near him. I was happy to let him hold me, but I still didn't hug him back.

"Thanks," I replied.

I pulled back, Jason stepped to my side, and I clasped my hand in his.

"So, what now?" Ren cocked his head to the side, looking inquisitively from me to Jason.

"It's time to focus. I need to protect the Magics from the king. Save the Magics. Time to find my mother before Sinder does," I replied. "And I think I know where to start."

I handed the piece of paper to Ren and watched as his thoughtful green eyes flitted over the words. He looked up at me, and I knew he knew exactly what I was thinking.

"This will be a hell of a lot harder than last time," I added.

"Well, we survived it before... Only this time, we have no idea where to look other than a guess, and I'm being hunted by crazy bounty hunters," Jason added.

I reached my hand out to Ren.

"Ready for this?" Ren asked, although I was certain he already knew the answer.

I looked at the portal tree that stood motionless in the breeze.

"I'm ready," I replied without a shred of doubt. "I'm ready."

To Be Continued...

ACKNOWLEDGMENTS

Thank you to my husband for always keeping my spirits high and my coffee cup full. I couldn't have done this without you.

I'd like to thank my Mom. When I was a kid, even if money was tight, she never, ever said no when I asked for a new book.

And to all of my family, my friends, my step-dad, my mother and father-in-law, your support means the world to me.

Last, but not least, I want to thank all of the hardworking Pandas that have spent so much time working on the edits, the cover, and the marketing for EVERLY. I was blown away by your talent! And a very special thank you to my editor, Rachel. Working with you has been one of the high points in my life. I'd also like to thank my publisher for everything she has taught me and for having faith in my storytelling. *Molad an Banron* Zara!

ABOUT THE AUTHOR

Author Meg Bonney is a paralegal by day, a TV reviewer by night, and a writer every moment in between. Meg enjoys stories with strong emotional relationships but that aren't necessarily romantic. Her TV watching and writing has always been more focused in the sci-fi/fantasy genre where the stakes are high and the consequences are dire and because fairies, mermaids, monsters, and witches make her happy. Meg lives in Wisconsin with her husband, her two young daughters, two cats, three hermit crabs, and one very spoiled fish. Meg enjoys impromptu dance parties with her daughters, strong coffee, baking, and getting way too emotionally invested in fictional characters.

Thank you for purchasing this copy of *Everly* by Meg Bonney. If you enjoyed this book, please let Meg know by posting a review.

Read More Books from Pandamoon Publishing

Visit www.pandamoonpublishing.com to learn more about other works by our talented authors and use the author links to their sales page.

Mystery/Thriller/Suspense
- *122 Series Book 1: 122 Rules* by Deek Rhew
- *A Flash of Red* by Sarah K. Stephens
- *A Tree Born Crooked* by Steph Post
- *Fate's Past* by Jason Huebinger
- *Juggling Kittens* by Matt Coleman
- *Knights of the Shield* by Jeff Messick
- *Looking into the Sun* by Todd Tavolazzi
- *The Moses Winter Mysteries Book 1: Made Safe* by Francis Sparks
- *On the Bricks Series Book 1: On the Bricks* by Penni Jones
- *Southbound* by Jason Beem
- *The Juliet* by Laura Ellen Scott
- *Rogue Alliance* by Michelle Bellon
- *The Last Detective* by Brian Cohn
- *The New Royal Mysteries Book 1: The Mean Bone in Her Body* by Laura Ellen Scott

Science Fiction/Fantasy
- *Everly Series Book 1: Everly* by Meg Bonney
- *.EXE Chronicles Book 1: Hello World* by Alexandra Tauber and Tiffany Rose

- *Fried Windows in a Light White Sauce* by Elgon Williams
- *The Crimson Chronicles Book 1: Crimson Forest* by Christine Gabriel
- *The Crimson Chronicles Book 2: Crimson Moon* by Christine Gabriel
- *The Phaethon Series Book 1: Phaethon* by Rachel Sharp
- *The Sitnalta Series Book 1: Sitnalta* by Alisse Lee Goldenberg
- *The Sitnalta Series Book 2: The Kingdom Thief* by Alisse Lee Goldenberg
- *The Sitnalta Series Book 3: The City of Arches* by Alisse Lee Goldenberg

Women's Fiction

- *Beautiful Secret* by Dana Faletti
- *The Long Way Home* by Regina West
- *The Mason Siblings Series Book 1: Love's Misadventure* by Cheri Champagne
- *The Mason Siblings Series Book 2: The Trouble with Love* by Cheri Champagne
- *The Shape of the Atmosphere* by Jessica Dainty

Made in the USA
Lexington, KY
11 March 2017